CHLOE THE CLONE

William E. Mason

CHLOE THE CLONE

DOUBLE DRAGON

PROLOGUE

Clonal Transplants, Inc. Sanitary Tech Marcus Washington pushed a broom along a narrow path between lines of clone crèches. They ranged as far as he could see in the dim light under the high ceiling of the Great Hall. At least that's what honorable president and CEO, Demetri Andropov liked to call it.

The Great Hall gave Marcus the willies.

Twenty thousand square feet of office-warehouse, it was one of many office-warehouses lining Havana Street in Denver. Offices fronted the warehouse and looked out onto a landscape of gravel, a couple of struggling junipers and a pot-holed parking lot. The ceiling towered twenty-five feet high with pre-cast double tee beams, an occasional skylight and swamp coolers that rattled when they worked at all. Floor mounted floodlights shone upward, making everything in the vast space seem upside down. Despite a new tar and gravel roof, drips fell from the ceiling, clear drops plunging out of the gloom and spattering onto the clear Perspex covers of the crèches.

Andropov shared one of the larger offices with a secretary. Clonal's technical staff took up the other two offices with their array of chemicals, beakers and tubes.

As far as Marcus could figure, they didn't need a lot of space to make an embryo.

Although he had worked for Clonal for a year, he had never met Andropov. It was a small company, not more than one of them cottage

5

industries growing look-a-likes. And with only six employees, counting his-self and Lamont plus the lab guy Andropov canned last week, Marcus figured he should have met the fat prick by now.

But Andropov kept to himself. He rarely came back to look at the clones, at least according to the lab techs. Andropov had his secretary handle all the public relations, usually stayed late, probably no home life, and only gave someone a raise when they threatened to quit.

As far as Marcus was concerned, Andropov could shove the Great Hall and all them wormy things up his arrogant ass.

Sanitary Tech Lamont Royale broomed from a cross isle and nearly knocked Marcus over.

Marcus grabbed Lamont by the lapels of his white janitorial suit. "What the fuck, dude?" He sniffed. "You been smoking that shit again, haven't you?"

"What's it to you?"

"I don't give a motherfuck if you get juiced on your time," Marcus scolded, "but if you screw up, we're going to get our asses canned."

Lamont tried to focus. "Okay, already. I'm cool." He clasped his broom tightly and propped it against his chest to keep from swaying. "But you ain't gonna believe what I found."

"Probably not."

"Seriously." A drop from the ceiling spattered on Lamont's shaved scalp. He ducked instinctively.

Marcus smirked. "Okay, what?"

"C'mere." Lamont scowled and wiped his head with his hand as he led Marcus over to a crèche on the far side of the warehouse.

The crèche was like all the other crèches in the hall, a shaped fiberglass mount that rose off the floor encasing a mass of machinery, monitors and feeding tubes from clustered bottles. Electronic cables and tubes snaked up and through watertight seals to an oblong bowl. The crèche bowls held amniotic fluid for the youngest clones, but were dry for the older ones.

This bowl was dry. A clone lay inside.

It looked to be about ten years old, naked, obviously female, white by racial reckoning, and very thin with blond hair splayed out around her head. Probably not more than two years in the tank. Andropov liked to accelerate growth.

"So?" Marcus gave Lamont a sidelong glance and was about to go after him again for smoking weed.

"She's sentient."

"No way."

"See them wires? I never seen wires like that connected to a product. They's stimulating her muscles. See...there...she jerks a little."

"That don't mean she's sentient."

Lamont put both hands on his hips and thrust his face close to Marcus. "Yeah? Then what the hell else do you think being hooked up to cable TV means?"

"We got cable here?"

"Fuck off." Lamont waved a dismissive hand, then bent to a knee and fingered a thick black co-ax that ended in a silvery male compression fitting. The compression fitting screwed into a black converter box partially hidden under the splayed feet of the fiberglass mount. From the box, wires traveled up the side of the support, slid inconspicuously under the Perspex cover and were taped to each of the clone's temples. "She's probably watching Animal Planet or something."

"Damn..." Marcus squatted next to Lamont. "How come we got a sentient? Them lab guys always nuke sentients, inject 'em with some shit and makes 'em brain-dead."

"We gotta tell Andropov," Lamont said. "He's going to be pissed if he finds out one of his lab guys let a sentient get by."

Marcus stood. "We don't gotta tell Andropov nothin'. I bet he already knows 'bout this. I bet that's how come he fired Nathan. I bet Andropov is walking a fine line down the middle of the road, right now. On one side he's got this here sentient female look-a-like who is ripe for a transplant. On the other side, he don't want no one to know she's sentient."

"So why don't he nuke her?" Lamont asked.

"Because, butthead, she's too old. You can only nuke 'em when they's little. If you nuke one as old as her, she's gonna die. And...if you let them live, then they's also gonna die unless you keep them stimulated. Hence, the muscle twitchers and the cable TV."

"How come you so all knowing, all of a sudden?"

8

"Yo, you oughta pay more attention to what you're doing than scrambling your brain. Nathan was real informative."

"Fuck Nathan."

"Amen. So, my man, as I sees it, motherfucker Andropov's got one helluva problem."

"He does?"

Marcus peered at Lamont like he was an imbecile. "Yeah, he does. Us."

Lamont frowned, confused.

Marcus did a little shuffle step. "If Mr. Andropov don't want no law on his fat ass, then he's gonna have to make us feel real good. Know what I mean?"

Chapter One

Sam Turner squinted at the alarm clock. 6:32 AM.

Why do I always wake up at 6:32?

His Colorado country home sat up high at a flatlander's nose bleed elevation of seventy-five hundred feet above sea level. It didn't seem high since the surrounding countryside, all part of El Paso County, was more or less the same elevation.

Red rocks loomed close to the house. Thick Ponderosa Pine carpeted smoothly to the plain below where a north-south rail line wound its way. A frontal range of mountains filled the view to the west with Pikes Peak dominating in the distance. To the east, high plains spread out flat eventually ending up in Kansas. A cloudless sky, giving over to first light, domed overhead.

Maybe it's a train. Maybe it's the sun rising and hitting the rocks.

But the sun's rising was always changing and his awakening was not. It must be a train. Still, the coincidence bothered him. Sam hated coincidences he couldn't explain.

He lay still. Getting out of bed was something he dreaded. His doctor had told him, "Don't rush getting out of bed. You'd be surprised how many people with your condition drop dead standing up too quickly. First, count to one hundred and fifty."

...One hundred forty-eight, one hundred forty-nine, one hundred-fifty. Okay.

He stood, feeling an ache in his back, cramps in his legs, but thankfully nothing in his chest. After

10

pulling on his robe, he made his way to the bathroom. With his bent over progress he thought he must look ten years older than his hard-fought fifty-six. But that's what heart disease will do to a person.

Brush my teeth. He sat down on the edge of the tub while guiding the electric toothbrush around his mouth. He followed the thirty second beeping guides the brush emitted--stay in one location until the beep--until the programmed instrument stopped after two minutes. Sam was locked into a routine. Sam liked routine.

Shave. Also sitting down. It eased his back, but forced him to rub his right hand--he held the electric razor in his left--over his face to monitor his progress in the absence of a mirror.

When everything felt smooth, he stepped to the washbasin, extra height to save him bending over for a face splash with cold water. Hair--what little was left--wetted and brushed.

Medications. Way too many.

Dead. Death. Dying. The thoughts always came after taking the meds. He hadn't thought much about dying before...before heart disease. But now it was an obsession. He supposed he could be excused the indulgence. After all, if he realized he could drop dead on a moment's notice, what else was there to think about?

He returned to the bedroom to dress.

At least I'm still cognizant enough to put my pants on before my shoes.

Sam smiled at his humor.

After pulling his belt tight, he went to the head of the stairs for the descent to the kitchen on the floor below, then paused out of habit. When he and Karen, may she rest in peace, had bought the house twenty years ago, they had never considered its vertical organization would become an issue. Garage on the lowest floor. Half a flight up to the living room. Another half to the kitchen, dining, TV room, then another flight of steps to the bedrooms.

At first, Sam had thought all this verticality would do him good. Keep him fit. Keep his heart pumping strong. But these days, forgetting to take the keys to the car from the bureau beside the bed precipitated an agonized climb back up.

At this elevation, his Colorado home had become a...health challenge. He questioned his euphemistic choice of words. He could have thought of his house as a *hazard* but decided health challenge was the better way to go. It seemed more in keeping with the times.

Damn heart disease. Sam knew his legs were strong from climbing stairs back and forth for every forgotten thing, but his heart wasn't up to pumping the energy his legs now demanded.

That Karen had preceded him in death always angered him despite doctor's orders to avoid thoughts that would anger him. She had been the more athletic, but cancer didn't know athleticism from dirt. Five years without her. About the same time his heart condition had been diagnosed.

This morning, he remembered to put his car keys in his pocket, so he took the stairs down slowly with a firm grip on the handrail. His doctor had encouraged him to install a mechanized stair-chair but the stair zigzagged between too many landings for that. A hydraulic elevator would have worked as well. He could afford it, and he had actually investigated putting one in, but never got beyond preliminary. Maybe he was too fatalistic.

Once in the kitchen, he started the coffee maker. Weak coffee, even though it was decaf, because even decaffeinated coffee had caffeine. Yesterday's mail sat unopened on the counter. A couple of magazines, a letter from Clonal Transplants, three missives of junk mail and a self-addressed stamped envelope that no doubt held a rejection slip. He had chosen to ignore it, yesterday playing out as a good day he didn't want to spoil.

While the coffee maker sputtered and dripped water through the coffee grounds, Sam sat and tore open the SASE. A quick glance at the salutation...Dear Author, and he knew the rest. He flipped the letter to one side.

Another two minutes for the coffee. He eased off the counter stool and stared at the appointment calendar hanging on the wall next to the refrigerator.

Doctor's appointment at 10:00 AM. Then nothing until a meeting with his cardiac support group at 7:00 PM. He hated days that had obligations in them, and this was going to be one of those days. He supposed his annoyance derived from his early retirement, which at first had provided him the free time he had sought. Golden

13

years early. But now, in retrospect, without Karen, he couldn't imagine his life getting much worse.

The letter from Clonal Transplants sat in plain view almost begging to be opened. He tore off the end of the envelope and pulled out the letter.

An ostentatious gold letterhead heralded Clonal Transplants with their motto underneath, *Personalized Attention to your Personal Extension.*

Corny. He read the letter.

Clonal Transplants, Inc.   *October 29, 2020*
3465 North Havana Street
Denver, CO 80239

Mr. Samuel Johns Turner
6634 Orion Drive
Monument, CO 80132

Re: House Joint Resolution No.54
Dear Mr. Turner,

As a valued customer, your satisfaction is our highest priority. To that end, we at Clonal Transplants feel it necessary to advise you of certain possible consequences that could derive from recent legislation passed by our government.

You are perhaps aware that on October 17, 2020, Congress passed H.J.Res.54 popularly known as The Control and Isolation of Clonal Transplanting Act of 2020. The President signed it into law last week.

Whereas, this legislation, now law, does not prohibit cloning for medical purposes, it does

14

promulgate very strict guidelines under which cloning can take place. We expect pressure will be brought to bear on our procedures, which hopefully will not alter or affect cloning that is already underway or near completion. However, given that the law is new and untested by the courts, we fully anticipate the more zealous members of Congress who supported the legislation will insure its statutes are pursued vigorously by federal law enforcement. The upshot of such action is that the smaller clone farms, such as Clonal Transplants, may be driven out of business.

Until such time as the law can be tested in the courts, our operations will necessarily proceed ambiguously.

We trust in the end, we shall prevail and continue to be able to offer our customers quality organs at a cost effective price.

Rest assured no matter what happens, your interests will always remain paramount.

We wish to thank you again for being a valued customer.

Sincerely,
Demetri Andropov
President and CEO of Clonal Transplants, Inc.

Sam reread the letter, trying to keep his hands from shaking.

I should have gone with one of the big clone farms.

But Doctor Collins had recommended Clonal Transplants, and he knew Doctor Walsh who did all their surgeries. It had been a package deal, twenty-five percent cheaper than the competition.

Andropov wasn't saying it, but there seemed to be a possibility he was going to be shut down. Then what? What will happen to the clones?

What will happen to my clone?

Sam had been waiting two years. His clone should be nearly ready. Maybe they'll test the law in the courts. But that could take months.

I could be dead by then.

***

Alice had just put Demetri's morning cup of coffee on his desk when the phone rang. Demetri thought to answer it, then decided that was why he had a secretary.

"Clonal Transplants," Alice said. She listened. "One moment, please."

She covered the mouthpiece with her hand. "FBI."

Demetri gave out a resigned sigh. Hopefully, this was a routine call. He stabbed the speakerphone button on his console and leaned forward. "Andropov, here."

"Mr. Dematry Androp?"

Alice smiled.

Christ, don't they ever get anything right? "I'm Demetri Andropov."

"Mr. Androp, this is Agent Bernard Wellstone with the Federal Bureau of Investigation. I'd like to ask you a few questions."

The voice was off-putting. Given its smarmy obsequiousness it sounded like it came from a small man. "Certainly, Agent Wellstone," Demetri said,

16

"or can I call you Bernard?" Demetri nodded at Alice. He could be smarmy and obsequious as well.

"Agent Wellstone will do," Wellstone said flatly.

"Then Agent Wellstone it is." Demetri tried to inject a lightheartedness into his voice he didn't feel. "How can I be of service?"

"Your cooperation is appreciated." Wellstone coughed. "Excuse me. I presume you've heard that the President signed HJR 54 into law last week."

"Yeah, yeah, I know all about it. That damn piece of legislation could put me out of business. And I didn't vote for our current President." Demetri hated the legislation almost as much as he hated the current President. The guy seemed to have a fixation on shutting down small clone farms like Clonal. Hell, it didn't hurt anybody to rent a warehouse, hire a few biology majors and set up shop. What was wrong with private enterprise?

But the feds were coming after him with the stealth approach. *We don't have any problem with you cloning people for their organs, but we're going to regulate you to death and put you out of business.* Of course the big clone farms had lobbyist. Demetri had squat.

"I'm sorry to hear that," Wellstone said.

"What did you say?" Demetri had been so far away in his personal reverie he had no clue what Wellstone was talking about.

"The possibility of you going out of business," Wellstone said. "As for the President, we don't comment on political matters. In any case, that isn't the intent of the legislation. You must understand

17

the Bureau has no position on legislation, but once it becomes law, we are beholden...by oath, actually, to uphold the law."

"You are forgiven."

"Sir?"

"Nothing. I was agreeing with you having to uphold the law."

"Thank you. Now, if I may, I'd like to proceed with a few questions. Just routine."

"Just routine. What objection could I possibly have to routine questions?" Demetri covered the speakerphone mike with his hand. "Alice, get me Simon." Simon Garulli was Demetri's lawyer.

"He's out of town, remember?"

"Damn." Removing his hand, Demetri said, "Fire away."

"Mr. Androp, I must advise you that you are being recorded and statements you make could be held against you in a court of law. Do you understand?"

This Wellstone was getting on Demetri's nerves. "Agent Wellstone, why is the FBI asking me questions? What gives federal law enforcement the right to meddle in this jurisdiction?"

"You ship across state lines."

"Oh." Demetri rolled his eyes at Alice. "Of course, of course, Agent Wellstone. I'm no fool. You guys have been after me for years."

"Sir, if you persist in displaying what I perceive as a flippant attitude, I will be forced to put it in my report."

"Okay, I get it."

18

"Thank you. Mr. Androp, are you the owner and chief executive officer of the clone farm known as Clonal Transplants, Incorporated."

"You know damn well I am."

"Please be patient. I have to ask some of these questions for the record."

"Yada, yada."

"I'm sorry, what did you say?"

"Nothing. Something from Seinfeld."

"Who?"

"It was a popular comedy series many years ago. You can catch the reruns at BroadTube.com."

"I'm sure. Now, Mr. Androp, having incubated over a hundred clones in the last five years, have any of them been sentient?"

Demetri closed his eyes and pressed his temples. He stared out the one window that gave him a view of the outside. *They can't possibly know. What to say?*

"Mr. Androp?"

"Yeah, yeah, I'm here. No, none. Absolutely none. I know the law." Demetri strode to the window and snapped the blinds closed. "I maintain a strict quality control on my operations." He raised his voice to be heard by the speakerphone on the desk behind him. "And I can assure you none of my clones have been sentient. In fact, the whole thought of a sentient clone giving up its organs to a client is abhorrent to me."

"I can barely hear you," Wellstone said. "Are you saying for the record none of your clones is or ever has been sentient?"

19

Demetri returned to his chair. His knees felt weak. *They know.* He sat down hard, stabbed a button turning off the speakerphone and snatched the handset. "You can be assured we at Clonal Transplants have only the highest ethical practices in mind."

"You didn't answer my question, Mr. Androp."

Demetri hammered the handset on the top of his desk leaving three dents in the polished wood. "I'm sorry, Agent Wellstone, there seems to be something wrong with the phone."

"Can you hear me now?" Wellstone asked.

"Just barely." Demetri spoke holding his nose.

"Sir, I wasn't born yesterday. Please let go of your nose and listen carefully. I don't want to take up any more of your time. Are you listening?"

"Yes," Demetri said still holding his nose.

"Good. Under Executive Order No.34Z, Transparency in Government, I must advise you we will be dispatching a team within the next forty-eight hours to inspect your facility. Our visit will be a necessary follow up on my report of this conversation."

"God damn it, Wellstone," Demetri shouted. "How can you fuck me over like that?"

But the line had gone dead.

Demetri slammed the handset back onto its carriage.

Alice cringed against a far wall. "Mr. Andropov, please."

"I'm sorry, Alice. That...that fucker upset me. You can go home early today. You know what I

20

mean. I'm giving you free time off. Alice, please go."

Alice grabbed her coat, shrugged into it and bolted for the door.

Damn. Damn. Damn sentient. I should never have kept her. I should have injected her right there and then. No. I made the right decision. She'd have died. Fucking Nathan. What was he thinking? Why? I wasn't mean to him. Okay, he was underpaid but I was trying to help him out, a deadbeat doctor from the old country, and without a green card.

But there must have been something else wrong with Nathan. Who would spend his entire time at Clonal growing a sentient? Not only growing her, but *raising* her. Demetri couldn't have been more surprised when he took one of his infrequent tours of the back warehouse. There was Nathan, clapping his hands dementedly as the clone ran around the warehouse. "Careful, deary, don't knock over any of the crèches." He was crazy. He fed her solid food every day. Talked to her. Saw she got her exercise. He even wired her to a cable TV feed from the break room. Who did stuff like that?

Demetri had asked but got nothing back but obscenities. He had no choice but to fire the bastard. Then the decisions. The clone only had a couple of weeks to term. No sense killing a viable product. No one would ever know she was sentient if he shipped her sedated. Only two weeks. A lot of money was at stake. Keep her wired and head for the finish line.

So who tipped the feds? Nathan wouldn't. He'd get deported. What about that janitor, Washington. Fucker comes in and says he wants cash to keep quiet about a sentient he's discovered in the back. But I paid him off. Sure, he wasn't happy, but what did he expect? I'm not made out of money.

Whose clone is she, anyway?

***

"Mr. Turner, how nice to see you looking in such good health." The receptionist at Doctor Collin's office pasted a brief smile on her face before the effort failed and she returned her gaze to the file in front of her. "Is your health insurance the same as we have on file?"

Sam pressed against the counter trying to get a look at the folder on the desk behind it. "I don't know what you have on file. But my health insurance hasn't changed for a year."

"You understand, Mr. Turner, we have to ask that question as a routine. You'd be surprised how many people with your condi--how many people change their health insurance without letting us know." She beamed another smile Sam's way. "If you'll have a seat, the doctor will be with you shortly."

Sam crossed to the far side of the empty waiting room, a bland ground floor room with off-white walls, gray level loop commercial carpet, green vinyl chairs, and side tables stacked with six month old magazines. Two windows gave a view to the parking lot.

Sam was about to pick up a copy of Good Home Maker, the only magazine available, when a nurse appeared at the door leading to the doctor's inner sanctum.

"Sam Turner?"

Surely the nurse must know he was Sam Turner. She could have said *Sam* without the question. She could have smiled. Sam hated being bothered by these little things. It couldn't be good for his heart.

He returned the magazine to the side table, counted to ten and stood, then walked to the door, which the nurse held open for him.

"How are we feeling today?" she asked.

"Tired. Weak. Not much change from last month."

"I'm sorry to hear that." She escorted him to a scale. "Could you slip off your shoes while I get your weight?"

Sam complied and stood on the scale.

"One hundred seventy-five." The nurse made a note on Sam's chart. "Now your height.."

Sam stood as erect as he could.

"Five feet, eleven and three quarter inches."

"I used to be six one," Sam said.

The nurse ignored his attempt at humor. "If you'll please follow me."

Sam shoved his feet back into his shoes and followed the nurse to an examination room where he was directed to take a seat on a paper-covered examination table.

The nurse wrapped a blood pressure cuff around his left arm and pumped the bladder tight.

She let the air hiss out as she pressed a stethoscope to his arm.

"One hundred forty over eighty-five. Could be better." She made another note on Sam's chart, then placed two fingers on his wrist to count his pulse.

Her fingers were cold, the nails painted blue with a white slashing stripe across them.

"Nice nails," he said.

She glanced up at him with a dull stare, obviously still counting. She finished, said a flat, *thanks* and flipped a page on his chart. "Same medications as last time?"

"The same." Sam tired of the nurse and the drill but he supposed they had their reasons.

Another note to the chart. "Doctor Collins will be with you shortly." The nurse left the room.

Cold bitch. Sam slumped on the table wondering why he couldn't sit in one of the chairs by the desk while he waited for the doctor. And he always had to wait, even when he was the only patient there.

Five minutes later, Doctor Collins knocked and entered. He crossed the small room to Sam and shook his hand.

"Sam, how are we feeling today?"

At least Doctor Collins had warm hands. "Tired. Weak. Not much change from last month."

"I suppose we can take that to be a good sign. A stable sign." Collins paged through Sam's chart. "Weight is good. Blood pressure is a bit high. You're taking your medications regularly?"

"I take them regularly."

24

"We should get that pressure down a bit. Anything bothering you? Any source of stress?"

"Yeah, as a matter of fact. I'm feeling a lot of stress from this cloning legislation."

"HJR 54?"

"That's the one. Andropov sent me a letter, which I interpreted to mean he was afraid he was going to be shut down by the government and lose all his clones."

"Really? I don't think anything as extreme as that is going to happen."

Sam felt a rising frustration. "Doctor Collins, you got me into this deal in the first place. You assured me Clonal was a legitimate outfit and Doctor Walsh a surgeon with a stellar track record of successful transplants. Now it looks like I won't have a chance to find out. My clone is in jeopardy."

"Let's have a look."

Sam hated it when doctors ignored him and changed the subject.

Doctor Collins eased him back onto the examination table and pushed and prodded. Had Sam breathe in and out. Thumped his chest a few times. Pushed at his liver and whatever else was in there.

"Have you been in touch with Clonal?"

"Not for a while. They should be ready by now. I thought they would have called." Sam sat up.

"I don't think we should let this go on. I worry whether we have weeks or even months."

"But I feel fine. A bit tired and weak."

25

"Stable, as I said. But you have cardiomyopathy. You can feel fine, even strong, then it can rise up and take a turn for the worse. God help us if the government gets involved."

"I don't believe in God."

The doctor stared at him. "It's an expression, Sam."

Sam tried to straighten up, but his spine felt weak. *Why don't they have back supports here?* "This letter has got me worried. I don't think *they* even know what effect this new law will have."

"I agree, it doesn't sound good. I'm going to fax a note to Clonal about your condition and the urgency of you getting your transplant now. If they are anywhere near term with your clone, then perhaps a push from me will speed things up."

"Thanks. Should I call them, too?"

"By all means. Get a firm date from Andropov. You can refer to my fax, and tell him I feel time is of the essence."

Sam sensed an urgency in the doctor's voice he hadn't heard before. "Am I that bad off?"

"Look. This kind of heart disease can be capricious. You feel good one day, then it kills you." Doctor Collins fumbled in his pocket. "I'm not supposed to be doing this but I'm afraid you're going to die on me if I don't. Take these." He held up a pill container. "If you have a heart challenge then one of these pills will get you through it. They're not FDA approved but they've been around Europe for a year. If you feel any discomfort, put one under your tongue. They're like nitroglycerin only a lot more effective."

26

Sam fingered the container. A heart challenge? His clone snatched away? Collins, Andropov and Walsh all in bed together on this deal?

If he was to have a heart challenge, then he was half inclined to surrender to the challenger, chuck it all in, be done with it.

Chapter Two

Back home, Sam stared at the phone. He hated phones. He hated calling. Especially if he wanted something. Maybe he'd be put off, refused, rejected. Sam hated rejection.

He picked up the phone and dialed.

Two rings, then a male voice. "Clonal Transplants."

"Hi, this is Sam Turner. Is Mr. Andropov in?"

"Sam! This is Demetri. I received a fax from Doctor Collins. How are you feeling today?"

First the receptionist, then the doctor and now Andropov. "I'm feeling weak and tired. No change from the last time we spoke. I want to--"

"That's great. That's great. You want to know about your clone, don't you? No problem. What is it you want to know?"

Sam's stomach gave a twitch, probably a reaction to Andropov's honey-sweet tone. Why was Andropov, president and CEO answering the phone? "Why are you answering the phone? Where's Alice?"

"She quit on me, Sam. Can I call you Sam?"

"I don't care what you call me." *No wonder I'm tired*. "How far are we from a transplant?"

"Not far, not far. A week, tops."

"You can see from the fax Collins feels I might not have a lot of time. I need my transplant now. And your letter about the consequences of HJR 54 for your business didn't help. I haven't felt this much stress in months." Sam drew a deep breath and tried to calm down.

28

Papers rustled at the other end of the line. "Do you have your surgery booked?"

Sam felt a wave of frustration. "Booked? How can I book surgery until you tell me you're ready with the clone?"

"I'm telling you now. We have you here on our calendar. If you hadn't called, we would have. You can call Doctor Walsh's office and set a date."

"Really?"

"Absolutely. Just let me know. Your clone will be sedated and transferred to the hospital where Doctor Walsh does his surgery." More rustling papers. "Denver Central. You have nothing to worry about. Walsh has performed dozens of transplants for us."

"I know all that," Sam said irritably. "That's why you and Doctor Collins recommended him. That's why I agreed. Will I see my clone before extraction?"

"Ahh, really, Sam, in all honesty, it's against company policy. It's not considered in the interests of the client to see his clone before transplantation. There are obvious reason for adhering to this policy, don't you think?"

Sam wasn't about to argue. He had only asked out of a fear he *would* see his clone. "I understand. I'll book surgery and get back to you."

"That's great, Sam. Really great. Is there anything else I can do for you?"

Sam frowned at the fatuous question. *What else could Andropov possibly do for me? Cook breakfast?* "No. Not right now. I'll be in touch. Good bye."

***

The conversation with Andropov played over and over in Sam's head. Here he was at death's door and everyone around him started acting like idiots. Especially Andropov.

Why didn't I catch on to the creep earlier?

Sam grabbed his keys, descended the stairs from his study and made his way below to the garage. Support group was next on his schedule.

He checked his watch. 6:30 PM. A half hour to drive the twenty miles to Colorado Springs to Debra Wallingford's house. She was hosting tonight.

His drive into the city was met with late rush hour traffic that still clogged the interstate. A light, early season snowfall dusted the highway and slowed everyone down even more. Sam checked his watch again. He was going to be late for the meeting.

Off the interstate, he maneuvered his way across town to Debra's house, a postmodern suburban plunked down at what used to be the eastern edge of Colorado Springs.

Sam parked his ten year old Toyota 4Runner and saw that the others in the group had already arrived. He did a slow walk to the front door, rang the bell and pushed through, not waiting for Debra to let him in.

The others were lounged in Debra's living room, probably chattering about their kids or grandkids, complaining about their spouses and generally complaining.

"Sorry I'm late," he said to no one's attention except Eddy Stormer, who gave him a nod before continuing with whatever he'd been saying to Michelle Green. The latter sat in rapt attention, nodding to whatever it was Eddy was saying. Eddy loved attention.

Sam took a vacant seat. Five members, including him, were present. One was missing. When Eddy took a breath, Sam inquired, "Where's Penny?"

A dead silence fell over the group, and they all looked at him as though he had appeared out of nowhere.

"Penny's two kids are sick," Harry Boregard said. He was the oldest member of the group and a neighbor of Penny's.

Penny Hunter was an engaging member whom Sam liked, but she was cursed like the rest of them with a sick heart. Sick kids would be the least of her worries.

When the silence lengthened, Michelle, never one to let a silence go unused, asked, "How are you feeling, Sam?"

Though they all had heart disease of one variety or another, Sam was the only one who was growing a clone to facilitate his transplantation. All the others were in line, waiting for some unfortunate to crash his motorcycle into an immovable object and become brain-dead...hopefully with a hundred percent tissue match.

Sam supposed it was kind of Michelle to inquire if it weren't for the fact he had already answered the question three times today.

"I'm feeling tired and weak. Not much change since last meeting."

"I suppose that's a good thing," Michelle said. "We all suffer the same dreadful symptoms and have to count our blessings when they occur. Unfortunately, we aren't all seeking the same alternatives to a cure."

"She still doesn't believe in clones, Sam." This from Harry, who at sixty-six was long on candor and short on tact.

Since the conversation had drifted away from Eddy's focus, he began picking through the mixed nuts Debra had put out on the coffee table.

"Are you actually going to utilize your clone for a transplant?" Debra asked.

She was the youngest of the group. Heart disease knew no age limits, and she was perhaps the sickest of them all. Her extra weight only made her personal health challenge worse.

"Of course I'm going to use my clone for a transplant," Sam said. "I don't know why you want to go over and over this ground every time we meet. I'm not about to change my mind. My clone will provide a perfect tissue match for the transplanted heart. You all would be wise to consider doing the same thing. You could die waiting in line before a good match becomes available."

Eddy drew a deep breath. "I think the reason we feel compelled to revisit this discussion is we all feel you are ignoring the moral implications of your decision." Eddy was big on morality.

"Really, Eddy," Sam said. "Where's the morality? It's all about mortality. I'm availing myself of the best medical solution to a medical problem. I have the means and the will to pursue this."

"I wish I had the means." Debra flicked her finger against the side of her nose in agitation. "I registered with the United Network for Organ Sharing two years ago. Thank God, I'm still alive. I must admit if I wasn't on National Care I might have been served earlier, but that's the way it is. We aren't all as fortunate as you are, Sam. It peeves me you can circumvent the system because you're rich and can afford to hire organ ghouls like Clonal Transplants."

Sam's heart rate increased. "I resent you calling them ghouls."

"Of course they're ghouls." Eddy shouted.

"Eddy." Michelle patted his hand. "I don't think we have to go over this again."

Eddy whipped his glasses off his head and stared at Michelle, his eyes almost bugging out of their sockets. Eddy hated being shut up. "I think we have a responsibility to ourselves--" He began an agitated wiping of his glasses with a tissue. "-- and as a service to an errant member of this group to revisit *ad nauseam* the arguments against cloning."

He finished by replacing his glasses, then glared at everyone in the room, bludgeoning them into silence, daring them to take him on.

"What about the obscene failure rate?" he asked when no one spoke. "We all know the so called *therapeutic cloning* Clonal Transplants does often end in failure, and when it succeeds there's no

33

guarantee the clone's organs are not subtly compromised."

"I wouldn't call the failure rate obscene." Sam felt heat rise up his neck. "Therapeutic cloning has come a long way and has proven to be the only way to grow organs. We all know cloning single organs hasn't been perfected. Besides, as regards cloning whole beings for their parts, failures are weeded out early on. It's no more immoral than advanced reproductive techniques, growing a number of embryos and using only a few while the others are discarded."

"You make me sick," Eddy said, beginning to warm to his argument. "Pretty soon we won't even need *advanced reproductive techniques*. We'll have ourselves cloned, then the clone will clone itself, leading inexorably to an inbred gene pool."

Sam shook his head in dismay. *How do I reason with this guy*? "I never said I was in favor of cloning humans in general. I'm in favor of therapeutic cloning. The clones are all brain-dead. They don't reproduce. Besides, you're overstating your argument. It's much, much simpler for a man and a woman to procreate. And, I might add, much more enjoyable...you should try it."

The two women in the group giggled but Eddy glared, his mood darkening by the second.

"You'll get nowhere with that kind of talk, Turner. It shows the speciousness of your argument when you have to resort to personal attacks."

"I'm sorry." Sam smiled, enjoying Eddy's discomfiture. "Did you take that personally?"

"I did." Eddy fumed. "Every life is precious in God's eyes. Clones are precious even though they're brain-dead. You can't grow them and harvest their organs any more than you can harvest organs from your next door neighbor."

Sam folded his arms across his chest and leaned back in his chair. "There are a couple of big fallacies in that statement. Number one, you'd have to believe in God in the first place for that to hold. Number two, because therapeutic clones are brain-dead, they're nothing more than compatible tissue. They have no soul, you might say. There are no moral issues involved."

Eddy snorted derision. "And that's the trouble with folks like you. Argue and argue until you have eliminated morality, then it's okay to proceed. But the fact remains, in the eyes of God, who is the ultimate moral authority, just because we can do something doesn't mean we should!"

The thudding in Sam's chest increased. *Are they trying to kill me off, here and now*? "Come on, Eddy," Sam said. "Let's leave God out of it. You know damn well there's no stopping cloning. The benefits are too great. Someone, somewhere will do it. I believe that's called human nature."

"Turner, you're so full of shit!" Eddy yelled, then made a face and rubbed his chest with his fist. "I don't know why we put up with your drivel in a God-fearing group like this." He finished in a croaking whisper.

Michelle tried to soothe him. "If you don't calm down you'll have an attack."

35

"I've had enough." Sam stood, felt faint, counted to ten, and regained his composure. "I've tried to address your concerns. But here's the bottom line. It's none of your business how I choose to pursue a cure for my disease.

"We're supposed to support one another here, not tear each other apart. Rather, tear *me* apart. If you want to sit and wait and risk dying while working through the National Care bureaucracy and UNOS, you're free to do that. But don't push it or God on me.

"And while we're on the subject, I'll let you in on a little secret. I booked my surgery today. By this time next week, I'll have a new heart and a new life. You can take this support group and stuff it, and I doubt God will even notice."

Eddy leaned forward with his mouth open as though someone had punched him in the stomach. "Mark my words," he wheezed, obviously still in pain, "God will notice!"

Michelle Green made the sign of the cross and put both hands to her cheeks in surprise.

Harry Boregard took out a handkerchief and blew his nose, then wiped his rheumy eyes.

Debra Wallingford moaned, clutched her chest and fell out of her chair.

***

Demetri was in a daze. He must have made a hundred calls that morning, urging clients to contact their doctors, saying he could no longer insure the maturity of their clones. Thank God for the hold-harmless clause his lawyer had inserted in all the contracts or he could be ruined. Clients paid half of the eight hundred thousand cost of the clone up front for a package deal consisting of pre-transplant care, the cloning and the final surgery. The remainder was placed in escrow to be paid upon completion of the contract. But if circumstances developed that were beyond the control of Clonal Transplants, like a raid by the FBI, then the client could not hold Clonal responsible for being unable to deliver the product. Furthermore, the client would forfeit all monies paid up to that point as compensation to Clonal for undertaking the complex procedure in the first place.

Pretty onerous, but people still lined up to sign on the dotted line.

He was mid-dial when he spotted a black van pulling into the parking lot at a reckless speed.

The van lurched to a halt. Blazoned on the side door was a red and white shield with the scales of justice above it on a field of blue and the letters *Department of Justice, Federal Bureau of Investigation.*

Shit.

The sliding door slammed open, and men dressed in black, with black ski masks, and wearing Kevlar body armor leapt out. He counted ten of them. They all carried automatic assault rifles.

Demetri stared in wonder, not only that there were so many, but also how so many could have fit in the van. He had little time to resolve the conundrum when the men barged through the door and fanned out into the room.

"Nobody move!" the lead man shouted. The business end of his weapon swung back and forth across the room, making Demetri's stomach twitch every time the pendulum-like motion of the barrel crossed his body.

Demetri looked around incredulously since he was the only one in the office, wondering why he was being addressed in the plural. He raised his hands. "Don't shoot!"

The line of the forward team parted, and a solitary figure, similarly dressed and armed, entered, then stood in the middle of the group.

"You the only one here?" the solitary figure asked.

Demetri nodded. There was something familiar about the voice.

"Okay. Over there." Solitary motioned with his gun toward a near wall.

Demetri eyed the neat Bureau patches stitched on each man's shoulder. *Fidelity, Bravery, Integrity*.

Right.

Solitary pulled off his hood. "Hi, Androp." He smiled. "I'm Agent Wellstone." He shoved out a hand to shake Demetri's.

"You're Wellstone?" Demetri couldn't believe his eyes. The guy was easily a yard taller than he was. Must weigh over two hundred pounds--all muscle. Chiseled features, short-cropped hair streaked with gray. Not a guy you wanted to mess with physically. "I thought of you as someone more...corpulent."

"Whatever gave you that impression?" Wellstone scanned the room. "Anyone inside?" He motioned with his rifle.

38

"The weekend tech is on duty. Otherwise, there's nothing beyond those doors but a bunch of brain-dead clones."

"That's what we're here to find out."

"Do you have a warrant for this?" Demetri cringed when Wellstone swung his rifle to point at Demetri's stomach, but it was only part of a maneuver to shoulder the weapon while Wellstone fingered into a chest pocket and produced a piece of paper.

"How's this?" He handed the paper to Demetri. "A warrant to search your premises."

For a moment, Demetri thought he had Wellstone by the short and curlies, the latter having had his name wrong on all occasions. But a glance at the warrant showed it was indeed made out for Clonal Transplants in general and Demetri Andropov in particular. "I thought you'd have my name wrong," Demetri said.

"I have a good secretary. Now, if you'll sit down, we'll be about our business."

Demetri sat at his desk and stared, still trying to reconcile the obsequious voice on the phone with the aggressive agent before him.

The commandos who had been securing Wellstone's flanks streamed past him into the warehouse.

Wellstone followed. "Jesus H. Christ," he said. "Can we get some light in here?"

One of his men hit a wall switch that turned on the overhead lights. Every recess, nook and cranny in the Great Hall was illuminated.

The weekend tech ran up. "You'll damage the clones with all that light."

"Stow it, kid," Wellstone said. "You got a name?"

"Jeremy. Jeremy Bishop.

"Well, Jeremy, you stand back over there with your boss. We aren't going to be here long." He motioned to his crew. "Wrap 'em up and let's get out of here."

"Wha...wha...?" Demetri stuttered. "You're taking my clones?"

"Correct. We'll test every one of them to see if you have a sentient. If none are found, these will be sent to a shelter for brain-dead clones where they will receive the care they deserve for the rest of their natural lives."

"Since when is *that* in the law?"

"Since we've been told that's how we are to interpret it."

"But I'll be ruined."

Agent Wellstone ignored Demetri's lament.

A large truck pulled up outside and two men clad in white uniforms, possibly doctors, jumped out and hurried into the building.

"We're going to take real good care of your clones, Androp. These guys are from the National Board of Health and Human Services. They'll oversee the transfer of the crèches to the transportation outside."

Demetri felt a rush of heat rising into his head. His eyes felt like they were straining in their sockets. "You're taking the crèches, too?"

40

Wellstone smiled what was obviously false sympathy. "How else are we going to take them out of here. On stretchers?"

Demetri and Jeremy watched in horror as the crèches were unplugged from floor mounted sockets, hooked up to portable uninterruptible power supplies and wheeled out the door.

One of the commandos stepped up to Wellstone. "Sir. We've found an empty crèche." He leaned close to Wellstone and whispered something more in his ear that Demetri couldn't hear.

With an expression that could have been a precursor of the wrath of God, Wellstone turned back to Demetri. "An empty crèche, Androp. Where's the clone?"

Demetri staggered to his feet. "We have lots of empty crèches. They can't all be full. We have deliveries made and clients signing up all the time."

The commando came back into the office pushing an empty crèche. A crumpled fleece blanket lay next to a tangle of wires and tubes.

With obvious distaste, Wellstone reached in and picked up one of the wires. He examined the end. "The tip of this hook-up looks to have tissue on it. Someone must have pulled it out in a hurry." He waved to one of the doctor types to take a sample. "I'm sure we're going to find out it's human tissue. Then we're going to get a DNA profile. Then we're going to go looking for the clone it was stuck in. Where's the clone, Androp?"

"This is ridiculous! You're making assumptions that are leading you way beyond the facts. That clone was released to its client and the surgeon of record. We haven't had time to sterilize the crèche for another growth."

"How about you, Jeremy? You got anything you want to say?"

Jeremy fidgeted and took a quick glance at Demetri. "No, sir."

Wellstone stepped over and peered down at Jeremy. "You know, lying is a federal offense."

"Get away from him, Wellstone," Demetri shouted. "He's not lying. He hasn't said anything. He's got a right to a lawyer."

Wellstone scowled at Demetri. "All right. How about I bring in someone who will talk to me?" He beckoned to one of his men who was standing near the door to the outside.

When Demetri turned, the commando had ushered into the office a man in a white janitor's uniform that carried Clonal Transplant's logo.

Fuck. It's Washington. I guess the two hundred dollars I gave him wasn't enough. "Who's he?"

"This is--" Wellstone consulted a piece of paper. "--Marcus Washington. Says he saw a clone he swears was sentient in this crèche."

Demetri gave off a dismissive harrumph. "You expect a man of his intelligence to be able to tell the difference between a sentient and a non-sentient clone? He's a janitor, for Christ's sake."

"He says the clone in the crèche in question was wired to cable TV."

42

"Absolute nonsense. Why would we have cable TV piped in here, into the dead brains of clones?"

Wellstone reached back, and an assistant slapped a piece of paper onto his hand. "This is a copy of a bill for last month's cable TV service to this address. I can produce similar bills for the last eighteen months."

Demetri stared at the proffered bill. "Yeah, we got cable in the break room. So what?"

"Then how do you explain the extra line charge?"

"Extra line charge? I know nothing of this. My secretary pays all the bills. Someone's fucking with me."

"I'll give you that," Wellstone said.

An aide stepped up to Wellstone. "All the clones are loaded up, sir."

Wellstone nodded. "Okay Androp, we're finished here. After the tests on the confiscated subjects, we'll get back to you. In the meantime, think about why this crèche is empty. Even clones leave traces of their existence. If that clone is sentient, we're going to find out. And that will be the end of you...unless you come to your senses and choose to cooperate. Am I understood?"

Demetri glanced at the determined men standing behind Wellstone, at his empty warehouse, at the grinning Marcus Washington. "Yeah, you motherfuckers. I get it. Now get the hell out of my private establishment."

Wellstone smiled. "You have the right to say whatever you want in your private establishment, so though we might be offended, there's nothing we can do about it. Goodbye, Androp." With that he motioned to his men, and they retreated as quickly as they had entered.

Marcus Washington was left behind looking bewildered.

Demetri rounded on him. "You little piece of shit. Do you know what you've done?"

Marcus gathered himself together in time to turn and dodge through the entrance door, thrusting his middle finger in Demetri's direction as he jogged across the parking lot.

Low life, Demetri thought.

"Can I go now, Mr. Andropov," Jeremy asked.

Demetri had almost forgotten the tech was still there. "Yeah. You did well, kid. You can go. I guess this is the end of the road for a while. But stay in touch."

"What about the...the reward you promised me."

"Oh yeah. I'm glad you reminded me. What was the amount?"

Jeremy chewed on a nail. "You said a year's salary. I wouldn't have done it for less."

"I must have been loopy if I promised that. But a deal is a deal." Demetri got out his checkbook and wrote out a check to Jeremy for a year's salary. "There you go. We square?"

"What about the all-inclusive month at Sandals in Saint Thomas?"

"I promised that, too? Look, kid, Alice quit--"

"I heard you fired her."

44

"Whatever. I'm not going to book you a reservation. How about another hundred bucks. That should cover it."

Jeremy frowned and shook his head. "I don't think so, Mr. Andropov. I hear those things run like a thou a week."

"That much. Must be the high season. Okay, I'm not going to quibble with you. You did good." Demetri wrote another check. "Now, Jeremy, we're done. Get the hell out of here."

"Yes, sir, Mr. Andropov. I hope it all works out well for you."

Demetri watched Jeremy go.

Nice kid. Hate to lose him. Smart, too. Had me by the balls. But I'm ruined, no putting a good face on it.

At least Jeremy had gotten the sentient out before the raid, wrapped her in a white sheet, put her in the back of the company car, then over to the back of the bakery that was also a tenant in the same industrial site. He had parked the vehicle between two large bakery trucks. Wellstone's men couldn't search anything that wasn't in their warrant, so Demetri had been home free.

Of course, he could have killed the clone any number of ways, and dumped her into a dumpster or cut her up into little pieces and flushed her. But, no, he wasn't stupid. If whatever means of disposal he used had been discovered he'd have spent the rest of his life behind bars. Plus there was the escrow account. Complete the contract.

45

Extreme sedation was the best course of action. She wasn't likely to cry out *help* as her chest was being cut open.

Chapter Three

The small town of Monument, twenty miles north of Colorado Springs, was five minutes from Sam's house. Aside from three fast food outlets, two gas stations, and a shopping center with a Great Foods franchise as an anchor, there was a Starbucks. It sat married to a local bank branch that had been built on the site of a former gas station.

His agent and mentor, JoAnne Calder, was already there for their morning meeting when Sam entered. She had chosen a table at a back corner, a defensive positioning. But if Sam had been first, he would have chosen the same spot. He liked JoAnne. They thought alike. In fact he had a crush on her. But she was fifteen years younger than he was.

"I'm sorry I'm late," he said as he slid into an empty chair opposite.

JoAnne looked up from her laptop. "Thirty seconds?" She pushed back a lock of blond hair and tucked it behind an ear, a gesture that was both tidying and a nervous habit, but one Sam liked, nevertheless. She was simply dressed, designer jacket over a knit blouse, slacks. With her good looks she didn't have to be ostentatious.

JoAnne had a steaming latte sitting in front of her.

"I see you've already ordered," he said. It still bothered him he had been late. He didn't like being late to anything. He liked being five minutes early. Sam signaled the waitress, a corporate capitulation to what used to be self-service.

47

He leaned toward JoAnne. "Can you believe it?" he said in a low voice. "A member of my support group dropped dead last night."

JoAnne pushed her laptop to one side. Two small wrinkles on her otherwise seamless forehead showed her concern. She blinked silky eyelashes. "But that's terrible. Was it Harry?"

"One would have thought so with him being so sick lately. I wish it had been that blowhard Eddy, but no, it was poor Debra. We had a knock-down-drag-out argument about me contracting to grow a clone. Debra got worked up and then, *pow*. She clutched her chest and collapsed."

"I'm so sorry to hear that. But why were you debating cloning? I thought you settled that a long time ago."

"It's never been settled. It seems every other time we meet, someone brings it up again, and we do the same dance over and over."

"And you keep going to the group?"

"I think last night was my last time. After the EMTs arrived, everyone blamed me for causing her attack. For Christ's sake, I almost had an attack myself."

JoAnne smiled. "I thought you didn't believe in God."

Sam felt caught. "He's not God. He's the son of God. Besides--" He searched for an out. "--it's just an expression."

The waitress came over and Sam ordered.

After the waitress went away, JoAnne asked, "You feel like talking business?"

"Sure," Sam said. "That should take all of about ten seconds. Publishing can drive anybody insane."

JoAnne laced her fingers in front of her and pursed her pink lips before saying, "I'm not your shrink. Do you have a shrink? Maybe you should get a shrink."

Sam glanced at the ceiling as if an answer lay blazoned across the drop-in tiles. He hated having to look at her when she was about to give him a lecture he knew he deserved. Her eyes narrowed. Her long, straight nose thinned even more. Then there were the lips. Nice lips. "I know, I know. You're my agent, not my psychiatrist. But you send out queries and nothing. Are they all boobs?"

"They're not all boobs," JoAnne said with a flip of her hand. "They run a business. They have to make judgment calls that will either make them money or not. I do that, too."

"Yeah, but somehow, I think of you differently."

JoAnne smiled. "At least I have that."

"You've got a lot more going for you. I wish I didn't have such a crush on you."

JoAnne sat up straight and eyed him. "I'm not sure how I'm supposed to take that. In a small way, I'm flattered you would think of me in those terms. But in a larger sense, I'm thinking I haven't served you well as your agent."

Sam's coffee came. He blew across the top of the steaming liquid, then tipped the cup back and forth, staring into the white reflection from the lights overhead.

She knows the pain I go through.

"They all say it's the economy," Sam said. "I think they're using that for an excuse."

"No, they're not. You know it's a tight market out there."

"But I'm not getting anywhere."

"Any time you want me to stop representing you, I will. I don't make any money unless you do."

"Come on, JoAnne. You know I'm not about money. I write because I like to write, from the heart."

"Speaking of hearts, have you ever considered writing a book about your experience. I mean something non-fiction. Heart disease. The options available. Your choice to go with a clone. I could sell that kind of book in a heartbeat, no pun intended."

Sam gave her a letdown look. "I know it would sell. But I like to write what I like. I'm not going to follow markets. I can't do that. Beside how could I write about this big thing that hangs over me all the time. I could be dead tomorrow."

JoAnne smiled. "Are you trying to intimidate me?"

"No."

"You could have fooled me. But I'll keep working for you as long as I think you have a quality product...and are still alive."

"Is that all I am to you, a potential meal ticket? I thought we might have more going."

She leaned back with a focused stare.

"I'm sorry," he said. "I didn't mean that. At least the first part."

She shifted in her chair. "Sometimes you say hurtful things."

"I said I'm sorry. I meant it." He looked at her imploringly. "Hey, why don't we get married?"

A blush came into her cheeks. "I know you're joking."

He eyed her. "Not really. But I'll give you your space. Think about it."

The blush deepened.

"You know this cloning is very controversial," she said, obviously hoping to change the subject. "I tend to agree with you on most things, but I'm not so sure about this one."

"It's not like these clones know anything. They're as brain-dead as a head on crash victim."

"I've heard this before from you. But my mom and dad would call it an abomination."

"Like in the Bible?"

"No. I don't know the Bible ever addressed cloning. They'd just think it was wrong. Maybe it is wrong. There must be a better way to grow organs than to grow the whole being and harvest organs out of it."

"If there is a way, they haven't perfected it yet. Look, I don't particularly like it either, but I'm going to die if I don't get a new heart. I'm not poor, just in poor health.

"Doesn't this new legislation worry you? President McAfee campaigned on the promise to shut down organ farms."

"Of course it bothers me. Hopefully, they won't get their act together before I get my heart.

I've been told my clone will be ready next week. I've booked my surgery."

JoAnne's eyes widened with surprise. "You did?"

"I did."

"I...I didn't know. It's so soon. There's a lot of risk in a transplant operation."

"I've been referred to Doctor Walsh at Denver Central. He's one of the best. I'm not worried. You shouldn't be either."

JoAnne leaned forward and grasped Sam's hands. "But I do worry. I worry about you, about the clone, about the right and wrong of what you're doing."

He savored her touch. He hadn't been joking about getting married, just thought it was a long shot she would feel the same way about him as he felt about her and say yes. He pulled his hands back. "What would you do if you knew two years ago you'd be dead by now if you didn't get a new heart?"

"I'd go for an artificial one."

Sam shook his head. "Artificial, organ donor. You know the survival rates. I'm fifty-six. I want to live to be ninety. I don't want something in me that will only give me fifty-fifty odds I'll live another ten or fifteen years. I want me. I want a perfect tissue match. The only way I get that is from a clone."

JoAnne closed her laptop. "You're pretty set in your ways, Sam Turner. If I didn't believe in your work, I'd drop you like a stone. I still might." She rose. "I've got a luncheon meeting in the Springs. We done here?"

"Come on, JoAnne, don't go away mad. You're the only person I can talk to nowadays."

"I'm not mad." She patted him on the head. "Finish your coffee. I've got to go."

***

Sam waited as JoAnne pulled away in her late model Proteus hybrid. After she merged with the local traffic and disappeared toward the stoplight down the road, he slid behind the wheel of his 4Runner, revved the engine and began the short drive from Starbucks to his home.

He passed through town, new police station on one corner of an intersection, graveyard on the other. *Odd juxtaposition*, he thought, but nothing more than a coincidence of land uses.

He turned at the cemetery and drove north, passing open fields on one side and a trailer park on the other before coming to the twisting streets of a small neighborhood. These in turn led to a more upscale development of larger acreages where he and Karen had bought their dream home twenty years ago.

He was thankful for the space, high up and surrounded as it was by trees, yet still having a view that gave him a sense of being connected to the outside world without compromising his privacy.

As he pulled into his garage, the extension phone on the wall rang.

He parked, hating the hurry-up the ringing phone induced. He could feel his heart picking up its beat. He counted the rings, trying to gauge the

53

amount of effort he would have to expend if he was to get to the phone before the answering machine picked up after twelve rings.

At ring number eleven he picked up. "Hello."

"Sam? Sam Turner? This is Demetri Andropov."

"Hi, Mr. Andropov. What's up?"

"Thank God you're home. Something has come up, and I need to see you."

Sam thought about going into his belief that God didn't exist, but figured Andropov wouldn't be amused given the tone of his voice. "Does this have something to do with the letter you sent me?"

"It does. But I don't want to talk about it on the phone even though I'm at a pay phone at the 24/7."

If Sam's heart had ticked up a notch getting to the phone, this news was bumping it up further. "You're making me nervous."

"No, no, nothing to be nervous about. Some complications. If you come up here, we can iron them out."

Complications? The whole legislation was fraught with complication. Who could have come up with such a perverse law even in their wildest dreams. Sam rubbed his chest, trying to will his heartbeat slower to no avail. "This is rather short notice. What's the rush."

"Like I said, I can't go into details on the phone. But I'm sure you're getting my drift. What more can I tell you than I already have. This can't wait until tomorrow. It can't. It won't. It's got to be right now. I'd come to you if I wasn't tied up. Believe

54

me. But I can get away for a few minutes if you can drive up."

Sam heard the urgency in Andropov's voice. Sam also heard the thundering of his heart. Maybe his clone was dead? What then? Two years down the drain. Not possible. "I'll come but it'll take me an hour to get to Clonal."

"Yeah, an hour is what I figure. But not at Clonal. I'm going to give you an address about three blocks away. We can meet there. Can you do it?"

"Of course. But you're beginning to scare the shit out of me."

"Sam, I apologize. It's like I said, this can't wait. It's gotta be now. You got a paper and pencil?"

"Hold on." Sam went back to the 4Runner and retrieved a pen and snatched up a bank deposit receipt that had a blank back. His hand started shaking as he poised pencil over the paper. "Okay. Shoot."

"Drive up Havana like you're coming to the office but turn right on Dakota. That's two blocks from the warehouse. Continue on Dakota until you come to Pretoria. Turn left on Pretoria. After about a block, there's a large parking lot on the right at 1680 Pretoria. I'll be parked at the back where the trees overhang the lot. You got all that?"

"I got it."

"I'll be there until one o'clock. I can't stay any longer."

"I'll leave right away."

"That's good. Look, I'm sorry about this, but it's out of my control. I'm doing the best I can."

"All right. I'll see you in an hour." Sam started to put the handset back on the hook.

"Sam!" Andropov's voice came out tinny and small.

Sam pulled the handset back. "What is it?"

"Could you make sure you aren't followed?"

***

The drive up the interstate seemed endless. Traffic was light, it being Saturday. Sam traveled in the right lane, content to move below the seventy-five mile per hour limit. He couldn't afford to be pulled over now.

On hitting east west I-70, he turned west, then north again at the Havana off-ramp.

By now the streets were deserted. He was in an industrial area with large volume warehouses, vast parking lots, truck-high docks with their collapsible wind screens. Here and there stood a parked eighteen wheeler. His 4Runner bounced over railroad tracks.

Sam followed Andropov's directions and slowed at the entrance to the parking lot. It was deserted except for a black hearse-like vehicle parked on the far side under overhanging trees.

Sam turned into the parking lot and drove diagonally across marked parking spaces. He slowed as he approached the trees. He parked, stepped out of his 4Runner and walked toward the vehicle.

Andropov emerged from the driver's side. Despite being well dressed in a dark suit, his dark hair combed flat and across his forehead, he resembled a Bulgarian weight lifter, a full head shorter than Sam and half again as wide.

Andropov hurried over and extended his hand. "Sam. It's good to see you again. How you feeling?"

Sam shook Andropov's hand. "What's so urgent you've made me come all this way? Is my clone dead or something?" Sam had trouble suppressing the horrible consequences of what he had asked.

Andropov glanced around, then grabbed Sam by a sleeve and urged him deeper into the shadows near the hearse.

"The feds raided me today," Andropov confided. "They took all of my clones."

That got Sam's attention. "All of them?"

"Yeah, all of them...but one. Yours."

"That's...that's awful...I mean all of them...but why not my clone?"

"She's special. I was able to--"

"She?"

"Look. I said she's special. The *she* is part of her being special...you being a male and all."

"Are you sure she's my clone?" An icy feeling locked into his brain, a feeling that told him he maybe should have gone with a National Care transplant. A feeling that told him the man standing in front of him couldn't be trusted.

"There was a screw up during fertilization," Andropov said. "I've fired the tech who did it. Be that as it may, the clone is still viable. That she's female is irrelevant...it's only one chromosome after all."

Sam frowned, unable to believe what he was hearing.

"Well, not totally irrelevant," Andropov said. "Her heart is still a perfect tissue match to yours but gender matching does increase the odds of a fit by a small percentage. Nothing to worry about. What did you want me to do? Let the feds cart her off?"

"Ahh...no...definitely not. But why not? I mean why out of all the clones you have did you save mine?"

"Look, Sam...can I call you Sam?"

Andropov had asked the same question the day before. What was with this guy? Did he always ask that same question of everyone he met, then forget he had asked? Sam nodded anyway and thought Andropov a bit unbalanced.

"Good. Look, Sam, when I talked to you yesterday, you told me your condition was dire. I don't think I have another client whose clone is so close to maturity and whose condition is so dire. So, what am I supposed to do? I'm standing here trying to help you and you're looking at me as if I was a gift horse with bad teeth."

"I'm sorry if I gave you that impression," Sam said. "You have to understand, all of this is rather sudden."

"Yeah, yeah, I know, sudden. I'm still reacting to it all myself. But we'll get through it. You *do* want to get through it, don't you?"

Sam felt he was being drawn into something he didn't quite understand but didn't have any choice

58

about. Play along. "Okay, I'm cool." It was the best he could come up with but it seemed to relax Andropov.

He ushered Sam around to the back of the hearse and opened the rear door. "There she is." Andropov pointed.

Lying on the bed of the vehicle was an elongated bundle, wrapped in a white sheet, almost mummy-like.

"That's my clone?"

"Yeah. Isn't she beautiful?"

Sam thought to challenge *beautiful* since he couldn't see the clone. He thought about having the sheet unwrapped, but there was Clonal's policy. He had to agree it was a good policy. He didn't want to think about someone who might look like him being carved up on an operating table. "Why did you bring her here? Why are you showing me this?" Sam asked the questions and feared the answers at the same time.

"I'm going to give her to you."

"What!"

Andropov looked around, alarmed. "Don't shout," he said in a whisper. "I'm going to give her to you because I can't be caught with her. If I'm caught with her, then they'll take her away and we'll never see her again. But, if I let you take her, you can go to Mexico where you'll still be able to have your operation. All you have to--"

"Mexico?"

Andropov gave Sam a shove. "Dammit, I told you not to shout. Now, are you going to listen to me or am I going to get in my car and drive your white bundled clone over to the feds? It's your heart we're talking about."

"I'm sorry," Sam said. And he meant it. Andropov seemed sincere in wanting to help him, help him survive. But...

"That's better." Andropov dug into a pocket. "Here's the business card of your contact in Mexico. This is not the doctor who will perform the operation. It's the name of a middleman. You can understand due to the sensitivity of these sorts of things, I can't give you the doctor's name outright."

Sam had never experienced quicksand, but began to think the sinking sensation that was coming over him was similar. "I know nothing about clones. How do I care for her even if I do try to get her to Mexico?"

"No problem. No problem. First things first. She's sedated. So it should be easy. If she wakes up you mix some of this--" Andropov pressed a small bottle containing a colorless liquid into Sam's hand. "--Mix it with some milky bread and poke it down her throat."

"But won't she starve to death?"

"Look, even if you don't feed brain-deads, they keep living a long time. How about the woman in...I forget. They pulled all the plugs and she wouldn't die! You're good to go."

"I don't want to go anywhere."

"Figure of speech, but in this context, yeah, you're going to have to go. That is if you want a heart. That clone lying there is ready. She's ten years old--that's physically age-progressed. Her heart can replace yours, although at first you'll still have to take it easy until it grows to adult size. After that you're golden."

"Why Mexico?"

"Simple. The contact on the card I gave you will set you up with a surgeon who has done work for us in the past when there's been too much bureaucracy up here, if you get my drift."

Sam didn't want to get Andropov's drift. He didn't want to go to Mexico, either. He wanted to stay home, be called when his surgery prep was ready and go in and have a transplant. All this other stuff was making everything too complicated.

"How am I going to get her to Mexico?"

"You can fly. You can drive. You can float her over the Rio Grande."

Sam was beginning to dislike Andropov. "That's not what I meant. How do I get her across the border? Aren't they going to wonder what's in the bundle?"

"There's no law prohibiting the transportation of clones across international borders as long as you have the proper documentation certifying the clone's birth and your medical condition. We do it all the time." Andropov reached into the side of his vehicle, rummaged around and returned with a folder stuffed with papers. "Here are copies of medical reports Doctor Collins provided. They attest to your need for a transplant. There's also a birth certificate. It's not a real one, of course, I didn't have time to get one, but it looks real, and who's going to know? The Mexicans don't care. I named her Chloe Turner. I hope you don't mind me using your last name."

61

Sam shrugged, befuddled, trying to keep up with the fast talking Andropov.

"Obviously, we couldn't swing a passport for the clone. But you're the only one who will need a passport coming back into the US. It will be only you, won't it?" Andropov smiled conspiratorially.

"I don't like any of this."

"Hey, I feel for you Sam. But if I had your condition and given the present circumstances, I'd be packing my bags. Now, let's get going. I don't know how much time I have before the feds are onto me for not being in my office or at home. Give me a hand. We'll transfer this here Sam-survival-bundle over to your 4Runner."

Andropov pulled on the end of the bundle.

Sam stumbled to grab the other end.

"Don't drop her," Andropov said.

The bundle slid out of the hearse, and Sam grabbed his end. The clone was lighter than he had thought, so light he wondered if she was still alive and if her heart would be big enough to save him.

They walked the bundle to Sam's car and lifted her inside the back.

"That's it, Sam. Real simple. Oh. One more thing." Andropov pulled a folded sheaf of papers out of his coat pocket. "This is your contract with Clonal. Now that I've delivered the clone, do you think you could sign at the bottom here indicating that we have fulfilled the contract? Just a formality."

"I don't know about that," Sam said, trying to stall. Things were moving awfully fast. "I thought I only had to sign after the transplant."

"Well, yeah, technically. But the situation has obviously changed."

"I don't think I want to sign."

"God dammit, Turner. You don't fucking know your ass from a hole in the ground!" Andropov reached for the bundled clone and began to draw her out of the 4Runner.

Sam fought down a sense of panic. No clone. No transplant. *I'm good as dead.* "Okay, okay. You don't have to swear. I'll sign."

Andropov immediately stopped his pulling on the clone and steadied the contract in front of Sam for his signature. "Thanks Sam. It's been great doing business with you. Don't lose that card I gave you. You won't get anywhere in Mexico without my associate's help--" Andropov stared past Sam to the street where a dark sedan had slowed. The two men inside were looking their way. "Gotta go."

Sam reached into his pocket for the card to ask Andropov a question. But when he looked up, Andropov was halfway to his car. "Wait!"

Andropov kept on going. He disappeared into the hearse and a moment later gunned the engine to life and sped out of the parking lot.

Sam watched the red taillights bounce as the car hit the street, then traveled down Pretoria and disappeared around a corner. The dark sedan did a slow U-turn and followed.

Sam walked over to his 4Runner and peered into the open back.

The bundle lay still.

He gave it a poke. Nothing.

He closed the door.

I'm screwed.

Chapter Four

Sam turned into the five hundred foot driveway that wound up to his house. Globed lights lining the drive came on mid-way up when his 4Runner tripped the electronic security sensor buried alongside the path. This calmed Sam somewhat. At least something was working as planned.

On the way home via the interstate, all he could think about was the clone lying in the back of his 4Runner. She hadn't uttered a sound or given any indication she was alive. Andropov must have really knocked her out.

What a jerk. Sam had his suspicions when he signed the contract. Something about Andropov exuded sleaze. Now Sam wouldn't even buy a used car from the man. But Doctor Collins had stood by the organization saying there had never been a problem with Andropov meeting his contractual commitments.

Sam parked, hit the button that closed the garage door, then walked to the back of the vehicle. He opened the hatchback and stared at the white bundle on the floor.

I can't leave her here. Obviously. Take her inside. Leave her in the basement? No, that won't do. Take her up to the bedroom. Unwrap her and see her condition. Go from there.

Thankfully, she was light. She couldn't weigh more than a couple of bags of groceries. He could do it.

He thrust his hands under the motionless bundle and hugged the clone to his chest, then made his way up the various levels of his health-challenging house to the top floor where the bedrooms were.

Feeling his heart screaming a protest after the effort, he lay the bundle down on what had been Karen's bed. He had never motivated himself to get rid of the bed Karen had occupied next to his. Perhaps it was too much of an effort, or maybe a reluctance to let go.

The clone lay immobile, a still chrysalis. A dead chrysalis?

Sam tipped the bundle over a bit until he located the end of the wrap encasing her. After pulling the end free, he removed the sheet.

Once the sheet was gone, a skinny, naked child lay before him.

How can something that puny harbor the means to my survival?

Then he saw the wounds, small and big sores, looking angry red around the edges where presumably the various wires and tubes that sustained her had been ripped out. A grouping of pinpricks lay around the crown of her head. Larger sores showed on her chest and torso, then other sores farther down, probably from catheters for evacuation of waste.

Damn that Andropov. He must have been in one hell of a big hurry if he yanked all the tubes out.

This annoyed Sam. He was beginning to feel gypped. Not only had Andropov mistreated the clone, he'd produced the wrong gender.

I paid four hundred thousand down for a perfect match. If she's a she, then obviously the match isn't perfect.

66

Still angry, he reached for a cover and threw it over the sleeping clone, then adjusted the top edge so she could breathe freely. He didn't see how she could have been breathing before, her face being covered. Maybe clones didn't need a lot of air.

He supposed she was breathing. To make sure, he leaned close and put his ear near her nose and mouth. A faint intake and exhalation of air confirmed she was at least alive, which made him wonder, how did she breathe in the crèche?

Probably clones were like babies. They floated around in the womb, fed by a tube, until birth, at which time they had to open their mouths and suck in air...and eventually food.

Since Andropov had said clones didn't need much in the way of care, Sam felt he had a few days if not weeks before having to worry about what she needed.

He went to the medicine cabinet in the bathroom and picked out an antiseptic cream as well as a packet of Band-Aids.

When he returned to the clone, she had soiled the sheet she was lying on.

At least her internals are functioning. That's all he needed was a constipated clone. That would kill her faster than not having any nourishment.

Christ. I haven't changed a diaper in thirty years.

The thought depressed him as it reminded him of Karen. She's the one who had infant nieces who had to be changed when her sister visited. He never figured out how he had been pressed into diaper duty, but he had.

He put down the antiseptic and Band-Aids and pulled an old sheet out of the linen closet. After a bit of thought, he tore the sheet into a number of squares and folded one into a diaper. Back to the bathroom for two wet cloths, then to the clone to clean her up. That done, he diapered her, tying off the long ends of the diaper rather than pinning them. He didn't have pins big enough to cope with the bunched cloth.

The clone had lain lethargic throughout the whole diapering. At times Sam felt he was diapering a frog, her legs were so long and skinny. Not a sound out of her. Not even a moan. No movement of eyeballs beneath her delicate eyelids.

Must be one hell of a sedative.

Sam concentrated next on the Band-Aids. He didn't see how he was going to be able to take over her care, not with fifteen different penetrations having monitored and sustained her before.

When he finished tending to the sores, the clone looked like she'd been sprayed with buckshot given all the flesh colored Band-Aids covering her body.

He was washing his hands in the bathroom basin when the clone moaned, the first sound she had made since he'd taken possession of her. It wasn't an unpleasant sound. Somehow it struck a chord in him. Did it have to do with her being him?

After drying his hands he approached.

Her mouth was open and a little pink tongue poked out, running back and forth on her lips.

She must be thirsty.

Sam went to the bathroom, retrieved a glass and filled it with cold water. Back at the clone, he lifted her head off the bed and poured a sip of water into her mouth.

The first sip went down smoothly. The water slid to the back of her throat, hit her swallow reflex and she gulped. No problem.

Emboldened he poured another larger sip into her mouth.

This one didn't go down.

She gagged, then made a strangled hissing sound as she tried to inhale. Her body jerked spasmodically.

Terrified she was choking to death, Sam turned her over and patted her back. When that didn't seem to help, he rolled her back, stuck his finger into her mouth to make sure she hadn't swallowed her tongue, tipped her head back to open her air passage and clamped his mouth onto hers. He blew.

Her small chest swelled with the air he was giving her.

He disengaged and allowed her to exhale. At the same time he checked her pulse. It was strong. He repeated the mouth to mouth a few more times before she spit the water up. She coughed and began to breath regularly.

He changed her sheet, then sat down on his bed, hunched over, head down, his hands between his knees. He'd worked up a sweat with all the rescue breathing, then rolling her back and forth to slip a clean sheet under her.

This is not going to work.

If he kept the clone, then she would surely die on him, or conversely, she would end up killing him. He couldn't even give her water, much less milky bread. If she died on him, what then? He didn't want to think of the consequences. Had he committed a crime taking her from Andropov? He hadn't had time to think about that.

The feds had confiscated all the other clones and were probably looking for this one. Was it a crime he had it, like felony child abduction? But he hadn't abducted anyone. Andropov had given him the clone. Maybe aiding and abetting. But he was a reluctant aid-er and abett-er. What nonsense. She was his clone. He'd paid for her. There was no law against taking possession of a clone. There was just a new law restricting the way clones were grown. Besides, did clones even qualify as people? Some argued they did. In fact, most probably thought that way, even though clones were brain-dead.

Go figure.

He took out the card Andropov had given him. Guadalajara? That's over two thousand miles away. He couldn't take a plane. Too public. He'd have to drive. Impossible. The clone would more than likely die on the long trip. Then there was the heat. Primitive conditions. Risk of illness.

Then what? Back to the feds hauling him away for some unknown infraction.

Solutions. Solutions. Returning the clone to Andropov is the only option.

Return her before she died. Since he didn't know when she was likely to die but thought it could be sudden, he'd have to return her soon. Like now. Of course once he returned her, the feds would get her and he'd be out a new heart, and out his initial payment with nothing to show for it.

70

Forget the money.

He could always get in line with UNOS. But with the government's encroachment into the whole field of healthcare a decade ago, wait times had quadrupled. Maybe he could buy his way forward in line. He'd heard it was possible. At least it was better than jail time for being caught with a dead clone.

Damn that Andropov. But damning Andropov *here* wouldn't cut it. He had to damn Andropov in person. Better yet, he had to grab him by the neck and shake him till he dropped. How Sam had agreed to take the clone in the first place eluded him.

He snatched up his cell phone and punched in the number for Clonal Transplants. After twelve rings someone picked up but said nothing.

"Hello, hello!" Sam shouted. "This is Sam Turner. I want to speak to Mr. Andropov!"

The line went dead.

***

Sam stood in the middle of his bedroom. The clone lay bandaged on the bed. Late afternoon. The sun was sinking toward the horizon.

Decision time. It had to have been Andropov who picked up the phone. He's avoiding me. I'll drive up to Denver. He won't expect that. Then confront him and demand he take the clone back.

Sam re-wrapped the clone, making sure there was a space for her to breathe through, then staggered down the stairs with her. Unable to see the treads, he took them slowly, not wanting to trip.

This was getting old real fast. He was risking his life on the damn stairs. A fall could cripple him.

At the bottom level he laid the bundled clone into the back of the 4Runner.

Why me, he thought. *It had been so simple. I sign a contract. I wait two years. I get my transplant operation.*

The anger and frustration he felt when this thought wedged into his consciousness and wouldn't leave was enough to occupy him all the way to Denver.

As he neared the end of Havana Street, he slowed.

The warehouse complex in which Clonal Transplants was one of the tenants, sprawled on his right.

Andropov's black hearse gunned out of the parking lot, made a right turn north, then another right on 56th Street. The hearse picked up speed.

Shit. Sam accelerated after him, flashing his headlights. The Rocky Mountain Arsenal slid by on his left, small suburban cookie cutter homes on his right.

The hearse didn't stop.

Trees and sunlight blinked overhead like strobes, alternately lighting and shading the interior of his 4Runner through its moon-roof.

Sam powered down the passenger side window, leaned across the seat as he drove one handed and hollered at Andropov, who glanced once his way but kept going.

In desperation, Sam swerved his 4Runner into the hearse, the two vehicles rocking back and forth on the road with a screech of metal on metal.

Andropov, a grim determination on his face, slowed.

Sam punched the 4Runner forward and cranked a hard right, cutting off the hearse.

Both cars came to a stop on the side of the road.

Andropov rolled down the driver's side window. "You fucking idiot! Are you trying to kill me?"

Sam leapt out of his car and rounded on the hearse. He reached into the window and grabbed at Andropov. "I've got the clone in the back. I don't want her. You've got to--"

Andropov put his car in reverse and backed up almost taking Sam with him. Once he was clear of the 4Runner, he gunned the vehicle down the road.

Damn him.

Sam climbed back into his car and gave chase. This time Andropov didn't slow down, leaving Sam trailing behind.

After five miles, Andropov screeched into RNO Airport Shuttle, an off-site airport parking lot.

What the hell?

Andropov sped up to the gate, lurched to a stop as he grabbed a parking ticket, then waited for white and red barrier to lift before proceeding into the lot.

Sam turned into the entrance drive.

Do I go after him? I have no choice. He collected his own ticket, went through the gate and followed the hearse.

73

It wound its way through the lot, directed by signs indicating where to park and where the next shuttle would be.

By the time Sam pulled in beside the hearse, Andropov was already out, a duffel bag of sorts in his hand.

The black and red RNO van idled next to him.

"We need to talk!" Sam shouted as he hurried from his vehicle. "You've got to take the clone back. I can't take care of her. She's going to die on me!"

The shuttle door was open with the driver waiting. Other passengers were already on board, their faces plastered to the windows watching and listening wide-eyed.

Andropov confronted him. "For Christ's sake, Sam. Keep your fucking voice down. People are listening."

"So what!" Sam glanced about wildly. "Where the hell are you going?"

"Can't say. Don't want to say. I'm just going. You don't want to know."

Sam was incredulous. "You can't. What am I supposed to do?"

Andropov stepped closer. He thrust his face within inches of Sam's. "That's not my problem," he said in a low, tight voice. "It's yours."

"Sir," the driver called from the inside of the shuttle. "Are you going to the airport or not?"

"I've gotta go, Sam." Andropov slung his bag up into the shuttle, where the driver retrieved it and put it on a baggage shelf. "Your best bet is still to get to Mexico. Your clone has no future here. It will either die, or the feds will confiscate it. Go to Mexico. If you make it, you can have the operation there, or wait until we get the results of a court challenge."

"But that could take months!"

"Sir...?" The driver said. "I've got passengers waiting."

Andropov peered at the driver's name tag. "Look, Abdul, I'll be there in a second." He turned back to Sam. "I don't know how long it will take. But it won't take months. If you don't proceed with an operation, you'll have to hold tight. It's your choice."

Andropov started to extend his hand to shake Sam's, seemed to think better of it, then climbed aboard the shuttle.

The door closed and the shuttle eased away toward the exit.

Sam stood gulping in frustration, his hands clenched at his sides. This was not what he had anticipated.

He stomped back to the 4Runner, glanced at the wrapped clone, who hadn't moved, and drove to the exit.

He handed his ticket to the attendant, a very black man with a name tag identifying him as Mustapha. Probably Ethiopian. They'd been moving into the area and taking over all the airport jobs.

"That will be seven dollars, please," Mustapha said in passable English.

"What?" Sam felt a stab at his heart. He counted. *This is going to kill me*. "I've only been

75

here five minutes," he managed to say in a calm voice.

"That's the minimum daily charge, sir."

Sam paid, then glanced out the exit. A black sedan with two men in it sat parked on the other side of 56th Avenue. *Cops.*

Sam tossed the receipt on the passenger seat and pulled out onto the otherwise deserted avenue.

The two men in the sedan craned to watch him go. One of them put a cell phone to his ear. A moment later, they pulled out in the direction the shuttle had taken to the airport.

Sam breathed a sigh of relief. They were obviously more interested in Andropov than they were in him. But they also must have taken down his license plate number. It would probably only be a matter of time before they did a trace and showed up at his doorstep.

***

Agent Wellstone's office on the eighteenth floor of the Federal Building in downtown Denver looked out over the city with a backdrop of the Rocky Mountains in the distance. Each year, over the twenty years Wellstone had been an agent working out of the Denver office, the haze of afternoon pollution that hung over the city had increased. Where once the skies had been pristine and clear, they were now tinged in yellow.

His office was small with wood paneling up to waist height topped by framed glass. This gave him a view into the general office area where his agents occupied desks arranged to face him. That way he could keep a close eye on his agents. Of course,

76

they could also see him, but he figured they were more afraid of him than he was of them.

But at the moment, Wellstone wasn't worrying about the skies over Denver or the size of his office. He was worrying about the lack of progress he was making on the Clonal Transplants seizure. He had taken a special interest in the case, because he agreed wholeheartedly with the new legislation. It was about time the government stepped in and took a stand against something that was fundamentally, categorically, and obviously wrong.

A knock sounded on the door to his office, and he looked up. "Come."

Agent Marshall stuck his head in the door, then when Wellstone beckoned, stepped inside. "Sir, we received a call from surveillance team Alpha. Andropov boarded an airport shuttle at an off-site parking facility and is currently heading for Denver International.

"Alpha also reported Andropov made contact with an unknown person driving a 2010 model Toyota 4Runner. A first contact with the unknown was made along 56th Avenue on the way to the parking facility, and a second contact at the facility. Alpha was not able to discern what they talked about."

"Did Alpha get a plate number?"

"They did, sir. I'm having it traced as we speak."

Wellstone rested his chin in his hand, thinking. He gazed absently at a photo of a woman, his ex-wife, a Rubinesque blond in a one piece bathing suit, sitting with their two young kids, a boy and a girl. Next to the photo sat a lithograph of Jesus Christ. Jesus had one hand raised and the other on his heart. Wellstone came back from his reverie to the present. "Have Alpha follow Andropov. We can catch up to the 4Runner later."

Marshall nodded. "I took the liberty of telling them to do that, sir. They report they are tailing the shuttle as it enters the airport district."

"Excellent. Let me know about the 4Runner as soon as you have any information."

"Yes, sir." Agent Marshall ducked out of the room and returned to his desk.

Wellstone had turned back to paper work, part of three, six inch stacks of paper that cluttered his desk, when he was interrupted again by a second agent.

Agent Mike Peterson had been trained as a lawyer before joining the agency. He now tracked the legal issues Wellstone's division faced.

Peterson entered and sat when Wellstone indicated a chair. "We've got a problem, chief."

"We always have problems, Mike. If we didn't have problems, we'd be out of business."

Peterson pulled out a sheaf of papers. "These are copies of a filing made in Denver Superior Court late this afternoon by the two clone farms in our jurisdiction. The filing asks the court to impose an injunction on our efforts to enforce HJR 54. They argue their businesses will be ruined by the time a formal court challenge can be adjudicated."

"Damn." Wellstone tapped the eraser end of a pencil against his teeth as he thought through the consequences of an injunction. "How long before they get it, if they get it?"

"A couple of days, maybe a week if the judge needs more information."

"And if they get it, what impact is it going to have on our case?"

"That will depend on the details of the injunction. But it shouldn't stop us from moving forward with our investigation as long as we don't infringe on anyone's civil rights. Anyone associated with these guys could cry foul if we press too hard, and the ACLU would be onto us like fleas on a dog."

Wellstone winced. "Cut the metaphors, Mike."

Peterson focused his attention on the papers in his lap. "Yes, sir."

"What about the clones we confiscated?" Wellstone asked.

"I suspect we will have to release those clones who are ready for transplantation, so as not to be seen as disrupting the business of either of these farms. Retaining possession of the remaining clones is immaterial as long as we take good care of them. Once the final judgment comes down after a trial, we'll either have to give up the clones or process them out to a shelter."

"But in the meantime we'll still be able to test to see if any of them are sentient?"

"I don't see why not."

Wellstone leaned back in his chair, clasped his hands over his midsection and eyed Peterson. "Still, we don't have a lot of time. It burns me up we might have to release these poor creatures so they can be butchered for their organs."

"Yes, sir. My feelings exactly."

Marshall reappeared and rapped on the door.

Wellstone waved him in.

"Sir, we've got the trace. The 4Runner belongs to a Samuel Johns Turner, 6634 Orion Drive, Monument. He's a retired civil engineer. Writes novels."

Wellstone came forward in his chair. This was beginning to get interesting. "What's he write?"

"Sir?"

"You said he writes novels. What's he write? Is he published?"

"I...I don't know, sir. I'll find out."

Wellstone waved a hand. "A personal curiosity. Not relevant. Odd he was seen with Androp as the latter is making tracks to presumably leave the country."

"Yes, sir. We thought the same thing. We also have a tentative make on Turner having met Andropov earlier in the day at a parking lot not far from the offices of Clonal Transplants. Our surveillance team couldn't get a plate ID, but the vehicle fits the description of a 4Runner."

"Well done, Marshall. I want you to put a tail on this Turner...that is if you haven't already done so."

"No, sir. I mean I haven't yet, sir."

"That's okay." Wellstone turned back to Peterson. "Mike, it's okay if we put a tail on Turner, isn't it?"

"I suppose there's no law broken if we keep tabs on him while he's out and about in public. But we can't make contact or press too hard without violating his rights. Why go to the trouble of dogging Turner?"

"We found an empty crèche during our search and seizure operation. What if Turner is a Clonal Transplant client and Turner's clone is the missing clone? Why would it be missing--"

"I don't know, sir."

"--It was a rhetorical question, Peterson. Let me finish."

"Yes, sir."

"Could it be that the missing clone is the sentient the tipster Washington saw? If it is, then Androp didn't want to be caught with it, so he pawned it off on the unsuspecting Turner."

"You might be right, sir," Marshall said. "But wouldn't Turner find out the clone is sentient?"

"It could have been sedated," Peterson said.

Wellstone glanced over at Peterson. "Exactly. Unfortunately, we can't nail Turner since he hasn't done anything wrong if the clone is his. He paid for it. That is unless, he discovers the clone is sentient and doesn't report it. Marshall, for starters, I want a check to see if Turner is a client of Clonal."

"Might be a tough one, sir, medical records being private."

"Where have you been, Marshall? They used to be private. Now we have a National Medical Records Databank that has saved thousands of lives and also given us, when we need it, easy access to everyone's records."

"Where there's a will there's a way," Peterson said.

"Nice, Mike. Ditch the clichés."

"Yes, sir."

"If Turner is a client, then I think my hypothetical begins to hold water." Wellstone thought about his own cliché, but Marshall and Peterson seemed not to have noticed. "All we have to do, now, is keep tabs on him until he gives us probable cause to reel him in."

***

Sam sat in his 4Runner in his garage, his hands gripping the steering wheel, head slumped forward.

Will this ever end?

After what must have been ten minutes, he unbuckled his seat belt, exited and trudged to the back of the vehicle. Dismay washed through him as he realized he was going to have to carry the clone up the stairs again.

He took the steps to the living room level slowly, then decided it was not worth the effort to haul her all the way to the bedroom above.

He lay her on the sofa and sat to catch his breath. He was at his wits' end. After a full roundtrip to Denver, he was back where he started three hours ago.

He went over to the sliding doors that led out to the south deck and opened them. Fresh air. A sharp drop in temperature. Fall. He turned on the floods that lit the rocks outside, competing with the failing sunlight, but even that didn't lift his mood.

He returned to the sofa and stared at the resting clone. He needed help. He needed advice. If

Karen had been alive, she would have known what to do. Now he was on his own, or was he? What about JoAnne? *She'll know what to do.*

He knew it was a copout, but he had no choice. JoAnne had been around the block a few times. From what little he knew of her, she hadn't always been a staid literary agent. Not having graduated from Vassar.

He reached for his landline phone, then thought better of it. Using the cell might be harder to trace. Trace? Had he come to that already? But the conclusion was obvious. Hadn't Andropov been raided by the FBI, and hadn't he withheld evidence that Sam now had sleeping on the sofa? Wouldn't the FBI like to know what happened to the missing clone? How much time did he have before someone knocked on his door, or more probably, barged through it?

When JoAnne picked up and said hello, Sam thought her voice was the sweetest he had ever heard. "I've got a problem."

"Are you okay?"

Good. Some show of concern. "I'm okay. It's not about me. Yes, it's about me. It's complicated. Can you come up here?"

There was a pause on the line. "I don't know, Sam. Should I bring a chaperone? It's six o'clock on a Saturday night."

Lost her. She's not taking this seriously. "I understand your reluctance. It's not about chaperones. Trust me. I don't want to go into it on the phone. I can't. Someone might be listening, if you know what I mean."

83

"Oh."

"Please."

"All right. I'll be over in a bit."

Twenty minutes later the driveway alarm set off chimes from the wireless receiver screwed to the wall in an upstairs hall closet.

It took about two minutes from the time the chimes sounded to the time JoAnne drove the rest of the driveway, parked, climbed the front steps and rang the doorbell. Sam was there to greet her.

"Thanks for coming," he said.

She nodded, gave him a brief hug and proceeded into the foyer, where he helped her out of an L.L. Bean jacket. Underneath, she had switched out of her designer clothes, opting for jeans and a sweatshirt. "Okay. What's this all about?"

"After our coffee this morning, I got an urgent call from Andropov...Clonal Transplants. He wanted to see me. Immediately. Since he sounded desperate, I agreed and drove up to Denver. He met me in a parking lot. The feds raided his business, confiscated all his clones except mine. Then before I could resist, he dumped my clone on me."

"What? That's crazy."

This isn't going well. Sam hung up her jacket. "I know it sounds crazy. But the reality is, I've got the clone."

"Where?" JoAnne peered into the living room and must have spotted the bundle lying on the sofa. "Is that the clone?"

"Yeah. She's sedated. I would have carried her upstairs, but I've already done that once and couldn't face doing it again.

84

"Did you say *she*?" JoAnne stepped into the living room.

"Andropov brushed it off like it was no big deal. One chromosome. Who could imagine one chromosome had such power? He said not to worry. The tissue match is still one hundred percent."

JoAnne sat on the sofa next to the clone. "She looks like an Egyptian mummy wrapped up like that. Can she breath?"

"It's loosely wrapped. The material is quite porous."

"So, what are you going to do with this one hundred percent pure tissue matched clone?"

Sam didn't like the way she phrased the question. "That's where I have a problem. I don't know how to care for her. As long as she's sedated I'm okay. Andropov brushed me off. He said she'll probably stay alive without the need for a lot of care in the near term. He said if she woke up to give her more sedative. Mix it with milky toast and poke it down her throat. Can you believe it?"

"I don't believe it, and neither should you. She's going to die on your hands if you don't do something quick. What else? Don't hold back on me."

"I tried to give her water. I almost drowned her. I had to give her rescue breathing. That was the last straw. I bundled her up again and drove back to Denver."

"You wanted to give her back?"

"It wasn't working. I guess I panicked. I called but Andropov hung up on me, so I drove up."

"Obviously he didn't take her."

"He was on his way to the airport. He told me my only option was to take the clone to Mexico and have my operation there."

"Mexico!?"

I guess that shocked her. "Yeah. He gave me a contact who would help me set up a transplant."

"He expects you to cart this brain-dead, sedated clone to Mexico and have an operation where her heart is cut out and inserted for yours...in, in Mexico?"

Sam pulled up a chair and sat opposite her. "Come on, JoAnne. They have good doctors in Mexico. It's nothing different than what I would have had done here. As far as I can tell, my clone is nothing other than that. A clone. A non-sentient agglomerate of tissue that will cough up a vital organ for me. All I have to do is make sure she stays alive long enough for me to get her south of the border. Guadalajara, the card reads."

"They have transplant hospitals in Guadalajara?"

"I guess. There's a huge American retirement community around Lake Chapala. There must be plenty of business."

"But that's like two thousand miles away. How are you going to manage?"

"I...I..."

"You don't know, do you? Admit it. Crossing international borders. Dealing in a foreign country. The feds probably looking for you. All this sounds way beyond your means of coping."

Sam felt desperate. His shoulders slumped. His chest heaved. "I don't think I have a choice," he whispered.

The clone moaned.

"She doesn't sound very comfortable. Should I unwrap her? I'd like to see her, anyway."

Sam eased forward and helped JoAnne unwrap the sheet.

The clone lay looking deathly pale, her arms straight at her sides, her blond hair matted to the sides of her head.

"Why all the Band-Aids?" JoAnne asked.

"Andropov pulled out her tubes and monitoring wires. I think he was in a hurry."

"Poor thing." JoAnne fanned the air with her hand. "I think she needs a diaper change."

Sam felt defensive. "I already changed her once. I've got clean diapers upstairs. I tore up a sheet." Sam stood and took the stairs slowly to retrieve a diaper. On the way back he stopped to wet paper towels in the kitchen.

"She's beautiful," JoAnne said once he returned to the living room and sat down again. "Your spitting image."

"Comments like that aren't helpful at all."

She gave his knee a shove. "Come on. Lighten up."

"How can you tell me to lighten up? This isn't a game. It's real. Lives are at stake." Sam shut up, cutting off his frustration as his blood pressure rose, at least his cheeks felt flushed, and he supposed it to be the result of rising blood pressure.

"If you don't calm down, you're going to have a heart attack," JoAnne said. "Here, I'll change the diaper."

"Thanks."

JoAnne busied herself with the changing.

Sam closed his eyes and leaned back in his chair, trying to concentrate on his breathing, something Zen.

"You know," JoAnne said when she'd finished. "You're bringing all this on yourself. All you have to do is take her to the feds. Explain what happened. It's not your fault."

Maybe. After all, I haven't committed a crime. "Negative. The feds rounded up all of Andropov's clones. Who knows if and when he will get them back. The feds would do the same with my clone. I could be dead by the time the legal issues get sorted out."

"All right. Let's assume that's true. Where do you go from here. What do you want from me?"

Sam took a deep breath and let it out, an obvious sigh of resignation. "I don't see I have any choice but to go to Mexico to have my operation. Given the secrecy with which Andropov gave me my clone, I'll have to travel with a bit of discretion."

"Discretion?"

"Okay, clandestinely, secretly. I'll have to be able to lay low for a while. I'll need a place to stay. I'll need money...which I can supply. I'll need a means of private communication with the world I leave behind." He looked at her pleadingly. "I don't know how to do this. I thought you might."

She finished tying the diaper, then leaned back on the sofa. "Suddenly, you need me?"

Sam felt a welling frustration. An urge to throw something. He counted.

"You're counting aren't you." JoAnne smiled.

Sam finished his counting. It hadn't done any good. "Dammit. Help me."

She studied the clone for a moment. "Okay, I'll help you. This stuff is coming from my days with the Weathermen Underground."

That caught Sam's attention. "Really?"

"Sam. The Weathermen were a 60's group. I wasn't even born then."

"I'm sorry. I should have known. There's too much going on right now. What do you have?"

"Communication is the easiest." She took out a pencil and paper from her purse. "Give me an ID and a password you want to use, and I'll set up an email account through a remote provider. Total privacy. Third party."

Sam thought for a moment. "ID...STurner64."

"What's that, your birth year?"

"So what?" When JoAnne didn't respond, Sam continued. "Password...counterculture."

"Too long. Has to have some numbers."

"Mudslide69."

"That'll work. I won't ask how you got from *counterculture* to *mudslide69*, but I will assume there's a relationship that will help you remember it. Next. Place to stay--" JoAnne wrote on a slip of paper and handed it to Sam. "--Here's the address of a friend of mine, Heidi Bergman. She runs a small, three bungalow resort in Playa de Cerro

Bonito. That's a tiny fishing village on the Pacific coast about two hours' drive from Guadalajara.

"I'll email her to let her know you're coming. Hopefully, she'll have a vacancy. She's not too busy this time of year. You can hang out there until things clarify up here, or you decide to proceed with your operation." JoAnne made a face.

"You still don't approve, do you?" Sam said.

"I'm sorry. Your clone is such a lovely looking little girl. It's hard for me to imagine her on a table next to you, and a surgeon slicing into her chest to remove her heart to restore yours."

"You have too much imagination." When JoAnne started to protest, Sam hurried on. "Thanks for this." He waved the notes she had given him. "I'm going to leave tomorrow. I don't think I'll have a moment to spare."

Chapter Five

The next morning, Sam awoke at 6:32 AM.
Figures.

JoAnne had wished him luck and left after eight o'clock. The clone had remained quiet all night.

Sam dressed, then went downstairs to the living room where he had left the clone asleep on the sofa. She seemed to still be sleeping, presumably still sedated.

He ate breakfast and thought about giving the clone something to eat, then decided against it in view of his experience the night before with the water. Of course he was only putting off the inevitable. He'd have to feed her sometime, just not then.

The sun was well up by the time he had thought through and laid out what he would need for an indefinite stay south of the border. He packed a single suitcase and loaded it into the back of the 4Runner, then carried the clone down the stairs and placed her in the back of the vehicle beside the suitcase. She was still wrapped in the sheet with part of it lying loosely over her face.

It was already past noon when he backed out of his garage and proceeded down the driveway. As the trees slid by on either side, his home receded behind him in the rearview mirror.

Will I ever see it again?

No time to dwell on that. His first stop was the local Great Foods. He parked a distance from the store where there were few other cars. The clone hadn't made a sound or moved, so parking at the edge of the lot was just a precaution. The only other shoppers who preferred the outlying parking spaces were young kids with baggy pants sliding halfway down their hips probably selling drugs.

Inside the store, he roamed the aisles, loading his cart with foods that were packaged or canned. There would be places to shop along the way, but if he was on the run, and it began to feel that way, he might have to hole up somewhere for a few days or weeks.

Next, he pulled into the Great Foods gas station and topped up, using his grocery card credits, and immediately regretted doing so since using them would leave behind a trail of what he had done. For that matter he'd used his charge card in the store. But he must be getting paranoid. Why should routine purchases attract any attention?

After gassing up, Sam drove to the local bank branch. He needed cash. Lots of it.

He wrote himself a check for fifty thousand on his Schwab account and put it into the drive-up tray along with his driver's license for identification.

The teller was all smiles until she saw the amount. She retreated from the window, presumably to talk to her supervisor. A few minutes later she reappeared. "We will have to put a hold of three business days on this check. If you'll sign the form I'm giving you to acknowledge the hold, your money should be available in three days."

Sam felt a flutter of panic. *No way.* "I can't wait three days. I need the money, now."

"I'm sorry, sir. I'm afraid that's our policy for amounts this large."

"I want to see your supervisor."

"Certainly, sir. You're welcome to see my supervisor, but you'll have to park and come inside."

A single parking space was open, nestled in a line of eight other cars. What if the clone woke up and started moaning? What if one of the other drivers came back and heard her? It was a chance he would have to take. He parked and entered the bank through a vestibule that was shared by the Starbucks next door. Had it been only yesterday he and JoAnne had sat there talking?

The bank supervisor turned out to be a young woman, almost as young as the teller. She stood to shake his hand and indicated a seat in front of her desk.

"I'd like to cash this check, now--" Sam peered at the name tag of the supervisor. "--Miss Keller."

"It's a very large amount."

"I've deposited checks here larger than this and never had a problem. Is it only when money goes out of your bank you put holds on checks?"

"It's a general policy," Keller said. "But we can make exceptions. One moment." She typed something on the keyboard in front of her, then perused the computer monitor. "I see you have cashed a number of checks over time that are as large or larger than this one. No bounced checks. You've been a customer of the bank for almost twenty years. Are you sure you have sufficient funds in this Schwab account to cover this check?"

"Of course I'm sure. It's my account." Then something clicked with Sam. "Do you have to report this transaction?"

"Indeed we do, Mr. Turner. We'll have to file Form 104 with the Department of the Treasury since the transaction is over ten thousand."

Sam stared at the supervisor in wonder. Since he had never run away before, it had never crossed his mind that this sort of requirement could be a real nuisance. "What if I want nine thousand?"

Keller graced Sam with a sympathetic smile. "The law says once you request a sum over ten thousand, then reduce it to avoid us having to file a report, we have to file a report, anyway."

"I guess they gotcha coming and going." Sam saw his attempt at humor was lost on the supervisor. "Ah, how about if I took out nine thousand from my checking account with your bank, here?"

"I'd have to say you are in a gray area. You have access to funds in your account with us that we can verify. That you have resorted to taking them instead of accessing an outside account raises suspicions. What's going on here, Mr. Turner?"

"I'm planning an extended stay south of the border and thought it wise to carry cash for the duration rather than have to wire it, banking between the two countries being what it is."

Miss Keller threaded her fingers together and leaned forward conspiratorially. "I hear you. Anecdotal word has it that sometimes you have to bribe bank officials down there to complete a legitimate wire transfer."

Sam leaned in, too. "You don't say?"

They were eyeball to eyeball when Keller blinked. "I think you heard me, Mr. Turner."

"Right, then. I'm making this check out for nine thousand. I guess I don't need your initials for me to cash it."

"No, you don't. Show the teller a photo ID, and she'll take care of you."

Sam rose and shook the supervisor's hand, then returned to the teller. Off to his left, through the glass partition of the supervisor's office, he could see she had picked up the phone and was talking to someone while looking at him.

Sam collected his money in twenty dollar bills and tucked the large envelope the bank provided under his arm. He thanked the teller and hurried to the 4Runner.

An elderly couple was peering into the back of the vehicle.

"Can I help you?" Sam asked as he came up to them.

"This your car?" The man's hair was shockingly white. He was bent over, used a cane for support and wore thick glasses.

"It is."

"What's that wiggling in the back? Looks like a child wrapped in a sheet or something."

Sam cupped his hands against the 4Runner's window and made an exaggerated show of peering inside. "I don't see any wiggling. You're imagining things." He stepped to the driver's side door and got in, powered down the window and started the engine.

The elderly couple shuffled out of the way when he backed out of the parking space. "I know what I saw! You're a kidnapper!" The old man waved his cane in the air. "Helen, call 911!"

Sam eased out of the parking lot and pulled onto the main street. When he looked in his rearview mirror, the woman had her cell phone to her ear with one hand and was pointing at him with the other.

He sped away, caught one green light, then waited impatiently at a red before being able to hit the on-ramp to the interstate. He accelerated to the seventy-five mile per hour limit and merged with the metal tide that carried him along.

With the suspicious bank supervisor, the old couple and Monument far behind, he adjusted the angle of his seat, put the 4Runner into cruise control and tried to relax.

A midday haze was lifting from the lower elevations of Pikes Peak, cutting the view of it in half and making it look taller than it already was. A fall snowstorm had lain down a blanket of white that glistened above tree line.

A mile farther down the road, a large lighted sign hung over the southbound lanes. Pixilated letters were scrolling across its dark surface.

As he got closer, he could make out the text.

AMBER ALERT: DARK BLUE SUV.
LICENSE NUMBER ABT-926
CALL (303)555-4251
***

Sam careened off the interstate at the next off-ramp. He came to the end of the ramp, pulled over to the side of the road and stopped.

His heart was beating as though this was the last time it would, and he was going to go out with a bang. Pain radiated from his left shoulder into his left upper arm.

He fumbled for the pills Doctor Collins had given him and placed one under his tongue. He took several deep breaths, monitoring the pain's spread.

It rose to a crescendo, then dissipated. Great stuff those pills.

Calm down and think.

There must be a couple of thousand SUV's on the highways, so he shouldn't worry about that. They weren't going to stop every dark blue SUV. Besides, his was dark green. And his license wasn't ABT-926, it was AEF-829. Still, it wouldn't do to cruise the interstate. If state troopers were anywhere, they were there.

He threaded his way back toward Monument, fretting it was nearly noon. How could he have tried so hard to get an early start and still be in the vicinity of Monument? He followed the service road north, then turned west on smaller roads that led through a suburb of upscale homes on one acre lots. At the back of the suburb, which pushed up against the foothills, lay a dirt track that would take him into the mountains of the Front Range. By doing this he would avoid Colorado Springs and end up farther west. From there, he figured it would be safe enough to travel the less crowded State

Highway that ran due west then south where he could take one of the high mountain passes through the Rockies. Besides, it would be dark in five hours, then no one would notice him, anyway.

Three hours later, with the sun long gone behind the mountains, he came to the town of Poncha Springs, a mixed bag of roadside shops for tourists, period-looking eateries and general stores. It was a typical Colorado town organized along the main road through it. The fourteen thousand foot peaks of Tabaguache and Shavano towered over the town. Named after Indian chiefs, they stood sentinel to Poncha Pass, the only way south through the mountains to the San Luis Valley.

Sam was hungry.

He pulled into the parking lot of Charley's Diner, which was located on the edge of town and didn't have a lot of patrons judging from the two other cars in the lot.

The clone seemed to be agitated in the back. She squirmed and emitted mewing sounds. Must be hungry or something. Maybe the sedative was wearing off. A near panic gripped him as he realized he was going to have to feed her. Giving her water had been bad enough. What would happen with milky bread?

But the mewing increased, as did the twisting and turning.

Sam hurried into the diner.

It was so brightly lit he had to wait a few seconds while his eyes adjusted. Neat rows of tables ran the length of a rectangular space with an old fashion counter and floor-mounted stools with chrome pedestals running on the long side. Behind the counter leaned a heavily made up brunette in a pink and white checkered dress with a red apron.

She eyed him as he walked up to the counter, then at the last moment shoved off, leaned on her hands on the countertop and gave him a ruby red-lipped smile. She had nice teeth.

"Do you have take out?" Sam asked.

"Sure do." She turned serious as she took out her pad and poised her pencil.

"I'll have a BLT and fries," he said without looking at the menu, then regretted the choice. Bacon and fries were two of the no-no's his doctor had told him to avoid. "And an extra slice of bread and two servings of milk. You can leave the milk in their containers."

"Will that be white or dark?" the waitress asked. She stood with her pencil in the air.

Sam had been glancing over his shoulder, out to the parking lot at his vehicle, lest another elderly couple start to take an interest. "What? What did you say?"

She brought the pencil down and sighed with bored impatience. "The bread, white or dark?"

"Dark...no, white." Sam tried to smile in the face of the stern glare from the waitress. Dark would be too coarse. White would mush up better. But he couldn't tell that to the waitress. So he stood there feeling like a fool.

"You can take a seat over there. It'll be about ten minutes."

Sam stepped over to an empty table, pulled out a chair and sat. He fidgeted, glancing often out the

99

window to the 4Runner, not that he could see what was going on with the clone on the inside. At least no one was paying the vehicle any attention.

Patrons came and went. Two Highway Patrol officers entered, glanced around without giving him a second look, and sat at a table nearby.

Sam stole a nervous glance at the officers as they perused the menu. He stepped to the counter. "Is my order going to be much longer?"

The waitress put down the coffee carafe she was about to pour and gave him a tired look. "It takes five minutes to fry the bacon. Then the cook puts the sandwich together." She eyed him. "If all goes well, you'll have your order in under ten minutes, like I said."

Standoff. Sam wasn't going to get his order sooner, and if he left without it, he would attract attention. "I'm sorry, I'm in a bit of a hurry, that's all."

"Aren't we all, honey."

Sam returned to his chair and drew the back of his hand across his brow where a rivulet of sweat threatened to cascade down.

The officer facing him looked up from his menu at Sam, then back down again. Fortunately, the waitress came over to take their order, and Sam felt he was forgotten.

A few minutes later, the cook shoved Sam's BLT and fries through an opening behind the counter and slapped a bell.

The waitress glanced over at Sam, who bolted out of his chair.

She arranged everything in a box, closed the lid and shoved the box toward him. "That will be seven dollars and fifty-six cents, please."

Sam took out his credit card.

As the waitress reached for the card, Sam drew it back. "I'll pay cash. It isn't much."

"Suit yourself."

He handed her a ten. "Keep the change."

"Why, thank you, Mister," the waitress graced him with a plastic smile. "You have a nice day."

That it was dark out and past six made Sam wonder why the waitress hadn't said something to the effect of having a nice evening. He hated these kinds of inconsistencies.

He was still sorting through what the waitress could have said when he got to the car.

The clone was beginning to act up, turning from side to side. More of the mewing came through the wrapped sheet.

"Shhh!" Sam said, then felt foolish, given that the clone wouldn't know what he meant. But to his surprise the clone stilled.

"That's a good clone." Sam leaned into the back and loosened the wrappings, thinking they might be too tight and be the cause of the clone's agitation.

He exposed her face and was brushing her hair out of her closed eyes, when they blinked wide open. Sky blue. Her delicate nose sucked in a long breath of air. Her mouth opened, and she ran a pink tongue over her lips.

He stared transfixed.

"Grandpa," she said.

Sam jerked back and hit his head hard on the hatchback door above him.

"You all right, sir?"

It was one of the policemen from the diner. They had finished their coffee and were headed back to their cruiser.

Sam rubbed his head. "Just about knocked myself out. But, yeah, I'm okay. Gotta be more careful. You guys have a nice evening."

But they were not to be put off. "What you got there?" the other officer asked as he stepped closer, trying to peer beyond Sam.

"It's...it's my granddaughter. I brought her food from the diner. She wanted to sleep."

Both officers were now at his side. "Cute kid," one said.

The clone stared up at them unblinking with her deep blue eyes.

Sam stepped back, not wanting to look like he was hiding anything. Though he didn't believe in God, the thought crossed his mind he should offer thanks that the Band-Aids on her head were concealed.

"You know," said the other officer, "you shouldn't have left her alone in the car."

Sam raised the palms of his hands in a gesture of defeat. "I know. I've read all the stories about kids suffocating, but she didn't want to come in. So I ordered takeout. I was only over there--" He pointed. "--I could see the car."

"Just a warning, sir. Next time you could be in real trouble."

"Thanks, officer. Warning taken."

102

The officer leaned closer to the clone.

"You okay, little lady?"

I'm cooked. But to Sam's surprise, the clone smiled and nodded.

"She doesn't look very comfortable there," the officer said. "You sure got a lot of stuff in back here."

"We're on a road trip."

Officer one glanced at officer two, then back at Sam. "Mind if I ask where?"

"Ah...Phoenix."

"Nice weather down there this time of year."

The radio in the cruiser behind the officers squawked.

"We got a call, Greg," the other officer said. "You have a nice evening, sir." He headed back toward the cruiser, but the other lingered.

"If you intend to drive out of here without me stopping you, you're going to have to move the kid into the back seat. She's got to be buckled in."

"Of course," Sam said.

The officer took out a pad and pen and peered at Sam's license plate number, then wrote it down.

"What are you doing?" Sam's attention was divided between the officer and the clone whom he had picked up to transfer to the back seat. She stared at him.

"Just routine, sir. It'll have to go in our log. We talked to you, saw you had left a child unattended in your vehicle and gave you a warning. No big deal. You have a nice evening." He caught up with the other officer, who was already in the cruiser, the engine running and the lights on top flashing.

***

Sam gave them a little wave as their cruiser accelerated out of the lot with its siren blaring. They headed north. He was going south.

When they were out of sight, he turned back to the clone. "How come you can talk?" he demanded, as he sat her up in the backseat and drew the seat belt across her lap. He arranged the sheet around her face.

Her eyes never left his. "Where are we going?"

Sam almost banged his head again. "I asked you a question."

She pursed her lips and shook her head.

That doesn't help. No time now. I've got to get out of here.

He rushed to get behind the wheel, then eased out onto the highway. Though it was late, he had to get as far from Poncha Springs as he could. Up over the pass, then down into the San Luis Valley. The road would be nice and flat there, a straight line all the way to Monte Vista.

Get to a motel. Get her inside. Sort this all out then.

He drove as though furies were after him, the landscape flashing by, a blurred memory, his BLT and fries getting cold on the seat next to him. He kept glancing back at the clone who sat staring at him.

How can she be sentient? Maybe sentience in clones was a temporary thing, like in that movie where they gave comatose patients an experimental

104

drug and they all woke up and were normal for a while before they regressed.

But he was fooling himself. Andropov must have known. The feds would have crucified him if they could have pinned a sentient on him.

Now Sam had the sentient. Anger welled up, making his eyes water.

He tore into Monte Vista, saw a trooper's cruiser parked at the edge of town and slammed on his brakes to drop from fifty to the thirty miles per hour that had begun at the city limit.

Shit.

The cruiser's lights flashed a warning, but the officer didn't make any attempt to pull him over.

Sam ran his fingers through damp hair and checked his heart rate, which hadn't had time to elevate yet. He kept his speed slow, looking for a place to pull in to spend the night. Something dark and non-descript.

Motels lined both sides of the highway, all well-lit with gaudy neon signs hawking low rates, free WiFi, waterbeds and continental breakfast. After a break in the visual confusion, the Monte Vista Drive-In Motel loomed up ahead. Weird, but it caught his attention. Very dark. He slowed and read the small sign out front.

FIRST RUN MOVIES SEEN FROM THE COMFORT OF YOUR BEDROOM

The show must have already started since the place was dark except for light coming from the office, the roadside sign and a large flickering

105

outdoor screen downrange. A line of trees separated the motel from the highway. The rooms were built in three consecutive arcs, each one lower than the next and facing the screen.

All Sam cared about was dark.

He pulled up to the office.

The clone's eyes were closed. Maybe she was sleeping. Hopefully, she wasn't dead.

Sam hurried into the empty office and rang a bell on the counter.

The proprietor came out from a back room. "Howdy. Welcome to the Drive-in."

"I need a room for the night."

"We got lots of rooms, unfortunately." He reached to a rack behind the counter and retrieved a key. "One-oh-five. Front row seat."

Sam glanced out the window. He didn't want to be in the front row, not with everyone in the upper rows able to see him park and carry the clone into the room. "You got something near the highway?"

The proprietor gave him a questioning look. "I got tons of those, too." He replaced the key and pulled another one out. "That'll be sixty dollars. I need you to fill out this form."

Sam shoved sixty dollars across the counter and filled in the form, name, address, phone, license plate. "Thanks." Sam turned to leave as the proprietor spun the form around and read it.

Go back to you TV, Sam thought as he walked to the car.

The clone hadn't changed position.

Sam glanced at the number on the key and drove to the room. He parked, then ducked around to the back, checking he was alone. He carried his suitcase into the room first.

The room was large for a motel room. King size bed against one wall facing a large window with the curtains drawn closed. Beside the bed sat a small console with two knobs, one labeled volume, the other a channel selector. Probably for the movie and radio stations. Small kitchenette. Closet. Bathroom.

He turned the lights off and opened the curtains allowing dim light from the flickering screen to filter into the room.

He returned for the clone. Still dark. No one in sight.

Once back inside, he laid her on the bed and began unwrapping her sheet.

"Grandpa." She was awake and not dead.

"Is that all you can say?" She looked so innocent, blond hair and blue eyes, skinny and frail and...naked. He popped open his suitcase and took out a t-shirt. As he pulled it over her head, she threaded her arms into the sleeves, drew it across her chest, then lifted her hips to bring it down to her knees as if she'd been dressing all her life.

"Grandpa, I'm scared."

What am I supposed to do? Try to comfort her. He patted her head. He rubbed her shoulders. "You have nothing to be scared about." *This isn't real.* Her voice was clear and concise as though she had been talking all her life. "How come you can talk?"

"Nathan talked to me all the time."

"Who's Nathan?"

107

She folded her hands in her lap and blinked her blue eyes. "He used to work at Clonal Transplants before Mr. Andropov fired him. I liked Nathan. He'd wake me up and talk to me about movies and things and let me run around the warehouse. Then Mr. Andropov found out what Nathan was doing and fired him. I haven't been able to run around since."

"How long ago was that?" Sam worried if it was too long, her muscles might have begun to atrophy.

"It's only been a couple of weeks."

Sam gazed at the bright little girl in front of him. *Amazing.* "So, all the time I've had you, you've been able to talk but chose to lie there and say nothing?"

"No. Only since the sedative wore off."

"And when was that?" Sam couldn't believe Andropov had been so clumsy administering a sedative that it would only last a few hours.

"Last night."

"How come you didn't talk to me earlier?"

"That's when I was scared."

"What scared you then?"

"That maybe you'd take me back to Mr. Andropov."

Sam found himself locked in her gaze. Luckily she couldn't read his mind and had no way of knowing he had tried to give her back to Andropov. He peered out the window. The flickering image of the movie *Alien* graced the screen. Somehow appropriate. But why *Alien*? It was a forty year old movie. So much for new releases.

"Grandpa?"

"What?"

"Do I have a name?"

Sam was struck by her directness. "Yes, in fact you do. It's Chloe Turner. I have a birth certificate to prove it."

She smiled. "I like being called Chloe Turner. What is your name?"

"I'm Sam."

She put one hand to her chin and wrinkled her brow in thought. "I do like Sam. But I can't go around calling you Sam. It wouldn't sound right. Besides I like Grandpa better."

"I'm not your grandpa," Sam said without much emotion. But what was he? A father? No. A much older brother? That didn't fit either. Grandpa was probably the best fit, given their age difference and that they were related.

Sam felt he was trapped in a surreal world, somewhere between Denver and southern Arizona in a drive-in movie motel talking to a clone who had decided to come awake and engage the real world. Feeling self-conscious, he asked, "Are you hungry? I brought you some bread."

"I'm hungry, but I don't want bread. I want cereal."

Sam felt a moment of relief. He had cereal from Great Foods and milk from the diner. "I'll be right back."

He ran out to the 4Runner and grabbed a box of cereal and a container of milk. He considered the box with his cold BLT and fries, then grabbed it, too. *Better than nothing.* When he came back into

109

the room, Chloe had selected the movie channel and turned up the volume. She was propped up on pillows in the bed, snuggled in a blanket, watching the movie. Her mouth formed the words silently as they were pronounced by the actors.

"I've seen this, like a thousand times," she said. "This is the part where the alien comes out of the man's chest."

Sam lowered the volume a few decibels. "This is an R-rated movie, maybe you shouldn't be watching it."

"I saw lots of R-rated movies at Clonal Transplants. I also saw lots of X-rated movies, but that was late at night after everyone had left. I think Mr. Andropov was still in his office."

"You know all that? How?"

"I don't know. But I know." She smiled.

It was the most beautiful smile Sam had ever seen. All innocent and nice. Trusting.

"I've got the cereal and milk. I'll go over here and put it in a bowl."

"Thank you, Grandpa."

Her calling him Grandpa still unnerved him. He sought to distract himself by going into the small kitchenette, taking out a bowl and mixing her cereal.

"Here," he said. "Cheerios."

"I think I'm going to like Cheerios."

"Most people do." Sam sat and watched her devour the Cheerios. When she finished, she held up the bowl.

"More."

Feeling foolish, Sam said, "Say please."

Again the smile. "Pleeeeze, Grandpa."

No arguing with that.

He went to the kitchenette, refilled the bowl with cereal and returned to Chloe.

"Here's your cereal." He thrust the bowl in front of her.

She took it with both hands and gazed at him with her deep blue eyes. "Thank you, Grandpa."

When she resumed watching the movie, Sam grabbed the box with the BLT and fries, and went into the bathroom. He closed the door and took out his cell phone, then speed dialed JoAnne's number.

"Hello, Sam?" JoAnne's welcome voice.

"The clone is sentient!"

"I didn't make that out. What?"

Sam lowered his voice. "I said the clone is sentient. She talks. She eats. She's propped up in bed watching the movie *Alien*."

JoAnne started to laugh, then cut it off. "Are you serious?"

"I'm serious. You should see her. She knows the entire dialogue of the movie. It's...it's disconcerting to see her mimicking the words coming out of the actors' mouths."

"I do believe you're serious."

Sam stared at the ceiling in frustration. "None of this is working out the way we planned."

"I guess not. She's supposed to be brain-dead."

Sam sat on the closed toilet seat, balancing the BLT box on his lap. "Now what?"

"You're asking me? Have you told her what you have in mind for her?"

111

"Of course not." *This isn't working.* He swallowed cold bacon, lettuce and tomato.

"What *do* you have in mind for her?"

He almost gagged on the cold bacon fat. "I don't know. The situation has changed. I haven't had time to think it through. Clonal was supposed to be clean. Maybe her reaction is just a reaction to all the TV she says she had to watch at Clonal."

"You're grasping at straws. She's sentient. You know it. I know it. Now what are you going to do with her?"

He pulled out a long string of toilet paper, waded it up and wiped his mouth. He put the rest of the BLT in the wastebasket along with the untouched fries. "Obviously, I can't use her as a transplant source."

"I'm glad to hear that."

"It's easy for you to be glad about it." Sam felt a rising frustration tinged with anger. "What about me? I've been hung out to dry. Two years waiting for a heart and now this."

"I'm sorry," JoAnne said. "You know that's not what I meant. I understand your frustration. You want my advice?"

"That's why I called."

JoAnne took a deep breath. "Okay, here goes. I see two options. The first is that you contact the feds and give her up. Then get in line for a transplant and hope for the best. Up to now you haven't done anything wrong, but if you knowingly cross state lines, not to mention an international border with a sentient, you're in a heap of trouble as far as federal law enforcement is concerned."

112

Sam shook his head, knowing she couldn't see him. "I know the law, but I simply can't give Chloe up."

"You've named her already?"

What was it with JoAnne? He was talking about a walking talking clone, and she was wondering about how the clone got named. "I didn't. Andropov named her. I have a birth certificate with Chloe Turner on it. Maybe he has a sense of humor--Chloe, clone--I don't know. Be that as it may, I've heard that because sentient clones aren't legally real people, the feds drug them into a coma and consign them to what they euphemistically call a shelter until they die." He thought it might be true. It was all over the blogosphere.

"That's nonsense," JoAnne said.

"Maybe. Then consider this. Chloe has always been mine. I paid for her. But now that I know she's sentient, I feel she's even more mine. She's me. Do you see what I'm getting at?"

"Sort of."

Why is this so hard? "I can't take a chance giving her up to the feds even if they don't drug her. I'd never see her again."

"What about Andropov? How's he fit in? He must have known Chloe was sentient when he gave her to you."

"I thought about that. He'd be in a heap of trouble for growing a sentient. Fortunately, the last time I saw Andropov he was headed out of the country."

"How do you know he left?"

113

Damn. "I don't. But I signed off on the clone contract. He's got his money. What more possible interest could he have in this?"

"Sam, I can hear you breathing. Calm down."

"Yeah. Give me a minute." He put the cell on the toilet seat and went to the wash basin where he splashed cold water on his face. After patting himself dry he returned to the phone. "Okay. I can't be certain that Andropov is out of the picture. That just complicates my life a bit more. What was option number two?"

"Number two is that you go to Mexico as planned. Their laws regarding clones are more liberal than ours and are silent as regards sentients. I guess they figure places like the US will see that sentients aren't produced. You'll be breaking US law crossing the border, but once in Mexico, you're home free. Then you sit tight and wait until the situation clarifies. Let the dust settle on this new law. Hopefully, you'll stay alive long enough for that to happen. If you have trouble, they have good hospitals in Mexico like you said. And they're not as strict about waiting in line for a transplant as they are here. You're rich. You could buy your way forward."

A knock sounded on the bathroom door.

Sam opened it, cell phone still pinned to his ear.

"Grandpa, can I have more cereal?" Chloe stood before him on spindly legs that shook with the effort to hold her up, the empty cereal bowl clutched in both hands.

"Is that her?" JoAnne asked. "She calls you Grandpa?"

114

"Yeah. I don't know why. Maybe I look like a grandpa she saw on TV." He put the cell against his chest. "Who said you could get out of bed? You're going to hurt yourself."

"But I want more cereal."

"You've had enough cereal for one night. Go back and finish watching the movie. I'm talking to someone."

Chloe eyed him, but said nothing. Instead she turned, wobbled back to the bed and clawed her way up into it. She adjusted her pillow and resumed watching the movie.

"I can't believe she's able to walk, or talk and eat," JoAnne said.

"There was a lab tech at Clonal named Nathan, who took her out of her crèche and let her run around."

"That sounds weird to me. Why would a guy do that?"

"I don't know. I haven't seen any indications he might have done anything else to her. It seems his beef was with Andropov, and Chloe was a way to get at him." Sam ran his fingers through his hair. "I know one thing, Chloe is going to need clothes.

"That would be a good start."

"Why am I thinking you aren't taking this as seriously as you should? You've got to help me here. I don't know anything about sizes for little girls. She looks to be about four feet tall, very thin."

"That would be about a child's medium ten but you might have trouble finding a good fit if she's so

115

thin. Why not buy loose stuff, stuff you can draw tight around her waist, or let hang on her."

"Great. I thought there might be more to it."

"Look, Sam, I--uh-oh. There's a dark colored sedan parked across the street."

"You think they could be the law?"

"I don't think it's the mafia."

"Maybe they've got your phone tapped."

"You're getting paranoid. They couldn't get a judge to approve a tap. I've done nothing wrong. And neither have you, yet."

Sam didn't like, *yet*. But there it was staring him in the face. "I'm going to take your advice and go with option two. Another day, and I'll be south of the border, free and clear. Hell, the feds don't even know Chloe is sentient yet. I'll be in touch by you-know-what."

"Uh-oh," JoAnne said. "Two suits just got out of the sedan and are coming up the walk. I gotta go."

Chapter Six

Wellstone sat, feet up on his desk, working the crease of a new Stetson hat, classic styling, Sahara tan color. He'd always wanted to wear a Stetson but Bureau dress code prevented him from doing so, at least in the Denver office.

"Chief!" Marshall poked his head into Wellstone's office. "We picked up a signal from Turner's cell."

Finally. Wellstone tossed the Stetson onto the desk. "And?"

"We've been able to pinpoint the cell somewhere in Monte Vista. On top of that, at about four-thirty this afternoon, two State Troopers talked to him in Poncha Springs. That's in the mountains well west of Colorado Springs."

Wellstone impaled Marshall with a stare. "I know where Poncha Springs is." If Marshall felt impaled, he didn't show it.

Resilient son of a bitch.

"My fault, chief. I knew you knew."

"Enough with the chief," Wellstone said.

"Yes, sir."

"It's now six-thirty. Why the delay in reporting?"

"It turned up in the officers' daily log," Marshall said. "A cross check wasn't done until a few minutes ago when the log was transcribed into the computer."

Computers. Sort of like women, love 'em or hate 'em, you still couldn't do without them. "Why the stop?"

117

"That's where it gets interesting." Marshall struggled to contain his excitement. "They gave him a warning for leaving a child in his car unattended. A little girl who appeared to be about six or eight."

"The missing clone."

"We can't be certain about that until we catch up to him but I do believe you're right. He's on the run."

Wellstone dropped his feet to the floor and leaned over his desk clasping his hands in front of him. "And what leap of faith brings you to that conclusion?"

"We turned up a Form 104 report filed by his bank in Monument. He withdrew nine thousand from his checking account after trying to cash a check for fifty thousand on a Schwab account."

Wellstone frowned. "That doesn't mean he's running anywhere. Since when does driving to Monte Vista with money in your pocket constitute *running*?"

"There's a pattern of activity." Marshall stepped farther into the room. "Sir, may I sit down?"

Wellstone waved to a chair.

"Thank you, sir." Marshall glanced at papers he was carrying. "The pattern starts with him buying eighty-nine dollars and forty-three cents worth of food stuffs from Great Foods in Monument this morning. Then he used all his gas credits to fill up his vehicle. Then he went to the bank. About the same time, a 911 call was placed by an elderly couple who reported seeing what they thought was a child-size body wrapped in a sheet in the back of an SUV. Though the vehicle was reported to be an SUV, the vehicle color and license plate partial didn't match Turner's, but the coincidence of time and place can't be ignored."

"Interesting." Wellstone started to lean back, then stopped and brushed dirt off his desk his shoes had left. "So we have a person of interest who met with Androp, spent one night at home before loading up with cash the next morning, then was spotted in Poncha Springs with a child. Assuming the child referred to in the Poncha Springs report is our clone, was there anything in the report to confirm she was sentient? Did they speak to her? If so, did she answer?"

"The report is silent on that issue, sir. I could do a follow up."

"Please do. Now the sixty-four thousand dollar question. Where's he going?"

Marshall blinked, as though he suddenly realized he was being asked a direct question. "Mexico?"

Wellstone graced the eager Marshall with a smile. "My thoughts exactly. But why Mexico?"

"That's the only place he can get an operation?"

"Very good, Marshall. Now--" Wellstone thought hard. "--from what we know of Turner, he seems like a normal kind of guy. He's not some whacko, insensitive monster who would go to Mexico with a known sentient to have a heart transplant. I'm thinking, when Androp gave him the clone, Turner didn't know she was sentient. Maybe she was drugged or something."

119

"That's a possibility, sir. Do you want Turner profiled? Maybe he *is* a monster."

Wellstone frowned. "Waste of time. Those psychologists make up their stuff as they go along. What we need now is a follow up on the police report. If it indicates the child was sentient, then we have to wonder why he's still heading for Mexico. Maybe its inertia. Maybe too soon for him to decide to break the law. We'll have to be alert to the possibility he might want to come in. After all, he hasn't done anything wrong, yet. But if he does have a sentient, and he takes her across state lines, not to mention a national border, we'll be able to reel him in."

"I'll get right on it, sir." Marshall started to get up.

Wellstone held up a hand. "What's the status on Androp?"

Marshall re-sat and glanced at his sheath of papers. "Alpha tailed him to the airport, but all he did was get off the shuttle, wander around the baggage claim for twenty minutes, then exit to the pickup island and get on a shuttle that returned him to the RNO lot."

Wellstone steepled his fingers as he thought that through. "My guess is Androp wanted to get away from Turner, and the easiest way was to ditch him at the RNO lot and return once he thought Turner was long gone."

"Do you want surveillance continued on Andropov?"

"Indeed. Androp is going to realize we know the approximate whereabouts of the clone and that

120

she is sentient. It will be interesting to see what effect that conclusion has on his actions."

"Yes, sir."

"Now back to Turner. If he's gone that far west, then he can't be thinking to cross the border at El Paso. If he had been, then he'd have taken I-25 all the way south through New Mexico. I'm guessing he's going to cross Arizona and go into Mexico at Nogales. Anything farther west means he'd have to backtrack once in Mexico."

"My thoughts exactly, sir."

Wellstone gave an impatient sigh, resigned to Marshall's eagerness. "We'll need another positive trace to confirm our assumptions. Let me know when you get an indication he has crossed into Arizona. He's going to use his cell again, or his credit card. Maybe get a speeding ticket or something." Wellstone put the Stetson on his head and pulled on the brim to adjust it. "If we get a hit, I'm going to Nogales."

***

Sam awoke to sunshine pouring into his room through the window that faced the movie screen. He had forgotten to close the curtain. He pulled it halfway across the window to reduce the light in the room since Chloe was still fast asleep on her side of the bed.

He had called JoAnne back a number of times the night before with no answer until she finally picked up.

"They were FBI," she had said in answer to his question. "They apologized for the late hour visit. Said they wanted to do an identity check. Said they knew I had been talking to you, and advised me under a government transparency regulation they would be conducting an in-depth interview in the morning."

She was understandably stressed, wanted to take a shower and go to bed, and was not looking forward to what would be a sleepless night.

Sam had wished her well and apologized for getting her into his mess. Though she told him not to worry about it, he understood from the tone in her voice she was not pleased with the situation.

He crossed the room to the bathroom, dressed and returned to Chloe. He gave her a nudge. "Chloe, we've got to get going."

She awoke, stared at him with disorientation, then smiled. "I fell asleep before the end of the movie."

"Sorry about that. We can watch it again sometime later."

She rubbed the sleep out of her eyes. "That's okay. I know how it ends."

"Yeah. I forgot you've seen it a jillion times."

"Can I have more cereal, now?"

"Sure, but be quick. We have to get a move on."

Chloe trudged over to the kitchenette. Her nightgown, consisting of Sam's shirt, dragged on the floor. She filled a bowl with cereal, poured in milk and sat at a small breakfast table.

She seemed very independent, but why shouldn't she be? There was nothing wrong with her physically, aside from the wounds from the crèche. She obviously knew a lot from having watched TV. She seemed very intelligent Sam thought with a modicum of admiration. Of course she would be. She was his girl. Or something like that.

Band-Aids still spotted her head. "Let's see how these are doing." Sam pulled off one of the Band-Aids. The skin underneath had begun to heal. It hadn't been a big sore to begin with. "We can take these off. You can hardly see where the wires were pinned to you." He couldn't very well go out in public with her looking like that, anyway.

Chloe brushed her hand over her forehead. "They feel okay, Grandpa."

"Good." Sam took out the road atlas and pointed. "We're going to drive to Durango. That's a little over a hundred miles from here. It's a medium-sized town. I'll shop for clothes for you there."

Chloe followed his finger on the map, then glanced at the shirt she was wearing. "I guess I need duds."

"Where'd you get that expression?"

She put her hand to her chin and slouched in an obvious thinking posture.

"Never mind," Sam said. "Probably from one of the TV series you watched."

Sam loaded up the 4Runner with the stuff he had brought into the room. Fortunately, there wasn't much.

When Chloe was ready, he seated her in the front seat and buckled her in. She still wore his shirt. He had found a necktie to pull tight around her waist so her shirt wouldn't drag. "You get to sit up here, now."

"I think I'll like that." She beamed.

The road to Durango was narrow by most standards but pleasant, no prime views, lots of coniferous trees.

Upon entering Durango, Sam searched out a Wal-Mart. Found one and parked. He rolled down the windows. "You stay here and wait for me. I'm going inside to buy clothes." He thought to humor her with *duds* but decided he shouldn't come down to her level. She should come up to his.

Inside Wal-Mart, it took him most of five minutes to find the location where little girls' clothes were displayed. He went through the aisles, pulling clothes off the racks, checking their sizes and dumping them into his cart. He added packages of socks and underwear, a one piece swimming suit and two fanny packs. One was for himself for his medications, passport, license and credit cards, as well as the thick stack of cash he couldn't very well leave in the 4Runner. The other was for Chloe since he anticipated if he had one she might want one, too. He then proceeded to the checkout.

"That will be ninety-six dollars and seventy-eight cents," the clerk said.

Sam thought this to be very reasonable in view of the cart having been filled to overflowing.

Sam paid cash and gave himself a mental pat on the back for not using his credit card. He collected his bags and returned to the car where he threw the packages into the back.

"What's the matter, Grandpa?" Chloe asked after he got behind the wheel.

He stared at her in wonder. How could a clone determine something was the matter? Was it so obvious? "What...how do you know I'm bothered about something?"

"It was in the second season of Seinfeld. The fourth episode when Kram--"

Sam held up a hand. "Forget it. I'll accept that you recognize stress. Look, we'll go to the next rest stop, and you can check out the clothes I bought. We can also have a little talk."

She looked at him quizzically. "Talk?"

"Yeah, there's a bunch of stuff we have to discuss."

He didn't wait for her to respond but put the 4Runner in gear and drove off.

It was another cloudless, fall day in Colorado. The air was crisp with a temperature in the low fifties. The road came clear of the forests as Sam drove farther west.

Chloe sat up and twisted around, looking at something that flashed by on the left. "That was the entrance to Mesa Verde, Grandpa!"

"So what? There's a rest stop ten miles up the road."

"But it's Mesa Verde. I've always wanted to see it."

How can she say stuff like that?

He supposed Mesa Verde was as good a place as any to stop, change her clothes and have a talk. He slowed, did a U-turn and pulled into the access road that led to the park entrance. At the gate he flashed his National Parks and Federal Recreational Lands Access Pass, a privilege bestowed on him due to his age and heart condition.

Once in the park, he pulled into the first deserted overlook he came to.

"Why are we stopping here?" Chloe asked.

"So you can change and we can talk."

"I don't want to stop here. I want to see Cliff Palace."

"But it's at the other end of the park."

Chloe folded her arms across her chest and stared straight ahead.

Sam hadn't seen that behavior in a while. Not since Karen's nieces. He'd forgotten how to deal with it, then remembered there was no reward confronting it head on, just more trouble. Better to lose this battle with a view to winning a subsequent war.

Twenty minutes later, he came to the pull-off where Cliff Palace could be viewed across the canyon.

Chloe leapt out of the car and hurried to the edge of the lookout, barefoot and on wobbly legs. It didn't seem to bother her not being in full control of her walking.

Sam had thought to have her try on first the clothes he had bought, but she seemed comfortable for the moment in his shirt. Fortunately, this late in the season there weren't any other tourists about. He came up to her and took her by the hand. "There's a path over there that leads to a lower level lookout. We can go down there. I think the view is better, and we can talk in private."

126

At the lower lookout, they sat on a bench and gazed at the ancient ruin across the canyon. At its zenith, it had housed over a thousand inhabitants. Circular kivas dotted the lower parts of the ruin. Terraced layers worked their way up and back into the overhanging rock, which formed a high natural roof.

"Isn't it magnificent, Grandpa?"

"I'm impressed every time I see it."

Chloe hugged her knees, a scowl on her face. "You said we were going to talk. What are we going to talk about?"

Sam leaned against the back rest of the bench. "All this is new to you, isn't it? I mean everything. Being out here, being in the sunshine, being in the car."

She glanced up at him. "It is new. Somehow it's also old. That doesn't take away from what I'm feeling."

How can a child so young, much less a crèche bred clone, be so precocious?

He decided there could be no beating around the bush. "Do you know you're a clone?"

"Yes. Nathan told me."

"Do you know you are my clone?"

"I kind of figured that out. But I'm a she and you're a he. That part I don't get."

Sam waved his hand in the air, then stopped, thinking he must look like Andropov trying to explain away the obvious anomaly. "The she part was a mistake, but you're still my clone."

Chloe seemed to take the information under consideration.

Now the hard part. "Do you know what clones are...made for?"

She looked up at him. Her eyes watered. She brushed away tears with the back of her hand. "Organs."

"How do you know this?"

"TV."

What to say? Chloe wasn't stupid. He'd have to be straight with her or lose all credibility. But how to be straight? He didn't even know where he was coming from these days. So much had changed.

"Do you know I'm sick?" He decided on trying a different angle into a difficult subject.

"No."

"I have heart disease. Cardiomyopathy to be exact. My heart muscle is dying and will be unable to pump blood through my body. I will die unless I can replace my heart. That's why I had you cloned."

Chloe put her chin on her knees and seemed to think about what he had said.

Sam didn't rush her. If she was thinking, that was okay. What she was thinking about could be another matter.

"You still want my heart?" She didn't look at him, just stared at the ruin across the canyon.

"I...I..." Sam stopped trying to give her an answer. Nothing in his long life had prepared him for these kinds of questions. Here was a child, not more than ten. She was a part of him, an almost identical part of him. She wasn't supposed to be asking these questions. Why wasn't she brain-dead? It was all supposed to be so simple.

128

"Grandpa, are you all right?"

Sam realized he was sweating, despite the cool morning. "I didn't answer your question, did I?"

"No."

Tears streaked down her cheeks.

He put his arm around her and hugged her close. "I promise you, I'll never take your heart."

She didn't say anything in response to his promise, but it was obvious his taking of her heart had been on her mind.

"Where are we going?" She wasn't going to let him leave anything out.

"We're going to Mexico to a small village on the coast called Playa de Cerro Bonito. Originally, I thought I could hole up there until I had my heart transplant. That was when I assumed you were a normal kind of clone. One that...couldn't think."

"You mean brain-dead."

"Yeah, that's what they call it."

"If I'm not brain-dead and you aren't going to take my heart, then why are we still going to Mexico?"

The thought crossed Sam's mind Chloe would make a good lawyer. Of course, he had thought once about being a lawyer. So it probably ran in the family. "There are two reasons. First, the FBI...you know about the FBI?"

"Of course."

"Good. The FBI seized all of Andropov's clones, except you. I suspect the FBI is currently looking for you. If they find you, they will take you away from me and put you with all the other clones

129

they have. I may never see you again. I wouldn't want that to happen.

"Second, it's possible, though I think highly improbable that Mr. Andropov could be looking for you. He might be afraid that if the FBI gets to you first and finds you aren't brain-dead, they will put him in jail for growing a sentient."

Chloe pondered what Sam had said. "Is that what I'm called? A sentient."

"Unfortunately. I'm sorry I used the term. But yes, that's what people normally call people like you."

Chloe gulped. "If Mr. Andropov gets to me first, what will he do with me?"

"He...well, he...he might try to make you brain-dead."

Chloe gasped a shrieking sob, startling Sam. She clutched his arm hard, her whole body shaking.

Sam hugged her tight. "I'm not going to let that happen. Listen to me. Chloe? I'm not going to let that happen."

She gulped back her sobs and scrubbed at her cheeks. Her shaking stilled. "Let's go to Mexico."

"Well," Sam said, feeling a moment of relief and at the same time realizing how fragile Chloe's world was. He continued with a false bravado. "I'm glad we got that cleared up. How about you try on your new clothes?"

"I'd like that."

Simplicity from innocents. Sam took her by the hand and led her back to the car. The overlook was still deserted.

"Do you have a preference?" Sam had no clue what a girl Chloe's age might want to wear, much less a clone who had only occupied the real world for a couple of days.

Chloe went right to the pile of clothes and in no time had picked out a tight top with frilly edges, underpants and a pair of shorts. She pushed aside heavier shoes and chose a pair of sandals.

Sam held up the second fanny pack. It was pink with the words *Chill Out* sewn on the front of it. "Check this out."

"Wow. That's pretty cool. You did good, Grandpa."

Somehow, Sam felt vindicated. He had said his fumbling piece about not wanting to carve her up, and he had done a reasonable job for a two generation gapper choosing her clothes.

***

Feeling a heavy burden had been lifted from his shoulders, Sam retraced his route out of the park to rejoin the highway heading west through Cortez, then on to Arizona. His promise to Chloe had come out so easily, without any agonizing debate. Had he changed that much in such a short time?

His support group would be pleased for all the wrong reasons. It wasn't that he had become opposed to cloning. It was that he had been presented with an unanticipated situation. To his recollection no one in the group had ever addressed sentient clones.

Despite JoAnne saying it was nonsense, he couldn't dismiss his fear that sentients, when they were discovered, were drugged into a brain-dead

131

coma and grouped with the rest of them. The moral issues in that were much more clearly defined. Even for him.

They had traveled for about two hours on US Highway 160, when Sam slowed.

"Why are we slowing down?" Chloe asked.

They had passed through the town of Kayenta in northeastern Arizona, all part of the Navajo Indian reservation.

"I saw a sign for a hot springs. Do you know what hot springs are?"

Chloe crossed her arms on her chest. "Of course, from the Discovery Channel. Hot Springs are produced from water that has been geothermally heated by the Earth's crust. Does this one have therapeutic powers?"

"Don't they all?"

"You didn't answer my question."

"I don't know about therapeutic powers, all I know is I have to immerse my tired body into something warm. I've been sitting and driving for two days. My muscles ache. I feel a lot of stress. So, how about it?"

"I'm ready."

Sam pulled off the highway into the parking lot in front of the hot springs.

After grabbing swim suits, Sam came around the car and took Chloe's hand. "I haven't been to this one before."

"Is that a problem?"

"No. I just hate going into an unknown situation."

132

Sam couldn't see the springs from the parking lot. A seven foot high reddish stucco-ed adobe wall blocked the view. On the wall various murals showed people soaking in pools of water.

At the entrance, a middle-aged Indian woman sat behind a pane of glass that had pasted to it the hours of operation of the springs as well as a list of prices.

The woman held a battery operated fan in front of her face and eyed them as they approached.

"Welcome to Hanover's Hot Springs," she said. "Just the two of you?"

"What you see is what you get," Sam said, trying to humor the dour woman.

"She your daughter?"

"No. She's my granddaughter."

"How old is she?"

"She's ten."

"Don't look ten. Too skinny."

Sam began to regret his decision to stop. "I don't think that's any of your business now, is it?"

The woman narrowed her eyes. "You want in or not?"

Sam glanced down at Chloe.

"Please," she tugged on his sleeve. "I've never been to a hot springs before."

Sam shrugged. "Hard to deny that sort of appeal," he said to the woman, but she wasn't buying any of it.

"If you want in, it'll be twenty-five dollars for you and six for the kid. You sure she's your granddaughter?"

Sam thought to make a snide remark, then stopped himself. "She's my granddaughter all right. Ask her."

This time the woman leaned forward and peered through the glass. "You his granddaughter, sweetie?"

"I'm a clone."

The woman looked perplexed. "What'd she say?"

"She said her name is Chloe." He felt a head rush and had to grab the front edge of the counter to keep from falling backward.

"You okay Mister?"

"Yeah, I'm fine." Sam fumbled for his credit card. "Can we go in, now?"

The woman took the card and pressed a button that buzzed a lock on the entry door, which swung open. "You go right ahead. I'll ring this up and catch up to you. Changing rooms are on your right. We've also got a small gift shop if you're interested."

"Thanks. Maybe later." Sam took Chloe by the hand and led her through the gate.

Once Sam felt they were out of earshot of the woman, he knelt down and took Chloe by the shoulders. "Chloe, you can't go around saying you're a clone. It could get us...it could cause a lot of trouble. Do you understand?"

Chloe nodded, but averted her eyes.

"Chloe, this is very serious. What is it you understand?"

"I'm not supposed to say I'm a clone even if I'm trying to make a joke."

"Not any time. Good. Now we can go look at those pools."

Inside, the area opened up. A red Santa Fe tiled floor spread out to encompass a number of steaming pools. Here and there were flowering Yucca plants, their bases ringed with white coral gravel. The seven foot wall surrounding the area dipped at the far side to a foot high, giving onto a view of a flat desert punctuated by towering Saguaro cactus in full bloom and yellow-tipped Palo Verde. Barren hills angled sharply in the distance. Someone had thought a lot about the layout.

The air temperature according to a wall mounted thermometer was a mild eighty-five Fahrenheit. The sky a cloudless blue.

"What do you think?" Sam asked.

She gave him a sidelong glance, probably still smarting from his lecture. "It looks nice."

"It does." He walked up to the nearest pool which was edged with rough Sedona sandstone. The sides and bottom of the pool, which were finished with a sort of bluish colored waterproofing, swept down to an inlet where new water eddied in. A small sign at the edge indicated a thermometer was attached.

Sam reached into the warm water and pulled out the thermometer. "One hundred two degrees," he said.

"Is that hot, Grandpa?"

"Not really hot, but after a while it will feel hot. Probably too hot for my heart."

"Excuse me, sir."

Sam turned to see the Indian woman standing over him. "Is there a problem?"

"Your card is flagged." She held out the card as if it were something dirty. "I put in the numbers and it's blocked."

Sam felt a clench to his heart. *Flagged*? Someone must be onto him. Someone who had access to credit card accounts. The FBI? More than likely, given JoAnne's recent visit from the Bureau. "I'm sorry about that. Some screw-up. You know computers. I'll give you cash." Sam dug into his fanny pack and produced two twenty dollar bills. "Here. You can keep the change. This is a nice place."

The woman accepted the money without a word, turned on her heel and headed back to the entrance.

Sam worried about the encounter, but figured it had been dealt with. The woman hadn't seemed put out. Except for a flag on his card, who would know? He turned to Chloe, who sat staring at the receding woman. "Hello! Let's get changed, then we can see if some of the other pools are cooler."

"I don't understand, Grandpa."

"It's nothing. My credit card didn't go through. She was concerned about payment. I paid cash. End of story."

"Do you have a problem with your credit? I can recommend a Web site that will--"

Sam handed Chloe her bathing suit. "Change."

She headed for the ladies changing room as if she'd been there before.

136

A few minutes later, Sam emerged from the men's changing room.

Chloe was already out and waiting. "Can we go in, now?"

"Of course."

Sam stepped over to a pool with a temperature of only a hundred degrees. "This one is better. It's a couple of degrees above body temperature, so it will feel warm at first, then you'll get used to it. He slipped into the water, came up and offered his hand to Chloe. "Get in."

"It's not too hot, is it?"

"I already told you I picked this pool because it was okay."

Chloe sat on the edge of the pool and dangled her legs into the water. "It doesn't feel hot."

Sam smiled and shook his head. "Come on."

She pushed off the edge and ducked into the water, then came up blowing. "This is wonderful. It reminds me of the bath I was in back at Clonal Transplants."

"If I thought this would remind you of Clonal, I wouldn't have brought you here."

"I didn't mind being at Clonal Transplants. While I was there, I felt no pain, no suffering. They took good care of me."

"I could go with that. Especially the no suffering part."

The woman at the gate strode into the pool area followed by a uniformed police officer.

"There they are." She pointed.

Sam eyed the officer as he approached. Dressed as he was in full Navajo Tribal Police

137

uniform he must have felt hot. A rivulet of sweat eased down the bronzed skin of his cheek from the hatband of his service cap. His tan shirt and slacks were a size too big for his frame. The green and yellow badge on his shoulder proclaimed, to Protect and to Serve. A lady in a flowing white dress held the scales of justice in one hand and a sword in the other.

A sword? Whatever happened to bows and arrows? Sam tried to keep the thought in mind as an underlying panic threatened to overcome him.

The officer knelt by the side of the pool and motioned for Sam to come across to him. "You got a name?"

Sam wondered if he had to give the officer his name, then decided not doing so would up the ante. "I'm Sam Turner. This is my granddaughter, Chloe. What's this all about?" Sam glanced at Chloe, trying to spot any Band-Aids that weren't covered up by her bathing suit. Everything clean.

"Could be about nothing," the officer said. "Could be something. Lady over there called in. First a credit card flagged, then the fact that you are old and your companion there is very young. You want to tell me about it?"

"I'm not sure what you want me to tell you. I'm probably overdrawn on my card. But who isn't these days. I paid her in cash. As for her suspicions that something is amiss here, what can I say? They're ridiculous."

The officer seemed very thoughtful, very patient. "Where you headed?"

"We're on our way to Phoenix to visit family."

138

"Your license plate says you're from Colorado. Whereabouts?"

"Monument. It's a small town north of Colorado Springs."

"She from there, too?" He indicated Chloe with a thrust of his chin.

Sam glanced over at Chloe, who was thankfully keeping her mouth shut. "Yeah. She lives with her mother. Her parents are divorced." Sam began to feel ill at ease as the lies crept in. He hadn't been prepared for a challenge like this. He glanced at the gate woman, who remained back by the entrance looking on.

Damn busybody.

"All right, Mr. Turner. It doesn't seem like anything untoward is going on here. You have to understand we get calls all the time. We have to check them out."

"I understand."

"Could I see your driver's license?"

Sam looked over to Chloe. "I've got to go to the dressing room and get my fanny pack. You going to be okay here?"

"I'll be okay, Grandpa." Chloe shaded her eyes with her hand and smiled at the policeman.

Sam climbed out of the pool and barefooted it to the dressing room. *This is bad. This is really bad.* His heart rate started to climb. He grabbed his fanny pack, counted to ten with a couple of deep breaths and returned to the outside.

He handed his driver's license to the officer.

"Thanks," the officer said, "I'm going out to the car and radio this in, just a routine background

139

check. You're not going to go anywhere while I'm gone, are you?"

Sam swept his hand indicating the desert beyond. "Really..."

"I didn't think so. Be back in a jiffy." The officer stood and went back out to his car. He didn't say anything to the gate woman as he passed her.

Sam thought he saw a flash of annoyance cross her face. As if she were disappointed that what she had perceived as something sick and perverted was only a grandfather and granddaughter taking a trip together to visit family.

Sam turned to Chloe. "Let's get dressed. I think we're done here."

"But Grandpa, I was just beginning to enjoy the water."

"Chloe."

"Oh, all right." Chloe climbed out and trudged to the changing room.

The officer returned and handed Sam his license.

"They're running a check on your ID. You said you were going to Phoenix?"

"I did."

"Mind giving me a contact?"

"What do you mean?"

"Look, I don't want to hold you up here. My sense is there's nothing amiss. If you could give me a contact, where you will be in Phoenix, that would be great. Better yet, when you get to Phoenix, you could give me a call. Here's my card."

Sam glanced at the card. "Officer Wendell Sicheii? I'm sure I'm not pronouncing it correctly."

140

Officer Wendell smiled. The first smile since he arrived. "Don't even try. Ironically, it means grandfather in Navajo."

"Is all this legal? I mean, me having to give you all this information."

That was the end of Sicheii's smile. "It's a request. You got a problem with that?"

Sam thought furiously. He didn't know anyone in Phoenix, much less their phone number off the top of his head. Time to dig in his heels. "I have your card. I'll give you a call. I don't think you have the authority to require any further information of me." As soon as he said that, he regretted it.

The officer scowled. "You and I were getting along real well, Mr. Turner, why the change?"

"I'm sorry. That just came out. I have a thing about being bullied. No big deal. You have your job to do. But I have to say that an enjoyable cross country trip is being turned into a nightmare by that overbearing woman." Sam indicated the gate woman. "Enough is enough."

"Really?" the officer said.

Chloe emerged from the changing room. "Are we going, now?"

The officer stepped between Sam and Chloe. "Chloe. Did I get that right?"

"Yes, I'm Chloe."

The officer gave Sam a sidelong look, one that said, I'm going to make your life a bit more difficult before I let you go. "Mr. Turner, I assume I don't have to remind you that you are on Navajo tribal land. Though we generally conform to US law, we do have our own laws and customs. Do you mind if I have a chat with your granddaughter?"

Sam shrugged. "Yeah, why not?"

"I gotta tell you," officer Sicheii said. "In my business, enough is never enough if I smell something fishy. And you're beginning to smell like two days old and out in the sun."

He took Chloe by the hand. "Let's you and me have a quiet talk over there." He pointed to a couple of chairs under an umbrella on the other side of the compound.

Chloe glanced at Sam, who nodded it was okay.

The officer and Chloe stepped around the pool and sat in the chairs.

Sam went into the dressing room and changed. When he came out the officer and Chloe were still talking. The gate woman had inched closer, presumably to overhear the conversation.

"What in the hell did you call in the police for?

She eyed him, narrow slits of accusation. "I could have lived with the credit card rejection. But, you know, I don't get cozy with guys your age travelling with little girls."

Sam stared at her. He felt what might rise to apoplexy had he not tamped it down. "You think I have an inappropriate relationship with my granddaughter?"

The gate woman gave a start and glared at him. "We don't get many dirty old men and young girls taking in the hot springs."

"Do I look like a dirty old man?" Sam splayed his hands out to his sides.

"Never can tell. Takes all kinds." She folded her arms across her ample bosom and stared into the distance.

After another five minutes, the officer stood and offered Chloe a hand.

The officer came over to Sam. "I think I'm done here. You and Miss Chloe have a nice day."

The gate woman started to say something then stopped at a glance from the officer.

"Come on, Chloe. Let's get out of here," Sam said.

Chloe swung her gaze from the gate woman to the officer and nodded. She clasped Sam's hand hard and fast-walked to keep up with his long strides out to the parking lot.

Sam strode to the 4Runner, started the engine, opened all the windows to exhaust the hot air and turned the air conditioner on high.

The officer exited the hot springs and stood with his hands on his hips as Sam drove away.

Chloe slouched in the passenger seat.

"What did you and the officer talk about?" Sam glanced over at her as he pulled onto the main highway.

"He asked a lot of questions about you and me. I didn't understand half of them. I told him we were like the Brady Bunch."

Sam searched back for the Brady Bunch and couldn't find a connection. "What's Brady Bunch?"

She climbed as best she could up onto her seat and leveled him with a stare. "You don't know about the Brady Bunch?"

Sam shook his head in defeat. "Chill. I don't know about the Brady Bunch. You do, and I'll accept that."

Could Sicheii have ticketed him for letting her sit in front, her being so underweight?

She seemed miffed. "Okay. You don't know about the Bradys. What I don't know about is what happened back there."

"It was people being cautious. There are a lot of weirdoes out and about. But the officer is going to find out who I am, then I think every trooper in four states is going to be looking for us. So we better get going."

Chapter Seven

A half hour out from the hot springs, Sam gunned the 4Runner southwest on US Highway 160. It was the quickest way to get to the border, meeting up with US Highway 89 past Tuba City, then down to Flagstaff and the Interstate all the way to Phoenix, Tucson and Nogales.

The road ran straight through level land with widely spaced mesquite backed by eroded red rock outcroppings, massive shapes that twisted and turned in response to eons-old floods of water washing away less dense sediment.

The 4Runner bumped up and over a rise, giving Sam a clear view back for at least three miles. He stopped and stepped out with his binoculars. Far back along the highway, Sicheii's cruiser drove slowly through shimmering heat waves.

"What are you looking at, Grandpa?"

"That policeman has been tagging along behind us. He's not going to let go until he gets his background check."

Sam returned to the 4Runner and accelerated to five miles over the legal limit. He wanted to put as much distance between him and Sicheii before the latter discovered who Sam was.

"Why are we going so fast, Grandpa?"

"That policeman is following us. If he decides to pull us over, I want to make sure I have a head start before he can."

The terrain became hilly.

Without warning, a second Navajo Police cruiser appeared over the crest of a hill, coming towards them. It was traveling at such a high rate of speed Sam hardly had time to react before it disappeared behind him down the back side of another hill. A moment later it came into view again, still heading away, on the plain beyond.

Sam slowed so he could get a look at what was happening.

The second cruiser came abreast of Sicheii's cruiser and stopped, two bugs meeting out in the middle of nowhere trying to decide what to do.

The blue and red lights atop Sicheii's cruiser lit up, and it accelerated towards Sam. At the same time the second cruiser also lit up, did a U-turn and followed.

"Uh-oh. Time to go!" Sam pressed the accelerator hard and watched as the speedometer climbed to one hundred miles per hour.

Chloe gripped a handle above her door to steady herself, a look of alarm on her face. "Where are we going, Grandpa?"

"Our only option is to cross into Hopi country." Sam gave Chloe one part of his attention as he careened the 4Runner down the road. "Navajo police have no jurisdiction there. It'll take them awhile to coordinate with their Hopi counterparts."

"What's Hopi?"

Sam glanced over at her, almost ran off the road and corrected. "You didn't learn that on TV?"

Chloe shook her head. "What's Hopi?"

The road leveled out and ran straight, not giving a true indication of their speed. "They're a native American Indian tribe, pueblo dwellers. When I was young--" The 4Runner hit a bump in the highway that elevated them for a brief moment. "--like in my teens, I spent a couple of weeks on the reservation as part of a summer program."

"You still have friends there?" Chloe pulled her seatbelt tighter across her hips.

"I have a friend. His name is Homer." To Sam's appreciation, Chloe was sitting quite calmly given the speed they were traveling. All wide-eyed innocence. "He knows me and I can trust him. We're going to need his help."

Sam sped past a sign that read,

YOU ARE NOW ENTERING THE HOPI INDIAN RESERVATION

He slammed on the brakes and brought the 4Runner to a fishtailing stop. He shoved it into reverse. The engine whined as he backed up, the reverse gear exceeding its safe range. Sam stopped and cranked a hard left onto a dirt track that led off toward a distant horizon.

"This is a shortcut to Hotevilla where my friend lives."

Sam kept checking his rearview mirror.

A minute later the two Navajo Police cruisers skidded to a halt where the dirt track met the highway. Both men got out and seemed to be conferring. Sam knew they couldn't enter Hopi land. The Hopis and the Navajo didn't like each other.

Sam slowed down. "The good news is they can't follow us in here," he said to Chloe who was

147

agog with interest. "The bad news is the Navajo reservation surrounds the Hopi reservation."

"Why?"

"I don't know. Someone in the Bureau of Indian Affairs must have thought about it a long time to come up with such a weird arrangement."

"Happy Hopi."

Sam thought it was a good thing the child was so lighthearted given their present circumstance of staying seconds ahead of the law. "Hotevilla Hopis weren't always happy. In fact they represent a breakaway group of clans. Didn't agree with everyone else and decided to camp out elsewhere. There are three mesas in Hopi land. Hotevilla is on the third one."

Twenty minutes later they came to a "T" intersection and Sam turned right. Another few miles and they were at the entrance to Hotevilla.

"I hope I can remember where Homer lives." Sam peered at a non-descript collection of mud brick dwellings spread out over the flat top of Third Mesa. The overall impression was one of red-gray adobe structures, sun-bleached poles, laundry hanging on lines and broken down cars rusting out in the open. Children ran helter skelter accompanied by barking dogs. The arrival of a vehicle, probably any vehicle from the outside world, was a welcome diversion.

Sam drove down an ill-defined track between rows of houses. He took a right at a fork in the path and a little later pulled up in front of a shabby dwelling. "This is it."

An old man pushed through a screen door and walked bowlegged toward the 4Runner. When he recognized Sam, his face broke into a wrinkled grin that showed a mouth missing half its teeth. "Sam Turner."

"Homer. It's good to see you. How has it been."

"Must be almost forty years. Hey, this beats Christmas cards."

"You haven't changed a bit."

Homer grinned even wider. "Neither have you."

They clasped hands, then slid into an embrace.

"Who's the little girl?" Homer asked.

Chloe had come out of the vehicle and stood watching them.

"This is Chloe my...granddaughter."

Homer glanced at Sam at the hesitation in his voice. "Nice looking kid."

"Say," Sam said, "how's your boy...Reggie?"

Homer stared straight at Sam, his eyes dampening with tears. "Reggie's gone. I never told you. Killed in the Iraq war. One of the first."

Sam was shaken. He had taken a real liking to the rambunctious kid. Played kickball with him. Tickled him before bed. Showed him tricks. "I'm sorry to hear that."

"Yeah, it was hard to take. Only good thing was he had a kid before he got himself killed in a white man's war."

"Then you have something."

"I do." Homer waved toward the screen door.

A young girl, maybe sixteen, eighteen stepped out shyly.

"This is Flower," Homer said. "She and her mother live with me."

This wasn't the visit Sam had envisioned. But it seemed like yesterday he had been a naïve teenager himself and Homer a wise old Indian. Homer had always looked old. And even though the visit had been for a couple of weeks, the memories and impression he had of the place had lasted all his life.

Homer shoved his hands into his pockets. "What brings you here, Sam?"

"Could we take a walk and talk? Maybe Flower here would be kind enough to look after Chloe."

Homer waved Flower over to Chloe, then started walking toward the rim of the Mesa.

Sam followed, like he had followed years ago when Homer had taken him out and shown him the view from the Mesa top to the fields of corn far below, the red rocks jutting up in the distance, a setting sun lighting up the sky and land in shades of orange and ochre.

"I've got a problem, Homer," Sam said. "First off, I've got a bad heart. I need a transplant or I'm going to die. Soon."

Homer nodded but said nothing.

"Secondly, to fix my heart I contracted with an outfit in Denver to grow a clone for me. You know what I'm talking about?"

"I know about clones," Homer said. "Seen them on TV."

150

"Well, the outfit I contracted with got nailed by this new legislation. The head guy there dumped my clone on me and told me to take it to Mexico to have my operation."

Homer looked up. "Chloe is your clone, isn't she? Even though she's a she. I could tell it was you. And she thinks, isn't brain-dead like she's supposed to be. What're you going to do?"

Homer wasn't stupid, never had been. It was almost like he was prescient in his ability to grasp a situation. "I don't know," Sam said. "I didn't know she was sentient when I got her. I started out for Mexico to buy time. Maybe have my operation there. Then she turns out to be sentient, and I'm still heading to Mexico, only now it's not to have an operation, it's to stay ahead of the law that wants the clone because they want to nail the guy who made her. The guy who made her could be after her as well, but I don't know for sure."

"How far back are the police on your tail?"

"As far as the border to Hopi land. I had a run in with the Navajo police, and they chased me to the edge of the reservation. I'm thinking it's only a matter of time before they sort out jurisdictional disputes and get someone to come looking for me here."

Homer smiled his crooked smile. "You got about forty-eight hours. That's about the time span for Hopi foot dragging."

"Then I'm going to have to be gone by then, but they've got me surrounded."

"Sort of. There's lots of ways out of here them dumb Navajos don't know about." Homer's eyes twinkled.

"My vehicle will be recognized as soon as I get out in the open. I'm screwed."

Homer batted away the statement with a hand. "Nah. Not to worry. I've got a nephew who's going down to Phoenix tomorrow. For a few extra bucks he can take you to the border. You can leave your 4Runner here until it's safe to come back for it."

Relief swept through Sam. Maybe they'd make it after all. "That'd be great."

They came to the edge of the Mesa.

"You remember coming here with me when you were a wet-behind-the-ears teenager?"

"Sure I do. You told me about *Tawa*, the Sun spirit, and how he created the first of four worlds out of endless space. I've not forgotten. Creating something from nothing. It's the mystery of our existence."

"And now you are facing that greatest of all mysteries. If you cannot cure your heart, you will embrace again the endless space from which the world was made." Homer never was one to mince words.

"I hope it doesn't come to that too soon. I have a lot I want to live for. These last few days have made me think again about things I thought I had resolved. Life, death, good and evil, innocence, Chloe's care."

"Yes, the young will make an old man young again in his thinking." Homer pulled on Sam's sleeve. "Come, let us return and have a meal together, then I will tell my nephew to take you to Nogales."

***

The next morning, Homer's nephew drove up to the house. A strapping young man, dressed in a denim jacket, jeans, cowboy boots and a shaped leather hat, he got out of an older model pickup.

"This is my nephew, Willie," Homer said when they met the young man at the front door. "You want some coffee, Willie?"

"Nah. I want to get going before it gets too hot." He shook Sam's hand. "Homer tells me you want to go all the way to Nogales."

"That's right. I'll make it worth your while to take us there. Five hundred okay?"

Willie waved Sam off. "Keep the money. I'll take you there. You're a friend of Homer's."

Homer pulled Willie to one side but not out of earshot. "Don't you go being dumb, now. Sam's got lots of money and you don't. Take it."

Willie turned back and took off his hat. "I'd be much obliged if you'd let me change my mind about the money."

Sam dug into his fanny pack and counted out five hundred in small bills. "You're going out of your way to help us, Willie. I wouldn't feel right not compensating you for it."

Willie took the money and shoved it into his pocket. "You ready to go?"

"Suitcase is right here. I'll call Chloe."

"She the clone?" Willie asked.

Sam was at first startled, then remembered there were no secrets in Hotevilla. If you told one inhabitant, the whole town would know within hours. "Yeah, she's the clone but you'd never know it looking at her."

Sam ducked inside. "Chloe, we're about to leave."

She was standing with Flower near the stove. "Can't I stay a little longer? Flower is showing me how to make fried bread."

"I'm afraid not. Flower, thanks for looking after Chloe. I hope we can come back this way sometime and visit again."

Flower nodded and gave Sam a shy smile.

Sam took Chloe by the hand and led her out to the pickup. "Where do you want us?" he asked Willie.

"Don't much matter. You can sit up front with me and the little girl can sit in the jumper seat behind. Ain't nobody going to see us until maybe we get back on the main roads, but that won't be till we're down Winslow way. I ain't going near Flagstaff. After that, we'll see what happens."

Sam thanked Homer and said goodbye. The reunion had been short, so much to talk about in so little time. That the friendship had endured at all was amazing. It probably had to do with the contact being made when he was young and impressionable. Two weeks. Homer had been in his thirties that long time ago. Maybe he was still young on the inside.

The drive to Nogales took all day, with only a couple of stops for bathroom breaks and food. Willie drove with very little in the way of conversation. Sam dozed most of the way, as did Chloe.

As the sun was heading low to the horizon, Willie came to the outskirts of Nogales.

"Where you want to be dropped off?" Willie asked.

Sam felt a wave of anxiety sweep over him. He'd been lulled into a mindless condition for the past hours and now had to confront the real world again. "How about near the border. Maybe near a travel agency so we can book a tour or something. We'll need a hotel for the night."

"There's plenty of those places." Willie began threading his way through town.

Sam couldn't believe a major town could look so shabby. Nogales was Nogales on both sides of the border unlike other border towns that had an American name on the north side and a Mexican one on the south.

The pickup slowed and stopped in a huge, mostly vacant parking lot.

"This here's an overflow lot for traffic if it backs up trying to cross the border. Any closer and they got cameras. Over there--" He pointed. "--is a travel agency."

"This is perfect." Sam helped Chloe out while Willie slid Sam's suitcase and the bag with Chloe's clothes in it over to him. "I best be on my way. I'm expected in Phoenix tonight."

"Thanks for the ride, Willie."

Willie shoved his hat up and pumped Sam's hand. "No problem. You sure you going to be all right here?" Willie seemed almost reluctant to go.

155

Willie had just doubled the amount of conversation he had engaged in all day. "We'll be okay. I'm going straight over to that travel agency."

Willie waved, got back into his pickup and pulled away.

"Are we going to Mexico today, Grandpa?"

"It's too late to go today. More likely tomorrow morning." Sam picked up the suitcase and took Chloe's hand. "I'm thinking we can get across the border on a tour bus."

But how was he going to get across the border with Chloe? It was one thing to have thought he could pull it off with her in the backseat and under a blanket in his 4Runner, quite another to have her sitting beside him on a bus.

Sam came up to the travel agency and set down his suitcase. He glanced at the posters plastered on the windows of the small office, posters showing people sunbathing while sipping exotic drinks with slices of pineapple sticking out the top. Hobie Cats knifing through clear blue waters. Chefs with tall white caps offered appetizing dinner dishes. "Okay, Chloe, we're going to give it a try."

He pushed through the glass entry door and welcomed the cool air-conditioned interior. A girl who appeared to be half his age sat behind a desk surrounded by more gaudy travel posters. A computer monitor glowed off to her right. But she didn't seem to be doing anything other than filing her nails.

Sam walked up to the desk. "I'm interested in a bus tour to Guaymas."

The girl put down her nail file and smiled up at him. She was Hispanic, darker skinned than most, striking red lipstick to match the nails she had been working on. "Please, *Señor*, have a seat. My name is Maria--" She grabbed the nametag attached to her blouse and tilted it up so Sam could see. "-- Cabrerra. You have come to the right place. I can book your motor coach and all the stops along the way as well as your hotel in Guaymas. It's beautiful this time of year, not too hot, not too cold. Where you from?"

"Colorado."

"Colorado. *Que bonito*. But getting cold about now, *si*? You want some sun and the beautiful ocean, I can tell. Your little girl is going with you?"

"She is. She's my granddaughter."

"Lovely girl. How old? Eight?"

"Close. She's ten."

"I should have known. I have children of my own. Okay. Let me show you our premium tour. Five nights. Leaves every day at 10:00 AM from right out front. We cross the border, then have a walking tour of Nogales on the Mexican side. Nice town, Nogales. You been there before?"

"No I haven't. How long is the walking tour?"

"An hour, tops. Then lunch. We have it catered at the *El José's*, the best restaurant in Nogales. After that it's siesta time...on the bus, of course! You can sleep for the next three hours and not miss much. You know our northern Sonoran Desert isn't very interesting. Your destination that night is Hermosillo. Nice little town, lots of colonial architecture. Lots of churches. You like churches, *Señor*?"

"I try to stay away from them."

"*No problema*. There are a lot of bars in Hermosillo, too. You can go there instead...even with the *niña*. *No problema*. Mexico is a family-oriented country." She smiled even more broadly. "Next day, to Guaymas and the ocean...Sea of Cortez *actualmente*. Your hotel--"

"How much?"

"How much what?"

"I'll take the tour. How much do I owe you?"

"Five hundred dollars for you. Half price for the child since she's under twelve. All-inclusive including alcoholic beverages."

Sam counted out seven hundred and fifty dollars.

"You don't use a credit card, *Señor*?"

Sam thought he detected a note of suspicion in her voice. "Don't trust them. Here--" He pushed the small pile of money over to her. "--I think I counted right."

She took the money, bent it in half around a finger and flipped through it with her thumb, counting as if she were a machine. "*Perfecto*. Now, I'll need to see your passports."

Sam knew that was coming and wasn't quite sure what he could do about it. "I have a passport. My granddaughter doesn't have one. But I have her birth certificate."

Maria eyed him, then said flatly. "*No problema, Señor*. We don't ask a lot of questions here at South of the Border. A birth certificate will

158

get you into Mexico, but I must tell you, your granddaughter will have trouble crossing back into the US. She'll need a passport for that."

Sam nodded. "Yeah, I know. I was hoping we'd be able to get across with the birth certificate. We applied for a passport before we left but it didn't arrive on time. Her mother will FedEx it to us. I hope." He smiled.

Maria gave him a blank look. "It's your vacation. We're almost finished." She shoved two forms at Sam. "If you sign them, I'll fill in the rest. They are Mexican Tourist Visas. You'll need them since you are staying for more than seventy-two hours."

As Sam was signing, she continued. "Here's how it's going to work. We collect all the passports when you get on the bus. Sometimes, a US Customs and Border Patrol agent will stop the bus and want to check passports, especially now since one is needed to get back in. If he finds out your granddaughter doesn't have a passport, he may make you get off the bus. But that is a chance I see you are willing to take. We will not be responsible. After that, the bus passes through Mexican control. A National Immigration Institute official will board the bus and check IDs and make sure everyone has a Tourist Visa. Then you are in Mexico."

"Do we meet up here tomorrow to get on the bus?"

"The bus will load up out front. Try to come early as it takes time to load the luggage and get everyone checked in and seated." She stood without smiling. "That's it. Have a nice trip."

When Sam extended his hand to shake hers, she did not respond. Instead, she patted Chloe on the head. "She looks so sweet and innocent. You really his *nieta*, child?"

Chloe glanced up at Sam.

"That means granddaughter in Spanish," Sam said.

Chloe nodded and turned back to the travel agent. "I'm Grandpa's granddaughter, all right. We're going to go swimming in the ocean."

"I'm sure you will enjoy your trip," Maria said, not looking very convinced.

Sam left the office wondering if Maria would call in the law like the Indian woman had at the hot springs. But when he glanced back before shutting the door behind him, the girl had reverted to filing her nails.

Maybe she's waiting until we get out of sight.

Too late now. It was getting dark and they still had to find a place to spend the night.

***

The next morning, Sam had no trouble getting to South of the Border Tours Central on time. The hotel he found had been terrible. It seemed like long-haul trucks cruised through their room all night. Despite heavy curtains over the windows, lights from outside seeped in around the edges. The city of Nogales, a city that never sleeps.

Sam got up for good around 4:00 AM. Chloe snoozed through it all, until he woke her up at 8:00 AM.

As they approached South of the Border, the bus that would transport them on their tour was

160

parked at the curb, its motor idling, its air-conditioning going. It looked to be state of the art for tour buses, all red and black with silver pin-striping and a huge windshield in the front behind which the driver sat at a level below the passengers. Sleek vertical rearview mirrors that were almost as tall as a person protruded on each side. Probably even had toilets on board for both sexes. Doors were open to the undercarriage where baggage was being loaded.

A small crowd of fellow travelers milled around the entrance to the office and the door to the bus. One by one, everyone got processed and boarded.

Sam handed over his suitcase to the driver, then his passport and Chloe's birth certificate to Maria. The smile she had been giving everyone else sagged when she recognized him.

"Aren't you going to wish me a pleasant trip?" Sam said facetiously.

Maria avoided his stare. "Next."

Sam ignored the rebuff and boarded the bus, Chloe's hand gripped firmly in his. He climbed the ten steps to the upper passenger level.

"I want to sit up front," Chloe said.

Two seats were empty in back of the driver. Sam glanced down the aisle as the other passengers began filling seats. "Looks as good as any." He slid in by the window. The seat was well upholstered with a white cloth Velcro-ed to the head rest. Chloe sat on the isle and immediately tested the button to recline the seat, the flip open ashtray that had never been used, and the footrest that ratcheted out from underneath.

"All systems go?" Sam asked.

"Ready for ignition," Chloe said.

Where does she get all the lingo? TV.

A staid woman in her late forties climbed the steps with a little girl and made her way to the back of the bus.

"That little girl looks about you your age, Chloe," Sam said. "Why don't you go back and try to make friends? We're not scheduled to leave for another twenty minutes."

Chloe stared at Sam, then at the other girl. "What do I say to her?"

"Something will come to you. Don't little girls always find something to talk about?"

"They do in the movies."

"That's a good start. Talk about the movies you've seen."

Chloe eased off the seat and disappeared to the rear.

The bus filled up slowly but by the appointed time it was full.

Tours to Guaymas by way of Nogales must be popular, Sam thought.

After Maria waved and wished everyone a fun trip, the door closed and the bus pulled out.

Chloe returned to her seat.

"How'd it go?" Sam asked.

"Good."

"That's all? You talked to her for almost half an hour."

162

"She's going to Guaymas to visit an aunt who moved there because it was cheaper there than living in the US."

"Figures."

The bus ground through morning traffic lining up six lanes across in front of the American border checkpoint. After inching forward for twenty minutes, the bus stopped. The door opened and a Border Patrol officer stepped on board.

Sam's heart skipped a beat.

"Everyone here looking forward to a relaxing trip to Mexico?" the officer said, trying to break whatever tension his appearance had produced.

"Yeah!" A chorus of cheers went up.

"All right!" Then his jolly demeanor faded, and he got down to business. "My name is Bill Walker. I'm with the US Customs and Border Patrol. Let me tell you what this is all about. Every once in a while we board a tour bus like this and make a random check.

"I'm going to do a few checks here of your passports. I expect my checks to be routine, and it shouldn't take more than a few minutes. I apologize for any inconvenience."

Bill took a stack of passports from the driver. "How about we start with you, little lady?" He stood over Chloe and glanced at Sam. "You got a passport in here?"

Sam's heart skipped more than a beat. *They're on to me.*

Chloe glanced at Sam, then started rifling the passports one by one. She stopped at one of them. "This is my passport."

163

Sam felt a sharp pain in his chest and decided this was the end of them, right there and then.

The officer snatched the passport out of Chloe's fingers. "What's your full name, child?"

"Abigail Laurie Fisher."

The officer glanced at Chloe then back at the passport as though he were disappointed. "That's what it says here, but the photo doesn't look too much like you."

"It's an old photo. I got the passport five years ago, when I was five."

The officer brightened.

Sam cringed.

"When were you born?" the officer asked.

"I was born on February 16, 2010 in Toledo, Ohio."

The officer raised his eyebrows, then frowned, obviously not hearing what he expected to hear. "Okay, little lady, you can sit back down." The officer pulled another passport from the stack. "Samuel Johns Turner?" He looked around.

Just then, one of the officer's peers leaned into the bus.

"Bill, we got a problem over on Aisle Five. Need some backup, ASAP."

"Gotta go, ladies and gentlemen...boys and girls." Walker nodded to Chloe and dumped the passports onto the driver's lap. "You all have a nice trip."

Walker descended the steps and jogged away with the other agent.

As the driver started the bus and pulled forward to the Mexican side of the border, Sam leaned close

164

to Chloe and whispered, "How'd you know to say all that?"

"I heard you lie to Maria about me having a passport, so when I talked to Abigail back there, I asked her about when she was born and where she was from. She likes to talk. I listened. Her mom's name is Eva."

Sam shook his head in disbelief. "I suppose you know who her father is and what she had for breakfast."

"George, and cheerios, just like me."

Chapter Eight

The tour of Nogales on the Mexican side had started slowly and gotten slower. Chloe didn't complain, but Sam could tell she was becoming impatient with the tour commentary about people and places that may have been interesting to an honest-to-god tourist but not to her.

Mostly, the tour guide directed his entourage to pricey shops where he entered and engaged in friendly banter with the owners before waving the group in for what seemed like extended stays. No doubt he received a cut from whatever anyone bought.

In a silver shop, Chloe pulled Sam over to a glass case and pointed to a silver cross on a thin chain. "Grandpa, isn't it beautiful?"

"It is. What do you know about crosses?"

"I know they were used for crucifixions."

"And?"

"And, Jesus died on a cross."

"Quite so." Sam looked up. "I think the tour guide is ready to move us to the next store."

"Will you buy me that cross? Please."

"What's so important about having a cross?"

She thought a bit about the question. "It will protect me and keep me safe."

"If you're a believer, then you'd have to wear a Saint Christopher medal for that."

Chloe scowled. "I don't want a Saint Christopher medal. I want a cross."

The tour guide was waving to them. The others were already out on the street.

"Okay. But only the cross, no bracelets or anything else." Sam motioned to the proprietor who hurried over and took the cross from the display case.

"How much is it?" Sam asked.

"Three hundred pesos, *Señor*."

"That's way too much. I've gotta go. The tour is moving on."

"One hundred pesos, *Señor*. I cannot go lower."

Sam pulled out a ten dollar bill. "This okay?"

"It is okay, *Señor*. *Muchas gracias*."

Sam took the cross and gave it to Chloe, who slipped the chain over her head and adjusted the cross on her chest. "Now I'm really safe."

They proceeded to the restaurant for lunch, which was okay, but not what might have been expected of *El José's* if it was indeed the best restaurant in all of Nogales. Sam thought he had seen the owner José somewhere before. With his good looks, faded by age, he could have been a movie star. He circulated among the tables, shook hands with the men and squeezed the women's shoulders as he leaned forward to indulge their every word.

Sam breathed a sigh of relief when they boarded the bus and the driver announced facetiously it was siesta time for the next few hours. *Indeed.*

The outskirts of Mexican Nogales were poverty stricken barrios filled with trash, run-down adobe buildings, a scattering of beat up cars, wandering chickens and burros. What people he saw seemed downtrodden, the men dressed in baggy pants and sleeveless shirts, the women tough and stocky. They carried firewood or laundry on their heads with infants wrapped on their backs.

Chloe sat with her face glued to the window the whole time. "Why are they so poor, Grandpa?"

"There are a lot of reasons people are poor. Unfortunately, in Mexico people tend to stay poor, whereas in the US there is the hope of moving out of poverty."

Sam pulled a pamphlet guide for the Sonoran Desert out of a seat side pocket. "Here, why don't you look at this and see what it says about the desert we're about to cross."

"I guess that will be better than looking at poor people."

Sam figured she was probably right but didn't want to belabor the point.

An hour out of Nogales and two hours to go to Hermosillo, the bus began a series of erratic backfirings, which degenerated into a lurching and finally a complete slow rolling stop to the side of the road.

The driver leapt out of the bus and went to the back where he opened the panel to the motor. Gusts of oily black smoke drifted in the breeze to one side of the bus. Not a good sign. So much for state of the art.

He climbed back in and held his hands up for attention. "The bus is broken. I will call for help. Don't you worry. The office will send another bus."

He sat in his driver's seat and thumbed his cell phone, then spoke earnestly into it.

168

Sam gazed out at the bleak desert. How anything could grow there was beyond his imagination. What vegetation there was spread thinly. *Cholla* cactus that was especially prickly according to the pamphlet. Organ pipe cactus. Creosote bushes as well as sage and a scattering of Palo Verde. Probably no shortage of rattlesnakes, the only viper out of a stated population of three hundred fifty different animal species. But where were they?

The driver finished his call. "They are sending help," he said. "We will be here for maybe an hour. I am sorry it is getting stuffy inside the bus. Because it is normally AC, the windows cannot be opened. If you want, you can wait outside. It is very nice weather this time of year. Also, I know you are thinking about the toilet. It is not a good idea to use the toilets on the bus. Better to do your business outside. *Señoras* to the right, *Caballeros* to the left." He waved his arms to indicate the respective directions on the side of the road.

Most of the passengers, including Sam and Chloe filed out of the bus, picking up bottled water from the front as they exited. The air temperature felt like it was about eighty, very dry and pleasant. Still, people hunkered down in the shadow cast by the bus.

This isn't going to work, Sam thought. Despite JoAnne's assurances that once he got into Mexico he was home free, he didn't want to test the hypothesis so close to the border. He felt like a proverbial sitting duck. The feds definitely seemed interested in him, given the response of the Navajo

169

police and the near escape crossing the border. If they also had arrived at the conclusion Chloe was sentient, then it might not take much to induce the Mexican police to detain him for whatever reason. He didn't know how those things worked. He couldn't squat there waiting to see if the law would arrive, sort through the crowd, discover him and Chloe and haul them away.

"Chloe." Sam leaned down to her ear. "We've got to get out of here."

Chloe looked at him questioningly, enough so that he thought maybe leaving the tour was a bad idea.

Instead, she said, "Okay, Grandpa. If you think we should."

Her undivided trust in his judgment was sobering. But he also divined that underneath all her innocent exterior, an undercurrent of perceptive thought ran very deep.

"No one will notice us if we take a bathroom break, then keep going."

Chloe surveyed the desolate landscape. "Where will we go, Grandpa?"

"Maybe we'll disappear for a while, then come back to the road after they've left and hitch a ride."

Chloe didn't seem convinced, but Sam realized he wouldn't know convinced on Chloe from skeptical. "What about our clothes?"

"We'll have to leave them behind. We can buy new ones when we get to a town. I've got all our necessary documents, money and my medications in my fanny pack."

Chloe peered up at the sun.

170

Sam could see she was thinking about being out in the desert. "It's not that hot out there," he said nodding toward the desert. "We've got two bottles of water that should last us."

She nodded, and he took her hand as he led her to where the black asphalt ended and the sand began. "You head over there where the ladies are supposed to go. I'll go over here. When no one is looking, head for--" He scanned the desert beyond and pointed to a large cactus that stood out above the rest. "--for that cactus."

She nodded and skipped away from him as though she'd been doing this sort of subterfuge all her short life.

As Sam entered the bush on the men's side, a child's voice carried through the heated air.

"Chloe, I'm coming with you."

Sam peered around. Abigail Fisher had taken off after Chloe. Nothing he could do about that, now. Hopefully, Chloe would ditch the girl and still make the rendezvous.

Sam arrived at the cactus. No sign of Chloe. Immediately, he started to fret she had become lost or also as bad, snared by Abigail.

"Boo!" Chloe said, coming up to him from the side.

He jumped, felt a rush of adrenaline, then the accelerated beating of his heart. "Chloe, you can't do that. I'll have a heart attack."

"Oh. I forgot. Sorry." She stuck out her lower lip.

"We've no time for that. Come on." He took her by the hand and checked they were still alone, then headed deeper into the desert. "How'd you get rid of Abigail?"

"She doesn't like snakes, and I told her the desert was crawling with them."

Sam kept up a good pace for what he thought to be about a mile out from the highway where a well-defined dirt road running parallel to the highway cut across their line of travel.

Sam turned south onto the road. "We'll follow this for a ways. It'll be easier than walking through all that cactus."

Chloe said nothing but fingered the cross hanging around her neck.

After another half hour, Sam called for a rest stop. He pulled Chloe over to the side of the road and sat in the relative shade of a large thorn bush. They were on a slight rise in the landscape, one that gave them a good view of the desert they had come through and the desert they would still have to cross. The tour bus remained in the remote distance behind them. "One bottle of water left." He handed it to Chloe, and she took a sip.

The distant sound of an approaching vehicle drifted to him through the still air. Sam looked north at an approaching cloud of dust that resolved itself into the dark speck of a vehicle.

It came toward them at a high rate of speed, then blew by them, big and black, flashing chrome wheels. An H2 Hummer.

Sam leaned over Chloe, trying to protect her from the suffocating dust. It drifted to the side of the road as the Hummer sped south without slowing.

Chloe gazed up at him with concern.

It was obvious she was feeling some apprehension. After all, Sam was the only person she knew connecting her to the real world. "You all right, kid?"

"I worry more about you, Grandpa."

"That's nice of you to say. I'll be okay, maybe a little tired."

After about a mile, the Hummer's taillights came on and the vehicle slowed to a stop. A second vehicle appeared farther south. It closed the distance to the Hummer and stopped in front of it.

Barely discernible figures emerged from both cars and met in a group between them.

Bright flashes of light, like sparkling fireworks went off. Then, drifting on the dry air, the popping sound of gunshots, some of it automatic weapons fire. A haze of blue gun smoke drifted in the air. Silence. No figures were left standing.

Chloe cowered at his side, muttering and clutching her cross, almost as if she were reciting penance. It had been obvious, even to her, what had happened.

"It's okay," Sam said. "The shots are way over there. They have nothing to do with us. Nobody even knows we are here."

Sam debated about what to do. He couldn't go back to the bus. But they had to get a move on. If they were still in the area when the second bus arrived, they would be missed and probably looked for. Detouring into the desert to get around the unknown obstruction ahead would waste time and energy. Maybe if they approached cautiously they'd

173

be able to tell if it was safe to continue or would have to detour.

Sam waited. And waited. After fifteen minutes, with no further sounds or movement coming from the two cars down the road, he turned to Chloe. "We're going to head down that way. It's our most direct route."

"I don't think that's a good idea."

Sage Chloe. So young. So knowing. "If we go cautiously, we'll be okay. Anyway, whatever happened there is long over."

Twenty minutes later, Sam took Chloe's hand as they approached the two vehicles.

A maroon Mercedes with gold trim and white leather seats, issued flames and smoke out of its engine compartment, which was riddled with bullet holes. The Hummer sat looking undamaged, its diesel engine ticking over as if it were waiting for them.

Sam edged to the far side of the road with Chloe clawing at his leg, her whole body shivering, the cross clutched in her fist.

Four bodies lay sprawled near the Mercedes, another two closer to the Hummer.

"Grandpa, there are a lot of bodies over there."

"I see them. You stay here. I'm going to check if anyone is still alive."

After prying Chloe's hands away from him, he walked to the nearest body and knelt to feel for a pulse. But as he rolled the man over onto his back, it became obvious the dark skinned man, probably Mexican, was very dead. Half his face was blown away by a large caliber bullet. His chest showed

174

four neat holes in a line from lower left to upper right. His legs lay crookedly. His right arm, tattooed from the shoulder to his wrist, ended with a hand gun still gripped in his fist.

Sam moved to the other three bodies and found similar carnage. These guys hadn't been playing hide and seek. It was *mano a mano*, the Gunfight at the OK corral, high noon.

"They're dead," he called back to Chloe.

Chloe came over and sat beside him. He put his arm around her and pulled her close. "We're going to be okay," he said. Although she nodded, she didn't seem to calm down any.

He went to the Hummer where the remaining two bodies lay. These guys were better dressed but just as dead. He went to the passenger side of the Hummer and opened the door.

Cool air from the air-conditioned interior flowed over him. What a delight. He reached in and shut off the ignition. No sense burning fuel. Then he noticed two stacked aluminum attaché cases on the passenger seat. He pulled one over to him, slid the latches and lifted the lid.

One hundred dollar bills in tight wrappers, marked ten thousand each were packed into the case. *Must be a million dollars here*. He presumed the other case was similarly stuffed.

After closing the case, he walked to the driver's side and pulled down the visor, then extracted the Hummer's registration from a clear plastic envelope. The vehicle was registered in Arizona to a Jorge Batista, whose home address was in Nogales on the US side of the border.

He rounded to the back of the Hummer and swung the door open. The rear cargo area was empty. He closed the door and motioned for Chloe to come to him.

She shook her head.

She's afraid. He walked to her, knelt down and took her into his arms. "How's that cross working?"

She tried a smile but kept rubbing the crucifix. "I don't know," she said in a small voice.

"Look. I'm scared, too. But I think this is our lucky day. These were all bad people. We had nothing to do with what happened here. Now they are all dead and they've left behind that Hummer that looks like it's waiting for us to use it. Maybe your cross has been helping us out after all."

Chloe brushed away a tear and nodded.

He took her by the hand and led her to the passenger side of the front seat and buckled her in. When he rounded the front of the Hummer, he paused. The body nearest him lay stretched out with a machine pistol still griped in its hand. Though taking the pistol seemed a morbid thing to do, it didn't rank much below taking the Hummer.

He eased the weapon out of man's grip. As he started to turn away, reflected light gleamed off of something in the man's rear pocket. Sticking out of the pocket was the pearl handle of a very small pistol.

Sam retrieved the gun, which he decided was a Derringer or something close to it.

He put both weapons on the floor in the back seat and climbed in behind the wheel.

"It's time we got out of here and on our way," he said to Chloe. "The good news is, we don't have to try to hitch a ride. The bad news is, I don't know what's in store for us."

***

Wellstone had arrived in Nogales earlier in the day aboard a government issue 2009 Learjet 85. He didn't often travel in style, but this was an exception. His quest to bring the sentient clone home and to drag its conspirators into a court of law had been cleared by the highest authority. In his dreams he fantasized the Vice President had been given a briefing on the case and issued specific instructions to process it to the fullest capability of the Bureau. Hence the Learjet.

Wellstone sat behind his desk at his hastily organized base of operations, an office in a non-descript building near the border. A very rundown part of town. But he didn't require much comfort, just top notch electronics and communications. Nothing worse than being in the metaphorical dark when it came to pursuing a person of interest. And this Turner was becoming more and more interesting all the time.

The intel had Turner using his credit card at a hot springs west of Kayenta, Arizona. When Navajo police ID'd him, they were requested to pull him over for further questioning. That was before he disappeared into the Hopi reservation. Finally, local police had relayed a call from a Nogales tour operator that she had sold a bus tour to Guaymas to Turner and a young girl named Chloe, whom he claimed to be his granddaughter.

Wellstone's pleasure evaporated when he learned Turner and the child had boarded the tour bus and entered Mexico. All this was despite the best efforts of an alerted US Customs and Border Patrol.

Wellstone fumed, and took his frustrations out on the Stetson hat he had brought with him. He worked the shape of the brim. At least once he got the brim right, he'd be able to wear the hat, this being a field operation.

Damn that Turner.

Wellstone didn't like playing catch up, especially to a target who was an amateur. But he had to admit, amateurs could give you fits and throw you all sorts of curves.

"Sir?" The ever present Marshall made his presence known. "The pizzas are here."

Wellstone nodded, laid the Stetson to one side and indicated Marshall could deliver a pizza to his desk. "I'd like to think we have better things to do than decide on pepperoni or cheese."

"Yes, sir. We're monitoring all links. If Turner so much as sneezes, we'll know about it."

Wellstone wondered about the sneeze. Turner seemed in good health despite having a bad heart. Wellstone raised a pizza slice to his mouth.

"Sir?"

Wellstone stopped mid-bite. "This had better be good, Marshall."

Marshall looked confused. "I'm sure it is, sir. We asked around and Barry's True Italian was said to be the best pizza in the area."

Wellstone stared. *What else can I do?*

Marshall finally caught on. "I'm sorry, sir. We have a Maria Cabrerra here for questioning. She's the travel agent who sold Turner his tour ticket south."

Wellstone took two bites from the pizza, then shoved the box with the rest of the pizza to one side of his desk. "I'd like to talk to her. Show her in."

A heavily made up Hispanic girl was ushered into Wellstone's office. She wore a too short skirt and a tight, red top that left her shoulders exposed. She was a bit overweight with no waist to speak of, probably had two kids already. She clasped her hands in front of her and glanced around, obviously in awe of being asked into the FBI's command center for an interview.

Wellstone thought to ease the tension and get her to relax. "Please, Miss Cabrerra, have a seat. We want to ask you a few questions. It won't take long. Routine stuff."

Cabrerra sat down, the skirt rising on her hips to mid-thigh.

For Christ's sake, she looks like a whore, Wellstone thought, finding her looks personally offensive.

"I'm Agent Wellstone, and this is Agent Marshall. Would you like a slice of pizza? We were just having lunch."

Cabrerra shook her head, then turned back to glance at Marshall, who stood six feet behind her.

Wellstone picked up a paper on his desk and pretended it had something to do with the questioning. "You sold a tour package to a Samuel John Turner, all-inclusive, to Guaymas."

179

"*Si, Señor.*" Cabrerra crossed her legs, showing a bit more thigh and black stiletto heels. "He came in two days ago with a little girl."

"But you didn't call the authorities until after the tour bus left."

"That is right, *Señor*. The first day, when I sold him the tour, I had my suspicions something wasn't right. Then after he boarded the bus...and didn't give me a tip or nothing...not that we expect it, but some do, you know...I decided to call it in."

"And I'm glad you did." Wellstone gave her one of his best smiles. "Could you give us a description of the girl?"

"*Si, Señor*. She was blond. She had blue eyes and was very skinny. Her skin was very pale, *también*. The *señor* said she was ten, but she was very small for that age, maybe four feet, fifty-five, sixty pounds."

"Thank you, Miss Cabrerra. You're very perceptive. That's an excellent description. Could you also tell us how they were dressed, any jewelry?"

"The man was dressed casually, nothing real classy. Also, in my opinion, the girl had taken more time to choose her clothes, sort of mix and match, if you know what I mean?"

"We do. Thank you." Wellstone pretended to write something on the paper in front of him. "Did they have any luggage?"

"*Si*. There was a suitcase and a duffel bag."

"So they intended to stay in Mexico a while?"

"The tour was for five nights, *Señor*. Maybe it was odd they had so much luggage."

180

"Excellent observation, Miss Cabrerra. We could use someone like you on the force."

Miss Cabrerra waved a hand in dismissal and blushed. "*Gracías, Señor*. I have to be alert in my business, you know, you could not image the number of *cabrones* we have coming into the office with all sorts of stories just to get a trip to Guaymas or Mazatlan or Acapulco. Some prefer Huatulco, or Ixtapa. And--"

"Did they book any side trips, which might indicate they would only be passing through Guaymas?"

"Unfortunately, no side trips. I get a bonus for booking those."

"Miss Cabrerra," Marshall said, stepping close and leaning in. "What did you perceive the relationship to be between Mr. Turner and the girl?"

"Perceive?"

"In your opinion, what was the relationship between Mr. Turner and the girl?"

"That is what made me make the call...besides not getting a tip. But you know like I already told you, I don't expect a tip. You know, we don't have many old men coming in and requesting a trip to the beach and having such a young girl with them. You know what I mean. We get the drunks that want all-inclusive because they can drink all they want. And also, you know, we get the--"

"I think we understand," Wellstone said, feeling if Cabrerra didn't shut up he'd have to throw what remained of his pizza at her. He gave Marshall a look that told him to distract her.

181

"Miss Cabrerra," Marshall said with a sly smile to Wellstone, "did you observe any sort of untoward behavior between the two of them, inappropriate touching, nervousness on the part of the girl, aggressiveness on the part of Mr. Turner?"

"*No, Señor*. Mr. Turner and the girl seemed to get along real well...but one can never tell in these types of situations."

"But you did talk to the girl," Wellstone said, "and she answered you as though she understood everything you were saying?"

"I did. She was very nice and engaging. Oh, the poor *niña*, she's in trouble, *no*?"

Wellstone could only sit and wonder at the woman's total naïveté. She seemed unaware of the impression she was making on them. "It's not something for you to worry about, Miss Cabrerra. She's not in the kind of trouble you are imagining if that's any consolation to you. But there is trouble."

"I'm so glad for that, *Señor*. I mean, not that she is still in trouble, but that she is not in *that* kind of trouble."

"I want to thank you, Miss Cabrerra for coming in to talk to us--" Wellstone waved to Marshall that the interview was over and he could escort Cabrerra to the door. "--if we have any further questions, will you be available?"

"Of course, *Señor*. You know, I want to help. Always, I want to help."

Marshall touched her shoulder, and she rose, smoothing her skirt. She smiled at Wellstone and let herself be directed to the door.

182

When Marshall returned, Wellstone said, "Those are the most difficult kinds of interviews, Marshall. They want to help, but don't know how they can, which puts a lot of pressure on us to get the answers we seek."

"Yes, sir. I felt that pressure, too."

"I'm convinced this girl Turner is traveling with is his clone and she's sentient. Somewhere along the way, Turner ditched his 4Runner. Maybe in Hotevilla. Then he booked the tour as a way to get across the border. I'm guessing Guaymas isn't his final destination. Problem is getting to him. Our Mexican liaison will only go so far as to keep track of them since they are in the country legally. But, boy, I'd like to haul them in. If we could do that, we'd have that son of a bitch Androp by the balls."

"Yes sir, by the balls."

***

Sam climbed up into the driver's seat of the Hummer after buckling Chloe into the passenger side.

She craned around, wide-eyed. "This is huge, Grandpa. Much bigger than your old car."

"These Hummers *are* huge. Especially the older ones, like this one, before the Chinese started downsizing them to meet the market."

Chloe frowned.

Sam realized either *Chinese* or *meet the market* or both had been lost on her. When she didn't follow up on her frown, he studied the array of controls in front of him. He scrunched around feeling the smooth leather at his back. He breathed in the cool air-conditioned air. What luxury. But this was probably a drug dealer's car with bulletproof windows and side panels. Maybe even James Bond defenses, rockets, or compartments in the back to drop tacks on the road. Sam would have to be careful what buttons he touched.

The sun was below the western horizon and a cool darkness settled onto the desert. Not that it would help the dead much. Another desert species had made itself known. Vultures with huge wingspans circled high overhead, still in sunlight, waiting for Sam to leave before descending to the buffet of flesh.

Sam switched on the headlights, put the Hummer in gear and eased it forward in the direction of the highway. At the edge of the highway he waited, lights off, until traffic thinned. There wasn't much traffic anyway this time of the evening.

When nothing was coming north or south, he drove onto the road and headed south at a moderate speed.

He studied intermittently the CD changer and stereo system on the dash. *Bose Cabin Surround Sound System* read a little label. Sam pushed a button, and was practically thrown back in his seat by a blast of thumping *Mexicana Urbana*. He stabbed at the off button.

Chloe picked up an iPoddle from the floor. "Can I play this, Grandpa?"

"Of course you can. In fact you can keep it. I don't think whoever owned it has any use for it, now."

184

She grinned and twisted earphone plugs into her ears. She thumbed buttons on the face of the iPoddle, then must have hit something she liked because she started jiving back and forth to what Sam assumed was music.

He left her alone. It had been a long, hot, traumatic day. She probably needed time to herself. Time like she used to have in her crèche, no pain, no worries, no suffering.

A half hour later, ghostly shapes wavered at the far edge of the Hummer's high beams on the right hand side of the road.

Sam slowed and the shapes became distinct figures waving for him to stop.

Sam counted a man and two young boys. A woman sat with an older woman on the side of the road cradling a young girl in her lap.

They were all dressed in what could only be described as rags. The man seemed half crazed, his black hair unruly, no hat, which was odd for a Mexican. His shirt and pants used to be white at some point in time long ago. He wore sandals made from the treads of old tires.

The two women weren't dressed much better.

Sam came to a stop and pushed the button that powered the window down on Chloe's side.

The man stepped up to the Hummer and let loose an agitated stream of Spanish Sam couldn't understand. The women chattered in the background in what almost seemed like wailing instead of speech.

Sam powered the window back up a couple of inches. "I don't speak Spanish. *No hablo español.*"

185

The man gripped the window and nodded violently. "*Lo siento, señor. Mia niña* is sick. I must get to Hermosillo to a doctor. *Por favor. Ayudame.*"

Sam debated taking a chance with these people, but they seemed in dire need. On the other hand, if he left them there, who would know? But the girl might really be sick.

"I'm sorry," Sam said, his first thought being he needed to be on his way and picking up these strangers would only slow him down. "I don't have time for this."

Chloe removed the earphones, looked at the women and the prone girl, then at Sam. "Grandpa. We have to help them." That said, she re-plugged the earphones into her ears.

Of course we do. What am I thinking? Why do I need a ten year old reminding me? But she kept amazing him with her grasp of reality and single-minded attention to what might be most important.

"Okay," Sam said to the man, "you can load up in the back. But you'll have to move those two suitcases and the guns on the floor way back to make room. That's the best I can offer."

The man nodded profusely, then opened the door to the rear seat. "*Aye dios mío!*" He made the sign of the cross across his chest.

"Look," Sam said, revving the engine. "If any of that bothers you, you can wait for the next car to take you in."

"*No, no problema, Señor.* I have seen guns like this before. I will move them to the back." He

186

turned to the younger of the two women. "*Maria, ayudame!*"

Maria transferred the limp girl to the older woman and hurried to the man's side. "*Aye dios mío!*" she said upon seeing the guns. She, too, crossed himself.

The two of them struggled for a minute transferring the cases and guns into the back of the Hummer. Then they all loaded up on the passenger seat, plenty of room for the adults with the kids standing between their knees or sitting on their laps.

The girl did look very ill. Her eyes were glazed with fever, her face sallow.

Chloe roused herself from her iPoddle and leaned over the seat. "If that little boy moves over to your left," she said to the man, "then the girl can lie all the way down. I think she would be more comfortable."

The man gazed at her as though he was looking at an apparition, certainly a saint with blond hair, then quickly complied.

Sam shook his head in wonderment and got underway. Why in the world had he become such a soft touch? Maybe it was Chloe. Maybe his own sense of mortality was getting to him. There was also a rising anger born of frustration that the winds of change were blowing against him, that his perfect little world, excepting his bum heart, was coming apart before his eyes.

The man tapped Sam on the shoulder and leaned close to his ear. "*Señor*, I saw drugs in the back. But your secret is safe with me."

187

Not knowing what the man was talking about, Sam stifled the urge to turn around. "Look, whatever your name is--"

"I am Juan, *mi mujer es Maria, mi madre es Estella, y mis tres niños son Gabriela, José, y Miguel.*"

"Thanks," Sam said, "I'll try to remember all that. There are no drugs in this car, the guns aren't mine, this Hummer isn't mine. *Comprende?*"

"Not yours. *Si, Señor. Yo comprendo.* You speak very good *Espanish.*"

Juan leaned back in his seat and began a heated argument with his wife, who kept pushing on his shoulder and waving an exasperated hand in the air, trying to shut him up.

Sam caught a few words in Spanish. Juan, it seemed, was concerned about being in what he thought was a drug dealer's car. Whereas Maria could care less about what they were in, her only concern being to get Gabriela to a doctor as soon as possible.

Eventually, Juan and Maria quieted down and fell asleep, probably exhausted from their ordeal with Gabriela. The Hummer purred along the road as if it was meant to be there. Sam slouched back, hit cruise control and glanced over at Chloe, who sat belted in. She had her iPoodle in front of her and was busy flipping through screens.

An hour later they came to the outskirts of Hermosillo. The town glowed in the distance. But bright lights intruded nearer to home. The road ahead was awash with high intensity floods. Two guard shacks constricted the flow of traffic between

188

them and a steel barrier arm flanked by concrete abutments blocked the way. As they approached, an armed sentry stepped in front of them and held up his hand for them to stop.

"Hey," Sam said trying to get Chloe's attention.

She tilted her head, enough to let him know she was listening.

He leaned in close to her ear, pulled out the earphone and said, "We've come to a police checkpoint. You'll have to be in this world if we hope to make it through."

Chloe glanced up, nodded and pulled out the other earphone. She put her hands in her lap and waited.

189

Chapter Nine

Sam slowed the Hummer. Behind the approaching sentry lounged three federal soldiers with what Sam thought were automatic assault rifles hung over their shoulders. Aside from that initial conjecture, Sam didn't know the guns from sticks, but these guys were toting heavy stuff.

"Control," Sam said over his shoulder.

His hitchhikers rose from their sleep and pulled themselves together. There was no possibility of avoiding the checkpoint. He eased up to the heavy steel barrier arm with its red and white striping.

The sentry came over to Sam, glanced inside, then stepped back and examined the exterior of the Hummer.

"*A donde esta Jorge*?" he asked.

Sam felt his stomach clench. Not his heart, thank goodness. Maybe that was a good sign. "Jorge? Look, my Spanish is a bit weak. Do you speak English?"

"I speak English. Where Jorge?"

"He's in Matamoros."

"How come you have his Hummer?" The sentry tried to peer deeper into the vehicle, but could probably see nothing distinctly, given the tinted glass. All Sam could hope for was that the peasants he had reluctantly helped wouldn't give him away.

"We...we did a deal," Sam said. "It was quick."

"Did Jorge tell you about me?"

Sam glanced at the man's name tag. "Yeah, he did, ah...Guillermo. He said to give you whatever you asked for...as a gift. But he also said you should be temperate...if you know what I mean." Sam smiled and hoped the sweat cascading off his brow would be attributed to the lingering heat of the day.

Guillermo nodded knowingly. He glanced over his shoulder at the three guys behind him, then with what seemed to be an immense effort, said, "Okay, five hundred US, *ahora*."

Sam was beginning to appreciate the benefits of being thought a drug dealer. "*No problema*." He dug into his fanny pack to withdraw five hundred dollars from his dwindling personal cache and handed it to the sentry.

"Can I go now?" Sam hoped to speed up the process as Guillermo shoved the money into his pockets without counting it.

The sound of a car door opening and shutting intruded.

Guillermo didn't turn around but his eyes went wide.

Sam peered past the farthest guard shack at a parked black Mercedes he hadn't noticed before.

A police Colonel in full uniform had exited from the backseat. He tugged the bottom edge of his jacket to straighten it, then smoothed his mustache with thumb and finger.

He was a stocky man, very stern, mid-forties, polished boots, shiny belt buckle. A diagonal strap cut across his chest and ended at the holster for his service revolver, pearl handled.

A regular George Patton.

Sam figured Guillermo was always on a prescient alert, always needing an extra few seconds warning before his superior appeared.

Guillermo, pitiful as he was, came to a rigid attention and saluted.

Sam slouched back in his seat, figuring he had come to the end of his rope. Here he was sitting in a murdered drug dealer's vehicle, a sentient clone beside him, and a clutch of locals with a sick girl in the backseat. But imbedded in his psyche was the assumption all south of the border police Colonels were corrupt.

Maybe there is a way out of this.

"*Que pasa aqui?*" the Colonel demanded of Guillermo.

Guillermo seemed to shrivel to half his size. "*Nada, Colonel.*"

The Colonel stepped up to Sam. "What are you doing here, *gringo*?"

"I'm on my way to Guaymas. Is there a problem?" Despite Sam's retort, his heart was going at a giddy-up pace.

"Is this your car?"

"No. A friend loaned it to me in Nogales."

"You are lying."

"I'm not lying. Why should I lie to you about the loan of a car?"

"I think I have seen this car before. Guillermo, have you seen this car before?"

"*Colonel*, it is Jorge's car."

"It is Jorge's car," the Colonel mimicked. "Are we supposed to prostrate ourselves on the road and let Jorge's car through?"

"Pros...?" Guillermo said.

The Colonel hooked his thumbs into his belt and turned his attention back to Sam. "I am Colonel Tulio Ingles. I am in charge of this entire region. I know all the drug dealers here. You, *Señor*, are not one of them."

"You're right about that. Jorge, whom you seem to know, loaned me the car. You got a problem with that, I suppose you'll have to take it up with him."

Ingles smiled. "I will, *muchacho*. But for now, you can show me identification. *Por favor*."

Sam dug out his driver's license and handed it to Ingles.

He tilted the license to the light and read. "Samuel J. Turner. Colorado. Nice place Colorado. Who's the girl?"

"She's my granddaughter."

"I assume you have identification for her, too?"

Sam started to dig out Chloe's birth certificate, but Ingles raised a restraining hand. "That won't be necessary *Señor* Turner. I believe you."

"Thank you." *What game is Ingles playing*? It seemed the feds would have radioed ahead long ago and given the Mexican police all the information they needed to identify him and Chloe. Certainly a policeman of Ingles' rank would know.

"You can give me twice what you gave Guillermo."

"I..." *Is it so simple? Ingles wants money*? "You want me to pay you money, so we can be on our way?"

193

Ingles rolled his eyes, disgusted. "Did I say anything about money?"

Sam realized this wasn't the United States of America, and if he wanted to proceed, he'd have to cough up more money, even though money hadn't been explicitly mentioned. Then it hit him. If he wanted something down here, everything had a price and if you had an endless supply of money then nothing could stand in your way.

Sam produced a thousand dollars and handed it to Ingles. "This isn't money," he said facetiously. "It's a gift."

The Colonel stared at Sam, a look that told him not to push the boundaries of what was happening there. He counted the bills then peered at Guillermo. "You get this much every time Jorge passes here?"

"*Si, Colonel.*" Guillermo lowered his gaze, looking very forlorn. "I am sorry. I have a family. But in the future I will give you half of what I receive."

Ingles slapped Guillermo across his face. "You will give me everything you receive, and I will decide what to give back to you. Understood?"

"*Si, Colonel.*" Guillermo held his cheek. "*Muchas gracias.*"

"Now, since we all understand each other--" He motioned to Guillermo. "--search this entire vehicle."

Ingles must have seen Sam's startled look, for he smiled.

As Guillermo headed for the back of the vehicle on one side, Ingles walked on the other side

194

and stopped when he must have seen movement in the backseat.

"You have passengers?" He stepped to the rear passenger window, cupped his hands to peer through the tinted glass, then rapped on the window.

Sam flipped the button that would lower the window.

"Who are these people?"

"They waved me down from the side of the road," Sam said. "The girl is sick and needs to see a doctor in Hermosillo."

Ingles said something in Spanish to Juan to which Juan nodded, then leaned back so Ingles could get a better look at Gabriela.

Her breathing had begun to come in short gasps, her face very flushed and wet with perspiration.

"It looks like she's about to die," Ingles said.

"And she will if we can't get her to a doctor." Sam didn't want to pressure Ingles, but he figured even a corrupt police Colonel didn't want to have a child die because he obstructed getting her to a doctor.

"Guillermo, never mind," Ingles called to the sentry. "We can search them another time."

He stood back and waved Sam through the gate.

***

The phone rang, and Demetri picked up. "Andropov."

He was in his office, the only place he felt comfortable. He couldn't bear sitting at home. It wasn't in his nature. No wife. No children.

195

Actually, he had lots of children, but the feds had taken them all away.

"Hey, Demetri." It was Simon Garulli.

"Yeah, yeah, what's up?"

"We got the injunction!"

Demetri put the receiver to his chest and counted to ten. *Could it be true?* Was he going to be able to defeat the feds in a court of law?

"That's great. Really great. What are the details? I need details."

"Lots of details, but not to worry, most of them are irrelevant."

Demetri didn't like irrelevant. "Tell me."

"For starters, we've got a complete freeze on any further federal seizures."

"That's fucking bogus!" Demetri said with a burst of anger. "They already have all my clones."

"Calm down. If you can't remain calm, I'm going to hang up and call you back later."

Demetri counted to twenty this time. "Okay, I'm calm. Tell me what we've got."

"I addressed the seizure of your clones in my presentation to the judge. He was very sympathetic. Thank God for liberal appointments. He came down on our side and said any clone within six months of maturity had to be returned to you."

"That's great. That's great. Six months. If they give me all those clones back, I can avoid bankruptcy." Demetri laughed. "Hell, I mean I could save the lives of a lot of my clients."

"I'm with you on that. The upshot of the judge's ruling is that after the feds give you back your clones, they also have to stand aside as you proceed with your legitimate business, your *deliveries*."

"Yeah, deliveries. What about the sentient clone I gave to Turner?"

"It's a good thing you're protected by lawyer-client confidentiality or we'd have a problem with that clone."

"Huh? What did I do? It was that shit Nathan, who nurtured her. Besides, the feds don't now she's sentient. Neither does Turner. Once he gets south of the border and has his operation it's all history."

"Did Turner sign off on the transfer of the clone?"

"Yeah, yeah. He was so confused he would have signed anything."

"Good. At least you can draw your share of the contract amount out of escrow. Maybe get around to paying some of your legal fees."

"That's not funny, Simon."

"Okay, not funny. You said it's all history after the operation. It is, unless the feds or Turner find out she's sentient."

"Shit. You think they will?"

Simon chuckled. "You pay me to think of the possibilities."

"You're telling me I have to get to the clone first."

"Demetri, we're not having this conversation."

"How the hell am I going to find them?"

There was a long pause on the other end of the line. "Okay. Just this once. But we never talked."

"Cut the shit, Simon. This isn't the Sopranos."

197

"I don't know Sopranos. Here's the sweet part of the judgment. The feds have to make you whole, that means restore your business to the state it was in before Wellstone first made contact with you. That call he made precedes your premature transfer of the sentient. By court order the feds will have to assist you in restoring your business to the state it was in before their intervention."

Demetri saw light at the end of the tunnel. "If Turner goes to Mexico, the feds will be at a disadvantage. They'll have to work with the Mexican authorities."

"Exactly. You aren't similarly constrained."

"Thank God for that." Having spent his formative years being schooled by Marxists, Demetri had no opinion on the existence of God, he only used the expression to go along with Garulli. "Anything else?"

"Like I said, lots of details, mostly irrelevant. I'll send you a copy of the judgment. In the meantime, you can fire up your crèches, sweep out your warehouse, rehire your staff...except for that snitch Marcus Washington. By the way, I've got a PI onto him. We'll see if we can dig up dirt that will put him behind bars for a few years. Give him time to think about what he did."

"I don't give a shit about Washington. Is it okay for me to call Wellstone and see what he's got on my sentient?"

"I don't see why not. He'll have a copy of the judgment. His hands are tied. The feds will have to cooperate with you in tracking down Turner and the clone. If they refuse, they risk being held in contempt of court."

Demetri wrapped up the conversation, said goodbye and hung up. It was obvious to him he now had Wellstone and his testosterone-pumped swat team backed into a corner. Not only would they have to return most of the clones, they would be obligated to help him find the sentient. He had the advantage.

He found the number to the FBI's Denver office and dialed.

"I'd like to speak to Agent Wellstone, please."

"Certainly, sir. May I ask who's calling and what you are calling about?"

"You can tell Wellstone it's Demetri Andropov. He'll know what I'm calling about."

"One moment please." The line went dead, and Johann Pachelbel's Canon in D came on.

Very amusing, Demetri thought. *Dreary.*

"Hello, Mr. Andropov?" The operator came back on the line. "Agent Wellstone is currently in the field and cannot be reached."

Demetri laughed. *Of course he's in the field, like somewhere between here and the Mexican border looking for my clone.* "Look, young lady, you connect me pronto to someone in charge, or I'll have my lawyer up your collective asses by noon tomorrow."

"Sir, I must remind you all conversations with the Bureau are recorded."

"I don't give a shit about being recorded. You heard me."

"One moment, please."

A minute later the second movement of the Canon in D was interrupted. "This is Agent Peterson, can I help you?"

"You know who I am?"

"I do."

"Then you know the injunction that was issued in my favor regarding your seizure of my clones compels Wellstone not only to cease and desist but to make me whole by restoring my business to the state it was in before he started messing with me. You understand the phrase--make me whole?"

"I do, Mr. Andropov. I have a copy of the injunction in front of me as we speak. Obviously, your lawyer has given you one interpretation of the language contained therein. We have a different interpretation in view of certain information that has come to light regarding a particular clone."

Demetri didn't like the, *come to light*, part. It sounded too much as if they already knew the clone was sentient. "You can sit there and blow smoke up my ass all day, Peterson, but that's my clone and I want her back. I want to know where Wellstone is and what he's found out. And don't give me any crap about not being able to contact him because he's in the field. A hundred years ago I would have believed you, but not today."

There was a pause before Peterson answered. "Agent Wellstone is in Nogales on the US side of the border. I suppose it's obvious he'd be on the US side. We have no jurisdiction on the Mexican side. He can be found at 234 West Arroyo Street, Suite B. That's all I can give you. You got that?"

"I got it." Demetri hung up, a smile on his face.

Options. Options. Only one thing to do. Help myself.

He had always been good at helping himself. All those years under the fucking communists had taught him how to take matters into his own hands and make things right.

He left his office and walked into the adjoining one used by the clone techs to stimulate DNA into making a clone. He was no slouch when it came to the finer points of cloning. Though he had no formal degree in the field, he had picked up, along the way, a thorough knowledge of what went on during the process.

He also knew that inadvertently, clones sometimes manifested sentience. Not often. But often enough that Clonal Transplants, with his full authorization, indulged in *clonal cleansing*...at least those were the euphemistic words for injecting suspected sentients with a cocktail containing barbital, and an overdose of morphine. The techs liked to refer to it as Hawaiian Punch. Demetri never could figure out techie humor.

Hawaiian Punch rendered a sentient brain-dead within seconds. Unless, of course the sentient was near term. Then Hawaiian Punch was likely to kill it. But rough times demanded rougher measures. Killing the clone was a chance he now had to take. No clone, no proof of raising a sentient. Everything became hearsay.

Demetri rummaged through a drawer until he found a neat little leather case the size of a large wallet. He drew the zipper open, then placed two syringes into it from another drawer.

Next, he unlocked the cabinet that held the various drugs and medications Clonal used in the course of their business and ran his finger across the labels as he read them. He came to a box that held five vials of barbital, then another box with vials of morphine. What he wanted was the premixed cocktail. He stopped at a box labeled HP. Simple enough. He took two of the HP vials and placed them next to the syringes, zipped the wallet closed and shoved it in his jacket pocket.

If he could get to the clone before Wellstone did, then he would have nothing to worry about.

***

Sam gunned the Hummer into Hermosillo. A blue road sign with a white cross and *Hospital* underneath pointed the way.

"Gabriela threw up, Grandpa." Chloe said it like she was a nurse or some sort of caregiver who dealt regularly with people vomiting.

"*Lo siento mucho, Señor*," Juan said. "Maria will try to clean up the mess."

"We'll clean up later." Sam scanned the road ahead from one side to the other, hoping the signs to the hospital wouldn't give out and leave him stranded somewhere.

He rounded a corner and the hospital building sat squarely in front of him. A bright white sign with red lettering indicated the Emergency Room entrance.

Sam pulled up to the ER.

Juan clambered out first, then cradled Gabriela. Maria and Estella were both crossing themselves

202

and praying. Juan seemed impatient with the praying. "*Andale!*" he shouted.

The women came to their senses and hustled the boys out of the Hummer.

By this time, hospital staff had emerged with a wheelchair. Gabriela was eased into it and rushed through the doors.

Hurrying after her, with Maria, Estella and the other two children following, Juan glanced over his shoulder and gave Sam a wave.

Sam raised his hand in acknowledgement. What more was necessary? Money? No. An effusive thank you? Why? They both knew what was happening and were each dealing with the situation in their own way.

Back in the Hummer, Sam made sure Chloe was still buckled in. "We're going to drive and drive and drive," he said. "I want to get as far away, as fast as I can from the likes of Colonel Ingles. It's eight hundred miles to Guadalajara. We can be there by midday tomorrow if I don't stop."

"But Grandpa, it's already dark, and we have to clean up Gabriela's vomit."

Chloe had a point. Sam was coming to realize the girl, although she was only ten by whatever reckoning, had a very logical head on her shoulders. Sam pulled out of the ER drive-up and parked. He rounded to the passenger seat and used a bottle of water and some paper towels he found in the door pocket to clean up the mess. Fortunately, Gabriela hadn't had a big meal. The mess disappeared quickly. Sam dumped the trash in a nearby trash can and got back behind the wheel.

Chloe scowled.

"Now what's bothering you?" Sam felt he was becoming over-sensitive to Chloe's every mood change.

"We aren't stopping at the beach in Guaymas?"

"There will be plenty of beach opportunities in the days ahead. Right now we have to get out of Colonel Ingles' territory, which I think extends only as far as the State of Sonora."

"Why don't you like Colonel Ingles?"

"First off, he's a corrupt police officer. That's never a good sign. Second, he seemed to know all about the drug trade in his jurisdiction but wasn't doing anything about it. That's the first time I've seen a Colonel being driven around in a Mercedes. There's always the possibility he's got other connections within the force. Connections with similarly inclined policemen. I can only hope his network doesn't extend as far south as we plan to go."

Chloe crossed her arms on her chest. "I'm sleepy."

"You can sleep. I'll drive and try to stay awake."

Chloe reached beside her seat and pressed the button that lowered the back in a smooth powered whine. How she knew how to do this Sam could only guess. But of course, one could learn a lot from TV. At least he was beginning to think so.

She closed her eyes and was asleep in seconds. The ease with which she could crash like that made Sam a little jealous. His own attempts at sleep were

204

more often than not met with endless tossing and turning.

He backed out of the parking space and wound his way through narrow streets to the main highway. After he consulted his atlas he headed south. It was going to be a long, brutal night.

**

Ten hours later, the sun breached the hills to his left, casting long shadows across the road. Early morning cooking fires from roadside hovels sent smoke drifting into the air, creating a gray haze with the distinctive smell of burning mesquite.

He was coming into the outskirts of Mazatlan. Beyond Mazatlan, it was another three hundred miles to Guadalajara. If one wanted to pay the tolls, the *Carretera Internacional* was a fast and efficient highway where one could cruise unimpeded, especially at night. Sam had made good time.

A Wal-Mart loomed up ahead. He had to shop for clothes, again. Everything they had, including the new clothes he had bought for Chloe in Durango had been abandoned at the bus.

Sam pulled off the highway, threaded his way through the parking lot and parked. He tried waking Chloe, but she was sound asleep. He debated leaving her in the Hummer and decided it would probably be okay if he locked the vehicle and cracked the windows open a bit.

A half hour later, he was back. Chloe hadn't moved. No one could have seen her anyway given the dark tinting of the windows. He figured drug dealers liked their anonymity.

He retraced his route to the *Carretera* until he came to a sign that indicated an access to a beach. He pulled off the main road and took a rough track west toward *Playa Cerritos*.

The road ended at a promontory overlooking the Pacific Ocean, the surface of which undulated with a deep pristine blue and curled into glistening white waves that rolled in to the sandy shore below.

The sun, still low in the east, cast an orange glow on the rocks and surrounding landscape. The air hung heavy with the salty spray from the sea. Gulls glided in low swooping dives that ended as they tucked in wings and plunged into the water after fish.

Chloe woke up and stretched. "Are we there, Grandpa?" Then she looked out the window. "It's beautiful. Can we go for a swim?"

The place was deserted and Sam felt exhausted. He could use a dip in the ocean to freshen up. "Okay. But we have to make it quick. We still have four or five hours to go."

He handed Chloe a new bathing suit, and she changed into it quickly as he pulled his on. Taking her hand, he descended barefoot down a trail that led to the beach.

The sand was a mix of ground coral and volcanic stone. The waves crashed on the shore, then shot up the slope of the beach with sudsy swirls before sucking back into the sea.

Sam sat and let the water wash over him while Chloe played a safe distance behind him. As far as he knew she didn't know how to swim, and this was no place to find out or try to teach her.

He was beginning to relax, when she pointed to the Hummer on the bluff above and cried out.

"Grandpa, there are men up there."

Sam scrambled to his feet and shaded his eyes to the angled light. There certainly were men up there. He could see three of them, and they weren't peasants looking for a ride.

"Come on. We're done here. Better see what they're up to." He climbed the trail not knowing what to expect. As he got closer he could make out that the men were military types with shabby uniforms and rifles slung over their shoulders.

At the top, he waved. *"Que pasa?"*

They had been peering into the windows of the locked Hummer. The guns and money were well hidden in the far back under a tarp. Otherwise, the only things of value that could interest them were the CD player and the GPS in the dash.

Two of the men stepped off and un-shouldered their rifles. The third, who seemed to be their leader, sauntered over to Sam.

"This is government land, *Señor*. You shouldn't be here. The beach is private."

"I'm sorry," Sam said. "I didn't know. I didn't see any signs."

"You are in big trouble, *Señor*. Trespassing on government land is a big offense."

"I said I was sorry. I'll leave immediately. Is that okay?"

"No. That is not okay." The leader checked the location of his two comrades. "I want you to walk over there." He indicated an area twenty yards

207

from the Hummer and at the edge of the cliff overlooking the sea. "Leave the girl here."

Sam's heart began to thump as all sorts of perverse scenarios flitted through his mind, most of them involving lewd acts on the part of these three as regarded Chloe.

"Look, I've got money in my car. Why don't I get it and share it with you?"

The leader seemed interested. "Why don't you give me the keys and I'll help myself?"

"No can do. Special locks."

The leader didn't look like he believed Sam, but Sam didn't wait for him to respond. Instead, he took Chloe by the hand and walked quickly to the Hummer while thumbing the key fob. "When I open the door, I want you to jump inside fast."

Chloe gave him a terrified look, but nodded.

Sam got to the door, opened it and gave her a propelling shove that sent her all the way to the other side.

The man yelled.

Sam jumped in, pulled the door closed and pressed the power locks.

The leader was close on to him and slammed his fist against the window as Sam fumbled with the key. When the man's fists proved futile, he used the butt of his rifle, then when that didn't work, he stepped back and fired a shot at the side of the Hummer.

The bullet thumped against the Hummer's door panel, but as Sam had surmised, the vehicle was armored. He slid the key into the ignition, started the engine and wheeled the Hummer around toward the main road.

As the leader stared dumbstruck that his shot hadn't penetrated the door, Sam gunned the Hummer into a fishtailing, dust-filled escape.

"I'm not hanging around this town," Sam said to Chloe. "We'll push on to Guadalajara."

Chloe stared at him wide-eyed, fingering her cross. "Is that going to be better?"

"I hope so."

Chapter Ten

After gassing up on the other side of Mazatlan and having two police cars pass by without incident, Sam concluded the soldiers hadn't reported the encounter, maybe for fear of reprimand from superiors for discharging a weapon without being able to substantiate why.

By mid-afternoon, he was cruising through the outer suburbs of Guadalajara. He pulled into a modern shopping mall where a Sam's Club dominated one end, flanked by other American name brand stores.

Just like home.

He parked and dug out the business card Andropov had given him. Sam wasn't at all sure if he should make contact. And if he did, it wouldn't be for the reasons Andropov had stated. But Sam was in a foreign country, and although he was no longer looking to have a heart transplant from a clone, he could at least check in with the contact. If he had a heart attack or other crisis he wouldn't know what to do. The guy on the business card must have connections.

Sam typed the address into the car's GPS system. A second later, a route from where he was parked to the office of the contact showed on the screen. Fortunately, the office was not far away. Sam hated driving in Mexican urban traffic despite being inside what amounted to a tank by comparison with the other vehicles on the road.

Chloe examined the GPS screen. "Where are we going, Grandpa."

"I've got to check in with someone. It's about my heart."

"Oh."

Sam thought he saw a flash of concern cross Chloe's face. "It's not what you think. Mr. Andropov gave me the name of a contact in Guadalajara. I was to look him up once I got to Mexico...with a clone."

Chloe started whimpering.

Sam leaned over the Hummer's center console and put his arm around her. "Come on. We've been over this already. I'm not going to let anything happen to you. I don't even think of you as a clone anymore. You've called me Grandpa so many times, I feel like I am your grandpa."

She swiped a tear off her cheek, then folded her arms across her thin chest, a scowl on her face. "Then why do you have to see this man?"

"If something happens to me here, like if I have a heart attack, it would be a good idea to have a contact like this guy who is tapped into the Mexican medical system."

"If you have a heart attack, what is going to happen to me?"

Good question.

Sam had been so busy evading people he'd forgotten to consider that if the worst happened, Chloe would be on her own, in a strange country, with no one to turn to. Hopefully, he'd be okay for the next couple of days, giving him time to set up a safety net for her.

"You're right. I haven't thought about that, but I should, and I will. Let's take it one step at a time.

211

First, I have to see this man. Then we'll drive to Cerro Bonito. Once we get to Cerro Bonito, I'll make sure you'll be well taken care of if something happens to me."

Chloe choked back a sob. "What if something happens to you in the next hour?"

"We'll have to take that chance."

"I don't want to take that chance."

Sam realized she had a point. *What to do*? "Let's set up a survival kit for you." He dug out a wad of cash and counted out five hundred dollars. Then he added her birth certificate to the pile. Next he wrote down JoAnne's name, and her phone and cell numbers on the back of the birth certificate. He also used the GPS to look up the number of the American Consulate in Guadalajara. He unzipped her fanny pack and put everything he had collected into it.

"You're set. There's money and your ID. There are phone numbers of a trusted friend of mine. Her name is JoAnne. She already knows about you. She's the one who gave us the address in Cerro Bonito where we are going to stay. Finally, there's a number for the American Consulate in Guadalajara. But use it as a last resort. Understand?"

Chloe nodded.

"Feel better?"

Chloe nodded.

"Good. I guess we can go now and see my man." Sam drove out of the parking lot into traffic.

Ten minutes later, he pulled up in front of a narrow two story building with whitewashed walls, wrought iron grilles over the windows, and a sloping red-tiled roof. A low wall topped by more wrought-iron and a gate in the middle lined the property at the sidewalk. The building was similar to other buildings on a street that seemed to form a transition from more urban Guadalajara to the start of residential properties.

"Looks like he works out of his home," Sam said. "I'll be right back."

"I want to come, too." Chloe was out of the Hummer before he could respond.

Doesn't she trust me? Maybe she doesn't want to be left alone. He took her hand. Together they entered through the gate and traversed a short walkway flanked with multi-colored flowers to the front door. He rang the bell.

A woman answered the door. She had a bandana around her hair and a broom in her hand. The cleaning lady.

"*Que quieres*?" She smiled when she spied Chloe.

"I'd like to see Victor Gallego."

"*Si. Señor Gallego. Momentito.*"

Sam squeezed Chloe's hand and thought maybe it wasn't such a bad idea she had tagged along after all.

A man appeared. He was dressed in sandals, a loose fitting Hawaiian aloha shirt and shorts. He was about the same height as Sam, maybe a bit taller, with a slender build, thin face, dark hair and a pencil mustache.

"Can I help you?" he asked.

213

"I'm Sam Turner. This is Chloe. Demetri Andropov gave me your card and said I should get in touch when I got here."

"Sam Turner." Gallego rubbed his chin in thought. "Yes, Demetri told me about you. He put you on the list. Come in, come in. Please excuse the mess. I wasn't expecting you."

"I'm sorry for not calling ahead. But we were so close, I thought I'd drive over."

They passed through the vestibule to an open air courtyard, bright with slanting rays from the afternoon sun. The courtyard was well appointed with a small fountain, cascading bougainvillea and other tropical flowering plants Sam couldn't identify.

"Please sit down." Gallego indicated a rustic iron table with similar chairs. "Can I offer you refreshment. *Cerveza, tequila*?" He laughed and waved his hands. "Does Chloe want a Coke?"

"Thank you, we're fine. I don't want to take up too much of your time." Sam shifted in his seat. "I thought you'd be Mexican with a name like Gallego, but you have an accent...something I can't place, but almost like Mr. Andropov's."

"You are very observant, *Señor* Turner. Demetri and I are both from one of the *stans* of the old Soviet empire. We grew up together. When life there became intolerable, we emigrated. Demetri went to America. I came here and changed my name to something people could pronounce. I like it here. You can understand that."

"Of course."

214

"Good. That is good. I came here, but Demetri was always the business one. You know what I mean?"

Sam nodded.

"So after he started up his little clone farm, he foresaw the laws would change. So he contacted me and asked me to set up a support network down here for the operations. You know, just in case. We've done a lot of business in the last few years."

"That's good to know," Sam said. "I mean, your track record with transplants is important."

Gallego waved his hands as if pushing away the compliment. "*Señor* Turner...or can I call you Sam?"

Sam waved, too, indicating he had no problem with being called Sam. *Regular butterflies we are*.

"Sam. I'm glad we got all that history stuff out of the way. But this is Mexico. We are never in a hurry down here. Did you bring your clone?"

Chloe gave a start, and Sam decided *hurry* in Mexico had many degrees of subtlety.

"I...to be honest, Chloe is my clone. But as you can see Chloe is sentient and a quite normal little girl. This was not what I was led to believe when I took her from Mr. Andropov. Be that as it may, I can't use her for a heart transplant. That is out of the question."

Gallego leaned forward and peered at Chloe. "She's really a clone? I never would have guessed. When others arrive with their clones, the clones are always sedated. They look half-dead."

Chloe squirmed away from him.

215

Gallego straightened up, almost as though he was offended by Chloe's show of aversion. "Then why have you come to see me, Sam? I cannot put you in touch with a surgeon who will give you a heart transplant if you do not have a heart to transplant."

"I thought I'd check in," Sam said. "We will be here for a while. Something might happen to me...after all I'm a sick man. You have medical connections. You might be able to help in an emergency."

"But without a clone?"

"Without a clone." Sam stared at his hands in his lap.

Gallego reached to a side table and picked up a sheet of paper. "This is a list of clients Demetri has sent me. There are over thirty of them and counting. They are all supposed to show up here within the next few days or weeks with their clones. I must arrange operations for all of them." He tossed the sheet of paper back onto the table. "You come here and tell me you have a clone, but you don't want to use her...by the way, why isn't she a he?"

"It's a long story."

"Yes. I don't have time for long stories. Anyway, as I was saying, your request that I provide standby in case something happens to you does not sit well with me. I get paid by Demetri when I have made the arrangements for an operation. I get nothing for being a standby."

Sam almost breathed a sigh of relief. It was all about money. It was always all about money. "How much do I have to pay you to be a standby?"

"Three thousand US will cover it...for one month."

Chloe gave Sam a nudge.

What? Now she's telling me what to do? But Chloe was well ahead of him. She knew he had money, lots of it.

"That seems fair," Sam said. He didn't feel he was in a position to bargain, so he scrounged in his fanny pack for the money. He could only find half of it. "I've got to go out to the car for the rest."

Gallego waved away Sam's concern. It seemed all communication could be clarified and amplified with hands. "*No problema.* Chloe and I will wait for you here."

That didn't sit well with Sam, but what could Gallego do in the three minutes it would take to retrieve the money? "I'll be right back."

Sam sweated as he hurried out to the Hummer. He fumbled for one of his pills and popped it into his mouth. He didn't want to take any chances. He grabbed a bundle of one hundred dollar bills and hurried back inside.

Gallego had been in a close conversation with Chloe, or so it seemed when Sam re-entered.

"Got it," Sam said, as he counted out what he hoped to be fifteen hundred dollars from the stack.

After the money was handed to Gallego, he counted it, too. "Here," he said, handing back a couple of bills. "You miscounted. I'm an honest man."

217

Sam was impressed. "Thanks."

Gallego handed him a business card. "Keep this with you at all times. It has all my contact numbers."

He took out a pen and paper. "Do you know where you will be staying? In case I have to get in touch with you?"

When Sam hesitated, Gallego said, "Your choice, of course. I was thinking if there was a problem, no telling how your location would be communicated to me. If someone gave me the wrong address, by mistake, then I'd never find you in time. But you're the one paying for standby. I'm just trying to do my job."

Sam saw Gallego's point and felt silly being so secretive. "I'm sorry. I didn't mean to give the impression I didn't trust you. We'll be in Playa de Cerro Bonito, at Heidi Bergman's inn, *Casa Mirador*. You should have no trouble finding it. Cerro Bonito is a small town." He dug into his fanny pack for Heidi's phone number.

Gallego wrote it all down. "Cerro Bonito, nice place. A lot of *federales*, that's people who live in Mexico City, go there for vacation. A bit too primitive for my tastes."

Sam nodded and concluded there was nothing more to say between them. "We'll go now. I hope we don't meet again. I don't mean that in a derogatory way."

Another elaborate wave of the hands. "Sam. I know what you mean, and I thank you for coming here and introducing me to sweet Chloe. She's a

218

dear. I wish you all the best." He stood and shook Sam's hand, then showed them to the door.

After they pulled away in the Hummer, Sam asked, "What were you and Mr. Gallego talking about when I came in?"

"He said I had lovely skin. That it was almost translucent."

"Did he touch you?"

"Only with his finger. Here." She showed Sam the pale skin of her forearm.

"What else?"

"Nothing, Grandpa."

That sounded evasive. "Chloe?"

She harrumphed. "He said I reminded him of his daughter. He said she got sick and died in the old country before he immigrated to Mexico. He said if anything happened to you he would be more than happy to take care of me. He gave me his card. I put it in my survival kit."

***

Demetri slowed the rented Cadillac XTX as he came to the cross street indicated on the car's dashboard-mounted GPS screen.

"Turn right on Arroyo," the soft female voice of the GPS said.

Demetri began looking for building numbers. 234 Arroyo was one of the taller buildings mid-block. He parked, entered the vestibule and pushed the intercom button for Suite B. Not the fanciest building he'd ever seen. But as far as he knew, the government was trying to cut back on overhead costs. As far as he was concerned, he could tell them a whole lot more ways to cut costs, one of which was to stop bugging him.

"May I help you?" a voice said out of the intercom.

"Demetri Andropov to see Agent Wellstone." Demetri rocked back and forth on his heels, relishing the discomfort his appearance at the FBI's doorstep must be causing as word got around Suite B.

The door lock buzzed. Demetri pushed through and took the stairs to the second floor.

A uniformed guard met him at the top of the stairs, had him stretch out his arms and passed a magnetic wand over him. Then he was ushered inside and met by a female receptionist.

The office suite looked rundown. One big space with a clutter of desks, chairs and filing cabinets. Banks of computers with glowing monitors. Maybe three agents tops, manning various positions around the room.

Demetri spotted Wellstone talking to another agent at a desk by a window.

The receptionist led him over and left him standing in front of Wellstone's desk.

After a long minute, Wellstone finished his conversation with the other agent and acknowledged Demetri's presence by indicating he could sit in either one of two visitor's chairs.

Don't piss me off more than you can swallow, Wellstone.

Demetri thought to shake Wellstone's hand, but since Wellstone made no effort to greet him, Demetri sat.

220

The two stared at each other.

He's even wearing a fucking cowboy's hat. A regular Wyatt Earp.

After two minutes, Wellstone leaned forward, rested an elbow on the desk, chin in his hand. "What can I do for you, Androp?"

Demetri wasn't normally a person to hate anyone, but he knew he hated this smug, self-assured, athletically fit, urban cowboy. "You've read the injunction?"

"I have. So what?"

"You owe me my clones."

"I don't owe you shit."

Such belligerence. Was he stupid or bluffing? "You owe me my clones, or I will get a judge to clarify what you owe me. And you know if a judge has to explain his injunction to a recalcitrant law enforcement officer, he will hold you in contempt of court. You don't want that now, do you?"

Wellstone's eyes became even narrower. Color rose into his cheeks, setting off the gray that streaked his temples. A bead of perspiration slid down one side of his face where it became lost in a two-day growth of beard.

"Let's start again," he said. "What is it you want from me?"

"You owe me my clones."

Wellstone nodded. "Arrangements are being made to have them returned to you."

"Super. What about the clone I was induced to ship prematurely because of your actions."

Wellstone smiled, a smile that reminded Demetri of a grinning shark. "Ah, that clone."

221

"That clone. Where is it?"

"She's in Mexico."

They must be onto something if he knows the clone is a she. "She?"

"Bite my ass, Androp. You know damn well the clone is a she."

"Bite my ass? Nice. What are you doing to get her back?"

"We're in touch with the Mexican authorities. From this end, we're assisting with whatever information we develop."

"Is there some way I can get in touch with the Mexican authorities?"

"That's Bureau information."

Demetri shrugged. "I suppose we could always let a judge decide. Might be awkward."

Wellstone glared angrily. Then he reached for a business card and scribbled a name and number on the back of it. "Our counterpart there is a Colonel Luciano Obregon. This is a direct line."

Demetri took the card and glanced at it. *Maybe Wellstone was going to loosen up after all.* "It doesn't sound like you're making much progress."

Wellstone sat back and waved hands to dismiss Demetri's assertion. "We're dealing with Mexico, Androp. It's the eighteen hundreds down there."

"It sounds to me like you've let Turner slip through your fingers."

Wellstone slammed his fist on the desktop, a motion that startled Demetri an inch out of his chair. "You disgust me, Androp. Your type is what's wrong with this country. We let in scum like you,

222

then the good guys have to spend their time cleaning up after you shit in your den."

Demetri felt heat rising up his neck. Now *he* was getting angry. "I...don't...shit--"

"Of course you do. The clone is sentient. We have multiple witnesses. I've got you this time."

"Sentient? You're bluffing. Grasping at straws."

Wellstone came forward, so abruptly Demetri jerked back. "We have a first report from State Troopers in Poncha Springs. Another from the Navajo Police from outside of Kayenta. Then there's a travel agent in Nogales who sold Turner and the girl a bus ticket to Guaymas. That was yesterday. The bus broke down outside of Hermosillo. We've got an eyewitness report from an Abigail Fisher, who says she saw the girl, named Chloe by the way--" Wellstone stopped and peered at Demetri. "--but of course you know that, don't you?"

Demetri remained silent.

Wellstone smiled and continued. "Abigail saw Chloe walk off into the Sonoran Desert to take a bathroom break. Chloe and Turner were missing from a later roll call at the bus. A search of the area by local authorities discovered what they surmise was a drug deal gone bad. Six dead. One disabled vehicle. Tracks from another vehicle leading away. We think Turner and the girl came upon the scene, then departed in the second vehicle to places unknown.

"That girl, that clone Turner is traveling with, is definitely sentient. Calls him Grandpa. Walks and talks like a real person. End of story."

Demetri didn't like *end of story*. He shifted in the hard backed chair, his mouth dry, his anger dissipating to be replaced with the beginnings of cold fear. "The clone I gave Turner was brain-dead. The girl he's traveling with could be someone else, anybody. I don't know. Maybe he has the clone in a suitcase."

"Really, Androp. That is too contrived to be believed."

Demetri squirmed. "I...I don't have to sit here and--"

With a disgusted look, Wellstone waved Demetri away, snatched up a document from his desk and began studying it, ignoring Demetri. The interview was over.

Wellstone didn't stand to see Demetri out, increasing his fury at the arrogant FBI agent.

Back in the Cadillac, Demetri checked his cell phone. One missed call. He pressed until the name and number came up.

Victor Gallego.

Bingo.

He punched in Victor's number.

"*Si*."

"Victor, it's me, Demetri. How are you?"

"I'm good Demetri. Real good. You?"

"Yeah, I'm okay. Business problems. You know, clones."

"I had a visit today from one of your clients. You know who I'm talking about?"

224

"I can guess."

"He's in Guadalajara with a product. You know what I mean?"

"I do. I'm surprised he's that far south. Last I heard he was outside Hermosillo."

"Well, he came by to say he was in town. You know real friendly like. He thanked you for giving him my business card. But he thought he wasn't going to use the service."

"He's going to die if he doesn't use the service."

"Hey, that's what I told him. But he said he has a thing for his product. The product turned out to be different."

"He's gone soft. A lot of them do if they see their product. That's why we have our policy."

"I know, I know. It's a good policy. I don't make any money when a customer sees his product and goes soft. But like I said his product is different. I think you know what I'm talking about."

"Yeah, yeah, for Christ's sake. I know already. She's different. That's why I don't have her and he does. What else did he say?"

"He wants to hang out down here. He's got a place...by the beach. He gave me the address."

"Perfect. Let me have it." Demetri scrambled for a pen and paper.

"Sure, sure Demetri. *No problema*. But it's going to cost you."

***

Sam drove halfway to the coast before he spoke to Chloe. "I don't want you to ever talk to that man again. If any contact is to be made with him, it will be because I need his help. Do you understand?"

Chloe pouted as though she had been practicing all her life. "You don't have to be mad at me, Grandpa."

"I'm not mad at you. I'm just telling you I didn't like that he touched you or that he gave you his card without consulting me."

"I'll throw the card away."

"That's good. We're in a foreign country. The people and customs here are different than they are in the States. I don't know them very well, and I'm certain you don't know them."

"But on the Travel Channel, I--"

"Sometimes there's a difference between real life and what you see on TV."

"How much longer before we get to Cerro Bonito?"

"It'll be another hour." Sam shook his head. *Where does she get all this? She's so grown up. You press her on something she doesn't want to talk about and she changes the subject. Karen was like that. So is JoAnne.*

"Are we done talking?" Chloe asked.

"For now."

"Can I listen to my iPoodle, then?"

"Yes, you may."

She stuck the earphone studs into her ears and fiddled with the buttons on the face of the iPoodle, then leaned back and closed her eyes.

An hour later, Sam reached over and shook her. She had fallen asleep. "We're coming into Cerro Bonito."

She looked around sleepily.

Sam pulled off the road at an overlook and got out. Chloe came up beside him and slid her hand into his. Below them lay a sweeping bay. A couple of small islands seemed to float on the horizon surrounded by the deep blue of the Pacific Ocean. Lines of waves undulated toward the shore, breaking close in. Fishing boats bobbed at anchor.

The town itself built along the beach in a single line of development bounded by a road that must have been the main street. Smaller roads climbed into the hillside until it became too steep to support any construction. A town square sat about midway up the street and was flanked by a church. The rest of the buildings appeared run down, typical Mexican construction--blocky, whitewashed adobe, red-tiled roofs, half-finished.

"That must be Heidi's place at the south end of the bay." Sam pointed to a walled compound with a garden and four buildings--three bungalows and a larger house with a pitched thatched roof.

As the sun neared the horizon, its slanting rays colored the overhead clouds red and ochre.

"We better get down there. It'll be dark soon."

Back in the Hummer, Sam drove a series of switchbacks down to sea level. The highway came to a roundabout with an exit toward the sea. A single sign with an arrow pointed to Playa de Cerro Bonito.

He turned into the side road and rolled down the windows of the Hummer to breathe in sea air with the smell of salt and an overlay of fishiness.

The access road angled a sharp left when it hit the main road through town, which paralleled the

227

shore. A nature preserve anchored one end of main street with a sign in front of a fence bordering a tangled mangrove estuary beyond. *Tenga Cuidado Con Los Cocodrilos.*

"What are *cocodrilos*, Grandpa?"

"Crocodiles. Odd such a small town would have a nature preserve. Looks like the bus station is across the street."

"Is that how they feed the *cocodrilos*?"

Sam glanced at Chloe, and she giggled.

"Very funny." Sam slowed the Hummer to a crawl. The unpaved road was rutted, the rainy season having just ended. Where they existed, narrow concrete sidewalks lined the road with curbs that dropped down as much as a foot in places. Various stores, selling all manner of goods and services, fronted the sidewalks. Vegetables, house wares, general groceries, liquor, bars and restaurants. When they passed a CD boutique, a wave of hard thumping *Mexicana Rap* engulfed them. The bars and restaurants competed with their own sounds.

The walks were well populated with pedestrians who stopped to stare at the passing Hummer.

Sam realized they were a spectacle. There were few other vehicles on the road and those that were looked old and beat up.

He came to the square, a desolate looking space, weeds growing through cracked pavement with a rundown bandstand at its center. The church, looking abandoned, squatted on one side. Sam skirted the square and continued on the road as it

228

narrowed and dead-ended at Heidi's walled compound.

By now the few streetlights that were still working had come on. At this end, the town was quiet. A single ornamental light in a star-shaped glass and copper housing hung above the heavy wooden gate giving entrance to Heidi's garden. To the right, the line of the wall broke for double doors that gave vehicular access to parking beyond.

Sam got out and pushed a button imbedded in a colorful blue and white ceramic tile next to the door. He couldn't hear a chime but hoped one was ringing inside the main house at the other side of the garden.

A few minutes later the gate opened and a stocky woman with a pleasant, round face, cropped, brown hair flecked with gray greeted them.

"Mr. Turner!" She embraced Sam and turned to Chloe. "And this must be Chloe." Another embrace. "Welcome to *Casa Mirador*. JoAnne has told me so much about you."

"Thank you." Sam peered over her shoulder. "What a beautiful garden."

"It is my pride and joy, but I owe all of it to Manuel, who fusses over it as though it was one of his children." She glanced at the Hummer. "Oh, my. What a marvelous vehicle. I bet you got a lot of looks coming through town. Let me open the gates so you can park." She descended side steps to the parking area and opened the gates.

While Chloe stood at the main entrance, Sam returned to the Hummer and drove it into the compound.

229

"You can park over there." Heidi pointed to a number of garage spaces under the raised structure of one of the bungalows. "As you can see, we have lots of room this time of year. Oh, we've forgotten Chloe. She's still at the entrance. Come in, come in." She beckoned to Sam as she retraced her steps to Chloe, then led them both along a level path that cut across the garden. It graced a number of terraces following the slope of the hill that anchored this end of the bay.

Large banyan trees with ropey aerial roots provided a green canopy over parts of the garden. Red and yellow hibiscus surrounded shorter plumeria trees in full bloom. Fragrant gardenia lined the path at intervals.

Sam couldn't see the other two bungalows, which must have nestled behind the riotous vegetation. The main house glowed ahead with light coming through square windows flanked with wooden shutters. A thatched *palapa* style roof peaked above it.

Heidi ushered them into the vestibule and from there into a large sitting room with rotating fans hanging from under an open-beam ceiling and the exposed underside of the thatched roof. Wide sliding doors were pulled back, leading onto a terrace that over looked the ocean thirty feet below. The rustle of small waves lapping onto the rocks provided a background of white noise.

"This is a beautiful house," Sam said.

Chloe seemed to be in awe as well as she wandered between rough hewn furniture draped with colorful Mexican blankets.

"Yes, it is beautiful. I have been here fifteen years and never want to leave. Please, come, we will have some refreshment to welcome you."

Sam started to follow Heidi toward what looked like a study with a bar when someone shouted behind him. He turned to see a young woman propelled down a short flight of stairs connecting the sitting room to a hallway.

She lost her footing, tumbled the last two steps and sprawled into the sitting room.

Heidi gasped and put her hand to her mouth.

The woman, more of a girl in her twenties and dressed in cut-off shorts and a tight tank top, twisted around and reached back to the open door at the head of the stairs. "Give me my baby," she pleaded.

A young man, also in his twenties, dark tussled hair, low slung jeans and shirtless stepped to the opening. "Go to hell, you bitch." He retreated into the hallway and slammed the door.

Sam rushed over to the girl and helped her to her feet.

She began crying, leaving Sam unsure what to do next.

Heidi came over and took the girl into her arms. "I'm sorry you had to see this," she said to Sam. "That was my son, Lukas. He's as bad as my ex. This is Aurelia, my daughter-in-law." Heidi stroked Aurelia's black hair that was pulled back into a ponytail.

"It's none of my business," Sam said, "but what was that all about?"

"He hates me," Aurelia cried. "He beats me. He won't let me see my child." She dissolved into sobs on Heidi's shoulder.

"Come," Heidi said to Aurelia. "You can stay in one of the bungalows tonight. I will talk to Lukas. We will see how it is in the morning."

"But I want my baby."

"I know, I know. Let me try." As she led Aurelia away, she waved Sam toward the study. "Please, make yourselves comfortable. Help yourself to the bar. I'll be right back."

Chapter Eleven

After Heidi and Aurelia had left the house, Sam wondered if he and Chloe were safe with the likes of Lukas and nothing but a door separating them. He took Chloe by the hand and led her into the study. "Let's see what they have to drink."

"Why won't Lukas let Aurelia see her baby?" Chloe asked.

If Sam ever thought Chloe wasn't paying attention to what was happening around her, her current recall of the situation dispelled that. "I don't know. Maybe when Heidi comes back she'll tell us. But if she doesn't, then we shouldn't intrude. Do you understand?"

"I guess so."

Inside the study, an ornate bar sat wedged into a corner of the small room adorned with bookshelves, Mexican pottery, woven rugs, and a couple of overstuffed chairs. Sam went behind the bar and opened an under-counter refrigerator. He took out a Coke and a Sprite and showed them to Chloe. "Which one?"

"I want Sprite."

Sam poured the Sprite into a glass and handed it to her. He scanned the shelves behind the bar, found a bottle of *El Jimador* tequila and poured himself a shot.

Heidi returned. "I think I could use one of those, too," she said. "I'm sorry about all of that."

Sam waved off her concern, poured Heidi a shot and handed it to her.

She tossed the tequila down, then held out the glass for another pour, to which Sam obliged. She tossed that one back as well. "Now I feel better. Maybe I will sleep well tonight. When you are finished with your drinks, I will show you to your bungalow. You both must be exhausted."

She seemed reluctant to explain the altercation, so Sam kept his peace, not wanting to pry. He supposed there would be time in the days to come to find out what it was all about.

Heidi led them out a side door of the main house and down a flight of steps to a concrete terrace. The far end of the terrace looked over the ocean and waves that beat against rocks below. On the near side, the terrace led to a patio that abutted one side of the bungalow. Two hammocks were strung between corner posts that held up a trellised roof. Bougainvillea climbed up from below and covered most of the trellis.

Inside, the bungalow's main room had two built-in sofas, long enough to sleep on in one corner and a round dining table with four stuffed, leather *Equipale* chairs. A pass-through bar led on the far side to a kitchenette. The walls were off-white with tangerine accents. The doors had arched tops. One such door led to a bedroom that was large enough for a king size bed. An elaborate painting of the setting sun adorned the wall at its head.

"We call this bungalow *El Sol*, for obvious reasons," Heidi said.

"It looks very nice. I like the colors."

Chloe jumped up on the bed and walked around on it. "Firm mattress."

234

"There is a back door off the kitchenette where you can take the stairs down to your vehicle."

Sam looked around. "I don't see a phone."

"Yes, I'm very sorry about that. If you want to make a call you can use the phone in the main house. If you have a cell phone, there is coverage here, but it is prohibitively expensive. It's the same with Internet. Cerro Bonito has a single Internet Cafe, but it is open irregularly. If you want, you can use my computer for email. I'll have to charge you extra, though."

"That would be much more convenient than having to go into town. Thanks, so much. I hate to ask this, but is there a safe or lock box for our valuables?"

"Yes, of course," Heidi walked over to the built-in closet in the bedroom and slid back the door.

A safe, about a foot cubed, was built into the masonry of the wall.

Sam examined the safe and saw that the lock was programmable. "Perfect."

"I think that covers it," Heidi said. "Oh. I almost forgot the most important thing. How would you like to pay for your stay?"

Sam had to smile. She was a professional innkeeper through and through. "Cash."

"That would be fine, of course. It's a hundred and fifty dollars per night."

"I think we'll be here at least two weeks if not more."

"Could you pay at least for a week in advance? I'm running a bit short of cash just now."

"I can pay you the whole amount." Sam dug the money out his fanny pack.

"That would be even better. It's been a terrible season. I fear it will be my last if things don't improve. I have already missed one payment to the bank. I think they have a three strikes and you're out policy."

"I'm sorry to hear you're so strapped. You've obviously put a lot of yourself into the place." Sam thought about the millions in drug money he had locked in the Hummer. Give some to Heidi? Maybe later.

Heidi handed him a key. "This key opens the door to the bungalow as well as the gates out front. If you have any more questions, please don't hesitate to ask."

"I do have one more question. Where is the best place to eat?"

Heidi smiled. "It is getting late, isn't it? There are a couple of restaurants I could recommend, but my favorite is Antonio's. It's a five minute walk from here. The other one isn't quite as good and is on the other side of town. Anything else?"

Sam shook his head. "I guess we'll bring what stuff we have up from the car, then go to dinner."

Heidi shook Sam's hand. "I hope you have a nice stay." She patted Chloe on the head and returned to the main house.

"Why does everyone pat me on the head, Grandpa?"

"Why? Because you're such a cute little girl. There are things in the Hummer I have to bring up."

"I'll help you."

Sam wondered about Chloe dragging an attaché case with a million dollars in it up the stairs, but figured if she was strong enough to lift it, and if she wanted to help, he shouldn't be discouraging her. Besides, it would mean less stress for him.

At the Hummer, Sam took out one of the cases and handed it to Chloe. "Can you carry that?"

She gripped the handle with both hands and leaned back to get it well off the ground. "I think so."

After Chloe started banging the case up the steps to the bungalow, Sam picked up the guns, thinking to take them inside. Then he spied a rear side panel cargo compartment above the wheel housing. Maybe leave them in the Hummer.

He opened the compartment and peered at six tightly wrapped packages of what must be drugs, cocaine from the looks of it. Juan was right after all. He must have seen some residue or something in the back to tip him off. Sam realized how close to disaster he had come if he'd been searched at the police checkpoint.

He couldn't very well stash the drugs in the house. Better to leave them where they were until he could think of a way to dispose of them.

He closed the compartment, wrapped the guns in a blanket, tucked them under his arm and followed after Chloe with the other attaché case.

She was waiting for him in the kitchenette. "Where should I put this?"

"Take it into the bedroom."

Once in the bedroom he put both attaché cases on the bed and opened them.

237

Chloe peered at all the cash. "Wow. Is that real money?"

"I think so. I'm going to take it out of the cases and stuff it all into the safe. Let's form a line. You take the money out and hand it to me. I'll stack it in the safe."

Ten minutes later, with Chloe enjoying every minute of the game, the safe was packed with packets of one hundred dollar bills. The second attaché case was still three quarters full with probably one half to three quarters of a million dollars. Sam reprogrammed the combination and locked the safe, then snapped the attaché case closed. "I have to put this back in the Hummer. I'll be right back."

"What's in the blanket, Grandpa?"

"Guns."

"Oh."

"I'm going to hide them under the bed."

Chloe peeked into the bundle and picked up the Derringer. "I like this little gun."

Sam lunged to take it away from her. "I don't want you touching that. It's dangerous."

Chloe pouted. "I know how to handle guns. I learned from watching Western Sportsman."

"I'm sure you know, but I still don't want you touching them." Sam slid the wrapped bundle under the bed. "Think about where you want to sleep, while I take this money down to the Hummer."

Sam descended the back stairs to the Hummer and emptied the cash from the attaché case into the other side panel cargo compartment. He grabbed what few clothes they had and locked the Hummer, then hurried as best he could back to Chloe.

She sat on the bed looking at him with a sly smile. "It's okay, Grandpa. You can have the big bed. I'll sleep on one of the sofas in the living room."

So grown up. "That's very nice of you," Sam said. "For that, I'll buy you dinner at Antonio's. We better get over there. I know Mexicans eat late, but I don't want to be that late."

***

Antonio's occupied a two story building with a thatched *palapa* roof. A bar was on the ground floor with the restaurant above. Sam climbed the two steps to the bar entrance, which was flanked by two potted palms with a red neon sign hanging overhead saying "Antonio's" in sweeping script.

Inside, tables scattered randomly over a concrete floor contained by a low bamboo railing. Beyond the railing spread a grass lawn interspersed with rustling palms.

Multi-colored lights hung throughout. *Perpetual Christmas*. The bar ran along one side of the stair leading to the restaurant above. A group of mostly men sat or stood at the bar talking over the blare of a Mariachi band issuing from a boom box.

Gray cigarette smoke hung low throughout. Heavily made up young women in short skirts and low cut blouses sat with legs crossed on the stools, cigarettes between fingers flashing red polished nails.

Sam was anxious to get upstairs. "Come on. The restaurant is up those stairs." He dragged on Chloe's hand as she gawked at the chaotic scene.

"Hey, *Gringo*," one of the men at the bar called. "Who you got there?" He was tall for a Mexican, very muscular with swept back greasy black hair. He wore a shirt with short sleeves rolled up tight, jeans and cowboy boots.

Sam ignored him.

The guy stepped away from the bar and blocked Sam's path to the stairway. "I asked you a question, *cabron*. Who's the little *chiquita*?

Sam stopped and glanced at the others at the bar. They had stopped talking and were now all looking his way.

"She's my granddaughter. Now, if you'll excuse us, we were going upstairs to have dinner."

The man poked a finger on Sam's chest. "How come you're driving a druggy's car? Eh, *amigo*?"

Word must travel fast. "I didn't know Hummers were known as a druggy's car." Sam began to wish they had stayed at the bungalow and eaten food he had brought.

"How much you want *por la puta chiquita*?" The man dug into his pocket and produced a large wad of one hundred dollar bills. "I give you five hundred US. It will be for one hour. Then you can have her back, unless one of my *amigos* here wants her, too." He laughed with the others joining in.

The man's crude audacity left Sam speechless. His heart began picking up its beat.

Chloe retreated behind Sam and clutched his leg.

Sam started to move back toward the door only to be cut off by a second man. "Don't leave," the man said with exaggerated sorrow. "You just got here. Don't you like our company?"

There was no way Sam was going to get out of the situation with any sort of physicality. He took out his cell phone. "If you don't let me pass, I'll call the police." It was a bluff since he didn't know the number, anyway.

His statement was met with loud guffaws and bar slapping.

"No need to call the police, *amigo*. He's right here." The first man swept his hand toward a diminutive man in uniform Sam hadn't seen who sat at the far end of the bar.

The policeman came off his stool, hooked his thumbs into his belt and sauntered over to Sam. "You got a problem with Miguel, *gringo*? You doing drugs down here? It's a long way from Sonora. You want me to take you and *la niña* into custody?"

"No, I don't want you to take us into custody. All I want right now is to get upstairs and have dinner."

Two other men closed in on Sam and held his arms. Miguel stepped forward and ran his hands over Sam looking for what Sam couldn't tell. When Miguel finished with Sam, he grabbed Chloe by the arm.

She shrieked.

He jerked her away from Sam, then looked past Chloe toward the entrance.

241

A light skinned Mexican, dressed in a black silk shirt with open collar, black slacks and dress shoes entered. He was about the same height as Sam, but with a heavier build that exuded authority. A young boy, perhaps ten or eleven, clasped his hand. Two thugs, probably bodyguards, brought up the rear.

The other men in the bar all stepped back to give the new man a wide berth.

"Marcelo," Miguel said with obvious respect. "*Buenas noches*."

Marcelo looked at Miguel, then at Sam and Chloe. He gave a slight waggle with his index finger to Miguel.

"*Si, Marcelo*," Miguel said, crestfallen. "*Los sientos*." He returned to the bar as did the others.

Marcelo proceeded past Sam, patted Chloe on the head and ascended the stairs.

Sam looked after him, stunned. He grabbed Chloe's hand and started for the entrance.

Miguel, now looking very worried and contrite, motioned to Sam to go to the restaurant. When Sam hesitated, Miguel said, "Go, go. It's okay, now. You can eat. No one will bother you."

They all waited until Sam decided he had no choice but to go up to the restaurant.

Once he took Chloe's hand and headed for the stairs, it seemed everyone breathed a sigh of relief and returned to their drinking and talking. Lighters flared and were put shakily to the ends of cigarettes.

Heart still pounding, Sam took the stairs slowly. At the top they were met by a man wearing an apron.

"*Hola, Señor*. Welcome to Antonio's. I am Antonio." He swept his hand and ushered them onto the restaurant floor of polished hardwood with six or eight tables lined up alongside an open air railing and covered with white table cloths. Patterned place settings were flanked by sparkling wine goblets and water glasses. Beyond the railing lay a manicured lawn and coconut palms. The rising glow of a full moon gave the background of sky a whitish-gray wash.

Marcelo, the boy and the two thugs sat at the far end. No one else was in the restaurant.

"Where would you like to sit?" Antonio asked.

"Here will be fine." Sam indicated the table nearest to him.

Antonio pulled out a chair for Chloe. "*Que bonita niña*. Is she your *nieta*?"

"She is," Sam said attempting a smile after all the stress. "You are very perceptive."

"*Si*, perception is my especiality."

"Those men at the bar wanted to buy her."

"Ah--" Antonio waved a hand. "--They were joking. They are all married and have kids of their own. Why would they want to buy another one? Besides, it's much cheaper and more fun to make them, *no*?" He made a crude gesture with his hand.

Sam thought of Eddy Stormer's argument and realized he missed Eddy.

Since Antonio was being so friendly, Sam felt emboldened. "Who's the guy at the end table? He got me out of a jam down there."

"That's Marcelo Lopez. All the guys downstairs work for him. The boy with him is his son, Francisco. The other two guys, I don't know, probably bodyguards. Marcelo changes them all the time or they get themselves killed."

"Killed? What does Mr. Lopez do for a living?" Sam felt stupid asking since the answer seemed obvious. But he wanted it confirmed by Antonio.

"Marcelo controls all the drug trade in this region. You must know this, or if you don't, then you must be *loco* coming here in that Hummer."

"Does everyone in town know I came here in a Hummer?"

"*Si, Señor*, of course. It is a small town, *no*?"

"Antonio!" One of the bodyguards called and waved for Antonio to come over.

"Excuse me, *Señor*. I must take their order. Here is the menu--you can read Spanish? I'll be right back."

"Why did that man want to buy me?" Chloe asked.

"I don't think he was serious," Sam said. "At least I hope not. I'm glad Mr. Lopez came along. I don't know what I'd have done otherwise." Sam took out his pill container and shook out a pill. At this rate, he'd run out of pills before his situation resolved itself. If Heidi was still up, he'd have to email JoAnne for help.

Antonio stopped by the table on his way back to the kitchen. "Have you decided what you want to order?"

"I've not had a chance to look at the menu, yet. What would you recommend?"

Antonio brightened. "For you, *Señor*, I would recommend you start with our *ceviche* appetizer. The fish we use is very fresh, caught today. Then follow up with a shredded beef *chimichunga*. We make the best *chimichangas* in all of Jalisco. For the *Niña*...does she like shrimp?"

"I love shrimp," Chloe said.

Sam gave her a questioning look, which she ignored.

"Excellent," Antonio said. "For you I recommend the *camarones rebosado*. They come with a *salsa*, but we can make it mild."

"Sounds good." Sam handed back the menu. "Do you have a wine list?"

Antonio produced a wine list. "I'll be back." He disappeared in the direction of the kitchen.

Sam was perusing the list when he sensed someone had come up to stand over him. He looked up. *Marcelo Lopez*.

"Good evening. I'm Marcelo Lopez."

Sam staggered to his feet and shook Marcelo's outstretched hand. "Sam Turner."

"I understand you are new in town. Staying at Heidi's?"

"Yes. We just arrived. Heidi has a lovely place."

Marcelo maneuvered Francisco out from behind him. "This is my son, Francisco. He is quite taken by your...granddaughter, I presume?"

Sam shook hands with the shy boy. "Yes. This is Chloe, my granddaughter. Chloe, this is Francisco."

245

The two children eyed each other without saying a word.

"It takes a while for kids to break the ice," Marcelo said. "Unfortunately, grownups all too often go right to the heart of the matter. I'm told you came into town in a black Hummer. It even has a bullet hole in the driver's side door. May I ask where you got the vehicle?"

Sam looked into Marcelo's steely eyes and decided this was not a time to lie. At least not overtly. "It belongs to a man named Jorge Batista. He's a Mexican national living in Arizona. I came upon the Hummer under...unusual circumstances after our tour bus broke down outside of Hermosillo. Jorge didn't need the Hummer any more...we needed transportation, so we...borrowed it."

Marcelo smiled. "That's quite a story, Mr. Turner...or can I call you Sam? You Americans are so informal."

"Sam is good." Sam could feel the perspiration oozing from the pores where his hairline used to be. He hoped a drop didn't form and embarrass him by streaking down his face.

"I have similar information from other sources. You are very clever, Sam, telling me all this without lying but at the same time not telling me anything. I'll let it go for now. I hope you enjoy your stay in Playa de Cerro Bonito. We like to think of it as our little paradise." Marcelo started to return to his table when he realized Francisco was not at his side. "Francisco, come."

The boy broke off his gaze with Chloe and hurried to his father's side.

"I think they like each other." Marcelo smiled and took Francisco by the hand before returning to his table.

Immediately, Chloe leaned forward. "Francisco stared at me the whole time you were talking, Grandpa. I didn't know what to do, so I stared back at him."

"He seems like a nice young man," Sam said. "His father didn't seem that bad, either. Very intelligent. Very fair minded. Well bred, polite."

"Can I have a Sprite?"

"Sure. And I'll have a glass of wine. I'm starting to get hungry now that things have calmed down."

***

Antonio served Marcelo and his group, then Sam and Chloe. They ate in silence until Marcelo's group finished and made their way out of the restaurant. Marcelo gave Sam a nod when he passed Sam's table. Francisco craned to keep an eye on Chloe and almost tripped going down the stairs.

"Francisco is kind of weird," Chloe said. "But I think he is nice, anyway."

They finished their meal and left the restaurant without a second look from the men downstairs. The walk back to Heidi's was a pleasant one, the air heavy with the smell of gardenias, a full moon overhead.

Sam opened the gate and followed the path, which led to the main house before branching off to their bungalow. As he crossed the patio to their front door a sob distracted him.

"Aurelia?" He peered into a dark shadow that fell onto the terrace beyond. A cigarette glowed followed by a gray drifting of smoke in the moonlight. "Are you okay?"

He walked over to her, but she turned her face away from him. He knelt down and took her chin in his hand. "What is it?"

When she looked at him, her left eye was puffed shut, her lip cut and swollen.

An anger Sam thought he had long ago purged from his repertoire of emotions welled up inside him. "Lukas did this?"

She nodded.

Sam rose, clenching his fists in frustration, knowing there was little he could do to Lukas physically. There was little he could do to Lukas, period. There was no police authority in town.

"Please, *Señor* Turner, do not get involved. It is my trouble, not yours."

"But this can't go on. What are you going to do?"

"You are right. It cannot go on. But I don't know what to do. He has my baby. I have no money. He gets drunk, and if I say something he doesn't like he beats me. The next day, he says he's sorry. But I know better."

Heidi came out of the house with a flashlight. "What is it?" She flashed the light onto Aurelia's face. "Oh my God, what has he done to you?"

248

Aurelia started to cry again. She stubbed out her cigarette and stood to face Heidi. "I will kill him if he does this again."

Heidi's hand went to her mouth in shock. "You don't mean that."

Lukas slammed open the screen door of the main house and staggered toward them, a bottle of tequila dangling from his hand. He almost fell, lurched, and regained his balance. "Did I hear my name?"

Sam walked Chloe over to the door of the bungalow. "Time for bed."

Chloe stared past him at Lukas, who burped and wiped his mouth with the back of his hand, the one with the tequila in it, almost dropping the bottle.

"But I want to stay here with you, Grandpa."

"Please Chloe."

"Oh, all right." Chloe trudged into the living room, then across to the bathroom.

Lukas turned on Aurelia. "C'mere bitch!"

He grabbed her by her ponytail and dragged her screaming up the path toward one of the bungalows. "Who's going to kill who? Eh? You going to kill me? You going to kill me?" He tripped and fell. The bottle broke, spilling tequila on the cobbled path. "Fuck!" He wiped blood from a glass cut on his foot but staggered to his feet anyway and resumed a limping drag of Aurelia.

"Shouldn't we do something?" Sam asked.

"It's over for tonight," Heidi said. But her eyes were full of fear. "In...in another five minutes he'll fall asleep."

"You have to talk to him," Sam said. "You can't stand by and let this go on. Aurelia isn't getting through to him. I certainly can't. You're the only one he might listen to."

Heidi looked up at Sam with tears in her eyes. "I will try. I have tried. But unfortunately, I know my son all too well. Let him sleep it off for now. In the morning." She sat on the concrete bench that ran the perimeter of the patio and put her head in her hands, her shoulders shaking with sobs.

"He's like his father. I came here from Germany fifteen years ago to get away from it all and now it is back to haunt me." She looked up at Sam imploringly. "I was married to a Count.

"Yes, Mr. Turner, a real Count. But it didn't last long. Unfortunately, we produced a son. When I got divorced I came here with Lukas. I had money from the settlement. I bought this place. Things went well for a while, then the town changed...and Lukas grew up."

Sam knelt and took Heidi's hands. He thought to say something, but she hurried on.

"I know this place is not good for him. It used to be nice, but now there are drugs and the people who sell them and police corruption. But what am I to do? I can't sell out. Who is going to buy a place like this, now?

"A year ago, Lukas met Aurelia, she's a *federale*, her family is from Mexico City, nice girl. She was here on vacation. Wouldn't you know it, she becomes pregnant. So a marriage, or we'd be in big trouble. Now a baby, and she and Lukas fight all the time. What am I to do?"

250

Sam felt sorry for Heidi. Sam felt sorry for Aurelia. Sam felt sorry for himself. He hadn't counted on all these complications when JoAnne had talked him into staying in Cerro Bonito.

The phone rang in the main house.

"I have to answer that." Heidi nodded thanks, withdrew her hands and heaved herself to her feet. After scrubbing tears off her cheeks with both hands, she padded back to the house.

Chloe pushed through the screen door wearing one of Sam's T-shirts for pajamas.

"I thought I told you to go to bed," Sam said.

"I want you to tuck me in."

Sam led her to the sofa she had chosen to sleep on.

"Why did Lukas hurt Aurelia?" Chloe asked.

"Sometimes people who are very close to each other end up hurting each other. When it goes as far as this, physical violence, the consequences can be very serious."

"We are close, aren't we, Grandpa?"

Sam started to answer yes, then realized the point of her question. "I would never hurt you, Chloe. I've already promised you that."

He tucked the covers around her and kissed her on the forehead, but she was already asleep.

Heidi came to the door. "Sam," she whispered.

He stepped out onto the patio. "What is it?"

"JoAnne just called on her cell. She's on the bus from Guadalajara, ten minutes out from Cerro Bonito."

The two ropey hammocks swayed in the cool evening breeze. The intoxicating scent of gardenia

251

floated in the air. How could all of this wonderful sensory input be corrupted by reality?

"JoAnne is on her way here?" Sam knew what he had heard but was still having trouble comprehending it. "Did she say why?"

Heidi gazed at Sam, obviously seeing the disbelief in his face. "You didn't know?"

Sam shook his head. "How's she going to get from the bus stop to here?"

"She knows where my place is. She said she'd walk."

"That's insane. Does she know what your paradise has become?"

Heidi harrumphed. "I resent that kind of comment, Mr. Turner, even though--"

"Heidi. I have to meet JoAnne. I fear for her safety. Am I making sense?"

Heidi wrung her hands, worried, confused, frustrated.

Sam checked that Chloe was asleep. She was, lying on her side, facing the wall with her knees pulled up in a near fetal position. He returned to Heidi.

"Please," Sam asked, "can you watch Chloe while I'm gone? I shouldn't be more than twenty minutes."

252

Chapter Twelve

Demetri descended the jet-stairs from the ancient Aeromar ATR-42 that had landed at Playa de Oro International Airport in Manzanillo. Horrible ride. Bumpy all the way. Seasonal thunderstorms. He'd been traveling since dawn, the latest leg out of Mexico City, where he had to explain the syringes and drug vials in his possession. "I'm a diabetic," he had said, and they believed him.

He collected the duffel bag that served as his suitcase and stepped out of the air conditioned baggage claim into suffocating humid air, dim street lights, and a full moon rising above distant tree tops.

Why does anyone want to live here?

Of course it was a stupid question. The Mexicans had no choice. He walked to the curb, set down his bag and was besieged by five taxi drivers who demanded to know where he wanted to go.

"Playa de Cerro Bonito," he said as he was pressed back against a wall.

Animals.

The biggest and strongest of the drivers grabbed his arm and propelled him towards a newer looking taxi, yellow, like in the States with black lettering giving the name of the cab company.

At least the biggest gorilla on the block is driving the best vehicle.

"*Cuanto cuesta?*" Demetri was proud of his Spanish. And why wouldn't he be, having come from Central Asia and having had to learn English? After that, any other language was a piece of cake.

253

He thought about cake and decided he had become too Americanized.

"Five hundred *pesos*!"

Everyone shouts. "Okay. Let's get out of here."

The taxi driver held the door for Demetri. "Where you from, *amigo*?"

"That's none of your damn business. Just get me to Cerro Bonito."

A big smile, for whatever reason. "*No problema*. You can call me Paco."

"I don't want to call you fucking anything. I don't even know you. Drive!"

Paco scowled and slammed the door closed after Demetri got in, then slid behind the wheel and turned up the volume on his CD player.

Demetri winced at the folkloric music that emanated from the speakers. He thought to tell Paco to turn it down, but they were already speeding outside Manzanillo on a narrow highway, passing tangled vegetation on both sides, and Paco was a lot stronger than he was. No sense upsetting the man any further, lest he get it in his mind to pull off the road and make Demetri into compost.

All this stress must be getting to me.

By the time the cabbie had negotiated the curving road in the pitch darkness and pulled onto Cerro Bonito's main street, Demetri figured he had lost ten pounds, not counting figuratively having defecated in his pants. But that was a joke he told himself.

"Where you want to go?" Paco asked with a malevolent smile, shutting off the CD player.

"I'll be staying at the *Marina Fiesta Hotel*."

"It's up ahead. Nice place, the *Marina Fiesta*, but *Casa Mirador* is better."

Paco pulled forward and stopped in front of the *Marina Fiesta*.

Demetri couldn't very well stay at *Casa Mirador*. Then again he supposed he could. Wouldn't that be a hoot? Another joke he told himself. His mood had brightened at the prospect of closing in on Turner and the clone.

He paid the cabbie and gave him a big tip. "Sorry, for the profanity back there."

The cabbie nodded but didn't smile. Probably nothing malevolent to smile about.

After checking in, Demetri ascended a flight of tiled stairs with no hand rail that curved to the second floor and his room. A misstep on those stairs and the only thing stopping the fall would be the floor below.

He opened the door to his room with the large antique key he had been given. The door also had a dead bolt. The room seemed adequate despite its diminutive size and a lingering odor of mildew. From a small balcony, there was a view across the main street to shops on the other side. If Demetri leaned one way, he could see the ocean. There was a single queen size bed, a dresser, an armoire and a chair. A ceiling fan twirled overhead at what must have been its lowest speed. He'd have to see if it could be set higher before he died of heat exhaustion.

Off to one side was the bathroom, a cramped affair of stained fixtures that smelled of sewer gas.

A sign on the wash basin warned him not to drink the water.

On the dresser sat a tray with three one liter bottles of water, an ice caddy that was empty and an assortment of two ounce bottles of liquor. He picked through them--rum, gin, scotch, tequila. No mixers, but that wouldn't be a problem.

There was a phone, a step below wireless Internet, but at least a link to the outside world. How much more primitive could things get?

He took out his cell phone and checked the reception. An icon on the display showed good coverage. But he'd heard rates were excessive in Mexico. He picked up the land line phone and dialed the number Wellstone had given him for Colonel Obregon.

"*Si.*"

"Is this Colonel Obregon?"

"I am Colonel Obregon. Who is this?" A gravelly male voice. One devoid of fear. One comfortable with command.

Demetri lounged back on his bed. *Got to be careful, now.* "This is Demetri Andropov. I grew the clone the--"

"I know."

News travels fast. I guess it isn't the eighteen hundreds down here after all. "Excellent. Agent Wellstone said you were the FBI's liaison down here. He is under court order to cooperate with me trying to get my clone back."

There was no response at the other end of the line, making Demetri wonder if Obregon had hung up.

"Colonel Obregon?"

"What do you want?"

Tough guy. We'll see. "I have information that indicates the clone and her sponsor are here in Playa de Cerro Bonito."

"So what?"

"Could you and I have lunch tomorrow? There are certain, ah...business arrangements I would like to discuss with you."

"Two o'clock. *El Pescado.*"

The phone went dead.

That was easy, Demetri thought. He replaced the phone and twisted the cap off a two ounce bottle of tequila. He sucked it dry, then picked up another one and stepped out onto the balcony. He glanced up and down the street, lit here and there by bars or restaurants that were still open. A gentle background rushing sound from the ocean beyond permeated the place. Not many cars this time of night. Colorfully dressed ladies lounged outside the bars, smoking.

At the north end of the street the bus from Guadalajara, with its large-lettered sign, pulled in and discharged passengers. One passenger caught his eye. She was obviously an American given her pale skin and blond hair. The tight white jeans and striped tank top she was wearing enhanced her overall beauty. Tall, slender build. Nice tits.

She slung a backpack over her shoulder and walked down the street in a direction that would take her right under his balcony at the *Marina Fiesta*. A couple of loud whistles emanated from

257

the recesses of the open air bars as she walked past, but no one came out to harass her.

As she was about to pass under his balcony, Demetri leaned over the railing. "Hey, you in the tight-ass jeans. How about coming up and having a drink with me?"

She continued on without seeming to hear, but when she was half a block away she raised her middle finger over her head.

***

Sam hurried down the path to the gate, went through and was on the main road in a matter of seconds. He forced himself to slow down. It wouldn't do to drop dead right about now. Not with all that was going on.

He passed Antonio's, now dark, then the church and the central square. The streets were deserted.

Why is JoAnne coming here? It couldn't be for a vacation. Had something happened in Colorado? She probably hadn't been to Cerro Bonito in years and didn't realize the changes that had taken place.

Halfway through town Sam made out a solitary figure walking toward him. *JoAnne.* As she neared, he shook his head in wonderment at the way she was dressed. It was a miracle she hadn't been accosted within seconds of her leaving the protection of the bus. But here she was, strutting down the sidewalk with a subtle sway to her hips and a backpack slung over one shoulder, as casually as if she had been in Colorado Springs.

She recognized him and waved.

258

He came up to her and gave her a heartfelt hug, which she returned. "I guess I'm glad to see you," he said. "It's quite a surprise."

"I couldn't stay home. Too much was happening. I had to get away."

"What are you talking about?"

"I'll tell you everything after we get to Heidi's. I think I'm being followed. A man propositioned me from the balcony of the hotel back there."

Sam peered up the street to a balcony that projected over the sidewalk, but it was empty. "What did you do?"

"I flipped him off, of course."

Sam shook his head. "Didn't your mother tell you never to do that? It infuriates men and can make things even worse."

"Yes, Daddy. Are you going to stand here and lecture me on protocol, or are you going to escort me to Heidi's?"

Sam took her arm and hurried her along. If someone was following her, he didn't know what he could do about it. He felt he was at the bottom of the feeding chain when it came to physical strength. "Is it any wonder you're being harassed the way you're dressed?" He regretted what he said as soon as it was out of his mouth. "I didn't mean it that way...well, yes I did. You look stunning. Always do."

"Why, thank you, Sam. I'll try to forget it sounded like you were scolding me."

They hurried until they passed Antonio's, then slowed, Sam feeling they were close enough to Heidi's, and that no one was following.

"How is Chloe?" JoAnne asked.

"She's doing very well. I'm amazed at what she knows. She's quite intelligent, great sense of humor. She's asleep in the bungalow right now. Heidi is watching her."

They passed through the gate, crossed the path to the bungalow and were greeted by Heidi outside on the patio.

"JoAnne. It's been too long."

They hugged each other.

"I assume you'll be staying here tonight," Heidi said. "Do you want the small bungalow overlooking the sea."

JoAnne looked flustered.

"No need to rent another bungalow," Sam said. "There's plenty of room here. I can sleep on the sofa next to Chloe."

JoAnne seemed to wonder about that. "Thank you, Heidi. We'll work something out."

"Then I'll leave you two alone," Heidi said. "You must be tired. We can catch up tomorrow. Good night." She turned on her flashlight and disappeared toward her house.

Sam took JoAnne's backpack and opened the door for her.

"Is that Chloe?" JoAnne whispered.

"That's Chloe."

"I think she's grown since the last time I saw her."

Sam felt a burgeoning impatience. Forces were afoot he didn't know about, and JoAnne could brief him on them. But here she was cooing over Chloe. "Can I get you anything?"

260

"No. Thanks. I just want to freshen up a bit."

Sam led her through the bedroom and showed her the bathroom.

Five minutes later she came out.

Sam sat on the bed with the door to the living room closed. "You said you'd tell me everything later. Now it's later. Please. I closed the door so we wouldn't wake Chloe."

JoAnne came around and sat on the other side of the bed facing him. She curled a leg under her, something that would be painful for Sam, but she was young and limber.

"The FBI is onto you," she said.

"I figured as much."

"After they knocked on my door and gave me their equivalent of a heads up, they returned the next day for an interview. Lots of questions."

"Like what?"

"They wanted to know if I'd been in touch with you. I had to tell them. If I lied, they could have arrested me and put me in jail."

Sam felt a giddy humor at her discomfiture. She had experienced nothing compared to what had been dogging him for the last seventy-two hours. "You did the right thing to tell them the truth. What else?"

"They asked about Chloe of course. I told them you said she was sentient. I got the impression that only confirmed what they already knew. Then lots of questions about Andropov. I didn't know much about that, just what you told me about your meetings with him and the transfer of Chloe. They

261

also asked if I knew where you were, and I told them."

Sam gave it consideration. "I'm okay with that. I don't think it matters. It's Andropov they're after. They only need me...and Chloe, so they can nail him for growing a sentient clone."

JoAnne flapped her hands as though Sam was saying nothing of any consequence. "That's what worries me, Sam. Andropov obviously knew Chloe was sentient when he transferred her to you. If he now suspects the FBI also knows, then he's in hot water if they can take her, or you into custody. He's in hot water unless he can get to Chloe first."

"Oh my god. You think he's looking for us?"

"If I were him, I'd be looking for you. I'd also have in mind of doing harm to Chloe."

Sam sat up. "Damn. I just thought of something. I've been really stupid."

"Is this a first?"

"No, seriously. I gave Victor Gallego--he's the Guadalajara contact on the card Andropov gave me--I gave him my address here."

"That was dumb. Whatever for?"

"I thought if I was to have a heart challenge, he'd be a good person to get in touch with. He's got to have connections in the medical community."

"I suppose it's six of one, half a dozen of another." She swiped a lock of hair out of her face. "I haven't told you Clonal and another small clone farm were able to get an injunction against the new legislation. I read it in the Denver Post. The feds have to return all the clones to Andropov that were within six months of term. That's so he'll be able to stay in business pending the outcome of a court challenge to the law."

"How's that six of one?"

"Since Chloe was well within six months of term, and the feds induced Andropov to give her up, I'm wondering if, armed with the injunction, he can force the feds to cooperate with him on getting her back. Essentially, they're responsible for seeing Andropov is made good, put back to where he was before they raided him."

"So it's okay if I was stupid?"

"I guess that's what I was trying to rationalize. If Andropov is looking for you, he's going to find out where you are one way or the other." JoAnne yawned.

"You're exhausted."

"It has been a long day. I got up at four this morning for a flight out of Denver International to Guadalajara. Then the bus ride here. I should hit the sack." She started to get up.

"I've got some stuff I have to tell you," Sam said. "I'm sorry. I don't think it can wait."

She sat back down, looking concerned. "Is this going to keep me awake?"

"Come look at this." He got off the bed and went to the safe in the closet, punched in the combination and opened the door.

JoAnne rounded the bed and gawked at the packed-in bills. "How much is in there?"

"Over a million."

"Where'd you get it?"

"We came upon the aftermath of a drug deal gone wrong in the Sonoran Desert south of Nogales.

Everyone was dead." He crossed to the bed, pulled out the guns and unwrapped the blanket. "Guns, too."

"Sam?"

"I've got a drug dealer's Hummer parked downstairs and six kilos of cocaine stashed in the rear cargo compartment."

"This isn't the Sam Turner I knew in Monument."

Sam sat on the bed and slumped. "I'm afraid it is. I don't know what to do with all this stuff. I came upon the vehicle and saw it as an opportunity. I had to abandon my car in Arizona and hitch a ride with an Indian friend to Nogales where I booked a bus tour to Guaymas."

"But what were you doing in the desert?" She sat down beside him.

"The bus broke down. I was afraid the cops would catch up, so Chloe and I hiked into the desert. Kind of risky I admit, but it's not blazing hot this time of year. I wanted to get down range, flag a vehicle and continue south. That's when I found the Hummer and this stash of stuff."

JoAnne stood. "I'm going to sleep on all of this."

"There's something else you should know. It's about Heidi. She'll probably get into it tomorrow, but I thought I'd alert you."

"I don't like the sound of alert."

"It's about Lukas. In the short time we've been here, he's shown himself to be a drunk and a wife beater."

"Lukas is married?"

264

"He is, and he has a kid, about a year old. A little girl."

"When I last saw him, he was nothing more than a twelve year old trying to find his way. Reclusive kid. Must have found the wrong way."

"Anyway, I thought I'd let you know."

"I'm sorry about all this. I wouldn't have sent you here if I'd have known."

"Not to worry. It's too late now. We'll manage."

"Now you've got me wound up. I don't know if I'll be able to sleep."

"I'm sorry. It's a bit much after what you've been through today." Sam stood and headed for the bedroom door. "But give it a try. You can sleep here--" He indicated the big bed. "--I'll sleep on the other sofa next to Chloe."

She gave him an *are you serious or just joking look*. She must have decided he was serious. "I can't take your bed. Besides you're the one who is sick. What if you were to die out there because the bed was too hard or something? I'd feel terrible."

"You're kidding."

"Sort of." She got up and headed for the door. "I'll sleep with Chloe. Don't worry about it."

Sam smiled. "Yeah, right. And how would I feel if you died out there because the sofa was too hard? Look, the sofa works for a little girl and absolute martyrs."

She paused, hand on the door knob. "Okay, that bed looks big enough for two, and we're adults. I'll sleep on one side and trust you to sleep on the other."

"I don't know..."

"Oh, stop being such a prude. You've already asked me to marry you like a hundred times."

"All right. We'll give it a try. But no monkey business."

She stretched out her hand and shook his. "Deal. No monkey business...whatever that means."

Ten minutes later with the lights off and moonlight streaming in through the open shutters of the door to the balcony, Sam slipped into one side of the bed, and JoAnne into the other.

"Good night," he said.

"Night, Sam."

He lay on his back and thought he hadn't slept in the same bed with a woman since Karen had died. He tried to listen for her breathing to see if she was asleep. If she was asleep, she wasn't breathing very heavily.

"Sam?"

He gave a start.

She snuggled up next to him.

He felt her breath on his cheek. "What?"

"Will it kill you to make love to me?"

"I...I don't know. I don't think so."

She brought her arm across his chest and pressed closer. "Shall we give it a try?" She kissed him lightly a couple of times, then stayed for a longer one.

"You promise to marry me?" Sam asked.

"I promise." She slid over on top of him.

The door to the bedroom creaked open.

"Grandpa, I have to go to the bathroom."

JoAnne stifled a laugh and eased off of Sam, back to her side of the bed. She propped herself up on one elbow and brushed back a strand of hair.

Chloe stared.

"This is JoAnne," Sam said, self-consciously.

JoAnne smiled and gave Chloe a little wave.

"The JoAnne in my survival kit?" Chloe asked.

"One and the same," Sam said.

"But I thought she was old like you, Grandpa."

***

Morning came with the muffled sounds of the ocean, a chorus of exotic bird calls, and the shouts from a propane vendor as his pickup truck made its slow way through the street with a roof top PA system broadcasting, "*Igas, Igas.*"

Sam had never heard birds competing so loudly for center stage. They had started before sunrise and were now still going strong at 7:32 AM. He had awakened at the same time he always did if he accounted for the time change.

JoAnne lay on her side next to him facing away and sound asleep.

He got out of bed, pulled on his robe and walked into the living room.

Chloe lay on her stomach, one hand dangling over the edge of the sofa, the covers half on the floor.

Sam pushed through the screen door and crossed the patio to the far edge of the terrace. The low angled sun gave the humid air a soft glow, lighting the beach nearby and tapering off into a white haze as the bay curved into the distance. Gray pelicans glided in rigid formations low over

267

the water, having to flap their wings once or twice for a trip across the expansive bay.

Early morning fishermen were already in their boats readying them for a trip farther out in the bay to check nets that had been left in the water overnight.

How can a beautiful place like this contain so much trouble?

Sam returned to the bungalow.

After Chloe had finished going to the bathroom the night before, he had escorted her back to the sofa and made sure she was comfortable.

She had reached up and hugged him. "Are you glad JoAnne is here?"

"I think so."

"I think she is a nice lady."

"So do I." Chloe's simplicity always amazed him. It had been years since experiencing it in Karen's nieces, now grown and living away. "Go to sleep."

"Goodnight, Grandpa. Please leave the light on." She had turned on the light that sat on the table between the sofas.

He had returned to the big bed in the bedroom and found JoAnne fast asleep. His reaction had been that this was probably for the best. Maybe slow things down a bit. But he'd been trying for years to get close to JoAnne, and now that she had opened up to him, why was he retreating? Maybe he was worried about how long he had to live.

Back at the bungalow, he went into the kitchenette and made a pot of coffee, then took two cups into the bedroom.

JoAnne stirred, stretched, and opened her eyes. She smiled a sleepy smile. "That coffee smells awfully good."

He handed her a cup and sat on the edge of the bed. "I guess we got interrupted."

She yawned and eyed him over the rim of her cup. "I fell asleep. But you could have wakened me."

"You're bluffing." Sam took a sip of his coffee.

"What time is it, anyway?"

"Almost eight," Sam said. "Isn't it nice not to have anything to do?"

The buzzer at the front door sounded.

"Typical." Sam stood, then headed into the living room.

Chloe was sitting up. "What time is it, Grandpa?"

What is it with females? "It's eight o'clock."

"Can I use the bathroom?"

"I think it's free."

Chloe grabbed her clothes and headed into the bedroom.

Heidi stood on the other side of the screen door with Francisco at her side. "Chloe has a gentleman caller." She eased Francisco to the forefront. "I told him it was early but he wouldn't be dissuaded."

"*Buenas días*, Francisco," Sam said. "*Que quieres?*"

"I speak English very well, Mr. Turner. I am sorry to come so early. I hope I am not disturbing you."

"It's okay. We were all getting up, anyway."

269

Francisco nodded, seeming to take heart at not having disturbed them. "I would like to take Chloe to see the crocodiles at the nature preserve at the other end of town. The best viewing is in the morning. Later, they become sleepy in the heat of the day and lie around doing nothing."

"That's very nice of you to offer to show Chloe." Sam gave Heidi a questioning glance.

"It's perfectly okay," Heidi said. "He came with a driver and a bodyguard. If Chloe is safe with anyone, she's safe with Francisco. Besides, if I were you, I wouldn't turn down an invitation from the son of Marcelo Lopez. He's the--"

"I know who he is," Sam said. "I met him and this charming boy last night at Antonio's." Sam turned to Chloe as she came back into the living room. "You want to go look at crocodiles?"

"The *cocodrilos* we saw coming into town? Yes. Yes."

"Okay, get something to eat first, then you can be off."

"I have sweet rolls and juice in the car," Francisco said, gravely. "We can share them as we drive through town."

"That would certainly be efficient. Chloe?"

"Let's go." She slipped into her sandals and ran to the door, where she stopped and gazed at Francisco.

"Love at first sight," Sam whispered to Heidi.

"Thank you, *Señor* Turner, *Señora* Bergman," Francisco said. "May we go now?"

"Yes, of course," Sam said. "I'll walk you to your car."

Francisco took Chloe by the hand, and with Sam trailing a few feet behind them, led her back to the gate where one of Marcelo's bodyguards waited for them.

Outside, a driver stood beside a black Mercedes with the door open.

Francisco helped Chloe into the back seat, then shook Sam's hand. "I will guard her with my life, *Señor*."

Sam thought that was an exaggeration coming from someone so young, then he looked into Francisco's eyes and saw the kid was dead serious. "I'm certain you will." He stepped back. The driver closed the door. The bodyguard climbed into the front seat, and the Mercedes pulled away.

Sam returned to the patio where Heidi lingered.

"Cute couple," Heidi said, then she looked at Sam. "I haven't had a chance to talk to Lukas. He's still sleeping. But I will."

Sam nodded. "Are you sure Chloe will be all right with Francisco?"

"Absolutely. He's a nice kid. Not like his father. Well, his father can be nice, too, but I don't like the business he's in."

JoAnne came out of the bedroom. "Who was that?"

"Francisco, the local drug dealer's son. We met him and his father at dinner last night."

"You have drug dealers in Cerro Bonito?" JoAnne asked Heidi.

"We do now," Heidi said. "Things have changed since you were here last. Why don't you

271

come up to the house, if that's okay with Sam? We can do some catching up over coffee and breakfast."

JoAnne looked at Sam for an approval that wasn't necessary.

"Go on," Sam said. "I'll find something to do. Maybe go back to bed."

***

Two hours later, JoAnne hadn't returned, neither had Chloe. Sam started to worry. Both women, if he could include Chloe, had disappeared into potentially dangerous circumstances. JoAnne into the main house where she might run into an unpredictable Lukas. And Chloe into town with a drug lord's son.

The screen door creaked open, and JoAnne walked in.

At least one of them is back. "Did you have a nice talk?" Sam asked.

"I didn't realize how much Cerro Bonito has changed from when I used to come here as a child. And Heidi has such a horrific problem with her son. She told me what happened last night."

"Did Lukas show?"

"No. Heidi said that after he's blown up like that, he's contrite for a couple of hours. That he and Aurelia were probably making up. But I think it's gotten to the point where Aurelia has to take control of her life and leave."

"I agree." Sam kept looking out the window toward the entrance gate. "I'm worried about Chloe. They should have been back by now."

"We can take a walk into town. It's ten minutes to the nature preserve. I'm sure someone will know where they went."

Outside, the air was fresh. It had rained the night before, enough to keep down the dust on the road. As they walked, JoAnne slipped her hand into his. It felt good. Almost natural.

At the town square, a small crowd was gathered by the bandstand. To one side were two jeeps painted in beige, green and black camouflage. In each jeep lounged three or four military types. Sam couldn't tell if they were soldiers or part of the regional police force. Though they looked bored, they still carried automatic weapons. On the other side of the crowd, two black Mercedes were parked next to each other.

Sam recognized one of the men leaning against the driver's side door as Marcelo's bodyguard. Sam's heart began thudding in his chest as he imagined the worst of possible scenarios involving Francisco and Chloe. "I don't like the looks of this." Sam angled over to the crowd.

With JoAnne in tow, he pushed his way to the front.

Marcelo, flanked by his other bodyguard, was in a fierce shouting match with a uniformed police Colonel. Behind the Colonel stood another policeman holding Francisco and Chloe by the shoulders.

"Chloe!" Sam took a step in her direction but was restrained by a soldier.

Chloe had her arms wrapped around her chest and seemed too terrified to speak.

273

The arguing stopped, and the Colonel motioned to the policeman behind him to release Francisco.

The boy ran to his father's side and clutched him. "Papa! They still have Chloe."

"It will be all right, Francisco. Colonel Obregon will release her after he talks to Mr. Turner about the circumstances of his presence here."

As Marcelo passed Sam, he said, "I do believe it is your turn, now. This imbecile, Colonel Obregon, has gotten it into his head that the best way to win cooperation from citizens and visitors is to harass their children." Marcelo pushed through the crowd pulling a reluctant Francisco behind him and climbed into his waiting Mercedes. A second later the two cars drove off toward the north of town, leaving Sam free to face Colonel Obregon on his own.

Sam stepped up to Obregon. "I'm Sam Turner, Colonel. You have my granddaughter there."

"Grandpa!"

Sam could see her shaking. "It's okay, Chloe. I'll work this out."

"Indeed." Obregon ran his thumb and index finger over his mustache. "I know who you are."

"You do?"

"You are the American your FBI wants to talk to, no?" He waved a hand in Chloe's direction. "And this is the little girl they are looking for."

Desperately, Sam tried to review the disparities in laws regarding clones in the United States versus Mexico. "I haven't done anything wrong."

274

"That depends on to whom you are talking." Obregon held out his hand. "Do you have identification?"

"Yes, of course." Sam dug into his fanny pack and produced his passport.

Obregon took a note pad out of his pocket and wrote down information from the passport. "And the little girl?"

"She's carrying her birth certificate in her fanny pack."

Obregon motioned to one of his men who stripped Chloe's fanny pack from her waist and handed it to the Colonel.

Obregon passed it to Sam. "Please."

Sam zipped it open and retrieved Chloe's birth certificate.

Obregon read it. "This is not a real birth certificate." He handed back Sam's passport and the certificate.

"I have no reason to doubt the certificate is genuine." Sam stared at Obregon. Was the man going to arrest him? Was he blustering and had no cause? Did he want money?

Obregon smiled. "Of course not. Who is the *señora* you have in your company?"

This is my friend, JoAnne--" Sam pulled JoAnne to the front. "--She arrived yesterday."

"Please, *Señora*, may I see your identification, too?"

JoAnne fumbled in the back pocket of her jeans for her passport and handed it to Obregon.

He made another note and handed it back to her. "Thank you. Now we are finished with the formalities and we come to the real questions. Why are you keeping such bad company?"

"I am?" Sam couldn't imagine to whom Obregon was referring. The only company he had been keeping was Heidi and JoAnne.

"Marcelo Lopez. The scum of the Earth. He perverts youth, sells them drugs. He squashes the competition in the dead of night."

"I assure you I haven't been keeping company with--"

"Colonel!" The policeman Sam had seen the night before in the bar stepped forward.

"What is it Sanchez?"

"Excuse me interrupting, Colonel, but Marcelo Lopez has done much here to help the--"

"Roberto," Obregon said. "If you continue to insult me with that drivel, I will have your head on a platter. Now, shut up. I am trying to conduct an interview." Obregon turned his attention back to Sam. "You have been walking a very fine line, *Señor*. But I do believe you overstepped when you crossed into our country under false pretenses. The girl really doesn't have a birth certificate, does she?"

"As I told you, I think it is genuine."

"Perhaps." Obregon busied himself brushing dust or lint off his uniform. "We have reports you drove into town in a black Hummer. But you left Nogales as a tourist on a tour bus." He thrust out his chin to indicate it was a question.

"Yes, I drove here in a Hummer. I'm certain you know how I came into possession of the vehicle. And Chloe is not my granddaughter, but she's close to it. I love her dearly. We are not

276

hiding. We are here because the US government has adopted an ambiguous law regarding children like Chloe. I would like to remain here until that law is clarified by the courts."

Obregon placed both hands behind his back and nodded that Sam should continue.

"I have a heart condition that needs close attention. Given the ambiguities I spoke of, my best recourse for treatment is here in Mexico...if it comes to that. Is there anything else you want to know about me?"

"No, Mr. Turner. You have been more than forthcoming." Obregon indicated the policeman behind him could let Chloe go. "I appreciate honesty. These, of course, are delicate matters. Some involve the State Departments of our respective countries. I am content to know, at least for the time being, that you are here in Cerro Bonito. You *will* let me know if your plans change."

"Of course." Sam took Chloe into his arms.

She clutched him.

JoAnne laid a hand on Chloe's head and smoothed her hair. "It's going to be all right. The Colonel was only doing his duty."

"I was afraid," Chloe said. "Francisco was so brave. He stood up to those soldiers when they stopped the car. They had guns and he was not afraid of them. The soldiers were very mean to Francisco's driver. They hit him in the face and stomach when he resisted."

"I'm sorry you had to see all of that," Sam said. "Sometimes the adult world is not a pleasant place to be in."

Obregon stepped over to Chloe and put his hand on her head. "I have two little girls like you, *niña*. I am sorry if my men frightened you."

Chloe nodded and buried her face in Sam's side.

"Can we go now?" Sam asked.

Obregon glanced at his watch. "Yes. We are finished here. I have a luncheon appointment."

Chapter Thirteen

Demetri had slept late. The heat and humidity were oppressive. The single ceiling fan pushed the hot air around but offered little relief. When he did open his eyes it was already 1:00 PM. He was to meet Obregon at two.

He got up and walked to the open balcony doors and peered down to the street. Cerro Bonito had come to a semblance of life. Vehicles maneuvered past each other, honking horns for no apparent reason. A thin mix of pedestrians walked the sidewalks. Shops were open. Music blared out of the CD store a block down the street. The air carried the fresh smell of the sea mixed with the heavier smell of fried food from the many sidewalk vendors.

He was about to turn back to shower when a black Mercedes shoved its way down the street toward a central square where a disturbance was going on. A large crowd had gathered. Soldiers with automatic weapons sat in two jeeps. A second black Mercedes seemed to be the object of the crowd's attention.

Demetri tried to make out what was happening, then gave up and padded into the bathroom for a cold shower. Cold didn't describe the warm water that issued from the shower head. At least there was water.

He finished his shower, dried off and put on a clean shirt and slacks. He slipped his feet into sandals. He didn't know how formal Obregon would be, but assumed he'd be in uniform, so Demetri thought he should at least look presentable.

Another look outside, and the disturbance at the square seemed to be breaking up. The two black Mercedes sped up the street and passed under his balcony.

Who owns Mercedes down here? Must be drug money.

It occurred to Demetri that Colonel Obregon might be at the center of whatever was happening and the reason the commotion was beginning to break up was that Obregon had to meet him for lunch. It also occurred to Demetri if he was late for lunch and kept Obregon waiting, then any request he might make of the Colonel would be dead on arrival.

Demetri hurried downstairs and asked the desk clerk for directions to *El Pescado*. A block north of the hotel on the same side of the street. Of course, directions in a dump like this could only be trivial.

El Pescado was a pleasant place. Bougainvillea grew from planter boxes out front, half covering open-air windows. Inside, the tables were arranged to provide client privacy. The background music was at an acceptable level...enough to mask conversation, but not loud enough to be annoying.

Demetri took a seat and told the maitre d' he was expecting someone. He then sat for five minutes with no one paying him the slightest attention until Colonel Obregon entered.

That precipitated a flurry of activity. If the place had seemed deserted and sultry before, it became a hive of activity with waiters rushing back and forth, plunking down water, and adding chips and salsa.

Demetri stood. "Colonel Obregon, I presume." He shook Obregon's hand.

Obregon nodded. He sat and waved to an attentive waiter. "Bring my favorite." He turned back to Demetri. "So, why do you want to have lunch with me?"

When Demetri started to answer the question, the Colonel held up a hand. "*Momento*."

The waiter brought a very expensive looking bottle of tequila and a small carafe of a red liquid Demetri couldn't identify.

Obregon poured two shots of tequila, then filled two other small glasses with contents from the carafe. He slid one of each to Demetri. "*Saludo*."

"What's this?" Demetri said, indicating the second glass.

Obregon frowned.

Bad start, Demetri thought.

"It is *sangrita*," Obregon said, tequila shot still poised. "A mixture of orange juice, grenadine and chilies. You toss the tequila and take a hit of *sangrita*."

Demetri smiled, hoping he hadn't committed a total faux paux. Who the hell had heard of *sangrita*, for fuck's sake?

He clicked Obregon's glass and tossed back the tequila.

"Now you may answer," Obregon said.

Demetri, who had followed through with a sip of the *sangrita*, choked out his proposal. "Despite

281

what you might have heard from the FBI, the clone belongs to me. I could make it very worth your while if you help me regain possession of her."

Obregon refilled the shot glasses, his face expressionless. "Señor Andropov," he said without looking up, "are you implying I am a corrupt policeman? A man who can be dissuaded from his duty to his country to work for the sole interests of some *gringo* who comes in here waving a lot of cash?"

Demetri felt flushed. "It was not my intention to suggest anything of the sort, Colonel."

Obregon tossed back his second tequila and indicated Demetri should do the same, then leaned forward and whispered, "Then, *Señor*, why the hell are you here talking to me?"

Could it be this easy? The Colonel, from what Wellstone had said, was highly placed, a direct liaison to the Bureau. Was all law enforcement down here so corrupt?

"I'm glad you made that clear," Demetri smiled and lifted his glass. "I love this tequila."

"*Gran Patron Platinum.* It is the smoothest sipping tequila produced. Three thousand pesos a bottle. You will pay."

"Of course, of course. Look, may I call you Luciano?"

"No."

Demetri gulped at Obregon's self-assurance. He would be a man who ground up anyone who stood in his way and think nothing of it. "You must understand, I'm not interested in Turner."

Obregon nodded.

282

"Just the clone," Demetri said. "The FBI would like to have them both. But, if they don't have the clone, then they only have Turner. It becomes his word against mine."

Obregon smoothed his mustache. "I can give you the clone, but it will be very risky. What are you willing to offer in exchange?"

Ah, Mexico, Demetri thought. *What a forthright country. If only it worked the same way up north. How much more progress could be made.*

"I'll give you fifty thousand US upon delivery of the clone."

Obregon leaned forward and steepled his fingers. "One hundred thousand."

Demetri poured another shot and offered it to Obregon, who shook his head.

Demetri downed the shot for himself. *Tough son of a bitch. But I'm in no position to bargain. Maybe.* "How about half now, half upon delivery?"

Obregon shook his head again.

A drop of perspiration formed on the side of Demetri's face and slid down his cheek. "I thought not." Demetri reached out his hand. "Deal."

Obregon remained immobile. He gazed at Demetri with hooded eyes. "*Señor* Andropov, now that we have agreed the price, how do you intend to pay for this...exercise?"

"You want your money, now?"

Obregon leaned back. "Do you expect me to undertake such a mission, a very complex mission mind you, without assurances I will be paid?"

"I suppose not. Can I write you a check?"

"Surely, you are joking."

283

"Yeah, bad joke. I don't have the cash on me. Do you have an account somewhere I can wire the money to?"

"Yes, of course." Obregon took out a business card and wrote on the back of it. "This is the number of an offshore account I have in the Cayman Islands. I have also written the name of the bank and their routing number. If you direct a wire transfer of the funds to that account, I will verify they have arrived later this afternoon. Do you have any problem with this time frame?"

"None. I can call from my room."

Obregon poured himself another shot. "This is very good tequila. Thank you for being so generous." He tipped his glass to Demetri.

Feeling a bit emboldened by three shots of tequila and now that business was out of the way, Demetri asked, "Colonel, I saw a disturbance in the town square earlier. What was that all about?"

Obregon stared at him for a moment, giving Demetri the impression he had overstepped his familiarity with the Colonel. But the Colonel waved a hand and said, "It was nothing. I had received reports Turner and his clone were in my area. I knew the clone, who is quite a charming little girl, had been seen in the company of the son of one of our more prominent citizens, a Marcelo Lopez. Anyway, to remind *señor* Lopez who runs this part of the country, I had his son and the clone seized. Of course, it wasn't but minutes before Lopez showed up. We had a heated exchange, and he went away with his son and a renewed appreciation of who I am. Then Turner, and a lady I

284

can only assume to be his girlfriend, arrived and I had the opportunity to introduce them to the way we do things down here."

Demetri felt weak. "You had the clone in your custody?"

"I believe that is what I said. But of course English is a second language for me, perhaps I mis-communicated."

Demetri wiped his forehead with his napkin. "No, no, Colonel, you were most clear. It's just that I have come so far to repossess my property, then to know you had her and let her go...it's almost too much to bear."

Obregon smiled. "You are overreacting to this matter. They are here and I control the area. They cannot leave without me knowing or letting them do so. If you wire the funds as I've requested then I can give you the clone tonight. Is that soon enough?"

Demetri nodded. "Yes. Of course. That would be fantastic."

"I don't know about fantastic, but it will be quick." Obregon stood. "When you get the clone what will become of her?"

Demetri stood as well. "She's sentient. She's not supposed to be. If the feds can pin that on me, I'll be spending a lot of the rest of my life in jail."

"Señor Andropov, you have told me what happens to you. I asked, what happens to the clone?"

"I, ah...I inject her with a solution of drugs that will render her brain-dead. No sentience. No criminal charges."

"Seems simple enough," Obregon said.

"Very."

"Do you have any children?"

Where is Obregon going with this? "Are you kidding?"

"I thought not." Obregon left the restaurant.

A waiter stepped up to Demetri. "Would you like to order?"

Demetri waved him away. "Nah, I lost my appetite."

***

Sam and JoAnne walked back to the bungalow with Chloe between them holding both of their hands.

The sun hung low on the horizon, sending slanting blazes of color into the clouds. The town was quiet. The air still. To Sam, Cerro Bonito seemed heaven on Earth.

In the bay, fishing boats bobbed at anchor. Gray pelicans glided low across the water, three and four in formation. Flocks congregated on the boats. Others swooped, then stalled midair to plunge into the sea to fish.

Chloe seemed unaware of the beauty Sam was enjoying. She had a light touch to her step, almost as if she was pleased with the day's outcome.

"I not only have a grandpa, but I have a mommy, too."

JoAnne glanced at Sam and laughed. "I guess that's possible."

Sam shook his head. It felt good having JoAnne at his side, even though there were unresolved tensions in their relationship.

286

Upon arriving at the bungalow, they found Aurelia sitting outside in the patio. She held her baby in her arms. "*Señor* Turner--" She noticed JoAnne. "—*Buenas tardes, Señora*. Welcome to Cerro Bonito. I am sorry to be causing so much trouble. My husband is not right in the head."

"You can call me JoAnne. And you must be Aurelia." JoAnne stepped forward to better see the baby. "You have a beautiful baby."

Aurelia tucked the blanket around the baby's face. "She is named Maria, after my mother."

Chloe pushed forward and smiled. "I'm Chloe because I'm a clone."

Aurelia looked up. "Yes, you have a beautiful name."

"Can we help you with anything?" Sam asked since Aurelia seemed to have been waiting for them.

"I have decided to leave Lukas," she said, her voice choked with emotion. "It will be better for me to return to my family until Lukas changes his behavior."

"I think that's a wise decision under the circumstances," Sam said. He almost felt like a preacher, giving advice without having a background from which to give that advice. But he continued. "Either he will work his way back to normality or his condition will get worse. You are better off somewhere else where you and the baby will be safe."

Aurelia stood, chewing her lower lip. "Since I have made the decision, I must ask for your help. I have no money. I cannot go to Heidi. If you could loan me enough for a bus ticket to Mexico City, I will pay you back as soon as I get there."

"Of course." Sam tried to wave away her anxiety. "Money is no problem. When do you want to leave?"

Aurelia choked back a sob. "I want to leave now. Lukas is into his tequila and will soon pass out."

Sam dug into his fanny pack.

The door to the main house banged open, and Lukas staggered out. "Well, well, well. What the hell is this cozy little meeting all about?"

Aurelia backed away, clutching the baby close to her chest. "I'm leaving you Lukas. I'm taking the baby and going to my family."

"Like hell you are."

Sam stepped between them. "Lukas, you're drunk. This is not a good time to talk this out."

"Fuck you, Mister. She's my wife. Get your fucking nose out of our business." He lurched forward and shoved Sam in the shoulder.

Sam stepped back to avoid another shove. "Lukas, be reasonable. We don't want any violence here."

"Violence? How about this?" Lukas swung a haymaker that caught Sam in the jaw.

Bright fireflies zoomed in a darkness that tunneled Sam's vision. He lunged at Lukas, wrapping him with both arms.

They fell to the patio floor.

Lukas jerked Sam around and sat on him, then grabbed Sam by the hair and gave him two quick jabs to the nose.

Blood gushed over Sam's face. He flailed his arms trying to block more blows. Out of the corner of his eye he saw JoAnne grab a potted plant and raise it over Lukas' head.

Lukas turned.

The pot banged off his shoulder and crashed to the floor. Shards of pottery scattered.

He leapt up and grabbed JoAnne by her blouse. As he pulled her toward him, her blouse ripped, then he shoved her hard against the wall.

Aurelia rushed to support her.

Chloe screamed and ran into the bungalow.

Lukas turned on Aurelia, hitting her with the back of his hand across her already swollen cheek.

Sam struggled to his knees as Lukas made a grab for the baby.

A shot rang out.

Everyone froze as tufts of thatch drifted down from the pergola overhead.

Chloe stood with the Derringer clasped in both hands. She leveled it at Lukas. "You going to make my day, *hombre*?"

Lukas stared unfocused at the gun, then staggered back, the booze finally taking its toll. He righted himself and leaned over the edge of the patio to vomit into the bougainvillea. Wiping his mouth with the back of his hand, he stumbled toward the main house.

JoAnne rushed to Sam's side and knelt. "Are you all right?"

Sam's concern wasn't for himself, but for Chloe. "I told you to leave those guns alone."

289

She lowered the Derringer, walked over to Sam and handed it to him. "I'm sorry."

He took it carefully. "What was that about *make my day*. And *hombre*?

"I saw it on TV."

"Sam," JoAnne said, "this is no time to talk about the movies. I'll get something to clean you up." She started for the door.

Sam clutched his chest as a familiar constricting pain began to make itself known. "I'm going to need my pills. They're beside the bed."

JoAnne nodded to Chloe, who hurried into the house.

Aurelia pushed forward, choking back sobs, the baby in one arm. She helped JoAnne ease Sam onto one of the benches. "I am so sorry, *Señor*. Lukas is crazy. I am so sorry."

"It's not your fault." Sam lay down and tried to control his breathing. He tilted his head back to stanch the flow of blood pouring from his nose.

Chloe reappeared and handed JoAnne the pill container.

She shook out a pill. "Ten left."

"Better than the average cat."

"It's not funny," JoAnne said. "That hoodlum should be arrested and put in jail." She knelt beside Sam and dabbed at the blood that seemed to be everywhere. "You're going to have to take off your shirt."

With the pill doing its miracle work and the pain subsiding, Sam let JoAnne help him out of his shirt. "Down here I think they beat people for sport."

"That's not funny either, Sam."

"I know. I'm just pissed off and hurting."

"I must go now," Aurelia said. "Lukas will have passed out. There is still time to make the six o'clock bus. Please, *Señor*--"

"Give me a minute," Sam said. "I'll get a clean shirt and come with you."

"Sam, you can't," JoAnne said. "You're a mess."

"Yes, I can. If there's any way to get back at that bastard, it's to see this lady onto a bus." He got up and walked as steadily as he could toward the bedroom. Before going into the bathroom, he took the Derringer from his pocket and after a moment's hesitation, shoved it under the pillow on his side of the bed.

He washed his face with cold water, put on a clean shirt and returned to the patio.

Heidi had arrived. "Lukas has passed out. Thank God. I'm ashamed to call him my son. Look what he did to you."

"I still look bad?" Sam said.

Joanne put her hands on her hips. "Your nose is swollen and red. Your eyes are watery. They'll be black and blue tomorrow. Did he break your nose?"

"I don't think so." Sam touched his nose. "But it hurts."

"She's leaving isn't she?" Heidi demanded, not to Aurelia but to Sam.

"Can you blame her?" Sam said.

Heidi turned to Aurelia and gave her a hug. "I'm so sorry, my dear. Do not cut me out because

291

of my son. I am a grandmother, too." She caressed the baby's cheek.

Aurelia nodded, then to Sam. "We must go." She eased the baby away from Heidi, who looked on longingly.

Chloe still clutched JoAnne.

"Do you mind watching Chloe?" Sam asked.

"She'll be okay with me." JoAnne clasped Chloe's hand. "But please, don't be long. I worry about you."

Sam led the way out the gate and along the main street. Few residents were about. When they arrived at the bus station, he let Aurelia step up to the ticket window to buy her ticket to Mexico City.

She had a quick exchange with the ticket master and turned to Sam. "It costs 700 pesos, *Señor* Turner."

Sam leaned close to the ticket window. "I don't have pesos. Are dollars okay?"

The ticket master nodded. Sam pushed a hundred dollar bill through the window and received change in pesos. He gave the ticket to Aurelia. "We just made it. Here comes the bus."

A red, yellow and green painted bus rumbled into town from the highway and rolled to a stop. As the bus released its air breaks, billowing clouds of dust blew past. The door hissed open.

With Sam close behind, Aurelia clutched her baby and hurried down to the sidewalk.

After the bus discharged its passengers, Aurelia, still holding the baby in one arm, extended her other hand to shake Sam's. "*Muchas gracias,*

Sam Turner. I will never forget the help you are giving me."

"Here." He pressed a wad of one hundred dollar bills into her hand. "This will get you started."

"Señor, I cannot..."

"You let me worry about that. And yes, you can."

Aurelia kissed Sam on the cheek. "Thank you." She mounted the steps and was gone into the dark depths of the bus behind tinted windows.

Sam touched his nose. He must look frightful. Residual heat in the air began to give him a headache. Better get back to the bungalow as soon as possible lest he pass out somewhere in between.

The bus pulled out.

Sam watched until it reached the roundabout at the main highway and turned north on a route that would take it first to Guadalajara, then south to Mexico City.

Feeling he had kept a mother and her daughter safe, he started walking back through town.

He had gone but a short distance when a beat up red jeep with dark tinted windows barreled past him at a reckless speed.

Sam muttered a curse at the foolishness of driving so fast in town. Ten minutes later he arrived at *Casa Mirador*.

***

The gates to the parking area were wide open. From the bungalow on the far side, JoAnne ran toward him with Heidi close behind.

293

"Lukas has taken Chloe!" JoAnne cried. "I left her for a moment. When I turned around, Lukas was dragging her down the stairs. She was screaming."

The jeep. Sam felt the blood drain from his face leaving it cold and clammy. "Where'd he go?"

Heidi came up, waving her arms in agitation. "I don't know. I don't know. If he took his jeep, maybe he means to go far."

Sam tried to think through a fog of fear and pain. "There must be a police authority we can contact? Obregon?"

"We can try," Heidi said. "I will make some calls."

She ran back to the main house. Sam and JoAnne followed with Sam the slowest, almost falling off the path a couple of times.

The phone rang as they approached.

Heidi answered. "*Si. Si.* That is wonderful. They will be right over." She hung up.

"What was that all about?" Sam asked.

"It was Marcelo Lopez. He has Chloe."

"Thank God," Sam said. "Where does Marcelo live?"

"He has a villa, a mansion really, on the other side of the nature preserve on the beach. At the end of the main street, there's a dirt track to the right that goes inland around the preserve and through the swamp. It's the only way into his place."

"We'll take the Hummer."

JoAnne gave him a sidelong look as he led her down to the vehicle. "Do you want me to drive?"

"Thanks, but I'll manage."

She slid into the passenger seat and looked around. "Wow. This dwarfs my Proteus."

"I don't think now is the time to compare makes of vehicles," Sam snapped, then apologized. Her detachment was probably a defense mechanism. People under stress spewing dark humor into a dark hour. Tension released knowing Chloe was not with Lukas.

Heidi pulled back the gate for them and stood off to one side.

Sam eased the Hummer out of the parking area.

"I find it hard to believe you're relieved a drug lord has Chloe," JoAnne said.

"You haven't met him. His business aside, he strikes me as a standup guy. In any case, I'd rather know that he, instead of that idiot Lukas, has Chloe."

Five minutes later, having found the rough track around the preserve, Sam pulled up to an ornate wrought iron gate, the only opening in a seven foot high wall. It extended on Sam's left to the beach and to his right as far as he could see before curving out of sight. To one side of the gate, the wall formed into a guard house. One of Marcelo's thugs stepped out and approached the Hummer. He held a machine pistol down at his hip.

"I'm Sam Turner. Marcelo is expecting us." Sam eyed the weapon. He was convinced if the man took it into his mind to shoot them on the spot, no one would ever know.

The thug peered across Sam to JoAnne, then into the back seat. He nodded, returned to the guardhouse and pressed a button. The gates swung open.

Sam drove on a cobbled drive that was flanked by small flowering plants, punctuated at intervals with towering Washington palms. A manicured lawn spread out beyond with scattered date palms hanging heavy with ripening orange fruit. The driveway curved toward a looming, two story villa with white stucco-ed walls and a red-tiled roof. Ornate decorative bars covered the windows. The railings of upper floor terraces were mounted by small statuettes.

Sam brought the Hummer to a stop under a tall portico. An expansive entryway led from the curb to carved double doors.

The doors opened and Marcelo strode through, crossing a Persian carpet with a glittering chandelier hanging high overhead. He stepped up to Sam's side of the Hummer. "So, we meet again, *Señor* Turner." He shook Sam's hand. "What the hell happened to your nose?"

Sam shrugged. "I ran into a door. Long story."

Marcelo seemed about to respond when he looked past Sam and noticed JoAnne struggling to find the latch on the unfamiliar door.

"*Momento, Señora.*" He rounded the Hummer and opened the door for her, offering his hand. "I am Marcelo Lopez. Who might you be?"

"JoAnne Calder. Thanks." She took his hand and stepped from the Hummer.

"You have lovely friends, *Señor* Turner."

To Sam, Marcelo's attitude seemed almost too casual, but if he was king of the jungle, what other attitude would he express? "Where is Chloe?"

"Yes, the girl," Marcelo said. "That is the most important thing, isn't it? She is inside. She is unharmed. Francisco is showing her his collection of sea shells."

"What happened here?"

"Actually, nothing happened here. The madman Lukas drove up and demanded to see me. He was drunk, of course. He would never dare come here otherwise. Since he had the girl, I let him in.

"In his befuddled mind, he seems to have thought if he delivered the girl to me, since she is sought after by the Americans with in all probability a reward offered, he would ingratiate himself, and I would bring him into my...business. Of course, this was all nonsense. I thanked him for the girl, then sent him on his way. When he refused to go, I had my men throw him out. His jeep is still parked, over there." Marcelo pointed.

"He's a loose cannon, that one," Sam said. "You aren't afraid of repercussions?"

"Me? Afraid? No. He made threats, but he is a small fish. We feed them to the *cocodrilos* as appetizers."

Is he speaking in metaphors or does he really feed his enemies to the crocodiles? "How can I thank you for helping us?"

Marcelo gave Sam a dismissive wave. "There will come a day, I am sure, then I will ask a favor of you. But don't worry about that for now. It is getting late. I would be honored if you and *la señora* Calder would join me for dinner."

Sam looked over to JoAnne.

"Yes, we'd love to," JoAnne said.

Marcelo smiled, probably at JoAnne's assertiveness. "Good. Please come this way." He led them into his villa.

The vestibule would have been more than adequate for a grand resort hotel. Polished tile floors. Aggressively woven tapestries. Mexicana art, obviously Aztec with serpent heads clutching hearts with pointed teeth. After crossing a second richly-colored Persian rug they came to an open air courtyard.

Marcelo ushered them toward a long table set for five. "We will eat in the courtyard. It is a pleasant evening. Not too hot, not too cold."

The courtyard was square, nicely proportioned, maybe sixty feet on a side with a sheltered walkway all around. Bougainvillea climbed columns at the corners. To one side, a fountain spit a gentle stream of water up into the air where it fell to a gurgling return. Smaller potted hibiscus and gardenia lined the perimeter. A soft glow of lights, from rooms beyond the courtyard, filtered into the space. Candles lit the table.

"Thank you," Sam said. "Will Chloe and Francisco be joining us?"

"Of course." Marcelo dispatched one of his ever-present attendants to call the children to the table.

"May I ask if there is a *Señora* Lopez?" Sam said.

"You may ask, of course. It is an obvious question. Alas, there was a *Señora* Lopez. She died giving birth to Francisco. I am not a lucky man."

"What a tragedy," JoAnne said. "I'm so sorry to hear that."

Marcelo gave her a slight smile. "Thank you for your kind words, *Señora*. Please, you will sit here, beside me, if you will do me the honor."

"Really, you do me the honor." JoAnne fairly gushed.

Sam took a chair offered him by a man who must have been the headwaiter. He was dressed in a high-collared white jacket with brass buttons up the front, white pants and shoes.

JoAnne seemed to be enjoying the attention. Well, so what, Sam wasn't going to be jealous, was he? Good for her.

Chloe ran into the courtyard and hugged him. "Grandpa, I knew you would come. I wasn't afraid...well not much, anyway."

"He didn't hurt you, did he?"

"I was most afraid Lukas would crash his jeep. He couldn't steer straight."

Francisco was close behind her. "Good evening, *Señor* Turner."

"Good evening, Francisco." Sam was impressed by the boy. As always, his manners and composure were impeccable.

Francisco took Chloe by her elbow and directed her to an empty chair, then pulled it out for her.

"Your son is amazing," JoAnne said.

Marcelo indicated a chair Francisco should take. "Well, perhaps not amazing, but he is a good boy." Marcelo clapped his hands.

Waiters, dressed in colorful Mexican folkloric uniforms, filed into the courtyard with platters of food held high. They lined up behind JoAnne as she surveyed each dish and helped herself. After she took a serving, the waiters worked their way around to Chloe and Sam, then Francisco and Marcelo.

Marcelo nodded to Francisco, who bowed his head.

When everyone else followed suit, Sam bowed his head, too. What would a little appeal to God matter?

"We thank the Lord for our food tonight. We thank him also for the safety of our friends who have joined us here. May the virgin Mary bless us all. In the name of Jesus Christ. Amen."

"Amen," Marcelo and JoAnne said.

Chloe looked at Sam, seemingly for direction.

"Amen," Sam said. A simple amen meant little in the scheme of things. Was God going to punish him for his hypocrisy?

One of Marcelo's thugs ran in.

"*Ejercito Mexicano*!"

A brief flash of alarm crossed Marcelo's face. He regained composure almost immediately and put his napkin down next to his plate. "Please excuse me. This should take but a minute. The Mexican army. If they are here, then they can be purchased, certainly bought, I don't know how to put it diplomatically in English."

300

Chapter Fourteen

Sam followed Marcelo out to the entrance, his platoon of bodyguards close behind.

Military jeeps, like the ones Sam had seen in the square earlier, roared up the drive, leaving muddy tracks on the cobble stones, broken hedgerows of hibiscus and skid marks on the grass.

A ranking officer jumped out and confronted Marcelo.

"By order of Colonel Obregon I am to take the American and the girl he calls his granddaughter into custody."

"You toad," Marcelo said. "These people are my guests."

"We have our orders, *Señor*."

"I care nothing for Colonel Obregon's orders. Come, *Señor* Turner, let us return to our dinner."

At a motion from the officer, soldiers leapt from the jeeps and spread out in a line, guns drawn, to confront Marcelo and his men.

"Please, *Señor* Lopez," the officer said, "do not make my job more difficult than it already is."

"Then what are we to do?"

The officer nodded to a soldier, who stepped toward Sam.

Marcelo's men cocked their weapons.

Francisco, Chloe and JoAnne streamed out of the house.

"Sam, what's happening?" JoAnne cried.

Marcelo put up a restraining hand and approached the officer.

"I do not want bloodshed here, at my house, in front of my family and guests."

"Then you will step aside," the officer said.

Marcelo walked over to Sam. "For the moment, we will have to comply with this idiot's demands."

The soldier snapped handcuffs onto Sam's wrists and led him to one of the jeeps.

This can't be happening.

A Mercedes eased up the driveway. It stopped and Colonel Obregon got out of the backseat. He walked over to Marcelo and extended his hand.

After a slight hesitation Marcelo shook it. "What is this all about, Colonel?"

Obregon surveyed the scene behind Marcelo. "Nice place Don Lopez."

"You flatter me unnecessarily."

"Yes, perhaps I do. I don't know why I would do that under the circumstances. Be that as it may, it is imperative that I take the American and the girl into custody."

Marcelo snorted a derisive laugh. "Really, Obregon. I thought you had all that sorted out this afternoon."

"Yes, but that was this afternoon. This is now."

Marcelo wagged a finger at Obregon. "Someone has paid you a lot of money to do this."

Obregon slapped Marcelo hard across the mouth.

Marcelo spit back.

"This is not what I wanted," Obregon said, his voice taut with anger. He motioned to the officer who stepped to Marcelo and cuffed his hands in

302

front of him. "I think you will benefit from a night in jail. A time for reflection on who runs things down here."

Marcelo awkwardly pulled out a handkerchief and dabbed at a spot of blood on his lip. "I know about your nights in jail. You have tortured my men in the past. Should I also be similarly concerned?"

"I have no intention of torturing anyone." Obregon waved a dismissive hand, then motioned to two of his soldiers. "Take the girl."

Chloe screamed as the soldiers pried her away from JoAnne.

"Why the girl?" Marcelo asked, neatly refolding the handkerchief and shoving it into his pocket.

"There are certain parties that have a vested interest in her as property. I have come to...an agreement, shall I say. Besides, it is time the property was returned. We all have a sense of the right to personal property, don't we?"

"You have been bought off!" Sam shouted from the jeep.

"Ah, *Señor* Turner," Obregon said, strolling over to Sam. "Please, I fear for your heart."

"You'll take Chloe over my dead body!"

"If you wish, it will be so." Obregon stroked his mustache.

Sam lunged forward only to be restrained by two soldiers.

"Grandpa!" Chloe screamed as the soldiers dragged her kicking toward the Mercedes.

"You can't do this," Sam shouted.

303

"No?" Obregon waved away the two men who were holding Sam. "Señor Turner," he said in a low whisper. "Let me be very frank here because we are dealing with life and death."

Sam strained at the handcuffs. He craned to see what was happening to Chloe, but she'd been shoved into the car and the door closed. All he could see were the whites of her palms pressed against the darkly tinted glass. "Okay. You've got my attention."

"I have not, as you and Don Lopez like to put it, been bought off. However, I am experiencing a certain fortuitous convergence of outside opportunity and my duty as a senior member of the police. Do I make myself clear?"

Sam nodded. "If I can sweeten your outside opportunity, will you consider leaving Marcelo, his men, Chloe, myself, JoAnne, and anybody else I can think of, alone?"

Obregon smiled, as if he had set the conversation up and knew where it would lead. "Of course. I am a reasonable man."

"Can we take a walk over to the Hummer?"

Obregon eyed him suspiciously.

"Please, Colonel. I want to show you something."

At a nod from Obregon, the soldier steadied Sam at the elbow as he climbed down from the jeep. Obregon followed him to the Hummer.

Awkwardly, with his hands still cuffed, Sam opened the back panel door, then indicated the right cargo compartment. "It's in there."

Obregon gave him a skeptical look.

"I'm cuffed, Colonel, or I'd open it myself."

Obregon opened the compartment and surveyed the money crammed inside. "That looks like a lot of money."

"It is. I reckon about three-quarters to a million US. It's yours."

Obregon smiled. "That's a lot of sweetening. You are being very generous."

"Do we have a deal?"

"Deal." Obregon waved for the officer to approach. "Free this man, then Don Lopez."

The officer gave Obregon a questioning glance, but did as he was told.

Obregon walked up to Marcelo. "*Señor* Turner and I have cleared up a misunderstanding. You are free to go, for now."

Obregon walked to his Mercedes and opened the door to the backseat.

Chloe sat rigidly with her hands in her lap, her eyes wide with fear.

"You can get out, now," Obregon said. "Your grandpa has bought your freedom."

Chloe leapt out of the car and ran to Sam. "I was so scared they were going to take me back to Clonal."

Sam hugged her. "It's okay. Colonel Obregon isn't going to hurt you or take you away."

JoAnne came up and embraced him. "How horrible. Chloe are you all right?"

Chloe nodded and worked her way into their embrace.

Francisco looked like he wanted to join them, but stood his ground.

Obregon retrieved a cloth bag from his Mercedes, then returned to the Hummer. While his men looked on wide-eyed, he transferred the packets of bills from the cargo compartment to the bag. When he was finished, he strode back to his Mercedes and tossed the bag onto the backseat. He gave a nod to Sam and climbed into the car.

The Mercedes pulled away with the jeeps hurrying to fall in behind it.

"I thank you, Sam Turner for...obtaining my freedom," Marcelo said. "Men like Obregon are not kind to those he takes into custody. I hope it didn't cost you too much."

"It didn't."

Marcelo gave Sam a knowing look, then he knelt and squeezed Chloe by the shoulders. "You have a very kind Grandpa, little one."

Chloe smiled and looked up at Sam.

Francisco rushed up to Chloe and stopped, almost over balancing. "I didn't know what to do," he said sheepishly. "I'm glad you're okay."

Chloe shrugged, glanced at Sam and took Francisco's hand, letting him lead her back toward the house.

"This evening has turned out well," Marcelo said. "Shall we return to our table? The dinner is getting cold."

***

Sam held JoAnne's hand as they walked back to the bungalow by way of the beach with Chloe playing on ahead. Marcelo had suggested the walk, saying the moon was full, the air still, a good night for the romantic. He would have one of his men drive the Hummer back to *Casa Mirador*.

Marcelo had been right about everything except the sea. The breakers were rough, pounding the shore and sluicing up the sand, pausing at their zenith, then receding with an all-encompassing sucking sound.

Chloe danced along the high tide line of the surf. Perhaps she felt a special freedom being away from the likes of Obregon. Sam had to admit he felt a certain relief having resolved the confrontation peacefully. What was a few hundred thousand dollars in drug money. Had Obregon been put up to it? He'd made references to property being returned. Did that imply a connection to Andropov? Could Andropov be here?

JoAnne leaned into Sam. "You're thinking too much. Look around you. This place is beautiful. Look at that moon. I love its light on the water."

"I feel at peace here, too. But I can't get away from a stark realization. People are out there who would kill us as soon as look at us, and for what? To get a hold of Chloe?"

"Sam, you know I feel the same way you do." She gave his arm a squeeze. "I don't think you can stay here any longer. It's too dangerous. Too volatile. There's money-mad Obregon, who won't be satisfied even though you've given him a fortune. There's Marcelo, who is urbane and nice enough, but he's a drug dealer, for Christ's sake. And now Andropov seems to be lurking somewhere behind the scenes."

"What are you suggesting I do?"

307

"You call the FBI, find out who's in charge of looking for you and negotiate your return with Chloe to the States. If they agree to let you keep custody of her and give you amnesty for transporting a sentient, then you can agree to testify in their prosecution of Andropov."

"It might work. I'll call the FBI when we get back to Heidi's. If they can give me assurances in writing, we can drive to Manzanillo and catch a flight to Denver." Sam looked ahead and worried Chloe was getting too close to the shore break. "That's far enough, Chloe!"

But she couldn't have heard a word he said over the pounding surf.

Sam released JoAnne's hand. "I have to get her. She's too close." He'd been monitoring the waves coming up to the beach. They came in sets of five to eight with the last couple of waves in the set the largest. He'd counted six in the current set.

The seventh wave reared up, a true goliath compared to the rest. It crashed and shot up the beach, its whitewater frothing.

Chloe's legs came out from under her.

The force of the wave pushed her up above the seaweed strewn high tide line on the sand, paused, then with an ominous sucking, it dragged her tumbling and screaming into the sea.

Sam ran, his feet sinking deep into wet, loose sand. He lost all care about everything, Lukas, Andropov, Obregon, his heart. He focused on Chloe, who bobbed as strong shore currents swept her farther out.

JoAnne's plaintive voice came to him from the dark beach, pleading with him to come back. But he barely heard her. He was on a reflexive drive. Adrenalin was kicking in. In the back of his mind, a worry alerted him he was up against something big, something very physical, something that could kill him. But Chloe was adrift. There was no one else to save her.

He kicked off his shoes and plunged into the surf.

The last wave in the set reared and knocked him over. He held his breath as the turbulent water shook him like a rag doll, rolling him over, pounding him onto the sand. It let him go as it raced up the beach.

He staggered to his feet sputtering.

JoAnne shouted hysterically behind him.

But he wasn't going to be beaten.

Be sensible. You can't force your way through this surf, you have to go under it.

Another wave reared and started to crash.

Sam dove into the bottom of it and let the water curl over him, its force barely reaching down to pull at his hair. He came up on the back side and shook water from his eyes, then stroked furiously to get out beyond the shore break.

"Chloe!" He struggled to tread water as he scanned the agitated surface of the sea, searching for any sign of her.

"Chloe!" She couldn't have gone under already. He refused to believe that. Once beyond the shore break, he kicked hard, rearing up on ocean swells, trying to raise his head high enough to see.

"Grandpa!" A brief scream cut short.

"Chloe!" He swam in the direction of her voice.

His clothes dragged him down.

"Chloe!"

Nothing. He stabbed at the water, pulling himself forward, fearing he was going in the wrong direction.

His hand hit a soft bundle below the surface.

"Chloe, Chloe!" He pulled her to the surface.

She floated limp in his arms.

He turned her toward him, kicking to keep them both above water. He blew air into her lungs.

She coughed and started to breath.

Her eyes stayed closed.

We're going to be okay.

Then, what seemed like a vise clamped down on his chest. It squeezed and squeezed until all thought of ever being free of it evaporated from his mind.

Not now godammit.

He tried to keep Chloe afloat in the shifting water. First he was close to her, feeling her small body in his arms, the brush of her hair against his cheek, then he weakened and began to sink. He extended her at arm's length, as his head went below water.

He let her go lest he drag her down with him. Air escaped his lips in tiny bubbles. He felt heavy. The clamp in his chest whispered to him of death and dying.

His lungs labored for air. His eyes bulged, open, straining and seeing nothing but darkness and feeling only the sting of the ocean's salt. Would his life flash before his eyes? What did anyone know? He guessed everyone died a little differently.

So this is how it will end. Me gone. Chloe gone. Our bodies washing up on the beach with tomorrow's tide.

***

A steady thrumming grew louder. A throbbing vibration. A drumbeat, heralding the entrance into the afterworld? The noise shattered all thought, all sense.

Rough hands grappled at his shoulders, pulling him up, dragging him hard against the gunwale of a boat.

"*Andale!*"

Fishermen. A fisherman's boat.

Sam felt like a sail-finned Dorado, hooked and drawn over the side. He would have flopped in gratitude but the energy eluded him. Water poured from his mouth, and when that was gone he coughed up more from his lungs in a heaving spasm.

"*Señor*, are you all right?" A dark skinned face, devoid of front teeth peered inches from him.

Sam couldn't answer, just waved a hand. So convenient, the hand wave. Universal coverage. Universal understanding.

"We have the girl, *tambien*."

The pronouncement seared through all else. They had Chloe. All would be well. All would, unless the agony in his chest rendered him before he could get to shore and down one of his pills. In retrospect, Doctor Collins hadn't done him a favor,

311

dispensing the pills. All they had accomplished was a prolongation of life, a prolongation of agony. But that was unfair. He wanted to live. Chloe needed him.

The boat, no more than a long skiff with an outboard thrumming at the back, did a wide turn and headed for the beach. It paused, the pilot judging the swells before accelerating on an incoming wave and roaring with the wash up onto the beach until keel met sandy friction and stopped.

JoAnne was beside him in an instant. "Thank God you're all right." Then she was over to Chloe.

"Sam!" JoAnne called back. "She's okay!"

Sam lay back and let the relief wash over him, a soothing balm, if it could only dull the pain that hammered his chest.

"JoAnne, my pills." He always carried them and they were in his fanny pack but he couldn't reach them. He felt uncoordinated and stupid.

JoAnne was back and in his face. "Be still. I'll dig out the pills. You relax."

It was nice someone was taking charge. He couldn't. "Thanks," he said.

She brought the pill container out and opened it, then shook out a pill. "One or two?"

"One," Sam said.

Sam felt the pill pushed into his mouth. He tried to lift his head to see Chloe.

JoAnne pushed him back. "She's good, Sam. Don't worry about her. We have to get you to a hospital."

"Okay." Sam lay back exhausted. Let someone else take charge.

"These fishermen saved your life," JoAnne said. "I'm going to give them some money from your fanny pack."

Sam waved his hand again, thankful it was all he had to do.

"Here comes Heidi," JoAnne said.

Heidi ran up the beach. She must have seen what had happened or at least been attracted to all the activity. Her villa, after all, overlooked all of Playa de Cerro Bonito. "Are they all right?"

"He needs medical attention," JoAnne said.

"Then we must get him to Manzanillo. It has the nearest hospital." Heidi withdrew her cell. "I have a doctor friend, here in Cerro. A moment." She pressed buttons, then spoke into the cell.

"Doctor Alvarez will come. He'll bring Cerro's ambulance. It is primitive, but it will take Sam to Manzanillo."

"Thank you." JoAnne turned back to Sam. "It's okay. We're taking you to Manzanillo. A doctor is coming."

Sam tried to focus. "JoAnne." He reached up and pulled on her arm. "Chloe. Don't let anything happen to Chloe."

JoAnne leaned down and embraced him. "Nothing is going to happen to Chloe. I will come with you and so will she."

Chloe brushed past the line of fishermen who were blocking her from seeing what they probably thought was a dying man.

"Grandpa!" She fell into his arms.

"You're okay." Sam reveled in her worried embrace. How wonderful to be needed so much.

313

"But you?" Chloe said. "You almost drowned."

"Nah. I wouldn't drown saving you, would I?"

She gazed at him for a second, then laid her head on his chest. "Thank you, Grandpa."

***

Naked except for his white boxer shorts, Demetri paced his small hotel room. The single ceiling fan twirling overhead gave little relief from the hot, humid air. He rubbed his face and neck with a wet towel in an attempt to cool off.

Why hasn't Obregon called?

Demetri grabbed the phone and dialed Obregon's number.

"*Si.*" Obregon's gravelly voice.

"It's me," Demetri said. "What happened?"

The clink of ice in a glass sounded at the other end of the line.

Obregon gave a little laugh. "Well, *Señor* Andropov, nothing happened."

Demetri's stomach gave a lurching turn.

I wired one hundred thousand dollars to this pompous ass and now he's telling me nothing happened?

"Would you mind expanding on that a little?"

"Not over the phone. I will meet you in ten minutes outside the *El Dorado*. It's a bar up the street from your hotel. We can walk down to the beach from there. I will tell you everything."

Obregon hung up.

Demetri threw the phone against the wall where it left a dent in the wallboard and fell to the floor. He threw himself on the bed and hammered the pillow with his fists, then rolled over onto his back

314

and dug the palms of his hands at his eyes, squeezing away tears. His hands came off his eyes and he pressed his temples.

What the fuck is he up to? Shit. He said ten minutes.

Demetri pulled on a faded aloha shirt and a pair of shorts, slipped into sandals and hurried out the door. His sandals slapped on the tiled surface of the stairs, the sound echoing off the plastered walls. He burst into the lobby and ran past the night clerk.

"*Buenas noches, Señor,*" the clerk said.

Demetri ignored him and rushed out onto the sidewalk. He looked up and down the dimly lit street. A block up, a red and yellow sign with half its tubes burnt out, blinked *El Dorado*.

He ran, stubbed his toe and nearly fell.

God damn sidewalks.

He got to the *El Dorado* and stood out front, gasping for air, waiting, trying to think. The thump of music that issued from the bar would have torn the cones out of the speakers anywhere else.

El Dorado was probably an appropriate place for him to meet Obregon. Why shouldn't he rendezvous at a location legend held to be a kingdom of gold, a place where any fool could acquire wealth and riches? Obregon had. Did that make Demetri the fool?

"*Señor*, you want sex?"

Demetri jumped. He looked to his right at a diminutive female, slightly shorter than himself, no waist to speak of, wearing a black leather skirt and a low cut loose fitting blouse.

315

"What?" He couldn't believe prostitution was practiced so openly. At least in the States there was an attempt curb it.

"You want sex? One hundred pesos or ten US."

"Go away."

The woman, for she wasn't that young to be called a girl, looked around, then pressed up against him and tried to grab his crotch.

"You don't take no for an answer, do you?" He gave her a shove.

One of her high heels caught and she sprawled onto the pavement. With a snarl of what Demetri could only guess were obscenities in Spanish, she pushed to her feet and started to turn on him.

A black Mercedes pulled up to the curb.

The prostitute took a quick look at the car and scrambled around the corner of the building as fast as she had appeared.

Obregon? Demetri bent down and tried to get a look through the tinted windows. *Nice car. The asshole can probably afford it with all the money he steals.*

Obregon got out and said something to the driver who eased the car down the street and parked. "*Señor* Andropov." Obregon shook Demetri's hand. "Nice shirt. It looked to me as if it was attracting flies."

Fuck this. "Let's get to the point, Obregon. What happened?"

Obregon took Demetri by the elbow and directed him to a sandy beach access on one side of

316

the bar. "Let us walk on the beach. It will be quieter and we won't be interrupted."

Probably not seen either.

Once on the beach, Obregon pulled a silver flask out of his pocket and offered it to Demetri. "Have a drink, *Señor*, there's a chill in the ocean breeze tonight."

Demetri shook his head. *It's like a goddamned sauna out here.*

Obregon shrugged and took a long pull from the flask, licked his lips and slid the flask back into his pocket. His countenance clouded as he assumed a thoughtful look, putting his hands behind his back as he strolled. A strong smell of cognac lifted off his body.

"*Señor* Andropov, you must realize that in matters of this nature, desired outcomes cannot always be assured. Be that as it may, we who must undertake exercises like this still expose ourselves to extreme risk."

"Level with me, Obregon. Did you get the clone or not?"

"Unfortunately, no. I did not get the clone. I made an honest effort. She and her guardian, *Señor* Turner, were dining at the villa of Marcelo Lopez. You know of whom I am speaking?"

"Lopez? No. Who's he?"

"He's a drug dealer. He runs the biggest operation in Jalisco."

That surprised Demetri. This Turner sure was getting around. "Turner is keeping company with a drug dealer?"

317

"So it seems. And that is where I ran into problems. Marcelo employs a veritable army of thugs...for security, you understand. Which meant I had to undertake this exercise with a veritable army myself. To make a long story short, it was a standoff. To avoid unnecessary bloodshed, I had to come away empty-handed."

"All right. I'm not in a big hurry. When will you make another attempt?"

"Another attempt?" Obregon stopped and peered at Demetri. "But you paid for only one."

Demetri's dinner teased the bottom of his esophagus. He swallowed hard. One hundred thousand dollars had about cleaned him out, and this little shit was going to walk away without delivering? "You fucking bastard! You're stiffing me!"

Obregon's thumb and first finger smoothed his mustache.

Does he do that when he gets angry? Or was it more a conditioned response, like a cat's tail twitching before it pounced on a small rodent?

"Is that what they call it in English?" Obregon asked, his eyes narrowing to slits, his irises disappearing altogether into an opaque blackness. "Stiffing? As in a rod shoved vertically into one's rectum?"

Demetri was developing a searing hatred for this arrogant man. He tried to keep anger out of his voice but failed. "This ain't funny, Obregon!"

"No, I see you don't find it so."

They came to a boardwalk that cut across the sand and led to a broken-down pier, the rotted

318

timbers of which were buffeted by waves. Obergon's Mercedes was parked at the town side end of the boardwalk.

"This is where I leave you, *Señor*." Obregon indicated the Mercedes.

"Leave?" Demetri felt apoplectic. "Where the hell are you going? We had a fucking deal!"

Obregon mounted the boardwalk and strode toward the Mercedes.

The vehicle's motor came to life and the headlights snapped on.

Demetri ran after Obregon and caught up to him at the car. He grabbed him on the shoulder and spun him around.

Obregon held a service revolver in his hand, low, pointed at Demetri's stomach. "No one will hear if I shoot you, now. Shall I find out?"

Crazy drunken bastard.

Resigned, Demetri thrust his hands out and up, backed up a step, then ran up the street toward his hotel. Behind him he heard the door of the Mercedes slam shut and the purr of its engine as it pulled away.

What am I going to do?

He barged through the lobby.

The clerk looked up but said nothing this time.

Breathing heavily, Demetri sandal-slapped his way up the stairs.

In his room, he ran to the balcony that overlooked the street.

The red taillights of the Mercedes receded to the end of the main street, made a right turn away from the beach at the nature preserve and headed for the highway.

Victor. I'll call Victor.

He ran back into the room and dropped onto all fours to scramble for the phone, which was still off the hook and now making a repetitive beeping sound. At least it was working.

He sat on the bed, dug Victor's number out of his wallet and dialed.

Please pickup.

"Gallego."

"Victor, it's me, Demetri."

"Demetri, how are you? No, don't tell me. Let me guess. I hear heavy breathing. You are in trouble."

Demetri tried to stop gulping air. "Yeah, I got trouble. Lots of it. I'm in Cerro Bonito."

"Ah...Cerro Bonito, lovely place. Have you tried dining at *El Pescado*? I hear it's a wonderful restaurant."

"Cut the crap, Victor. I've had lunch there already with Colonel Obregon."

"Obregon? Whatever for?"

"I made a deal with him to get the clone back. I just talked to the little shit. No clone. He's stiffing me. Taking my money and running."

Victor made sympathetic sounds at the other end of the line. "Demetri, I wish you had called me first. I could have told you Obregon is not reliable. How much did you lose?"

"A hundred grand."

320

"A hundred. That's a lot of donuts, no? You got anything left to pay me for all these clients you are sending down here?"

"Have I ever not paid you?!"

"True. But a hundred grand?"

"Never mind about that. There's more money where that came from. But I have to get the clone back or all bets are off."

"So, you call me to tell me these problems so I won't be surprised when you don't pay me?"

"Don't be a fool. Of course I'm going to pay. But I need help." Demetri reached for the now dry towel on his bed and wiped sweat that had begun to cascade out of his hairline, down his forehead to sting his eyes.

"I begin to smell day old fish," Victor said. "You want me to help you get your clone back."

Demetri squinted his eyes against the sting. "Yeah. Can you do it?"

There was a pause at the other end of the line. "Sure, Demetri, I can do it. We go back a long way...to the old country. What are friends for? I have an address, the *Casa Mirador*. Is the girl still there?"

"I don't know. She could be there some of the time. Obregon tried to get her when she was at a villa owned by a Marcelo Lopez. You know him?"

"Of course. Everyone knows Marcelo. Tough character. Well protected. Where are you staying?"

"*The Marina Fiesta.*"

"I'll be in touch."

"I knew I could count on you. How soon can you get this done?"

"A day. Maybe two. No problem. But it's going to cost you."

322

Chapter Fifteen

Sam breathed a sigh of relief when the ambulance rolled to a stop at the emergency entrance to the *Hospital General de Manzanillo*. The ride there had seemed without end, the ambulance in need of new shock absorbers.

JoAnne had clutched one of Sam's hands the whole way and Chloe the other.

Doctor Alvarez checked Sam periodically, but in the end seemed satisfied Sam was going to make it on the basis of the miracle pill he had taken.

Sam was wheeled into the ER, given a cursory examination by the physician on duty, then assigned to a room. Since he had stabilized, he was to be kept for observation while tests were taken to determine if he had indeed had a heart attack.

Despite all the commotion going on around him, Sam felt well. "I don't think it was a heart attack," he said to JoAnne.

"Since when would you know the difference?" JoAnne patted his hand. "Let the doctors do their job."

Chloe sat on a chair beside Sam's bed. She seemed especially quiet, as she fingered the cross on the chain around her neck. Sam could only surmise all the talk about his heart was disturbing her.

Doctor Alvarez came into the room. "We have the test results, and you did not have a heart attack. We aren't sure what happened. Perhaps excess stress set up cramps in your chest that seemed like a heart attack. We don't know. I've examined you and can't find anything out of the ordinary."

"That's good news." Sam glanced at JoAnne and squeezed her hand. "I think I'm going to live." He tried to follow up with a smile, but exhaustion kept his lips in a line on his face.

"How long will he have to stay here, Doctor?" JoAnne asked.

"I think he should rest overnight. We'll see how he is in the morning, and if everything is okay, I don't see why he couldn't return to Cerro Bonito tomorrow afternoon. Mind you, he'll have to take it easy for a few days if not weeks. His body did suffer a major strain."

"I was so afraid it was a heart attack," JoAnne said. "All we have is a number of a contact in Guadalajara if something real did happen."

"Guadalajara?"

"Sam was given the name of a Victor Gallego. Sam has been waiting for a heart transplant."

Alvarez frowned. "No one told me he had a history of heart disease. If indeed he needs a transplant, then he is very lucky to have survived this latest crisis. But Victor Gallego?"

"Yes," JoAnne said, concerned. "Is something wrong?"

"I don't know *el Señor* Gallego personally, but I do know he works in referring patients from the States to Doctor Mendoza. This is especially true now that the laws governing the use of clones as organ donors has changed in the States."

Chloe whimpered.

JoAnne came over and put an arm around her. "It's okay, Chloe. We aren't talking about you."

"Grandpa told me to stay away from Mr. Gallego."

"Is that true, Sam?"

"It's true. I had a bad feeling about the guy. But in retrospect, I think I still would have contacted him. To cover my options."

Alvarez looked surprised. "You've already contacted Gallego?"

"Sam was a client of the organ farm, Clonal Transplants," JoAnne said with a hint of distaste. "I'm relieved to say he no longer is. I never believed in the practice. But he did contact Mr. Gallego when he passed through Guadalajara on his way here to Cerro Bonito."

"*Señora*, in my opinion, Victor Gallego would be the last person I would turn to if I had a heart attack."

"But why?"

"I have heard stories about the collaboration between Gallego and Mendoza. This is hearsay, so I don't want to give them credence by repeating them."

Sam struggled to sit up. "Then what do you suggest? Manzanillo isn't setup to deal with a major heart attack, certainly not one requiring a transplant."

"*Señor* Turner, you are correct in that conclusion. Your only hope is Guadalajara. But I would caution you about Gallego. That is all I care to say. I'm sure it is obvious you would be better off in the States even if you are no longer a Clonal Transplant client. If you'll excuse me, I must get back to Cerro Bonito. You will be in good hands here, not to worry."

Sam was a bit surprised by Alvarez' rapid departure, but figured if there was nothing particularly wrong, then a regular staff doctor could check him over in the morning and sign a release form.

"Sam," JoAnne said. "I think it's time you called the FBI."

"I can't." Sam gave an exhausted sigh and lay back on his pillows. "I'm too weak to carry much of a conversation. You'll have to do it. You can speak for me. I trust you. Just get me out of here." He closed his eyes.

"You sleep." JoAnne pulled the covers up to Sam's chin against the chill of the hospital's air-conditioning. "I'll make the call outside in one of the waiting rooms. Chloe, do you want to come with me?"

"Can I stay with Grandpa?"

"Of course you can.

Sam felt Chloe's hand slip into his and gave it a squeeze.

***

Wellstone kept nodding off as he sat in his chair behind his desk. The long hours and the heat of Nogales had finally caught up with him. He hadn't received a break in the case for over forty-eight hours. Surely Turner and the clone had come to ground. And as surely Colonel Obregon must know where they were and what they were doing. Wellstone couldn't understand the lack of

326

information coming from south of the border. What was Obregon up to?

"Sir?" Marshall waved at Wellstone from his desk ten feet away.

Wellstone stopped nodding and blinked sleep out of his eyes. "What is it, Marshall?"

"Line three. Denver is patching through a call from Manzanillo. It's the woman, JoAnne Calder."

Wellstone lunged forward and picked up the phone. "Hello. Agent Wellstone."

"This is JoAnne Calder. Are you the agent in charge of the Andropov case?"

"That's not what we call it, Miss Calder, but if you have information on that case then I'm the agent you should be talking to."

"I'm calling from the *Hospital General de Manzanillo* on behalf of Sam Turner."

Wellstone grabbed a pencil and began taking notes. He waved to Marshall, who was listening in, to do the same. "May I ask the purpose of your call?"

"As you know Mr. Turner has a heart condition. Yesterday, he had what was thought to be a heart attack, but it turned out to be something less severe. In any case, he is being kept here in the hospital overnight for observation."

"I'm sorry to hear that. Is there anything we can do?"

"He wants to come back to the States as soon as he is well enough to travel. He has the clone with him."

"That would be Chloe. She's the clone we are interested in."

"As I told two of your agents when they interviewed me, Mr. Turner thought of bringing Chloe to Mexico so he could proceed with his transplant operation. Of course, that was before he realized she was sentient. Be that as it may, he continued on to Mexico out of a fear your office was after him and would take Chloe into custody with no assurances he would ever see her again. He intended to stay here until the legality of the new law regarding clones was clarified. Unfortunately, his situation has become untenable."

Wellstone scribbled *untenable* on his notepad and underlined it. "In what way, Miss Calder?"

"We believe Demetri Andropov is here."

"I figured he'd show up. Has he threatened you?"

"Not directly. But someone is trying to get hold of Chloe. This being Mexico, and Mr. Andropov being a person of little character, we fear he will find a way, that he will buy a way, to get at Chloe."

"Miss Calder, if I may be so bold to suggest, I think your best course of action is to return to the States."

"We've come to the same conclusion. However, Mr. Turner has two concerns in that regard. First, he's afraid if he returns to the States with Chloe, you will take her away from him. And, second, he fears prosecution for having transported a sentient clone across state and international borders."

This Calder is as cool as a cucumber.
Wellstone covered the mouthpiece. "Marshall, get

328

Peterson in here." He returned to his conversation with JoAnne. "Miss Calder, I can assure you the Bureau is not in the business of taking children away from their parents or lawful guardians. We also aren't in the business of compromising prime witnesses."

"You haven't answered my question, Agent Wellstone. If you can't promise me Chloe will be left alone and that Mr. Turner will not be prosecuted, then this conversation is going to end."

Shit. Where's Peterson. "Hold, on Miss Calder. I'm going to have to consult with my legal counsel. Can you hold a minute?"

"I'll hold."

Wellstone stabbed the hold button. "Peterson!"

"I'm right here, chief." Peterson had come up on Wellstone from the side.

"It's JoAnne Calder," Wellstone said, "the lady friend of Sam Turner. He's in a hospital in Mexico and wants to come home with the clone and be offered immunity from prosecution for his testimony. What's our position as regards taking them into custody?"

Peterson smirked. "We've got him dead to rights, sir. He's crossed State lines with a known sentient clone. He's crossed an international border. We could grab him and hold him indefinitely...after charging him of course. As for the clone. She'd be ours. She'd be caught up in the system and he'd never see her again."

"Really?" Wellstone was surprised. Seemed pretty harsh.

"Since she's a clone," Peterson said, "she has no legal status, despite her being sentient. The laws haven't caught up with the times."

Wellstone drummed his fingers on the desk, then raised his thumb to his mouth and started chewing a nail. "Turner won't come back unless we can assure him of immunity and that we won't take the clone away from him."

"I suppose there'd be a way to give him that assurance. As long as we know where the clone is, and he agrees not to leave the country again with her, whether she is in our direct custody, or he has her won't affect any case we bring against Andropov."

"Can you draw up something? We're going to have to fax it down there. Calder won't take my word for it."

"Yeah, I can type something up. You going to sign it?"

"Who else? We don't have time."

"Will do." Peterson returned to his desk on the other side of the room, shoved his computer mouse around while looking at the monitor, then began typing on his keyboard.

Wellstone released the hold button. "Miss Calder, are you still there?"

"I am. This call is beginning to cost me a fortune."

"I'm sorry to have kept you waiting. We can always have the charges reversed. I've discussed the matter of Mr. Turner's return with my legal counsel, and he is at this moment drawing up a document, which after I sign, will serve as a guarantee the Bureau will not attempt to separate the girl in question from Mr. Turner. As regards immunity, it will require Mr. Turner's full cooperation with the Department of Justice in the prosecution of one Demetri Andropov. Am I making myself clear?"

"Crystal."

Wellstone let out a silent sigh of relief. "Can you give me a fax number down there where we can send the document?"

There was a moment's silence, then JoAnne came back on the line and gave him the number. "That's to the hospital in Manzanillo. We will be here, until tomorrow afternoon."

Wellstone repeated the number. "Got it. Now, how does Mr. Turner and the girl intend to return to the States?"

"There are flights out of Manzanillo. But I understand the connections are horrendous. We might have to go to Guadalajara to get a direct flight."

"And when do you think you will be able to leave?"

"That's still to be decided. It all depends on how Sam feels."

"Of course, quite understandable. But I'm concerned about Mr. Turner's safety and that of Chloe."

"We're worried, too. What do you suggest?"

"We have a liaison down there who can insure your safety. You can trust him absolutely. You have my assurances. His name is Colonel Luciano Obregon. I'll be contacting him--"

331

Wellstone stared at the phone. "Marshall, what just happened?"

"She hung up, sir when you mentioned Obregon."

"That's odd. Call her back."

"I've tried, sir. She isn't answering."

"All right. If she wants to play cute, so can we. We have a direct line to Obregon. Call him and alert him to this new situation. I want Turner and the clone taken into custody. If they have to surround the hospital, then have them do it."

Marshall looked up the number and dialed. He spoke for several minutes with someone on the other end of the line, then hung up.

"Sir?"

"What is it, Marshall?" Wellstone was getting impatient with all the delays.

"I couldn't reach Obregon. When I dialed his number, it was transferred to another agency. After identifying myself, I asked to speak to Obregon. They said he boarded a flight to Cuba earlier this evening."

"Cuba? Why the hell is he going to Cuba in the midst of an investigation?"

"They suspect he was going to Cuba for good, like immigrating and never returning to Mexico."

"Are they all money grubbers down there? Someone must have gotten to him. Androp? Maybe. Turner? Possibly. He's a rich man."

"My thoughts exactly, sir. You still want the immunity faxed?"

Wellstone glanced over to Peterson, who was still typing away at his computer. "Yeah. Can't

332

hurt. While we're waiting, call the airport and get hold of our pilot. I'm going to Mexico."

***

Sam awoke the next morning feeling like he'd been hit by a truck. If there was a muscle in his body that didn't ache, he would have paid money to know about it.

JoAnne lay asleep on a folding cot that had been brought in for her. Chloe snoozed in one of the larger chairs.

A vague feeling of apprehension swept over him. *Where's that coming from*? Then he remembered JoAnne's conversation with Wellstone and his association with the corrupt Obregon. What was the world coming to? What good was an immunity document from this guy Wellstone? Did he even have the authority to sign one?

A nurse came in and checked Sam's vital signs. "Everything is very good, *Señor* Turner. The doctor will see you when he makes his rounds in about an hour."

Sam was served a light breakfast, which he didn't eat.

JoAnne awoke. "What a horrible night. Can we get out of here? All I want is a shower."

"The nurse said the doctor would be in shortly. I suppose if I check out okay, they'll release me."

"Are you going to eat that roll?"

Two hours later, after what seemed interminable delays, a hospital aid rolled Sam in a wheelchair out the door to the patient pickup area where a taxi awaited them.

Sam pressed ten dollars into the hand of the reluctant aid, and with his and JoAnne's help got into the back seat of the taxi.

JoAnne took Chloe by the hand and rounded to the other side to join him. She leaned toward the cabbie in front. "We want to go to Cerro Bonito. How much will that cost?"

"Cerro Bonito. Okay. Five hundred pesos. You can call me Paco."

"That's fine, Paco." She eased back onto the seat, as the cab pulled out into busy street traffic. "Are you comfortable?" she asked Sam.

"I'm fine, as long as I don't have to move too quickly."

Sam winced as they almost collided with a car coming from his side. That would be the supreme irony...to die in a traffic accident in Manzanillo. He supposed it was a step up the ironic scale from being found washed up drowned on the beach in Cerro Bonito.

"I'll call Heidi and let her know we are on our way." JoAnne took out her cell phone and punched in Heidi's number. After a brief conversation, JoAnne clapped the phone closed and turned to Sam with a frown on her face.

"What is it." Sam had given up trying to get comfortable on the small seat.

"She said she didn't think it was safe for you to stay at *Casa Mirador*. That Lukas was acting very strangely."

"Has Lukas ever acted normally? Where does she expect us to go? The *Marina Fiesta*?"

"She suggested Marcelo might put us up until we can get a flight out of here. It would only be for a day or two."

"We can try." Sam lowered his voice so Paco couldn't hear him. "I never thought I'd be asking a drug lord for protection, but there's a first for everything. We still have to go to the bungalow to get the money, and we can't leave those guns under the bed."

Forty-five minutes later they came to *Casa Mirador*. Heidi let them in. "I've called Marcelo. He agreed to take you. I think Lukas is passed out in his room. At least I haven't seen him the last hour."

"We'll only be a minute," Sam said. He got out of the taxi while JoAnne paid Paco. Sam climbed the back stairs to the bungalow with Heidi's help. The Hummer was parked underneath. Good for Marcelo. They entered and crossed the living room to the bedroom.

Lukas sat on the bed, a bottle of tequila in one hand and the machine pistol in the other. He waved it drunkenly in Sam's direction. "Welcome home, Turner."

"Lukas!" Heidi yelled. "Leave this room immediately!"

"Shut up, Mother." Lukas took a swig from the bottle. "Look what I found under the bed." He giggled.

"You've got the gun," Sam said. "What do you want?"

"Well..." He pulled the trigger and sent a burst across the wooden doors of the closet. "Works!"

335

JoAnne and Chloe crowded into the room. "What was that? Oh my god." JoAnne stopped short, hand to mouth.

Sam motioned her back into the living room. "I'll take care of this." Once they had retreated, he turned back to Lukas. "You're going to kill someone if you're not careful. I asked you what you wanted."

Lukas caressed the side of the pistol. "First off, I want to be paid for my jeep. It's over in Marcelo's compound, and I don't think he has any intention of giving it back to me."

"I'll pay you for your jeep."

Lukas' head snapped up. "You will?"

"How much?"

Back to the caress. "It cost me used ten thousand pesos."

"Sam dug into his fanny pack and pulled out a wad of one hundred dollar bills. He crossed in front of Lukas and sat at the head of the bed, where he proceeded to count out the money. "Here's a thousand dollars. That should cover it."

Lukas took the money and stared at the remaining wad in Sam's hand. "That looks like a lot of money you have there, Turner." He drifted the barrel of the rifle to point at Sam's legs.

"It is."

"How about I tell you a secret--" He burped, then giggled. "--and you give me that there wad."

"What makes you think your secret is worth as much as this wad."

"I'm sure all right. Chloe, Chloe, Chloe," he sang.

336

"What about Chloe?"

"That's the secret part."

Sam handed Lukas the remaining bills. "All right. Let's hear it."

Lukas stood. Shoved all the bills into a pocket and rested the barrel of the pistol on his shoulder. "You got any more guns?"

"What's the secret, Lukas?"

"Something big is coming down. Maybe today. Maybe tomorrow. Gang from Guadalajara. I heard all about it. I'd be real protective of your little girl, Turner." Lukas stood unsteadily and took a lurching step toward the bedroom door.

The bullet riddled closet door came off its track and crashed to the floor.

"Well, well, what do we have here?" Lukas stepped over to eye the wall safe.

Sam slipped his hand under the bed pillow and felt for the Derringer he had taken away from Chloe. His hand closed around the handle.

Lukas looked back over his shoulder. "You know how to open this?"

"I do." When Lukas turned back to the safe, Sam stood and closed the distance between them, the Derringer held at his side out of sight.

"Then open it," Lukas demanded.

Sam came up beside him and raised the Derringer to the underside of Lukas' jaw. "I think you're done here, Lukas," Sam said, his face inches from Lukas' ear. "Let me have the pistol, real easy, now."

Lukas strained away from the barrel pressed to his neck, but held out the pistol.

337

Sam grabbed the gun and stepped back. "Let's take a walk out to the terrace." He motioned with the Derringer.

Lukas stared dumbly, very drunk. He stumbled out of the bedroom, crossed the living room without looking at anyone and banged through the screen door.

Sam kept close behind him. "You're not going to be a problem are you?"

Lukas burped and wiped his mouth with the back of his hand. "I don't feel so good, Mister."

"Why don't you go up to the bungalow and take a nap?"

Lukas nodded, then stumbled up the walk.

Maybe I should have tied him up? Sam thought. But the man seemed pathetically out of it. In any case, Sam had the gun and didn't expect to stay long.

He tried to collect himself after the confrontation. All internal systems seemed to be functioning without breaking down. He took a deep breath, then another one.

Chloe was at his side in an instant. She grasped his leg in a desperate hug.

JoAnne hurried over to him. "Are you going to be all right? I thought he was going to kill you. I thought he was going to kill all of us."

Sam indicated the bed where JoAnne helped him sit down. "If he had, I don't think it would have been on purpose, just a result of accidentally pulling the trigger on that weapon. It's my fault for keeping the damn thing."

Heidi came over to them. "I am ashamed of my son. He is nothing but a petty thief, demanding money of you and for what, a broken down jeep and a fabrication about Guadalajara gangs. We always have pressure from those gangs here. Thanks to Marcelo, they stay away."

Sam striped a pillow case off a pillow. "I'm going to borrow this if I may."

Heidi seemed surprised, but nodded.

Sam walked to the safe, punched in the combination and opened the door, then began dragging packets of money out and stuffing them into the pillow case.

"Oh my God," Heidi exclaimed. "I have never seen so much money in my life."

"It's a good thing Lukas didn't make me open it," Sam said. "I got off easy giving him a few thousand dollars."

Heidi began to cry.

JoAnne put an arm around her and looked at Sam.

He realized he'd been so wrapped up with his own problems, he'd forgotten about Heidi's. He drew JoAnne to one side. "Do you know the balance of her mortgage?"

"I think it's about fifty thousand."

Sam walked back over to Heidi, took her hands and pulled them toward him palms up. "Hold them there for a moment." He stacked seven ten thousand dollar packet onto them.

She stared at the money, then looked up to him and started to say something.

He held up his hand. "Not a word. It's not my money anyway, and at this point you could use some of it better than I can. Just don't show it to Lukas."

Heidi nodded and pressed the pile close to her chest as she leaned forward and up to give Sam a kiss on the cheek.

"Now, where was I," Sam said, returning to unload the safe into the pillow case. When that was done, he took a deep breath before replacing the machine pistol and Derringer into the blanket and tucking it under his arm.

JoAnne had gone through the rooms and collected the few clothes and toiletries they had. "I think we're ready." She embraced Heidi.

Chloe embraced Heidi. Then Sam did so, again.

After two trips, everything was in the Hummer.

They eased out of the gate, with Heidi trying to wave good bye and only succeeding in dropping one of the packets on the ground.

***

"There are the *cocodrilos* Francisco showed me, Grandpa."

With JoAnne driving, they had come to the end of the main street and were about to turn onto the dirt track that would skirt the nature preserve and take them to Marcelo's.

Four large crocodiles lay on the near shore, which was separated by an estuary from the other side where three more crocodiles lounged. It being late afternoon, they slept, opening their mouths from time to time, a way to dissipate the afternoon

340

heat. Pink flamingos stood in the shallows a safe distance from the reptiles, stabbing their beaks into the water and coming up with wriggling fish.

Did Marcelo use the crocs as a human garbage disposal? Sam hoped he never had to find out for sure.

JoAnne bumped over the dirt track and came to a stop at the entrance gate to Marcelo's compound.

The same guard as before came out to greet them. This time, though he still carried his machine pistol, he wore a big smile on his face. "Welcome, *Señora*, *Señor*, *nieta chiquita*." He waved them through.

"What a difference a couple of days make," Sam said. "When we get there, I'm going to have to talk to Marcelo alone for a while, if you don't mind. I've got to make it clear we are in danger. I also have to think of a way to compensate him."

JoAnne gave Sam a quick nod, then concentrated on her driving, obviously not wanting to over-steer the unfamiliar Hummer into a flower bed.

Marcelo must have been alerted by the gate guard, for he was waiting for them at the entrance to the villa.

He opened the Hummer's door for Sam, probably having decided that between Sam and JoAnne, he was the more frail.

In the meantime, JoAnne had jumped out and come around to Sam's side.

"Thanks," Sam said to Marcelo, who gave him an arm. "I hate feeling so weak. I think as long as I take it slow, I'll be okay."

341

Francisco bounded out of the house and ran up to the back passenger side where Chloe still sat. She peered out the tinted windows as if she were waiting for Francisco to open the door for her.

He pulled the door open and extended his hand. "Welcome, Chloe. I have missed you."

"And I missed you, too, Francisco." This with a dramatic sweep of her hand before they both dissolved into childish laughter.

Sam had to smile at the give and take.

Francisco took Chloe by the hand. "I'm sorry to learn about your mishap the other night. From what little I have been told, you almost drowned."

"Yes," Chloe said, clutching his hand in both of hers. "If it hadn't been for Grandpa and those fishermen, I would have."

"Then let me make a suggestion." Francisco took her by the shoulders and peered into her eyes. "We have a pool out back. It is not very deep. I would like to take you there and teach you how to swim." He looked back at Marcelo, who nodded and gave them a *go do it* wave.

"We will join them at the pool," Marcelo said.

Chloe returned to the Hummer and rummaged in the back for her bathing suit, then she and Francisco disappeared into the villa to change.

The adults walked to one side of the villa on a path covered by a wood trellis. The open sides looked into tangles of exotic growth. Every now and then an iguana would pop up its head, eye them, then thrash back into the brush.

The trellised path ended at an open space with a broad line of three steps leading down to a tiled area around a kidney shaped pool.

"It's not really for swimming," Marcelo said. "We have the ocean for that. I sometimes float in the pool with a jug of Margaritas. Though it is small, Francisco has friends over and they seem to enjoy splashing around and trying to push each other in. Come let us sit over here." He directed them to a white powder-coated table and chairs with a canvas umbrella overhead.

As soon as they were seated a waiter appeared and took drink orders.

Moments later, Francisco and Chloe ran hand-in-hand down a grassy slope from the villa. They paused at the pool edge to kick off their sandals.

"I think it would be nice to be young again," Marcelo said, looking at the children. "I must say, Francisco is absolutely captivated by Chloe. He speaks of no one else since he first met her."

"You have raised a fine son," JoAnne said.

Two bodyguards took up positions on either side of the pool. The lifeguard, complete with a bush helmet and red shorts, leapt from the lifeguard chair and approached Francisco.

"I want to teach her how to swim," Francisco said.

"At the shallow end, Francisco," the lifeguard said. "I will sit nearby. Okay?"

Francisco nodded. "Come Chloe." He grabbed her hand and pulled her to the far end of the pool.

343

The drinks came, and Marcelo toasted Sam's continued good health.

After everyone had a sip, Sam nudged JoAnne with his foot under the table, hoping she would interpret it as a hint she should excuse herself so he and Marcelo could talk.

She proved to be very perceptive. "Excuse me, Marcelo, where can I find the ladies' room?"

"Of course." Marcelo snapped his fingers to an attendant. "Show *la Señora* Calder the ladies' room."

The attendant nodded and pulled out JoAnne's chair, then accompanied her to the house.

"Marcelo," Sam said without preamble, "I've got to talk to you about something."

Marcelo drew his gaze back from JoAnne. "What is it that troubles you?"

"I know this kid Lukas is a pain in the butt, a drunk, a wife beater and a non-starter, but before we came here, he warned us something big was afoot, something involving a gang from Guadalajara. Something directed at Chloe."

"He said that?" Marcelo leaned in close, looking concerned. "It is possible. I am constantly under pressure from the crazies in Guadalajara. If someone has gotten to them and paid them enough, then, yes, they would not hesitate to do harm to Chloe, and by extension me, since you are my guest and under my protection."

"I didn't want it to be this way. I thought to impose upon you for a few inconsequential days until we could get a flight out of here."

"In my business, one learns there are no inconsequential days."

"I would like to repay your kindness."

Marcelo waved his hand in dismissal, but his face showed a slight smile. "It is I who owes you."

"I paid off Obregon for Chloe. You came with the bargain. I think this time, I have to be more direct in my gratitude."

Marcelo shrugged. "Okay, Sam, if you insist."

"Can we go out to the Hummer for a minute?"

"We can. The children are well looked after here." Marcelo stood and waited until Sam also eased out of his chair.

Together they walked back to the front of the villa and to the parked Hummer.

Sam opened the rear door and turned the latches on the left side cargo compartment. He reached in, withdrew a kilo package of cocaine and handed it to Marcelo.

Marcelo hefted the package. "You know what this is?"

"Of course I do. I have been meaning to throw it into the sea."

Marcelo raised an eyebrow. "A kilo like this has a street value of over fifty thousand US."

"There are five other packages like that in the compartment. They're yours. Take them as an indication of my gratitude for all you have done for me and might have to do in the future."

Marcelo whistled low. "I appreciate this. But I want you to know you would have had my full support without it. If not for you, then for the love I see my Francisco has for your Chloe. It is a rare flower, this kind of love. I see it in his eyes, the way they look at each other. They are still young and cannot know what it is."

Marcelo motioned to one of his bodyguards to transfer the kilo packages to his Mercedes, which was parked next to the Hummer in the drive.

The bodyguard had placed the last package into the trunk of the Mercedes when shots rang out from the pool area.

Chapter Sixteen

With an agonized grimace, Marcelo sprinted down the trellised walkway toward the pool.

When Sam caught up, Marcelo was standing waste deep in the water clutching Francisco. "He's okay!" Marcelo shouted.

"Where's Chloe?" Sam staggered down the steps to the pool area, his fist rubbing his chest. *Not now. Not now.*

"They took her!" Francisco yelled.

Panic seared Sam's consciousness. *She's gone.* Then he spotted the dead. One guard floating in the pool, a red stain blooming from his body. Another guard slumped into a hibiscus bush, yellow flowers splattered by drops of crimson. The lifeguard sprawled on the pool deck. Another one of the attackers hung over the wall, like a blanket set out to dry. A steady drip of blood oozed from his wounds. No sign of Chloe.

Shots echoed from the front of the house.

This is surreal.

Sam left Marcelo with his son and hurried as fast as he dared back to the front of the villa. *I need a pill.* He fumbled in his fanny pack for the container, screwed open the cap and shook out a pill. Two more slipped past his trembling fingers and fluttered to ground. *No time.* He crammed the pill into his mouth. *Better than nothing.*

The gate guard slumped against the wall, clutching his bloodied arm. Beyond, a jeep sped away down the dirt track leading through the swamp and back to town.

347

Sam raged at his inability to do anything.

The kidnappers must have crept up to the compound unobserved and circled around the outside wall to the pool area. Then climbed over the wall, engaged in a shootout and abducted Chloe. Rounding again to the front, they were met by the jeep that had been waiting out of sight down the road. Precise timing. A very professional job.

In the dim light, Sam caught a glimpse of Chloe, struggling in the back of the receding vehicle, then her plaintive cry for help carrying back over the oppressively humid air.

JoAnne ran from the main house. "I heard shots!"

"They've kidnapped Chloe." Sam pointed to the jeep, now disappearing into the gloom. It slowed to a stop, then a second vehicle turned on its lights and headed back toward them.

Marcelo ran up to him. "Is that them? Quick. We will follow." He ran to his Mercedes parked by the side of the drive, leapt in and gunned the engine to life.

Sam lunged into the passenger seat as another of Marcelo's seemingly endless supply of bodyguards crowded in.

The bodyguard smiled as he cocked his machine pistol. *"Hola, Señor Turner.* You remember me? I'm Miguel."

Sam was nonplussed at Miguel's aplomb.

Marcelo accelerated down the drive and banged through the half open gates. "What is that?" He pointed to the bright lights coming toward him. He switched on the Mercedes' high beams, then slammed on the brakes.

Ahead of him, a large truck veered, then skidded across the dirt track. It lurched to a stop, straddling the road, its front and back tires sinking into the soft shoulder, its front and rear bumpers hanging over the algae filled waters of the swamp. A man struggled across the truck's seat, jumped out the opposite side and ran, arms waving above his head and screaming to catch up to the jeep.

"No chance of getting around," Marcelo said, looking for a way past the truck. He stepped from the Mercedes.

Miguel burst from his side of the car and ran to the truck. He flattened himself onto the ground and frog-crawled under the chassis, rose on his elbows and let go a burst from his machine pistol.

The truck driver's faint cry filtered back, as he pitched forward on his face.

Three more of Marcelo's bodyguards ran up to him.

"Get that truck out of the way," Marcelo commanded.

One of the bodyguards climbed onto the running board of the truck and tried the door, only to find it was locked. He took the butt end of his pistol and bashed at the window, breaking it. After brushing away the glass he reached inside and released the door lock. "No keys!" he shouted.

The other two bodyguards ran forward. "Release the brake."

Miguel squirmed from under the truck, and the four of them pushed. The truck moved, then picked up a bit of speed before its front wheels tipped into the swampy water beside the track. The rear wheels lifted off the ground.

"It is enough for us to get by." Marcelo climbed back behind the wheel of the Mercedes and waited for Sam and Miguel to get in, then he eased past the truck, the wheels of the Mercedes spinning in the soft shoulder. Once clear, he gunned the vehicle down the track at a reckless speed.

He came to the main road and skidded to a stop. The jeep sat at the entrance to the nature preserve, empty.

"They've changed vehicles. No telling where they have gone. Probably the highway. But north or south?"

"We have to take a chance. Go north," Sam said.

Marcelo looked at Sam as though the chase had become fruitless, but he sped out of town, joined the highway and headed north at a brutal speed that only slowed when he had cleared the switch backs leading up to the heights above the town.

Once there, the road stretched out before them, flat in the direction of Guadalajara. Not a car in sight. "We guessed wrong. They could be anywhere."

"No!" Sam shouted, then clutched his chest. Steel fingers dug into his heart. "I..." His hands went to his fanny pack. *My pills*. Then he slumped forward, knowing this attack was the real thing.

Marcelo pushed Sam back in his seat. "Miguel, tighten his seatbelt. Make sure he stays upright."

Marcelo turned the car around and sped back to Cerro Bonito.

Ten minutes later, he pulled to a stop in front of his villa.

Sam swooned in and out of consciousness.

JoAnne met them on the drive.

"He's had a heart attack!" Marcelo yelled.

"His pills." JoAnne opened the door and rummaged Sam's fanny pack. "Here they are. Sam, take this." She shook out a pill and put it into his mouth.

Marcelo looked on apprehensively. "Is he going to die?"

Sam closed his eyes and counted. The pain radiated out like it always did, then receded. But this time it only receded part way. "I'll take another one."

"No," JoAnne said. "One per attack. That's what it says on the bottle."

"Please. The first one isn't working."

JoAnne hesitated.

"Give him another one," Marcelo urged.

JoAnne shook out another tablet and placed it in Sam's mouth. "Is that better?"

"Better."

JoAnne twisted round to Marcelo, her face contorted with anguish. "He will die if we don't get him to Guadalajara."

"Use the Hummer. Lay him flat," Marcelo said. "My driver knows the way. He can get you there in under two hours. Do you think Sam can make it?"

351

"We have no choice," JoAnne said. "What about Chloe?"

"I will continue looking for her, but she could be anywhere by now. You should worry about the living."

"The living?" JoAnne's eyes filled with tears. "You think Chloe is dead?"

JoAnne's question hammered through Sam's fogged brain. He watched as Marcelo turned his head, closed his eyes briefly and gave a sigh, then looked JoAnne in the eyes. "You have to be realistic. If she is not already dead, then she might soon be. These men who kidnapped her were very determined. They left two of their own here. When the price is this high, then the consequences will be commensurate. Your place now is with Sam. Go with him."

After laying down the rear seats in the Hummer, a mattress was slid in and Sam eased onto it.

JoAnne leaned back from the front seat. "Are you comfortable."

"I think so," Sam said. But he was lying. The pain never let up. The pills, miracle capsules that they had been, were telling him they had done all they could do. And then there was the anguish. Chloe gone. Where? He couldn't tell heartbreak from heart attack.

"We can go," JoAnne told the driver.

He glanced at Marcelo for confirmation, and when Marcelo nodded, drove out of the compound.

Fighting fatigue and pain, Sam dug into his fanny pack and removed Victor Gallego's business card. "JoAnne."

"What is it?"

"Call this guy." He handed her the card.

"But this is one of Andropov's cronies."

"I know. But he's my only hope. I paid him to be on standby for this type of situation. If he can't help us no one can."

JoAnne pulled out her cell phone as the Hummer left Cerro Bonito behind and began picking up speed on the main highway. The road ahead was deserted, the Hummer's headlights opening an illuminated tunnel as it plowed forward in surrounding darkness.

JoAnne punched in the number from the card. Eight rings, but no one picked up. "There's no answer."

"Try his cell. I think it's there, too."

"I see it." She thumbed in Victor's cell number. JoAnne covered the microphone. "He answered. I'll put it on speaker."

"Hello, hello." A male voice emanated from the cell's speaker.

JoAnne held the phone out in front of her. "This is JoAnne Calder. I'm a friend of Sam Turner's. Is this Victor?"

"I am Victor. What has happened?"

"Sam has had a heart attack. He is stable for the time being. We are transporting him to Guadalajara as I speak."

There was a pause on the other end.

"You must bring him to the *Americana Hospital de Guadalajara*. Do you know how to get there?"

JoAnne looked at the driver who had been listening. He nodded. "Yes, our driver knows the way."

"Good. I will call ahead and alert them you are coming. I am out of town, but will return. I can be there shortly after you arrive. But that is okay as the emergency personnel at the hospital will take care of Sam until I arrive. We can then discuss how you want to proceed."

"What about specialist help?"

"The doctors on duty will see that Sam is stabilized. Once I'm there and we agree on how to proceed, I can contact my sources for further specialized treatment."

"I think he's going to need a transplant."

"Yes. Yes. I'm sorry if I'm being vague. Of course, further specialized treatment includes the option of a transplant. I wish you Godspeed."

Victor hung up.

"You trust this guy?" JoAnne asked Sam.

Sam had been half listening to all this talk about a transplant. The event he had always feared, loathed, came crashing down on him, complicated by Chloe being gone. That hit him hard. He tried to push the thought away and concentrate on his body, which hurt all over. Not working. Chloe's smiling face, her beguiling personality loomed in front of him. He thought to cry out, but couldn't.

"Sam, are you all right."

Sam shut his eyes tight, forbidding tears from streaking down his cheeks. He turned away and choked out a response. "No. But what else is there?"

***

Demetri stood under the blinking *El Dorado* sign for the second time in less than forty-eight hours. Victor had called. Was he going to bring the clone with him? Demetri couldn't contain his excitement. The packet that held the syringes was tucked into his back pocket. He was wearing the same shorts, sandals and aloha shirt he had worn when he had met Obregon. It was so fucking hot, and the shirt was of the thinnest material.

"Hey, Demetri."

Victor seemed to have appeared out of nowhere. They shook hands, then embraced. Demetri noticed Victor had come alone.

"You look well. You look well, Victor." At least Victor hadn't one-upped him in the wardrobe department. They were similarly dressed right down to the aloha shirts.

"And you, Demetri. How can you look so fit after all the shit that's been floating downstream? How you been?"

"It's been hard, real hard." *Enough with the glad handing.* Demetri peered around Victor, a motion he hoped would telegraph what he was about to ask. "Where's the clone?"

Victor let go of Demetri's hand. "She's safe."

"I don't want her safe. Where the fuck is she, Victor?"

An artery on the side of Victor's temple pulsed.

355

Victor never did like being yelled at.

"I have her in a safe house about thirty kilometers from here. Cute kid. Reminds me of the daughter I lost."

What the fuck? Is he going soft? At least he has her. Demetri reached to his back pocket for the packet and handed it to Victor. "There's a syringe in here and a drug cocktail that when injected into the clone will render her brain-dead. I'd do it myself, but you're the one who knows where she is."

Victor eyed the packet. "Isn't that going to kill her? She's full term." He took the packet.

"That's a chance I'm going to have to take. If the feds get to her first, I'm toast."

"I know, I know. Bummer. Can we take a walk and talk?"

Demetri felt his skin prickle. Talk was what Obregon had said in this exact same place. Did everyone use the same introduction before stiffing him? "What's to talk about?"

"Come. It's too noisy here."

At least Victor wasn't interested in the beach, and he didn't have a car trailing him, at least one Demetri could identify.

"You look good," Demetri repeated, trying to get the conversation back onto good ole boy terms.

"Yeah, thanks. Some things have been coming my way. Of course, some things haven't been. Look, you're not going to believe this, but I got a call from a JoAnne Calder. I think she's Turner's broad, though she sounded a lot younger than he is."

"Calder. Calder. Doesn't ring a bell."

356

"Not important. She calls and says after we, I mean, she doesn't know it was us, after we kidnapped the clone, Turner had a heart attack."

"He's dead? That's great."

"No, he's not dead. Almost dead. They were stabilizing him and transferring him to Guadalajara."

"So why'd she call you?"

"He hired me to be a *standby*, you know in case something happened to him, like what has happened. He was clear about not using the clone for anything like a transplant, but he figured I still had connections, which I do, with the medical community in Guadalajara."

"So she asked you to fix him up with our guy?" Demetri laughed and punched Victor in the shoulder. "That's rich."

"Yeah, I thought it was pretty funny myself," Victor said, "we having just kidnapped the kid."

"This is beautiful. Turner will die without a transplant. And, we've got the kid. That juice I gave you will send her to la-la land and beyond."

"Yeah, you're right about Turner. And I've got the kid...that's what I wanted to talk to you about."

Demetri caught the shift from *we* to *I. Here comes the stiff.* "What're you getting at?"

"I lost two guys doing the job. I'm not a very popular man right now with my contacts in Guadalajara."

"I'm sorry, Victor. Real sorry to hear that."

"Yeah, me too. But, hey, money can fix anything. These bozos come cheap. But when they're dead, then there's family and all sorts of other people to pay off."

"How much, Victor? How much you asking?"

"You're way ahead of me. You always were." Victor gave Demetri a sad smile. "But I'm going to need double what we agreed."

"Fuck no! That's one hundred fifty thousand. Where am I going to get that kind of money?"

"What about Turner's escrow account?

"What about it?"

Victor stopped walking and peered at Demetri. "My friend, I think we have a big time misunderstanding developing here. The heat is on me. It's not on you. Either you help me out here, or I'm a dead man."

"All right, all right. Calm down." Demetri glanced around and saw they were alone. "I can give you twenty percent more. That's it."

"That ain't worth squat, Demetri. These guys are leaning on me and will cut off my balls and shoot pool with them if I laid that number on them."

Demetri had come to a crossroads. *I'm tapped out. I can promise more money, but he'll only ask for it, and I'll not be able to produce.* "I gotta be honest with you, Victor. This is your problem."

"So much for friendship." The artery on Victor's forehead had picked up its beat. "Then I've gotta be honest with you. I'm sedating the clone and taking her to Guadalajara and giving her to Doctor Mendoza. Turner can have his heart transplant real easy, and live to testify against you."

Demetri felt his stomach start to churn. "You wouldn't dare."

"Oh, I'd dare all right. Now, if you don't want any of this to happen, then you can cough up the cash, in let's say, like an hour, and I'll stand down. You got it? Since we're being honest with each other."

"God damn it, Victor! This is my life we're talking about!"

"You can shout all you want. That ain't going to change a thing." Victor made a motion with his hand, and a dark colored sedan eased out of the shadows and stopped beside him. "I gotta go now. I have an appointment to keep in Guadalajara.

Before Demetri could get over the car having trailed them unseen, Victor had opened the door and slid inside.

He rolled down the window. "One hour, Demetri." He motioned to the driver and the sedan picked up speed and headed out of town.

Fuckers. They're all fuckers.

Then the reality of his dilemma came crashing down on him. He had no idea where he'd get any more money. He was broke. He tried to look at the bright side. Always had. Maybe the transplant would fail? The clone would be dead. If Turner died, too, then as far as Demetri was concerned, same result. He would be home free, and it wouldn't cost him anything.

Too many ifs. Only one way to go. Find the safe house. Kill the clone. No clone, no evidence of a sentient. Turner will die without a transplant. No Turner, no testimony. What about Gallego? No money, no Gallego. The Guadalajara gang would see to that.

There couldn't be that many villages thirty kilometers from Cerro Bonito.

I rent a car. No. No car rentals here. A taxi. That's a plan. Just get to the clone first.

***

Demetri hurried back to his hotel room. He grabbed the duffel bag, packed his clothes and cleaned out the bathroom of his toiletries. He checked the second syringe and vial of Hawaiian punch, then wrapped them in one of the bathroom's hand towels.

Tucking the rolled towel under his arm and hefting the duffel bag, he huffed his way to the lobby and slapped his hand impatiently on the deserted reception counter.

The clerk appeared from a room behind the counter, rubbing sleep from his eyes.

"I'm checking out," Demetri said.

The clerk nodded without much expression, probably having developed a dislike of Demetri from his hasty, wordless comings and goings.

"Hurry up, dammit. I got a train to catch."

The clerk must have understood the *hurry up* part and been confused by the *train to catch* part. Nevertheless, he produced a bill and a credit card receipt for Demetri to sign.

After Demetri signed, the clerk put the invoice and the receipt in an envelope and shoved it across the counter. Demetri grabbed it and without another word hurried from the hotel.

I'll never see the greasy fucker again. What the hell do I care what he thinks?

360

On the curb outside he looked up and down the street for a taxi. One stood parked in front of the *El Dorado*. Great. He clumped his way up to the taxi and banged on the roof to wake up the driver who was laid back in the front seat behind the wheel.

"I want to go to Guadalajara," Demetri said.

"*Si, Señor. Guadalajara. No problema.*"

"How much?"

"It is a long way, and I have to drive all the way back."

"How fucking much?"

"Two thousand pesos."

"Okay, let's get going. I'm in a big hurry."

The driver got out and opened the rear door for Demetri. "I will put your bag in the trunk."

"Never mind. I want it up here with me."

The cabbie shrugged, got back in and pulled out of town and onto the main highway.

"You look familiar," Demetri said once they settled down to a cruising speed.

"*Si, Señor.* I am Paco. I drove you here from Manzanillo."

"That's right. Now I remember." Demetri felt a fleeting sense of familiarity, like he belonged in this place, like he knew everyone. "Tell me, Paco, are there a lot of villages thirty kilometers from here?"

Paco glanced in his rearview mirror, then back at the road. "*No, Señor.* Most of the villages are either close to the coast or close to Guadalajara. But there is one village, Salsacate, about thirty kilometers from here."

"I'm going to want to stop in Salsacate."

"*No problema, Señor.* For two thousand pesos, you can stop all you want."

"Thanks." Demetri leaned back and closed his eyes. What was he going to do in Salsacate? There were probably a hundred buildings in any small village. How did he think he was going to find one with the clone in it? If indeed the clone was even taken to a safe house there. Maybe Victor had already snatched her up and was on his way to Guadalajara. No way to tell.

Twenty minutes later, Paco announced, "That is Salsacate up ahead. Where you want to stop?"

The highway went through the middle of town at a slight elevation above the surrounding development. "Slow down. I'll let you know." Demetri leaned out the open window as the taxi slowed. He didn't know what he was going to be looking for or whether or not it would be on his side of the road or the other.

About midway through the village, gunshots echoed from a compound a block off the highway. As the taxi neared, the shots became louder and more distinct. Automatic weapon fire. The din sounded like a Chinese New Year's celebration.

"Stop here," Demetri said.

"Here? But there is a war over there."

"That's what I want to check out. You're safe here. I'll only be a few minutes."

"But *Señor*, I cannot wait. It is too dangerous."

"God damn it, Paco. Here's your two thousand pesos and I'll give you another two thousand when we get to Guadalajara. Wait here for me."

"Okay. Okay. I do it."

362

Demetri grabbed the rolled towel and his duffel bag, which he had emptied of its contents onto the floor of the cab. He ran a long route around the worse of the firing.

A number of shooters were hunkered down behind three cars that were parked thirty yards from a rundown looking house. The shooters would pop up, exposing themselves to incoming fire, squeeze off a few rounds then duck down again. Bullets splattered against the walls of the building, sending chips of plaster flying. The windows had long ago been shot out.

Bright flashes from return fire stuttered from the otherwise darkened building. Probably Lopez men behind the cars had cornered the thugs Victor had hired.

The clone could still be here.

Behind the building under siege, sat a windowless structure that could have been a large shelter for equipment.

Victor's sedan was parked to one side of the shelter.

Hot damn.

Demetri ran low toward the equipment building. A single security light dangled from a wire over the front door. He tried the latch and found it unlocked. He opened the door and peered inside to a short hallway that was lined by two doors on either side. Storerooms. He looked back the way he had come and saw no one, then stepped into the hallway and closed the door behind him.

The clone had to be behind one of the doors. He unwrapped the syringe from the towel and held

363

it in one hand, the duffel bag in the other, then fumbled for the switch beside the entrance door and killed the overhead light. He felt his way to the first door.

***

Chloe sat on a bare floor, her knees pulled up to her chest, her hands covering her ears. Despite the pressure she brought to bear on the sides of her head, she could still hear gunfire from somewhere outside. There had been a sliver of light coming from under the door, and now even that had disappeared. The shooting never stopped.

She pushed herself into the corner of the small windowless room. The dirt floor gave off the smell of mildew, the plaster walls sweated dampness.

It was not unlike being back in the crèche. Total darkness. But she had been safe in her crèche. At least she thought she had been. Maybe not.

Who were those men who had climbed over the wall with guns? They shot everyone. She had been so afraid they would shoot Francisco, but they hadn't. They had grabbed her and taken her in a jeep back through the swamp, then into a bigger car that drove very fast to this place. She didn't know where it was. A house on the highway leading to Guadalajara.

She shook all over. She only had on her bathing suit but she wasn't cold.

A big man, whom she didn't know, had dragged her into the small room. It was square, about eight feet on a side, no more for a ceiling and completely bare.

Where is Grandpa?

Where were all the people she had come to count on? She didn't even have her survival kit.

The bolt on the outside of the door slid back. Someone pushed the door open and stood in the doorway. There was a fumbling sound, then the striking of a match. Whoever it was held the match high.

Chloe shielded her eyes trying to see who it was but the match was very bright after the pitch darkness, then the match went out.

"Hi, little one," a man said. "I'm here to help you." He seemed to fumble in his pocket, then produced a penlight that must have been attached to his key chain from the sound of the jingling keys.

Chloe stood, but did not move toward the man. Rather she drew her arms close to her chest, then pressed her back hard into the corner of the room.

Though she could not see the man's face, she could see in the glow of the penlight that he held a dark cloth or a bag in one hand and something else in the hand with the light.

A glint of reflected light flashed her way from the unknown object.

The man stepped into the room. "Listen. This is what we have to do to get you out of here. You do want to get out of here, don't you?"

Chloe nodded in the dark, not sure the man could even see her.

He held out the bag. "I'm going to put you in this bag, zip it up and carry you out so you can be free. Do you understand?"

Chloe understood him, but was none the less terrified. "Am I going to be all right?" Her heart was twittering fast. Something told her not to trust this man. But she had been thrown into this awful place, and now all she wanted was to get out.

"Of course. I'm the one who will get you out. Now, step into the bag."

Chloe knew the room was awful. This man was giving her a way out. He sounded sincere. "All I have to do is climb into the bag?"

"That's it. Real easy." The man lowered the bag and angled the penlight down to where she should step.

Chloe stepped into the bag.

"Crouch down," the man said. "I'm going to zip this thing up and we'll be ready to go."

He pulled the sides of the bag up and started to close the zipper, then stopped halfway. "One more thing." He brought his hand up into the light where she could see.

"That's a syringe," Chloe said.

"Yes it is. It's got some stuff in it that will calm you. I can't carry this bag with you in it if you might move or make a sound. There will be bad people watching. Know what I mean?"

"You're going to give me a shot?"

"Like I said. Just to relax you. Do you have a problem with that, Chloe...can I call you Chloe?"

Chapter Seventeen

Marcelo's driver gunned the Hummer up the curving drive to the Emergency Entrance to the *Americana Hospital*. He braked, got out and ran inside to alert the staff.

Two orderlies and a nurse appeared with a wheeled gurney and lined up behind the Hummer.

They slid Sam out and onto the gurney, then rushed him toward the entrance.

"Wait for us," JoAnne said to Marcelo's driver. "I'll call."

"Of course, *Señora*, I am at your disposal."

She ran into the hospital as the orderlies wheeled Sam onto an elevator.

After cramming herself in beside them, she reached down to take Sam's hand.

He squeezed it. "Everything is going to be okay. We're here. They will take good care of me."

"You're too much of an optimist," JoAnne said. "We're here, but I worry they don't have the technology or the know how to fix what's wrong with you."

Sam closed his eyes. *I worry, too*. But he felt very tired and couldn't keep his mind on anything for more than a few seconds. "Did Gallego say he would fix everything up?"

"I told you he said he would. He's about a half hour behind us in arriving."

They came to the fourth floor. The orderlies wheeled Sam out into a hallway and down to a prep room where he was lifted off the gurney and onto a hospital bed.

Staff descended on him, taking his blood pressure, inserting IVs, not one but three, threading a catheter into his bladder.

Then they all withdrew, and Sam was left to wonder, what next?

A doctor entered the room. "Hello, *Señor* Turner, I am Doctor Fuentes." He reached forward and patted Sam's hand as an alternative to a handshake. "A Victor Gallego called and said you would be arriving and that you have had a heart attack. You seem stable enough at the moment, but we will do tests, nevertheless, to ascertain the extent of your attack and how we might proceed. Am I making myself clear?"

Sam raised a hand to indicate he understood.

"Doctor Fuentes," JoAnne said. "Sam has a history of heart disease. He had one heart challenge a day ago. It was not diagnosed as a true heart attack, but for all intents and purposes, he needs a transplant. He has had a contract with Clonal Transplants in Denver for two years for them to grow him a clone and now is the time."

"A transplant. I am afraid, *Señora*, I am not the one who does those operations here at the *Americana*. That would be Doctor Mendoza. He handles all of the requests for transplants that come out of America. And I might add we are being flooded with them at this moment."

"Is Doctor Mendoza here?"

"I will check for you. In the meantime, I will have *Señor* Turner hooked up to a life support apparatus. Mind you, it is only used in the most

368

dire cases, but from what you have told me, *Señor* Turner fits that category."

"You bet he does."

"If you please, *Señora*, you can wait outside while we undertake this procedure."

"No," Sam croaked. "I want her to be here."

Doctor Fuentes looked at JoAnne and shrugged. "You may stay if you wish."

Sam felt violated in ten different ways. Then a large machine started sucking stuff out of him and pumping it back in. He supposed it was supplementing what his heart was not capable of doing.

"So now what?" Sam asked from his prone position, barely able to see JoAnne.

"We have to wait for Gallego. He seems to be the lynch pin in all of this."

The door to the prep room opened, and Gallego rushed in. He was in a total sweat and looking very crazed and nervous.

"Is that Sam?" he asked.

"Don't you recognize me?" Sam said through his tubes.

"Sure I do, Sam. You look awful. All those tubes. All those wires. How are you feeling?"

"I feel great, Victor." Sam winced. "I'd feel a whole lot better if I knew what you can do for me."

"Of course. That it is what is paramount on your mind. Here's the deal. Doctor Mendoza will do whatever is necessary to save your life. At this point, we need a tissue scan. We have to see if there is anything out there that matches you one

369

hundred percent. You don't want anything less, do you?"

"Let's cut the bullshit. If eighty-five percent works, I want to go for it. I'm going to die if you don't get this process going, ASAP."

"Acknowledged. I'm going to call Mendoza in now." Gallego waved a hand and left the room.

"Is he for real?" JoAnne asked.

"Please. He's the only hope I have. If he can't get something done in this godforsaken place then nobody can."

A doctor entered the room with a nurse trailing. "I am Doctor Mendoza. I do heart transplants. Victor has brought me in for consultation. First, we will take a tissue sample."

This Mendoza seemed like a total quack. He even talked like a duck. No, more like a total zombie duck. Sam endured a draw of blood from his arm.

"Do you think there's any chance of finding a tissue match," Sam asked.

"We can only hope," Mendoza said with a sidelong look at Gallego.

Gallego sat beside Sam and leaned in close. "Sam. If Mendoza can find a tissue match for your heart, it's going to cost some pesos, if you know what I mean?"

"I don't care what it costs. I'm going to die if I don't get the treatment I need."

"Perfectly put. I wouldn't have it any other way given that I had your means of paying."

Despite being debilitated, Sam picked up on *means of paying*. "How much do you want?"

370

"That's a very esoteric question. I have to ask, how much does Demetri charge for a similar service?"

"But he grows clones. It's different."

"Not really. Sam, you've got a few more minutes, maybe hours. This is not the time to play games. How much does Demetri charge?"

"Eight hundred thousand, but that's for the package. Pre-care. The clone. The operation."

Gallego sat back and let out a whoosh of air. "That much?"

"What? Is that too much?"

"Sam. When Demetri sends his patients down to me, I get five thousand and Mendoza gets ten thousand."

"You're getting screwed," Sam wheezed, then he thought telling Gallego he was getting screwed wasn't the best strategy if he was bargaining for his life.

Gallego was lost in thought. "Here's how it is Sam. I'm going to consult with Doctor Mendoza, and he's going to tell me how much he needs if he can in fact perform a transplant for you. Of course, it's going to depend on the results of the tissue scan."

"I got it," Sam said. "Just hurry up."

Gallego left the room.

"Can we trust these guys?" JoAnne asked. "All they seem to be concerned about is the money they will make."

Sam waved a tired hand. JoAnne wasn't where he was, at death's door. Being on that threshold focused vision, simplified what remained of life. "We'll see what they come up with."

Gallego re-entered the room. "*Señor* Turner, I have miraculous news. Mendoza has evaluated your tissue scan and ascertained it is a credible match with a donor who was delivered to the hospital earlier today. Can you believe it? It's a miracle. And. I've negotiated a price with Mendoza. He wants one hundred thousand. I will take the same for my...coordinative role."

"Are...are you serious?" JoAnne stammered.

Gallego raised his palms. "*Señora*, what is a life worth? If you don't want to pay, the donor's heart will go wanting. What can I say?"

Sam struggled to sit higher up on his pillow. "You said the heart donor was brought to the hospital earlier today. How early?"

"I'm not sure, *Señor* Turner. Late morning."

"Can you confirm that for me?"

"I don't know how anyone can do that," Gallego said, helping Sam with his pillow. "There are privacy laws. I took Doctor Mendoza's word for it. Why would he lie?"

Sam still had his doubts, but Gallego seemed sincere. "We're concerned, Mr. Gallego. Chloe was kidnapped earlier this evening. We don't know where she is, and we fear the worst."

"But that is terrible," Gallego ran his fingers through his hair in obvious agitation. "Who would do such a thing?"

"We don't know," Sam said in a sad, weak voice. "We suspect Andropov organized it."

Gallego nodded. "It could be. It could be. I have known Demetri a long time, and I must confess, I am not always one hundred percent going along with some of the things he does. But rest assured, Doctor Mendoza is above reproach."

"Pay him, JoAnne," Sam said. "Let's stop messing around."

"*Señor* Turner is right," Gallego said. "It's not time to be messing around."

JoAnne leaned close to Sam and whispered, "Two hundred thousand and you believe they are above reproach?"

Sam breathed out a long sigh, feeling every sigh could be his last. "Give it to him."

"All right. I'll be right back."

Sam clutched JoAnne's arm. "No. I don't want you to leave me. Call Marcelo's driver. Send Gallego down there. I don't care about the money. But if I was to die with you gone, I don't think I could bear it."

A play of emotions flicked across JoAnne's face. Sympathy? Sam couldn't tell. Miffed? Possibly. Nevertheless, she took out her cell phone and punched in the number for Marcelo's driver. "Jaime, this is JoAnne. A Victor Gallego is coming down to the Hummer and will take some money out of the back. You are to let him. Am I clear?"

She must have gotten a positive response because she said to Gallego, "We came in a Hummer. It's in the parking lot. In the rear cargo compartment is a stash of money. Sam doesn't want me to leave him. I have to trust you to go down there and extract the agreed two hundred thousand, then pay off Mendoza so he will proceed with the operation. Am I clear?"

"Very much so, *Señora*." Gallego left the room.

"Are you crazy, Sam?" JoAnne asked.

"I don't care. It's not my money, anyway. What am I going to do with it if I die?"

"Good point."

Twenty minutes later, Mendoza entered the room. "Everything is ready for your transplant, *Señor* Turner."

Sam was nonplused. "That quick?"

Mendoza leaned in close so only Sam could hear. "Money talks." He straightened up and motioned to an orderly to wheel Sam into the operating room.

Sam craned over his shoulder catching a glimpse of JoAnne, taut with nerves and concern, as the door closed behind him.

***

Wellstone checked his seatbelt, put on his Stetson and gazed out the window as the Learjet came in for a landing at *Playa de Oro International* in Manzanillo. The runway was a primitive affair by American standards, long enough, but narrow, its asphalt top looking more like a back country road than a runway for an international airport. It ran parallel to the sea with a span of dense vegetation in between. Long lines of breakers curled while moving across the blue ocean toward the pristine sandy coast.

The Learjet landed and taxied to a remote area where it was met by local law enforcement.

374

Wellstone had phoned ahead to let them know he was coming. The fact that Obregon had flown the coop to Cuba was the wedge Wellstone had used to pry the jurisdictional door open wide enough to allow him to come to Mexico.

He bounded down the jet-stairs and shook the hand of a police Colonel, one he hoped was not as corrupt as Obregon, whom he was replacing.

"Welcome to Manzanillo, *Señor* Wellstone. I am Colonel Tulio Ingles. I have been reassigned from Sonora, to replace Colonel Obregon. It is very unfortunate what happened with Obregon. I can't understand it."

"It happens, doesn't it," Wellstone said.

"I like your hat, *Señor* Wellstone. I have always wanted to own a Stetson."

Wellstone ignored the compliment. "What do you have on Turner?"

Ingles snapped out of his phony familiarity. "Because of the reorganization of our force due to Obregon's departure, we did not check the hospital until this afternoon. By that time Turner had been released."

"You--"

"We had no authority to hold him anyway, *Señor*. Unlike your country, Mexico still has laws protecting individual rights."

Wellstone felt he should say something to correct Ingles' misperception of the laws of the United States, but decided to let it pass. No sense riling up the natives. "Where'd he go?"

"It is our understanding he returned to Playa de Cerro Bonito."

"Well, let's get going."

Ingles smiled. "We are ready to go, *Señor*. I have a helicopter standing by. You can be there in ten minutes. Unfortunately, duties here prohibit me from coming with you. But Sergeant Sanchez here will accompany you. He is the police presence in Cerro Bonito and knows the town and its people like the back of his hand."

A thin policeman in a baggy uniform stepped forward with Wellstone's bag and saluted. "Roberto Sanchez, at your service." He shook Wellstone's hand.

"Please follow me." Ingles directed them to a waiting black Mercedes.

Colonels must get paid a good salary down here to afford a car like that.

Wellstone got in the back with Ingles. Sanchez sat in front. The driver sped across the apron to a helipad, where a helicopter was standing by with its rotors already picking up speed.

The Colonel said goodbye, and Wellstone and Sanchez ducked low as they ran to the helicopter.

Inside Wellstone had barely buckled up and placed a helmet with a boom mike over his head when the helicopter lifted off and was soon flying north low over the water.

Ten minutes later to the second, they landed on an expansive manicured lawn of what looked like a huge walled estate.

"Where are we?" Wellstone asked Sanchez as the rotors whined down.

"This is the villa of Marcelo Lopez. He is a very wealthy *patron*. *Señor* Turner was last reported staying at this address."

Wellstone leapt out of the helicopter and glanced around. "How does someone make enough money down here to afford a palace like this?"

Sanchez looked at Wellstone. "He sells drugs, *Señor*."

A well-dressed man strode up to them.

"*Señor* Wellstone." He stretched out his hand. "I am Marcelo Lopez. Welcome to my humble abode."

"Doesn't look humble to me. You a drug dealer?"

Marcelo waved his hand. "Whatever gave you that impression?"

"Roberto here told me you sell drugs."

Marcelo wagged a finger at Roberto. "You should keep your opinions to yourself, *Bicho*."

"*Si. Señor Lopez*. I am sorry."

Marcelo turned back to Wellstone. "But you are not here to discuss my business. You are here for Sam Turner and the girl. Unfortunately, there has been a...complication."

Wellstone didn't like the sound of complication. That usually meant a heap of trouble, a pile of manure, a game changer. "What sort of complication?"

"We were raided a few hours ago by a gang of thugs. From reports I have received, they were hired out of Guadalajara with the intention of kidnapping Chloe."

"The clone."

"I know nothing of a clone. She is the young girl who was with Sam Turner. She called him Grandpa, but I have no way of knowing whether or not he was her grandfather.

"Be that as it may, I regret to say the raid was successful despite the heroic efforts of my bodyguards, two of whom were killed."

"All this happened a couple of hours ago?"

"Yes. I believe I made that clear at the outset."

"What is this, the wild west?"

"No, *Señor* Wellstone. This is Mexico. You are from the wild west."

"You're telling me you have no idea where the clone is."

"We traced Chloe to a safe house thirty kilometers from here. There was a shootout...like in the wild west. When all was said and done, there was no trace of Chloe. Honestly, we don't know what happened to her."

"What about Turner?"

"That is most unfortunate. Upon witnessing her kidnapping, he had a heart attack. He has been rushed to a hospital in Guadalajara."

Shit. "Roberto, can this chopper get us to Guadalajara?"

"I will check with the pilot, *Señor.*"

"You got an address," Wellstone asked, "of this hospital in Guadalajara?"

"I do." Lopez took out a business card and wrote on the back of it. "I can call ahead and have one of my associates in Guadalajara meet you at the airport. The hospital is not far from there."

"That would be super," Wellstone said.

378

Roberto returned. "*Si*. The chop-ter can go to Guadalajara."

"Then we'll be off. Thank you for your help." Wellstone shook hands, thinking the last thing he would have expected was thanking a drug dealer for his help, but he was learning something new every day. "Roberto, you coming with me?"

"*Si, Señor*. Colonel Ingles said I was to go where you go."

"All right. Let's get a move on."

***

An hour later the police helicopter landed at a remote part of the Guadalajara International Airport reserved for law enforcement operations.

Wellstone cleared the blockhouse-shaped control building with Sanchez and hurried to the curb.

A man stood next to a black Mercedes.

They must all go to the same dealership.

The man waved and came up to them. "Marcelo sent me. We can go to the hospital whenever you are ready."

Wellstone got in the back, and Sanchez rushed around to the other side to join him.

Ten minutes later they pulled into the hospital parking lot. It was already past nine o'clock. A full moon had risen, casting the lot in distinct shades of gray.

The driver parked as close as he could to the hospital entrance.

Wellstone jumped out and was hurrying to the entrance when a commotion off to his right distracted him. He held his hand up to the closely

379

following Sanchez. "What's happening over there? Sounds like an argument."

In the dim light he could see two men, one in a dark sedan, the other reaching in through the driver's side window with both hands as if trying to drag the driver out. Both were yelling at each other in an incomprehensible foreign language.

"We better check it out," Wellstone said. "It looks like it could escalate into violence."

"It happens all the time here, *Señor*. Let us go to the hospital."

Wellstone frowned at Sanchez and was even more determined to see what was going on. He jogged toward the altercation.

The tires on the sedan squealed, laying down a strip of rubber with faint blue smoke rising, as it pulled away from the man standing outside. The man screamed what must have been obscenities at the departing vehicle.

Wellstone came up to the man. "Androp?"

Andropov spun around, his eyes wide, his expression contorted with suppressed rage. Then recognition hit. He shoved both fists hard on Wellstone's chest and ran.

Wellstone staggered back.

Sanchez came up to his side. "Who's that?"

"He's a fugitive. We have to get him."

Despite being skinny and wearing baggy pants, Sanchez sprinted after the lumbering Andropov, caught up to him and tackled him.

Andropov fell to the pavement, his hands outstretched, catching the full weight of his body.

He groaned and rolled over onto his back gasping for air.

Sanchez straddled him, grabbed one arm and rolled him onto his stomach to cuff his hands behind his back.

Wellstone ran up. "Good work, Sanchez."

"You can't do this to me, Wellstone," Andropov wheezed over his shoulder trying to get a look back. "You don't have any jurisdiction here."

"You're right, Androp. But Roberto does. What are you doing here at the hospital?"

"That's none of your fucking business."

"Who was that in the car?"

"Ditto."

"Fine. I guess you won't mind spending a few nights in a Mexican jail thinking about answers." Wellstone gave Andropov a shove with his foot having stifled the urge to kick him in the head. "You okay here, Roberto? I've got to get into the hospital and see what the situation is."

"*Si, Señor. No problema.* This fat man will be easy."

"All right. You sit tight. I'll be back as soon as I can."

Wellstone hurried into the lobby of the hospital and demanded to know where Sam Turner was.

The reception nurse punched into her computer. "He's in OR-6. Doctor Mendoza is the attending surgeon. A Miss JoAnne Calder is his contact person. She is in the adjacent waiting room.

"How do I get there?"

"Take the elevator over there." She pointed. "Go up to the fourth floor. There will be signs on the wall to direct you to the OR-6 waiting room."

Wellstone hurried off. He fidgeted waiting for the elevator, then while on the elevator until it came to the fourth floor. He ran out, glanced at the wall signs and came to the OR-6 waiting room.

As he rushed in, a good-looking blond woman stood.

"I'm Bernard Wellstone. You must be Miss Calder. We spoke on the phone."

She nodded, then stared at him without saying a word.

It dawned on Wellstone she was thinking about Obregon. "Look, when I talked to you, I didn't know about Obregon. He's skipped the country to Cuba."

"Cuba?"

"Someone must have gotten to him big time. Turns out he has a relative there in the regime. What we're trying to figure out is where he could have come up with enough money to make it worth his while to bolt. We figure Andropov."

"It was Andropov, initially," JoAnne said. "When Sam heard Obregon was working for Andropov, he outbid him. Obregon took the higher offer. But we never expected he'd bolt."

Wellstone shook his head. "Turner has that kind of money?"

"It's a long story." JoAnne gave him a sad smile. "I'll tell you someday. But now you're here."

Wellstone wanted to ask more questions, then thought better of it. "Yeah, now I'm here. Jet to

382

Manzanillo, helicopter to Cerro Bonito, then here. You got the fax we sent?"

"I did. Can I trust you?"

Wellstone indicated a chair and they sat. "JoAnne...is it all right if I call you JoAnne?"

JoAnne nodded.

"You're going to have to trust me. You and Turner are getting into this way over your heads. I know Chloe was kidnapped. I spoke with Marcelo Lopez. I'd like to help. Please tell me what's going on here." His plea seemed to work. JoAnne sat and placed her hands in her lap. She stared at them for a moment as though collecting her thoughts. "Sam is in the OR. Doctor Mendoza is giving him a heart transplant. They've been at it almost four hours."

"A heart transplant? They can do that here?"

"They can, and they do quite frequently. Andropov sends a lot of his patients here with their clones to have the operation."

Wellstone felt a moment of panic. "Where'd they get the heart?"

"It's not Chloe's heart if that is what you are thinking. Sam would never allow that." JoAnne's eyes started to tear up.

"Please, Miss Calder." Wellstone looked around and offered her a tissue from a box on one of the side tables. "I know it must be a tragedy for you that Chloe is missing, but how can you be sure Chloe isn't being used for the transplant."

"But it was all arranged. Gallego came--"

"Gallego?"

"Victor Gallego. He's Andropov's contact man in Guadalajara. Andropov sends patients down here

383

and Gallego sets up the transplants with Doctor Mendoza. When we got here, no one knew what to do...at least until Gallego arrived. He found Doctor Mendoza for us. Mendoza organized Sam's tissue scan. He's the one who came and said there was a good match with a donor."

Wellstone thought he smelled a rat. "That's quite a coincidence."

"I don't know what the odds are. Mendoza said the donor was brought in this morning. Gallego called it a miracle. He was very happy. It couldn't have been Chloe. She was kidnapped this evening."

"I bet."

"But it didn't stop him from negotiating payment for having the operation. Mendoza wouldn't perform it unless we paid up front."

"What? That's ridiculous."

"I thought so, too. In the end we paid. We had no choice."

"I saw Andropov in the parking lot. Did you know he was here?"

JoAnne stared at Wellstone as though she had been hit on the head with a brick. "Oh my God! You don't think Andropov got hold of Chloe somehow and provided her to the hospital?"

"I don't know what to think any more. But we've taken him into custody. We'll try to find out the truth."

Mendoza came out of the OR. "*Señora*, *Señor*," he said striping off latex gloves. "I am happy to tell you the operation has been a complete success. The finishing touches are being applied to

Señor Turner. He will be made comfortable, and you can see him in the recovery room."

Wellstone stepped up to Mendoza. "I'm Agent Bernard Wellstone, American Federal Bureau of Investigation." He shook Mendoza's hand. "Can you tell me the circumstances surrounding this transplant? We've been looking for Turner and the girl he was with, a girl we know to be a sentient clone. I understand you do a lot of transplants using clones sent here with their sponsors by one Demetri Andropov." Wellstone decided to drop the Androp in favor of clearer communication with a civilian.

Mendoza looked at Wellstone. "You American FBI have no jurisdiction in Mexico."

"That's correct. These are off the record questions you can choose to ignore."

Mendoza looked around for a wastebasket, found one and tossed the latex gloves into it. "I don't know anything about a clone in this case, Agent Wellstone. Honestly, in my business we don't ask a lot of questions. Once the operation is scheduled, I show up and take a heart out of one person over here--" He directed his hands to his left. "--and sew it into a person over there." He directed his hands to the right. "It is very simple."

"But the hospital must have records of who the donor was?"

"Most assuredly. But, unlike the United States where everybody's medical records are accessible by law enforcement, we here in Mexico still retain a semblance of civility and personal privacy. I cannot, nor can the hospital release any information in that regard."

385

JoAnne sat down, looking stricken. "Then it could have been Chloe. I shouldn't have believed Gallego. He said it was a miracle."

Mendoza looked ill at ease. "*Señor* Turner will have to remain here in intensive care for a few days, then we'll transfer him to a regular hospital room for another few days to make sure he is okay. If all seems well and good he can be discharged in a week. I will leave you for now."

After Mendoza left, JoAnne brushed away tears and stood. "I should have thanked Doctor Mendoza," she said to Wellstone. "It's just the circumstances leading up to this operation have been so traumatic. Chloe is still missing. I don't know what to think."

Wellstone felt a queasiness brought on by the suspicion that all the players here were dinking and dodging, and the bottom line probable fact was a sentient clone had been used in a transplant operation to save a man's life. Was Turner complicit? Goddamn him if he was. And this bubble-headed blond in front of him seemed to be making the most outrageous excuses for the conduct of all the responsible parties. His instincts pushed him to scream out the injustice of this, but he bludgeoned himself into a mental calm.

Keep focused on what you have. Don't let your emotions intrude.

"Mendoza said a week," Wellstone said. "I've got a private jet sitting at Manzanillo. I'll contact the pilot and have him fly up here. When Sam is ready to leave, I'll fly him back to the States."

"That's a very kind offer," JoAnne said.

386

"It's the least I can do. Sam is my star witness against Andropov. Speaking of whom. I've got to go out and check on him. I left him in the parking lot under the supervision of the Mexican policeman who accompanied me here on the flight up."

***

Karen stood on the opposite bank of a stream that separated them. Behind her spread rolling green fields, interspersed with towering Douglas Firs and a scattering of wild flowers. Birds flitted through the air. A low lying sun lit her hair from behind casting a glow around her whole body.

Her arm was outstretched, her hand reaching for him, encouraging him to cross the stream to her side.

The field, the trees and the stream dissolved in darkness. Karen lingered for a moment longer, then she too was gone.

Sam opened his eyes. Everything seemed white, until his mind sorted it out to walls, bed-coverings, the uniforms of nurses and a doctor's jacket. Banks of monitors and equipment loomed close with wires and tubes snaking up to his body and disappearing under the sheets to places he could only guess at. A large bandage covered his chest. Multiple IVs stuck to his arms. A breathing tube was clipped to his nose, another tube entered his mouth and found a home in his throat.

"He's awake," Doctor Mendoza said.

Sam did a mental check of his body. There was some pain in his chest but not as severe as he had feared it would be. He couldn't identify anything else different from before he blacked out. He recalled he was wheeled into an operating room. Before an anesthesiologist had administered drugs to put him to sleep, Sam had noticed a small body lying on a gurney to one side of the room. The top and bottom of the body were draped with sheets leaving the chest area exposed. It looked like it had been swathed with a dark colored disinfectant.

He tried to speak, but managed to produce nothing more than grunts.

JoAnne came into view. "Are you comfortable?"

How can I be? He shook his head.

"Mendoza says it will take a while for the drugs to wear off. The operation was a complete success."

Sam frowned and tried to give JoAnne a stricken look.

"We don't know whose heart it was," she said. "They won't tell us. They can't. The privacy laws down here seem to be even more restrictive than the ones we have in the States."

Sam began to shiver, a reaction to background pain or the surge of adrenalin that coursed through his body at the thought he might have Chloe's heart in him. "I...saw...donor," Sam said with intense effort.

"You saw the donor?"

Sam nodded.

JoAnne turned to Mendoza. "He says he saw the donor. How is that possible?"

Doctor Mendoza shook his head. "It is not possible. Although the donor was in the room when *Señor* Turner was wheeled in, the donor was

388

covered with sheets. If he saw anything at all, it would have been the donor's exposed chest."

"Oh, Sam, you're thinking it was Chloe, aren't you?"

Sam nodded as vigorously as he could.

"They wouldn't have done that to us knowing how we felt about Chloe."

Sam's eyes leaked tears. He thrashed his head back and forth.

Mendoza came over to him. "You must not agitate yourself, *Señor* Turner."

Sam gazed past Mendoza at a tall man, an American, six foot four, athletic with graying temples and wearing a cowboy hat.

"I'm Agent Wellstone. How's my star witness doing?"

"Star...," Sam croaked, feeling his fatigue.

"He needs rest," Doctor Mendoza said. "We should let him sleep."

Mendoza and Wellstone left the room.

JoAnne came over and sat on the edge of Sam's bed. She reached into her pocket and withdrew a silver cross on a thin chain. "I found this on the floor of the Hummer."

Sam reached for the cross.

JoAnne closed her hand around his as he held the cross. "I wonder why she took it off?"

Sam lay back and shook his head.

JoAnne patted his hand, then stood and left the room.

In his chest he felt a deep ache, an emotional ache. At least that aspect of his new heart was functioning.

Hot tears leaked out from the corners of his eyes and dropped to his pillow. Poor Chloe. Where was she? Was she here with him? Would he ever know?

Epilogue

Sam sat on a chair on the deck of his home in Monument. The view gave out to the distant south, high plains to his left, foothills to his right with Pikes Peak behind them in the distance. The temperature was dropping, so Sam pulled a blanket over his knees. He liked sitting there and wouldn't have it any other way. He abhorred the thought of moving to an assisted living home. Hell, he could still get up and down those stairs in his vertically challenged house. Why would he want to live anywhere else?

The driveway sensor chimed.

What a wonderful device, still working after all these years. Of course, he had to replace the batteries like every six months, but otherwise the damn thing kept on alerting him to people driving up.

He didn't get up from his chair, figuring whoever it was would find him.

"Sam, there you are."

JoAnne. Still lovely and still fifteen years younger than he was. Though he tried to do the math in his head, subtracting her age from what he was certain was his age at sixty-six eluded him.

"Hi." He waved a hand over his shoulder, wondering about the gesture...so long ago, so forgotten. Mexico. A wave did it all. "Take a seat," he said, indicating an empty chair on the other side of a small table. "I was enjoying the view. Autumn is nice. Not too hot, not too cool. The leaves changing color. Can I offer you anything?"

"I'm fine, Sam." She came over and gave him a kiss on the forehead before sitting down.

"I love it when you do that," Sam said. He often wondered why they had never married. Too big an age difference. Too big a difference in personalities. Too many traumatic memories of Cerro Bonito and Chloe.

"I didn't come all the way up here to hear you say you enjoy me pecking on your head."

"No, I suppose you didn't. Then what is it for?"

"I've sold the rights to your book."

Sam thought about that. It was a book he had to write, but hesitated to put out there. "I suppose I should be happy you did. But in all honesty, it broke my heart writing that book." The phrasing bothered Sam, but what else could he call the muscle in his chest that kept performing smoothly every day? After ten years, he had a right to call it his own.

"Maybe that's why I could sell it."

"It shouldn't work that way."

"No?"

"One shouldn't be able to make money off the misery of other people's lives."

"Are you becoming soft in your old age?"

"JoAnne, I've always been a softy. But here I sit, potentially the most successful first time published author on Medicare. I might even get an article on me in AARP's magazine."

"You should be happy, not complaining."

"All that pain." Sam pulled the blanket up tighter. "What happened? No one has ever been able to tell me what happened."

"You have to stop beating yourself with this. It can't be good for you. I don't think we'll ever know the truth."

"That cocksucker Andropov didn't give an inch, despite being sentenced to five years in the slammer. Can you believe it? Five years for what he did?"

JoAnne brought her sunglasses down off her forehead and positioned them against the glare of the sun easing lower in the western sky. "But that was the problem, Sam. The jury convicted him of obstruction of justice. We convinced them Chloe was sentient, but he denied any part in making her so, blaming that disgruntled lab technician."

"I never could get over the plea bargaining. A clinical error the tech said. Give me a break."

JoAnne turned her face to the sun and adjusted her glasses. "At least they deported him." JoAnne rocked back and forth in her chair. "These are really comfortable."

Sam glanced over at her. "Geez, JoAnne. I'm talking about a probable murder and you're focused on the chairs sitting on my deck." As always, when JoAnne or someone else brought up Andropov, Sam felt a welling agitation. "What happened haunts me every breath I take."

JoAnne stopped rocking. "Not knowing?"

Sam nodded. "I don't understand a man like that."

"Get over it."

"And what about that doctor, that...that...Mendoza. He wasn't any help. *I take*

393

the hearts out from over here and sew them up over there. How can anyone be so cynical?"

"Sam, he's a surgeon."

Sam saw JoAnne was going into her, I hear you but I don't have to listen to you mode. "Wellstone was pissed at the outcome of the trial. I think he thought nailing Andropov was some sort of mission from God."

JoAnne stared out at the view, her eyes shrouded. "He did express his displeasure at the outcome, but said he was going to move on. His one lament was being unable to track down Gallego."

Sam shook his head in dismay. "The guy vanished, and with all our money."

"You said you didn't care. That it wasn't your money, anyway."

"Still. He was nothing more than a common thief. I suppose you can hide pretty well if you have almost a million in cash to work with. That's what Obregon did. Whatever happened to him?"

"You know as well as I do he immigrated to Cuba."

"Yeah, I knew that. I just wondered if the dirt bag had died or something."

"Not to my knowledge."

"Do you keep in touch with Heidi?"

"An email here and there. She's still running the inn, thanks to the money you gave her."

A hawk cried high in the sky over the rocks. It glided on a thermal, then tipped its wings and fell off in a long slicing dive.

"Yeah, I did give her money." Sam marveled at the freedom a bird like a hawk must enjoy, being able to move through the vast space out in front of him without a care in the world. "I forgot about that."

"Lukas never did get better. He died of a drug overdose."

Sam didn't harbor any sympathy for Lukas. A cruel kid, caught up in a cruel world. "What of Aurelia?"

"*Nada*. Heidi never heard from her again."

"Wow. That must have been hard."

JoAnne nodded. "Last I heard from her, it must be two years ago, she wrote that Marcelo had been diagnosed with cancer. He'd left the drug trade and tried to go legitimate."

"I liked Marcelo. I'm sorry to hear he got sick. What of his son Francisco?"

"Heidi sees him around from time to time. She says he grew up to be a nice young man, but always seemed a bit sad. He took Chloe's disappearance very hard."

Sam remembered how the two of them had taken to each other. The attraction was immediate. "He liked Chloe, a lot."

"He did."

Sam leaned back in his chair, emotion threatening to overwhelm him. The thought of not knowing the truth gnawed at him. His eyes smarted, and he blinked back tears. His hand went to his chest where he fingered a silver cross that hung from a chain around his neck.

JoAnne looked over to him. "You've still got that cross."

"I don't know what I'd do without it. I keep it right here, on my chest, close to my heart. Maybe Chloe knows I do."

JoAnne lifted off her glasses and wiped her eyes with the sleeve of her shirt.

"You sure I can't get you anything?" Sam asked.

***

Victor Gallego leaned back in his leather recliner while watching the 2030 FIFA World Cup Soccer match between Costa Rica and Guatemala. He had come to think of Costa Rica as his home country since immigrating there. Mexico had always seemed temporary, and he couldn't even begin to remember the old country...too many horrors.

Someone rang the doorbell.

"Pilar!" Victor shouted. But the maid must have been on break or in the bathroom.

Victor crossed the living room of his modest villa, a nice house with an ample garden in a good suburb of Limón. There was a view over rooftops to the Caribbean Sea beyond. Not bad for a fugitive from the world.

He opened the door.

A young man, dark skinned, athletic, maybe mid-twenties stood before him. His black hair was sweptback. He wore impeccable black slacks, a black embroidered silk shirt and dress shoes.

396

"Can I help you?" Victor said in Spanish. He peered over the man's shoulder to a maroon Alfa Romero sport coupe.

"Are you Victor Gallego?"

They have found me. "I'm Victor Gallego. Who are you? Have we met?"

"My name is Francisco Lopez. We have never met. I believe you knew my father, Marcelo."

Oh God. He is here to kill me. "Knew? It was a long time ago but I still know him."

"He passed away last year. Cancer."

"I'm...I'm sorry to hear that. Come in. Can I offer you something to drink. Wine, beer, a coke?"

"Thank you. I'll have a beer if it's not too much trouble."

"No trouble at all. Pilar! I don't know where the help goes when you need them. Pilar!"

"*Si, Señor Gallego.*" The maid hurried in and made a little curtsy toward Francisco.

"Please bring this gentleman a beer. I'll have one, too."

If I'm going to die, then I might as well feel good about it.

"Sit down. Sit down. Over there is a good chair." Victor indicated one of the stuffed *Equipale* chairs he had shipped from Mexico. They had held up well.

Francisco sat and looked at the TV. "Who's winning?"

"Costa Rica but it's a preliminary match in their group. A long way to go." Victor grabbed the remote from his recliner and switched off the game.

"Nice place," Francisco said. "I like the view of the sea. It reminds me of the view from my bedroom in my father's villa in Cerro Bonito."

He seems like a decent kid. Do decent kids kill? "Ah, yes, Cerro Bonito. Lovely place. I'm sorry to say I haven't been there in years."

Pilar came back with a tray, glasses and two beers. She placed the tray on a table between Victor and his guest.

"Thank you, Pilar. That will be all." Victor dismissed her, thinking if Francisco was to shoot him then he could at least spare Pilar the sight of it. He poured Francisco's beer and handed it to him, then poured his own. "*Saludo*." He raised his glass and took a long swallow.

"Now, tell me, Francisco, what brings you all the way to Costa Rica. I'm sure you didn't come here to tell me your father had died."

"I thought my father's death would be of utmost interest to you. He never stopped looking for you, right up until the cancer left him bedridden. I myself have been looking for you, too. But as you can see, I found you."

"Such tenacity." Victor shook his head. "Why was your father and now you so obsessed with finding me?"

"I think we both know the reason."

"There could be lots of reasons."

"If you insist. Ten years ago you organized a raid on my father's villa. Two of his bodyguards were killed, and one of his guests, a young girl named Chloe was kidnapped."

398

Victor squirmed. *Will he shoot for my heart and kill me with one shot, or wound me in many places and watch me die?*

"It was a long time ago. I was younger then. I was mixed up with bad people. I've thought often about that night. For my part in it, I am sorry."

"Yes, it was a long time ago." Francisco took his glass from the table, leaned back in his chair and crossed one leg over the other. A shine reflected off his polished shoes. "My father's regret, besides losing two employees, was he never could find out what happened to Chloe. Some say she was forced to donate her heart to Sam Turner, the man she called her grandfather. Some say she was killed and dumped into the ocean to be torn apart by sharks or buried in the desert, a feast for *coyotes*."

"What do you think happened to her?"

"In my heart, I have always hoped she is still alive, even though what evidence there is points to the opposite conclusion."

"And what do you want of me, Francisco?"

"I think you know the truth, *Señor* Gallego."

Victor drained his glass. "Are you going to kill me?"

Francisco laughed and waved a dismissive hand. "No. No. If I were my father, then I might. But he got out of the drug business a long time ago. We are legitimate. I run the show now he is gone."

Victor felt a sense of relief, or was it disappointment. He had been living lies for so long, he might have felt their burden lifted from his shoulders in the brief moments before death took him. "What do you want to know?"

"Everything. On the day of the raid, I was in the pool. Men came over the wall, shooting. My father's bodyguards drew their guns but too late. The lifeguard ran and was shot in the back. The shooters looked at me and must have decided I was not a threat standing there in water up to my hips, a boy of eleven. They splashed into the pool, shoved me to one side and grabbed Chloe. Then as quickly as they had come they were up and over the wall. All I could hear were Chloe's screams. That's the last time I saw her."

Victor sighed. These were memories of times long suppressed. Ones he picked up and examined when he was drunk or they welled up and pushed into his consciousness in nightmares. "You have been honest with me. I will return the favor. It is like this." Victor leaned forward, hands clasped out in front of him, a posture of supplication, maybe one asking for forgiveness.

"She was taken to a safe house in a small village on the way to Guadalajara. I returned to Cerro Bonito and met the man, Demetri Andropov, who had hired me to carry out the kidnapping. You know of Andropov?"

Francisco nodded.

"I lost two men in the raid," Victor continued. "The people I had hired them from wanted more money for their loss. I confronted Andropov with a request for double what he had agreed to pay. I told him if he didn't come up with it, I would take Chloe to Guadalajara and let Doctor Mendoza transplant her heart into Turner. He was dying, of course. I

400

never heard from Andropov. Nor did I get the initial money he promised.

"I returned to the safe house to collect Chloe. That's when your father's men caught up to me. There was a shootout between my guys and your father's bodyguards. I grabbed Chloe and escaped to Guadalajara where I met with Doctor Mendoza."

Francisco's face reddened and a tear slid down his cheek but he kept silent.

"You are becoming distraught, Francisco. Please, hear me out. It was never my intention to do Chloe any harm. It would have broken my heart twice over. In the old country, before coming to Mexico, I had a daughter who was about the same age as Chloe was then. Because of my political activism, the State sought to punish me. They took my daughter away. I never saw her again. My wife died of a broken heart. Nearly so, did I.

"The first time I saw Chloe, she captivated me, so much she looked like my little girl. But that is a lot of sentimental history.

"When I met Mendoza he had already talked to Turner and his lady friend, *la Señora* Calder. Mendoza told me Turner would not survive the night without a transplant, and I thought then and there that was the end of Turner.

"Then Mendoza gave me a big smile. "Victor, we have a donor," he said. I couldn't believe my ears. "It is a miracle," I said. And it was. I cried for here was a way out.

"Earlier that day a young boy slammed his moped into a truck and suffered a fatal head injury. His body was rushed to the hospital as the family

401

knew the hospital paid for organ parts. A search of the records revealed no recipients with good tissue matches...until Turner came in. The match was near perfect.

"But Mendoza wanted money for it. Usually, Andropov paid and I got a cut. I went back to Turner and explained there was a heart available and that Mendoza was demanding payment. Turner agreed to pay. He had money in the Hummer. Lots of it. He didn't want it, so I'm ashamed to say, I took it all."

"You stole it."

"It wasn't his anyway." Victor waved his hands as if to dismiss the charge as irrelevant. "I paid off Mendoza and still had a fortune left over."

"So Turner did not get Chloe's heart?"

"No. No. That is what I am saying. A heart was available and Chloe was still in the trunk of my car. It was a miracle. Of course, I still needed another miracle myself, and I thought of the extra money I had as God given. The Guadalajara gang was after me and would see me die a slow death if I did not pay them. The American FBI was after Turner and would have done who knows what if they knew Chloe was alive. And God forbid Andropov found out. He would have injected her in an instant--with something to make her brain-dead. Then there was your father, who had his own beef to settle with me for organizing a raid that killed his men."

"You've heard Andropov is dead?"

Victor brightened. The first good news he'd heard in a long time. "No. I didn't know that. How?"

"After he was released from prison where he spent five years, he tried to make a go of cloning again but it didn't work out. He committed suicide four years ago."

Victor shook his head. "He used to be a good friend. But he changed. He became obsessed. After a while I didn't know him, anymore. I was afraid of him. That's why I ran. I walked out of the hospital, straight to my car and drove to Guatemala. I stayed there for a couple of years, but the political climate changed and I didn't feel safe." Victor laughed. "I didn't need that on top of everyone else who was looking for me. So I came here. Costa Rica has been good to me."

Francisco was now crying openly. "And Chloe?"

A key rattled in the lock of the front door.

Victor stood.

Francisco put down his glass and stood as well, brushing tears from his cheeks.

The door opened.

Sunlight from outside silhouetted a young woman in the doorway. "Papa, there's a fancy car in the driveway."

"Chloe, we have a visitor," Victor said.

Startled, she stared. "I...Oh my God!" she shrieked, rushing toward Francisco's open arms. "Is it really you?"

THE END

403